THE

GLEANER

Fayerweather Literary Services
Cambridge, Massachusetts
fayerlit@yahoo.com

Book design by Anne Leslie
Cover Photo Courtesy of Margaret Fanning

*For the Brothers of Weston Priory who once
lifted a young man out of a deep well.*

"And she said, I pray you, let me glean and gather after the reapers among the sheaves: and she came and hath continued from morning until now, that she tarried a little in the house."

The Book of Ruth, 2:7

"The voice I hear this passing night was heard
In ancient days by emperor and clown:
Perhaps the self-same song that found a path
Through the sad heart of Ruth, when sick for home,
She stood in tears amid the alien corn."

John Keats: "Ode to a Nightingale"

THE GLEANER

Stephen Leslie

PART ONE

<u>1</u>

Sugarbrook Farm, Stoneford, VT
February 1965

The tongue was blue and swollen and hanging out of the head. He could hear the cow's piteous bellowing as she strained to push the calf the rest of the way out, the head, shoulder and one leg already protruding from the dilated vulva. With a pail of steaming hot water in one hand and two lengths of chain in the other, the boy moved quickly from the barn back out to the yard where she lay in the snow. He knelt and pressed the calf's tongue. It had gone cold.

He took off his coat and flannel shirt, rolled up a sleeve of his union suit and washed his arm in the bucket. Then he stretched out prone behind the tremulous bulk and plied with his fingers until he reached the other leg caught behind the pelvic rim. It took more strength than he knew he had to grasp the inverted hoof, jam it backwards and pull it out through the birth canal to rest by its pellucid mate beneath the limpid chin.

He wrapped the chains around the calf's hooves at a point just above the dew claws and pulled on the grips, wincing as the cow tore. He lay back exhausted, the steaming calf between his legs, the mucous on his arm stiffening in the cold. As the cow eased out of her contractions, she heaved and sighed, a liquid froth gushing out of her, seeping a crimson melt in the snow.

He tried to get her to her feet but she was too exhausted to move, so he left her with a bucket of water and a flake of hay. It was almost dark now as he trudged back to the barn, hat pulled down over the tips of his ears and collar turned up against the freezing rain. He washed the birth slime off his arms and rinsed the chains before he hung them back up on the wall.

As he made his way through the barn he paused amid the random clatter of stanchion irons, cud chewing and the occasional splatter of manure hitting the gutters that ran down either side of the central alley. He could sense the cows sensing him. As quickly, he heard them ease back into their pattern of feeding and rumination, his presence as natural to them as daylight. He breathed in the familiar odors; the straw, the hay, the cattle. In the closeness of that animate dark the space around him seemed to extend outward toward some pervasive mystery as one might find in a cavern, a forest, or a church.

He usually passed straight through the well house linking the barn to the farmhouse kitchen, but tonight he paused for a moment to lean over the stone lip of the well to feel the vapors from the cold water below breathe an earthy air across his face. Then he slipped off his barn boots and went into the kitchen.

In a T-shirt, muscular arms crossed over his chest, his father leaned back on the counter by the sink, the good leg bearing his weight. His brother Tommy sat at the table with three beer bottles in front of him. Two empty, one half-full.

"There's beans and taters in the fry pan, Danny."

"Maggie dropped her calf outside. Bad presentation. Didn't make it."

"Bull calf?"

"Naw, heifer."

"Damn!"

He served himself, took a seat and drowned his food in ketchup and salt.

"How you doing, Danny?"

He kept eating and did not look up.

"Acknowledge your brother when he speaks to you, son."

Danny looked up at his father.

"Maggie freshened. The calf died."

"You said that. Why wasn't she in the maternity pen?"

"She was already down when I started chores."

"Is the cow still down?"

He nodded to say that it was. "She tore."

"Bad?"

"Not enough to stitch."

2

"If she isn't up by morning we'll' have to use the winch." His father made a clicking sound with his tongue and shook his head. "Hate to lose her. Been a damn good cow."

"She'll be up. I'll see to her at barn check."

"We'll have to be rid of that black bull. Throws big calves and few heifers." His father's thoughts turned to the next day's work.

"We'll hitch up the boys and do some skidding tomorrow. Need more timber for the sugar house."

"In this weather?"

Before his father could answer, his older brother interrupted.

"Christ Dad, can't you read the writing on the wall? Farming is dying out here."

His brother stuck a finger in the knot of his necktie to loosen it. He undid the top buttons of his shirt and tilted back in his chair.

"Shit! Listen to you talking about working with horses. Every one of our neighbors sold off his team years ago. You're liable to get yourselves hurt one of these days."

His father emitted a sigh. Eyeing his eldest, he took a sip of milk and wiped his upper lip on his arm.

"Tommy, you know as well as I do that there are more guys getting chewed up by contraptions on tractors than ever got hurt working a team. I'd sooner trust my life to those old horses out in the barn as to any machine. Besides, I know what you're driving at. I ain't selling."

Tommy's admonition brought both sons back to the accident as though it were yesterday. Patrick Sweeney had been driving horses since he was a boy and could handle plow and team before he turned twelve. However, all his skill and experience could not calm the horses on that high summer day ten years ago when the dump-rake tore through a nest of ground wasps. The horses spooked. Patrick was thrown forward into the steel tines of the rake and dragged over a hundred feet until the rake struck a stone, jarring the trip lever and releasing him.

Twelve-year-old Tommy was driving a second team on a wagon and six-year-old Danny was loading hay with a fork. The horses grew winded and slowed to a stop, no longer sure why they had been

3

running. When the boys reached their father he looked up and said through a pained grin, "Good thing you fellas missed one when I set you to picking rocks this spring." He was left with the peculiar twist thrown into his spine that day.

Tommy took a swig of beer, belched and pulled a Camel from the pack in the top pocket of his shirt. He lit his cigarette and puffed, shooting twin streams of smoke through his nostrils across the table.

"Look old man, the corridor is coming and with it, industry, tourism, jobs. Land prices will skyrocket. This is the chance of a lifetime. Gloria and I know there is a good life out there waiting for us and the twins. But as a farm this land is useless. If I were running this place, I'd have new equipment. I'd buy a tractor and I'd put a milk line and a bulk tank into that antique barn."

"You ain't running this place. It's not what you chose. We don't need any of that stuff."

"Well, you'll never get around the issue of the bulk tank. The Dairy Inspector will require it soon enough. You'll have to lay out several grand and shuck those old milk cans. I don't know what bank will even talk to you about extending credit."

His father uncrossed his arms and inched himself around, giving both sons a view of the snake the accident had made of his back. He began to methodically scrub the bean pot with a fistful of steel wool and suds. Two words came out of him like the growl of an animal in a trap.

"Ain't selling."

Danny looked at his father and saw fifty years of hardscrabble labor flash by. A lifetime on a hill farm carved out of spare granite and thick forest by his immigrant grandfather. Hard as it was, fifty years on that land had fed, clothed, and given his father everything that felt true to him. While men around him farmed with equipment and machinery, Patrick Sweeney farmed his fields with horses. The health of his fields and animals was his wealth. He had no need to justify what the grip of wooden haft or leather lines meant in the hands of a man born in the place where he intended to die. But Tommy didn't stop.

4

"We could go down to my office tomorrow and draw up some papers, get the place assessed and print up a listing."

"Ain't never gonna happen." Danny set his fork down and pushed away the uneaten portion of his supper. He looked at his brother.

"You must have a hole in your heart."

"Knock it off, Danny! What do you know about any of this?"

"I know what I need to know."

"You don't know jack-shit. You're not even going to finish high school. When was the last time you went to class? Don't tell me because I know. Your buddy, Levi Johnson---his mother the school nurse---she tells me they haven't seen you there in months."

"So what?"

"You're going nowhere fast, and it's a damn shame."

"Dad needs more help on the farm. Since you've been gone we're always behind, and I wasn't learning anything in school anyways."

"How do you suppose the farm debt gets paid? I assure you it isn't covered by the milk check. If it weren't for my job at the realty, this place would go under."

"I don't know anything about that."

Tommy was about to retort when Patrick spoke. Still facing away from them, his father said something barely audible.

"I'll think about it."

"Dad, what did you say?" Tommy asked.

"I'm saying if this place can't pay its own way, maybe it ain't meant to be a farm no more."

"Does that mean you'll let me put it up for sale?"

"I'll sleep on it."

Tommy stood, stamped out the glowing butt in a bottle cap, ran his fingers through his hair, placed his hands on his hips and shook his head. A shadow of uncertainty crossed his face but in an instant it was replaced with a triumphant smirk.

Danny stared at the empty space in front of him where his plate had been. His father coughed and rinsed a dish.

5

"What say we all have a beer!" Tommy spoke in a voice too loud. He opened the icebox and took out three more, popped the bottles open and set them on the table. Danny's mouth was agape as he watched his father grasp a beer bottle and take a long pull. Patrick set the bottle back down on the table half-empty and directed himself to his youngest son.

"Well, go on, Danny, drink up. Comes a time every man's got to have his first. By Jesus, your brother here had drunk more than a few by the time he was your age."

His father pulled up a chair and dropped heavily into the seat and took another sip, thoughtfully this time, swishing the beer around in his mouth and smacking his lips. Danny took hold of a bottle and tentatively raised it. His first swallow tasted bitter, the next sweet. He drank it too fast and could feel a buzzing behind his eyes but he could also feel the tension easing out of his body like the unclasping of a fist.

"A toast to our prosperous future!" Tommy exclaimed as he downed his beer. He caught his father's eye. "Why'd you quit drinking in the first place, Dad?"

His father inhaled deeply and frowned and his face turned pensive. "It was after your mother died. I'd seen your grandfather drink himself to death and I knew that if I didn't stop right then, I'd do the same. Then who would've run the farm? Raised you boys? I haven't touched a drop since the day we laid her in the ground. But hell, I haven't got that much time left and you boys are gone to men. Might as well have a taste." He cracked a grin and took another drink.

"No, Dad," Danny said.

"Easy, son," his father almost whispered.

Tommy looked hard at his younger brother and an old anger flashed across his face. "He's just like Mom was, always brooding on stuff. The angrier he gets, the less he speaks. It's the Indian in us. He's got it."

"I ain't like her. I can't even remember her face."

"Your mother died before you had the chance to really know her," his father said.

They all fell quiet for a moment, and then suddenly his father continued, and to his boys, so accustomed as they were to his long silences, it was as though a shroud had suddenly lifted and the dead rose to speak.

"I met your mother when I was stationed at the air base out west. I swear to God she was the prettiest woman I ever laid eyes on. Light brown skin, dark hair and blue eyes. She was serving tables in a honky-tonk. Her Daddy was some kind of an Indian outlaw, but her mother was of pioneer stock. Your granddad Aidan was none too happy when I brought her home. I guess he hoped I'd marry an Irish girl. Well, there weren't many Irish girls around here. Back in those days Stoneford was cut off from the rest of the world."

"It still is," Tommy chimed in. "But the highway will change all that."

"Anyhow, when your granddad saw how that woman could work, he changed his tune. Damned diabetes. How she fought it till the end." His father's voice trailed off in a wistful tone.

"I thank God Danny got the Indian side and not me. Nobody in my office knows about Mom. It's hard enough being a goddamned Catholic!"

"Christ Jesus, next thing you know he'll be voting Republican," quipped his father.

"She knew I wasn't at all like her. She always loved Danny more. She used to sing to him all the time, soft and slow. I can still hear those songs, though I never could understand the words."

An uncomfortable silence followed Tommy's reminiscence. Then in a dream-laden voice, Danny said: "Those weren't words. Those were the voices of clouds and rivers and trees."

His father and his brother stared hard at him but he continued on as if they weren't there.

"I remember her eyes. She only ever smiled through her eyes. She was always saying thank you to stuff---to the cows for their milk; to the bushes for berries; to the sky for rain."

Patrick spoke again, directing himself to Tommy as if he had no means to respond to the misty revelations of his younger son.

"Your Mother didn't take much to church going. But before your granddad Aidan passed, he insisted that you boys be baptized. He took you over to St. Joseph's. Said it was important that you see the

7

inside of the true church at least once in your lives. Your mother came along, to guard over you I think. But she kind of liked it in there---the paintings, the candles, the incense. Which is why her funeral was there."

A half-pint silver flask appeared on the tabletop and soon was passing from hand to hand.

His father continued. "Your granddad came to love her dearly. They were in many ways alike. Each of them was always at war with something. In the end I think they were at war with themselves."

Tommy smoothed back the close-cropped blond locks from his forehead and rubbed a hand about his round face. He lit up another cigarette. "Why do you suppose Granddad left Ireland in the first place?"

"Not for lack of money. His family were fairly prosperous farmers and shopkeepers. He wanted to make it on his own and America was the place to do it. Can you imagine? Just about Danny's age and all alone facing a new country."

His father went on to tell them of how their grandfather had found his first job in the coal mines in Pennsylvania and had worked and saved and bought a grocery store and gone on to buy more stores and invest in the stock market. Though he had a talent for starting up businesses, he'd not been very good at overseeing the day-to-day grind, spending too much time at the racetrack, drinking, playing poker, and chasing the ladies.

"That doesn't sound so bad to me," Tommy said.

"It all caught up with him. He lost nearly everything and that's when he decided to return to the land," said his father.

"That's what I'd call swimming against the tide," Tommy butted in, "Don't hear of too many businessmen hankering to become farmers."

"You know your Grandma's people were from up here. When times got hard, Stoneford was a place to come home to."

His father went on to tell them that for the most part their grandfather had been a cheerful man but that now and again dark moods would overcome him and he would take to drinking. He would be fine for months, sometimes even years, and then suddenly go on a binge for several weeks, losing their hard-earned money playing cards.

"Christ, I was practically running this farm by the time I was sixteen."

Patrick's face turned ashen with these recollections. He took another swig of the proffered flask, and continued on in a happier vein.

"Early on your grandfather had hired on as a hand at the Benson place. On the first day of work they asked if he could drive a team of horses and he jumped up into the seat of a wagon hitched to a team of chunks. And then the Bensons told him to go on up the skid trail and pick up a log and bring it back down to the mill. When he asked them how was he to load it up, Dicky Benson squinted at him in a mean way and told him to figure it out. Your grandfather went up the trail and found an enormous saw-log only three paces long but solid oak, the bole of a hundred-and-fifty-year tree. He got the team to tip the wagon on its side, chained the log to the bed, and then brought the horses round to the other side to right it again."

"Well, he drives back down to the mill and don't those Benson boys stare and Dicky asks, 'How we supposed to unload it?' to which your granddad is pleased to reply, 'Figure it out'."

The flask was empty. The weariness of the day had set in.

"The wife's going to be wondering what happened to me." Tommy stood and stretched, put on his jacket and placed the flask into its liner pocket.

"Yup, tomorrow's another day." His father remained sitting, rubbing his fingertips in half-circles beneath the sunken hollows of his eyes. Danny stood and made for the well house door.

"I'll be on to barn check."

"How's my horse doing, Danny? I haven't had much time to spend with her these days," Tommy asked him.

"Proud---but sweet under the saddle."

"Well, it's good night, then."

With the sounds in his ears of his father creeping up the stairs and the blue truck starting up in the drive, Danny stepped into the chill of the well house and slipping on his barn boots and slicker he stumbled toward the barn to do the last of the day's chores. After he swept in hay to the cows and watered and grained the horses, he went out into the yard. Though it was still winter, the heavy rainfall was setting the thaw in motion. The great unlocking had begun.

Maggie was standing over her dead calf, the after-birth still steaming where it had spilled out into the snow. She bellowed when she saw him. He went to her and wrapped his arms around her gangly neck. "What a good old cow," he said to her.

And the rain fell and he cried.

2

He awakened to a world enshrouded in fog. His father was already up. From his bedroom window he could see him tromping through the melting snow, pails in his hands, on the way to the chicken coop, the old black dog tagging at his heels. He dressed quickly and made his way across creaking floorboards down the narrow hallway and the steep stairs. He poured a cup of coffee topped off with thick cream and then ran to catch up with his father in the barn.

The morning fog was not as thick as the one in his head as he came to grips with the downside of his first taste of alcohol. Once into the routine of feeding chores, the queasiness began to subside and his natural health rebounded. He took note of Maggie at her place in the line-up. She was bright-eyed and eating hay, a sight that filled him with energy for the new day.

By the time he had his first cartload of corn silage loaded, he heard the sound of the vacuum pump in the milk house click on with a roar. The cows heard it too and many of the seasoned ones began to let down their milk. All bovine heads turned his way as he came along with the cart, tripping over barn cats, forking out heaping servings of feed. His father was into the rhythm of washing udders and placing on the machines. 'Kashunk, Kashunk, Kashunk.' The cylindrical inflations latched onto teats and pumped milk into the attached bucket. When a bucket was full, his father deftly tipped it into one of six milk cans on a standing cart. His movements were not swift but sure with an economy of motion made articulate through the years. Danny in turn fed out silage, grain and hay, then joined his father in the milking. Patrick was even quieter than usual, only making comments that related to the health of the cows, reminding his son of appropriate precautions and treatments. As the herd health was excellent, such admonitions were few.

When the last of the fifteen milkers was done and the milk poured off, his father straightened up with a groan and put his hand on Danny's shoulder, something he seldom did.

"I spoke some foolishness last night, son. Don't you worry about a thing. Come hell or high water, I won't sell the land."

His father almost smiled and then turned to the work of cleanup in the milk house. He leaned into the heavy cart, then stopped and called back over his shoulder.

"Hitch the boys up after breakfast. We've got logs to skid."

"Dad, all that rain. It's gonna be greasy up there."

"We'll just have to chance it. The sap's going to start running any day. We've got to get the roof on that sugar house."

When the cows were turned out, horses watered and fed, the myriad of morning chores completed, they made their way to the kitchen for a breakfast of bacon and eggs, oatmeal and toast before taking on the next round of tasks.

After breakfast Danny retrieved the dead calf from the yard and dismembered the stiff body with a meat saw and fed the pieces to the pigs. That done, he headed for the horse barn.

The two draft geldings, Liam and Rory, knickered low as he entered the stable. They were fifteen years old and in fine health. He haltered each in turn and put them in cross-ties to be groomed. Tommy's saddle horse, Tess, looked on jealously from her stall. He started with their feet, picking up each and scraping it clean. The horses offered up each hoof without protest. Next he brushed them down and combed out their manes and tails, and then put on their collars and work harness, straight bits and bridles.

"Step up Boys," and so they started out into the yard where his father stood waiting with a peavey slung over his shoulder.

"We won't be needing a saw today. I figure we got maybe a dozen good-sized trees already down. That should be enough board-feet to finish the trusses. Then we can get to tapping."

They made their way off the bottom land and onto the steep woods trail. The horses were feeling good and ready to work, yet they listened to Danny when he reminded them to walk. Old and arthritic but still eager to be part of the crew, the black dog came trailing behind.

Even with the heavy cleats on their shoes, the horses slipped as they climbed. Danny was uneasy with his father's uncustomary lack of caution. It was not like him to work the horses under such slick conditions. Heavy snow in December had collapsed the roof of the sugar house but with or without a finished roof, Danny felt sure they could get the boiling done. His father seemed to be driven by a sense of urgency Danny could not fathom.

The woods grew tall above the road and swallowed the boy and the man and the horses in the dance of a brisk south breeze on naked branches---the hard maple and smooth gray beech, yellow birch, white oak and hemlock, all awake to the uncharacteristic warming trend of the winds.

His father took over the lines while Danny did the grunt work, getting the slip hook and chain wrapped round the felled logs and secured to the hook on the double-tree. Danny worked with unhurried concentration and the horses stood calmly but with anticipation, ready for the pull. When his father smacked his lips, they leaned their weight into the collars with zest. The logs were twelve footers, many with sixteen-inch diameter tops or more but the horses pulled them as if they were matchsticks, only straining at the steepest grades. Patrick drove skillfully. Danny watched as his father helped the team anticipate when to surge or slow and to make use of standing dead trees in order to execute turns as they skidded the logs to the road. When it came time to work in the woods, his father's enthusiasm and knowledge transcended his old injuries and he stepped lightly, even hopping from side to side over the logs as they were dragged over the tumble of the forest floor. Once Patrick had the logs out of the woods, Danny would take the lines and drive the horses down the skid road, then return for the long dry run back up the steep incline.

In spite of the slick ground, the work proceeded smoothly. By mid-morning they had the better half of the needed timber down to the landing where the flatbed from the saw mill with its self-loading grapple could reach the decked logs.

Danny and team crested the hill when the sun burned through the clouds and a diffuse light unfurled across the valley. "Whoa!" he spoke to the team. The horses blew and he caught his breath, turning around to look over the fields. His father emerged from the shadow of the woods to stand beside him. They could see clear south to the singular slopes of Mount Ascutney. The shoulders of the old volcano

13

high enough to remain blanketed in snow were washed in a pink and golden hue by the breaking sun. Closer in lay the bridge that led into the valley through two steep knolls. To the east lay the Benson property, their black and white cows standing in the yard on the hillside watching for spring. On the Hart land sheep were drinking at the far side of the brook that flowed on through the bottom land that Aidan Sweeney had first tilled. That land was rich and black and free of stone. Danny saw a hint of a smile play on his father's thin lips.

"It's good land, Danny," he sighed. "Mellow and with heart. I'm lucky to have such a fine son to work it with me."

Danny's ears warmed at the unexpected show of affection. They both turned away and resumed the hike uphill.

As accidents will, it happened quickly. The bank that his father drove along was steep and the horses were pulling two heavy oak logs hooked together with the chain wrapped in a figure-eight. The load veered off the skid trail and the horses started to go with it. They pawed to regain ground and just as they seemed to be getting the haul back on track, his father got his left ankle caught between the skidding logs. He screamed out in pain and dropped the lines. Rory, hitched on the near side, lost his footing and started to slide back with the load. The rain-soaked bank gave way and the logs rolled over along with the team, catching his father in a crushing scissor-like grip and pulling the horses down in a neighing, flailing tumble. For twenty feet or more they fell, snapping through saplings and bouncing off boles, careening over a precipice of exposed shale and landing at last in a heap.

Danny heard the crash and came running. His father was unconscious and pinned beneath a log when he reached him. He placed an ear to his chest and heard the heart beating as from a distance, dim and far away. Liam was on his back and thrashing, all twisted up in his harness and lines. Rory, by some miracle, had landed cat-like on his feet and was standing calmly waiting for whatever came next.

Danny found a fallen branch and managed to pry his father free and dragged him clear of the wreck. He stood back to assess the horses. One look and he knew it was all over for Liam. He unsheathed the knife at his belt and cut Rory loose from his teammate and led him out of the tangle onto level ground. He hacked down two stout saplings,

14

lashed them onto the tugs of Rory's harness with some lengths of driving line and fashioned a crude travois. He placed his father on it and with the remainder of the lines, tied him on securely. Then he led Rory bearing his father upon the drags and in this way brought him down off the mountain. When they reached the farmhouse he tied the horse to the railing of the front porch and carried his father inside and up the stairs to his bed. He was amazed at how light he seemed. How diminished. He didn't stay with him long. He ran out and caught Tess in the paddock, put a bridle on her and swung on bareback. The five-year old Morgan filly's blood grew hot sensing the urgency of her rider. As they tore off down the gravel road, winter thunder cracked open the sky and rain threatened to fall again.

Danny rode as fast as he could down to the village to get the doctor, who contacted the boy's older brother. Tommy came quickly to drive the doctor up to the farmhouse. By the time Danny returned on horseback, the doctor had already gone into the house with his bag. Tommy was ambling around the farmyard with his hands jammed in his pockets, his shiny black shoes kicking at the melting snow and ice and emergent clumps of lawn.

Danny watered and turned out Tess and then unhitched Rory and led him to the barn. Rory kept looking with anxious eyes to the hill where his brother horse still lay. Danny put him in cross-ties and set about cleansing and packing tar on the cuts and scrapes. When the doctoring was done, he put the horse in his tie-stall, grained him, filled his water trough and stuffed the manger full of hay. Then he went into the house, got a rifle down off the rack in the parlor and headed back up the hill.

Liam didn't stir much as he spoke to him in low soothing tones. The horse lay calmly enough with three legs tucked under and the bad leg stretched out in front of him. Danny knelt and gently stroked the horse's long sleek face. He listened a moment as the labored breathing slowed and the eye whites disappeared. The right foreleg was broken in two places. A jagged shard of gleaming bone was poking through a loose flap of bloody hide. He thanked the horse for his many years of faithful service. Then he stood and stepped back three paces, braced firm, leveled the rifle and fired.

15

Tommy didn't know what to make of the single shot echoing off the valley walls. When he glimpsed his brother come striding off the hill onto the flat crop lands he remembered seeing that only one horse had returned and he felt a knowing pang.

Just then, the doctor came out of the house. He took off his spectacles and placed them in a holding case and slipped it into his coat liner-pocket.

"It doesn't look good, Tommy. I've given him what he needs for the pain. I'll be back first thing in the morning."

"Aren't you going to call an ambulance?"

"If that's what you prefer."

"What are you saying?"

"It doesn't look good."

"Okay, Doc. What shall I tell Danny?"

"Same thing I told you. He's not a boy anymore."

As the doctor spoke his eyes were on Danny who came walking into the farmyard, his face wet with twin streams of tears. He had the deer rifle in hand and Liam's harness draped over one shoulder and the peavey resting on top of that. Even in the trauma of the moment, he would not consider leaving a tool abandoned in the field, knowing that his father would frown on such an oversight.

Tommy called to his brother but Danny kept walking as if he hadn't heard. Tommy called again but Danny just walked on to the barn.

"Talk to him in a while, Tommy. He's taken a big bite today," the doctor said. Tommy threw his hands up in the air, his blue eyes flashing with both anxiety and anger. As he climbed into his truck, he heard the whinge of the silage unloader being turned on. Danny had begun evening chores and Tommy guessed that his younger brother would rather go it alone. Or so he told himself. In any case, he just didn't feel like going back into that barn.

With all the barn chores done for the night, Danny could no longer put off going into the house. He had seen the blue pickup parked outside again and his stomach turned into a closed fist at the sight. His brother was seated at the kitchen table. The radio was on.

"Gloria sent over some fried chicken and biscuits, Danny."

The cigarette smoke bothered his eyes, and the smell of the open beer bottles almost made him wretch. Then his stomach grew interested in the aroma of the chicken, but he denied it.

"I ain't hungry," he said, without meeting Tommy's eyes. He fled the kitchen and headed upstairs.

As he opened the door to his father's room, he tried to remember a prayer to say but the words that surfaced were in some half-forgotten language. He could hear his father breathing faintly in the dark. There was a clock ticking on the nightstand by the head of the bed. He averted his eyes from the pallid face framed in a swathing of bandage and backed out of the room, closed the door and went down the hallway to his own room. He stumbled in, fell on the bed and shortly slept.

Around midnight the wind began to blow up out of the south. The clashing of branches and a loose gutter woke him. He made his way again down the hall to his father's room and lit a kerosene lantern and knelt down by the bedside. His father was still breathing. Danny watched a slight vapor rise in the cold of the room, like the ascending sigh of a soul. He gently clasped his father's hand---held its cool roughness in his own for a moment before he let it go. Then he drew the quilt cover close up around the still form, rose and left the room.

He stealthily padded past Tommy's half-open door. He could hear his brother's fitful breathing. He went downstairs and put more wood in the stove, more out of habit than of need, as the wind was carrying an unsettling warmth that bore a premature awakening into the valley.

He went into the kitchen and poured himself a glass of milk. Then he went back into the parlor and pulled the old thirty-aught-six hunting rifle down off the gun rack, a hand-me-down from his grandfather, and stuffed some shells into the pockets of his coveralls. In the well house he laced on his leather boots and stepped through the side door and out across the yard. The old black dog barked once but did not follow. For the moment the rains had abated but wild tatters of clouds were scuttling across troubled skies like hungry ghosts.

The unseasonable warmth was disorienting, making his blood feel thick in his veins. The snow was melting off the bottom lands and the exposed earth was beginning to thaw, its scent raw and aching with nascent potency. Across the valley he could hear a roaring. The ice was breaking up with a groan and a shudder, the brook now a torrent, as a rush of flood waters descended with the snow melt off the hills. From every direction flashes of heat lightning etched electric details of the landscape in sudden erratic bursts, then pitched the world back into darkness. He crossed over the stubble of last year's corn and made his way to the field's edge, ascending the skirts of the hill until pasture gave way to woods. Then he picked up the trail of an overgrown road that had reverted to little more than a deer path through years of disuse. It wound steeply up into the hills. The forest growth was mature here, it being eighty or more years since this side of the mountain had been cut, and on its steepest bluffs there even remained some virgin timber. The woods were open and spacious with scant undergrowth.

He came to a place where an old fieldstone wall intersected the way and then ran parallel to the path up the hillside as he climbed. The stones of the wall were for the most part intact, only here and there toppled by frost heave, root growth or fallen trees. They were remnants of another time in the life of these hills when the woods had been cleared and flocks of sheep pastured in their wake. Sugar maples, two-hundred-and-fifty or more years old, stood as crumbling ruins along either side of his way. He could pick out darker hollows within the shadows of the forest floor that indicated the location of foundations--- farmhouses, barns, a schoolhouse, all swallowed by root grasp, moss hair, lichen, leaf and litter fall. An entire village under cover of trees.

He knew a little of the history of the region, of how wool prices had dropped after the civil war at the same time the prairie lands were opening up out west. But he wondered now about these particular people and what their days had been like on this land and what had caused them to leave. He passed their by-gone orchards, the decrepit trees grown spindly in a vain effort to compete for sunlight with the return of the native forest.

He came at last to an expansive clearing. There was a well on its eastern edge and he felt himself irresistibly drawn towards it. He lay down his rifle and got on his knees to remove the heavy flat stone cap. Beneath was a hole large enough to admit a water pail. This aperture had been chiseled clear through a flat slab of granite five feet in diameter that covered the circumference of the well. He leaned on his elbows and peered down through the opening to the water line a dozen feet below, though with the rains and the thaw it was on the rise. He could just make out the silhouette of his own head against the slightly lesser blackness of the overcast night sky. He had always marveled at the craftsmanship of the well, the intimately placed stones layered twenty feet down into the earth.

He looked deeper within. The reflected face below grew clearer and seemed to emanate a light of its own. This diaphanous light danced off the water and played on the surface of the stones. Spiders awakened and reluctantly fled to darker crevices to hide from the supernatural glow. There was one face and there were many faces like changing masks or film images flickering over a screen. Here was the visage of an ancient Celtic warrior of red hair and beard ablaze with battle fury, the faces of hooded druids and mediacval monks invoking the powers, the faces of women with flower garlands in their hair chanting lute-like songs that echoed within the stones themselves. He saw brown faces brightly painted with beaded braids and feathers in their hair. And then there was one face that almost made his heart stop with its sweet half-smile. It was a face he thought he would never see again. For just one moment, there in the depths of the well, he looked upon the face of his mother.

His ears alerted him to a stirring off in the brush to his right, the stamping and the blowing. He reached for the rifle, placed its butt on his shoulder and slowly wheeled it round with a deadly inquiry. He saw it as it saw him, a stately buck with an eight-point rack. The old warrior was caught unaware on such an unlikely night. Danny had an absolute bead on him. For just an instant he held the creature in his sights. Then the buck leaped and quickly vanished and Danny began to breathe again. Once more his eyes returned to the well, but only his own dark reflection remained. He set the well cap back in place and wearily turned to leave when he felt a sudden impulse to visit his other special spot on the hill.

19

At the crest just beyond the clearing there was a mound the size of a small house and within it, a chamber. The stone doorway was of post-and-lintel construction and the ceiling was made of seven rough-hewn blocks of granite fitted so snugly one next to the other that a leaf of note paper could not be slid between. The walls were of cobbled stone in beehive construction and the whole was covered by centuries of earth deep enough to sustain several towering hardwoods. There was a smoke hole cut in the rear of the ceiling. Surrounding the site outside in a wide circle, triangular standing stones were set, some cracked and broken, others fallen. Four of these stones stood at the cardinal points; others were set to mark the events of some long forgotten astronomical calendar. One was framed within the view out the door as seen from within the chamber, and it was from behind that stone oriented to the southeast that each December the solstice sun would arise in the center of the door, an alignment that illuminated the interior of the chamber with the light of the sun at the moment of its cyclical rebirth.

Over the course of his youth he had felt drawn to the site in search of some unknowable solace or sense of the holy, the way an urban dweller might duck into the quiet of a church to escape the hubbub of the city streets. No one seemed to know who had built the chamber or to what purpose. The local people said it was no more than a glorified colonial root cellar. Experts from the college across the river suggested a far greater antiquity to the structure.

He entered the chamber and curled up against the back wall of the subterranean room like a wounded animal taking refuge in its den. Every nerve and fiber in his body felt spent. He slept and then he dreamed.

A towering, muscular wild man burst into the cave, his long black hair swirling about a face framed in a ferocious smile, teeth gleaming white against his dark skin and black beard. He looked at the boy with fierce eyes:

"That from which you are running is that which you most need."

Danny sat up:

"From what am I running?"

The man laughed:

"You are running from me!"

Then he leapt to all fours and as Danny watched in horror, the man was transformed into a bear, grew a lustrous coat, his hands and feet sprouted dagger claws and with the lethal snap of steel trap jaws, the demonic creature fell upon him with an unabashed fury. Again and again the jaws incised and sheared and the paws lashed as the bear roared and the boy screamed. In agony he saw himself being dismembered and devoured to the last bone.

Once inside the belly of the bear, he experienced a deep sense of contentment, a feeling of wholeness that echoed of something remembered, something profound that had always existed, always been true. Then in another timeless moment the dream body of the bear rocked with convulsions and violently disgorged Danny from its innards. The bear turned away and exited the chamber. Danny examined his own form. His body was whole and glowing with renewed health and vibrancy.

Dawn was just creeping through the woods and into the ancient mound when he awoke, cold and stiff, yet feeling calm and resolved. He picked up his rifle and set off again for the farm to face what the new day must bring. As he walked, heavy raindrops began to drum a hard beat upon forest branches. He looked up at the thickening sky and saw a great horned owl soundlessly gliding down a deep ravine. He quickened his pace, and as thunder rumbled, ran the last mile home.

Almost out of breath he topped the last rise leading up to the barn and spotted the white ambulance. Tommy was speaking with the doctor. Danny stood stock still, unnoticed. He could just make out the voice of the doctor saying something about "little time left" and "the bridge." Then hefting the black bag, the doctor climbed into the passenger seat and slammed the door shut and the ambulance pulled out of the yard. With its roof light flashing red, the vehicle moved down the drive and onto the softening mud of the lane. Danny knew with a terrible certainty that his father would not be coming back.

Tommy turned and walked towards the barn, eyes to the ground, hands balled into fists. Danny noted that he was wearing coveralls and boots, the same ones that had been hanging in the well house since that day his older brother had left the farm, armed with an athletic scholarship to attend college. Tommy had come back sooner than expected; he had to drop out after three years to marry his pregnant girlfriend. Half-starved after his midnight sojourn in the woods, Danny ran into the kitchen to grab some cheese and bread and then ducking through the pelting rain, he made for the barn to join his brother at the chores.

3

It was evident that Tommy was out of practice. He got exasperated when a first-calf heifer kicked off her machine for the third time. He slapped the cow hard, and took the machine away to the next cow, leaving the heifer with an udder half full. Danny finished milking the cow he was on, hung his machine on the cart and walked past his brother to the milk house. He grabbed a pail and returned to the side of the nervous young cow. He spoke gently to her and stroked her flanks, consoled her enough to let him finish milking her out by hand. As he resumed milking the cows further on down the line, he could sense that his brother was fuming.

Tommy had brought along a radio and switched it on to a rock 'n' roll station. His father had never fancied a radio in the barn---held that the cows milked out best in the quiet. Danny figured he'd probably had that right. But he didn't say anything to his brother.

With morning chores done, Danny took on the task of pouring the milk down the drain. Today would have been the day to load the milk cans onto the buckboard, hitch up the team and haul the milk the three miles to the local creamery, but this day he stood and watched the rich fluid flow to waste as he tipped the cans one by one until all the milk was gone save enough for the calves and the pigs, the cats and himself. With one horse and his father gone, it was the best he could do. He might have asked his brother to haul the cans in his truck, but Tommy was already in the house getting cleaned up to go to his office, and anyhow in this moment Danny didn't feel inclined to ask him for anything.

He heard the creak of the hinges on the swinging door as it opened behind him.

"Where in hell's name did you run off to last night?"

"Up the hill."

"For Chrisssake, the old man laid out on his death bed and you out wandering in the woods. When are you gonna grow up?"

"Least I ain't a sell-out."

Tommy winced ever so slightly, trying to keep his face impassive like a boxer absorbing a lesser blow. He made ready for another round by taking a more reasonable approach.

"You've got to come to town with me, Danny, before the bridge washes out. All the old timers are saying that this is it, the hundred-year flood. It's coming."

With a bristle brush in hand Danny began scrubbing and rinsing out the cans. After finishing with the first he looked to his brother.

"What about the cows?"

"We'll turn the cows loose in the yard and feed out lots of hay. I'll soon take care of the cows."

"What does that mean?"

"It means you've got to face facts. I'm selling off the cows and I'm going to have to sell the farm."

Danny started in on the second can. "I ain't leaving," he said, as he furiously scrubbed.

"Listen to me. They've taken Dad to the hospital. He hasn't regained consciousness since the accident. He's in a coma. He also has multiple internal injuries. Doc didn't expect him to make it through the night, but since he did, he's decided to move him down to Springfield. So I guess there's still some hope, but not much."

Danny didn't speak.

"Do you know what that means?"

Giving his brother a look of deaf incomprehension, Danny kept on with the brush-work.

"Dammit Danny, talk to me!"

"He's already gone."

"What? You are hopeless. Worse---you're just like Mom --- damn stubborn squaw. You know she'd still be alive if she had taken insulin but she was sure she knew better; that her homemade remedies would work better than the 'white man's medicine'. Well, she lost. And so did the rest of us."

"I didn't know anything about that."

"Listen, Danny, I have to make some decisions. Dad never made out a will. Since you're not of age, Judge Benson has appointed me executor of the estate. I am trying to do what's best for both of us.

Danny stopped scrubbing and looked into his brother's eyes.

"Tommy, don't do this."

Tommy stepped back, placed his hands on his hips, looked to the floor and spat, then looked up again.

"Are you coming with me?"

Danny's face turned hard as a granite tombstone.

"I ain't leaving."

The elder brother spun on his heels and left. Danny could hear him racing the engine, spitting gravel as he pulled out of the drive in the blue pickup. He paused a moment to listen to the report of rain on the slate shingles, then resumed his work on the milk cans until he had cleaned them all.

He was sitting on the steps under the eaves of the front porch watching the rain form widening puddles in the drive when his brother's wife pulled up to the farm house in the gray Nash Rambler with its whitewalls and sleek lines. As she stepped out of the car, he stood up and came awkwardly down the steps, his body stiff from the vigil. His face was ashen, his dark eyes grown darker.

As their eyes met, the unspoken trust was still there, bridging the gulf that the loss of his father had gouged and the even wider chasm of her alliance with Tommy.

"The roads are bad. Mud season has begun. If this keeps up, the bridge will wash out by nightfall," she said.

He nodded in agreement but said nothing.

"Your brother will flip when he finds out I've come here. Danny, why don't you come down to the village and stay with us for awhile? We've got plenty of room and the twins would be delighted to have their uncle in the house."

They stood in silence then, with arms at their sides and rain falling on their heads.

He had always been shy around girls. He had few friends and no girlfriend. But with Gloria it had always been different. It was not just that she was his brother's girl and a longtime neighbor. There was simply an ease about her. Despite her striking good looks, she was without pretension, could laugh with abandon.

She stood before him now, the mother of babies, her hair close-cropped in the fashion of the modern housewife. And even in the depths of sorrow that was freezing the marrow in his bones, Danny could still be in awe of her lovely radiance, the curls of auburn hair framing high-boned cheeks, full and tender lips, level green eyes that pooled in depths of compassion.

She reached out to him and he tried to step towards her but the tumult raging in his breast transfixed his limbs. He felt shame because of the bodily attraction her presence kindled in him. He felt fear because of the aching hunger in his heart that cried out for a nurturing whose sheer magnitude could not be acknowledged. Beyond all, he felt a hardened anger at his brother for leaving him and his father alone on the farm, for condemning their lost mother, for being the husband of an angel.

He was walking headlong into this whiteout of confused feelings. He could neither understand nor express any of it, so he stood mute and only felt his flesh cave in to the slightest degree when she pressed her full body to his, her round breasts against his chest, her arms holding him close and tight, her hands kneading the taut cables in his neck, her voice softly speaking his name again and again, not trying to tell him it was going to be all right.

He was shocked by the intensity of their connection. She released him from her embrace and took a half step back and placed her hands on his shoulders. For an instant he thought she was going to kiss him and he was surprised at how much he wanted her to.

"He was so gentle" he said, his voice on the verge of breaking. "I never saw him slap a cow or raise a hand to a horse."

"I remember coming over here with my big sister when we were little. When my Dad came back from the war he sold our cows and took a job at the tool factory. How I missed those cows. This farm became my special place.

"You were just a baby then, an adorable brown nut. The little brother I never had. Your mother would lay you in a cradle by the wood stove and sing Indian songs to you while she went about her chores. She always found time in her busy day to greet us, invite us in for cookies or a slice of pumpkin pie. Sometimes she'd leave us to mind you while she went to the shed for wood or to the henhouse to collect eggs.

"But the barn was the main attraction. I'd climb up to the mow with Tommy. I had a crush on him even then. I was always losing my shoes jumping around in the loose hay. We would find out the secret places where the barn cat had her kittens."

She paused and their eyes met and all that passed between them felt free of guile. She talked to him then about his father. She confessed that Patrick had always frightened her a little; how he was always about his business in field or barn; how he said he did not believe in wasting daylight; how he seldom spoke.

"Your father was as much a poet as he was a farmer. His poetry was in the words he didn't say and in the way he responded so fully to the world around him."

Remorse rose in his gullet as if he'd swallowed a live coal he could no longer contain.

"It's all my fault. I knew it was too wet. I should never have agreed to go up there with him."

"And you seriously think that you or anybody else could stop that man once he'd set his mind on something? Listen, Danny, there is nothing you could have done to change what happened. Once death is stalking a person, it's going to have its way."

"I've got to stay on the farm."

"I know it's hard, Danny, but you've got to trust Tommy. This isn't easy for him either."

She lightly bit her lower lip and looked at him pensively.

"This land means nothing to him."

She could give him no true answer to that because she herself held no fixed certainties about the meaning of the land. But she had always felt like a sister to this slim raven-haired boy. So she acceded to his truth and to the music of the rain.

He watched the Nash roll down and away on the road to the village. As she rounded the bend, she leaned on the horn and he could imagine her lovely smile. In a moment she would be crossing the bridge and soon the rain would cause the brook to swallow the bridge. He was grateful for the rain.

Hands in pockets he walked in a desultory way across the farmyard. He paused by the equipment barn and stepped out of the rain and leaned against a support beam of the open-faced equipment shed. When he looked at all these implements, he saw more than farm machinery; he saw volumes of history.

Sugarbrook Farm had been like a world unto itself. All of the work was done with horses, no tractors to make payments on, no purchased feed, and just enough livestock that could be cared for properly. The cows were brushed at the morning milking, each was named and many remained in the herd until their fifteenth year or more. The farm house never lacked paint and the kitchen garden filled the larder every autumn. While his mother had lived, the place exuded a frugal prosperity. After she died, his father buried his grief in work. Alone with his boys, he barely kept his head above water. And these last few years he had fallen into debt. Ultimately his father had continued to farm with horses, not because he thought it was the only or best way to farm, but simply because he loved his horses.

As the afternoon waned, Danny walked down to the brook. The rain was falling hard and the waters were rising. As he watched, the bridge was taken. The flood crested and leapt over the fitted-stone piers, swept by planks and rail. The bridge had weathered such flooding before; the abutments were a masterful execution of dry wall construction, dug ten feet back into either bank. The storm surge broke out of the banks below the bridge and the spreading torrent fanned into leveling wakes as it began to pool onto the bottom lands. He marked the progress of the rising as the deluge came down. The bridge under, he walked back up the lane and set to mucking out the pig pen. With their tiny eyes gleaming mischief, wagging curly tails, talking all about it in their shrill voices, the pigs did everything they could to get in his way as he labored with flat shovel and wheelbarrow. After milking chores were done, he fixed himself a meal of cured bacon, canned green beans and mashed potatoes. He did not listen to the radio.

The next morning as he was milking the cows, he became aware of a sudden stillness. Then he realized the rain had stopped. Apprehension took him then; as long as the bridge was out he was safe, but once the waters receded, trouble would begin. Yet he felt oddly relieved. The endless rain had felt almost like a form of madness, like the incessant voice of a muse. Having spent itself, it opened up the possibility of resolution.

Vigilant now, he ate breakfast with one eye out the kitchen window and on the road. He saw a vehicle approaching and dropped the egg-laden fork and pulled the rifle down off the rack on his way out the door. He went around the barn, and then tracked through a corridor of white pines by the roadside. At a distance of fifty paces he could see them but he remained undetected. The black and white sheriff's car made its approach to the bridge. The sheriff parked the vehicle and he and his deputy got out. Tommy clambered out of the backseat. They examined the bridge. Danny could not hear their words above the torrent's roar. Tommy pointed in the direction of the house and the sheriff peered at it through binoculars.

Danny crouched behind a boulder amid the stand of pines and with his raised rifle placed his brother's head within the sights. He did not breathe. Then he swung the barrel and took a bead on the sheriff. He did not move. The men returned to the car, backed out and drove away.

He began to breathe again. He stood up and walked down to the sunken bridge and took a measure of the rising water level off a submerged dog-toothed aspen clinging to the opposite bank. Though the rain had stopped, the waters were still on the rise. "Good," he said to himself. "Good."

As he turned back to the farm house, he spied a lone figure crossing the fields beyond. He recognized the long lanky strides of his friend Levi. He went into the house, put the rifle on the kitchen table and ran back out to meet his friend. They wrestled with each other in the field. He got a leg hold and set Levi to one-legged hopping; then they both went over in a tumble, with roars, grunts and laughter.

"Stop, stop now, you're getting my school clothes dirty. My Ma will have a fit!"

"Nothing against your mother but that's a piss-poor excuse to keep from being pinned."

"Keep dreaming, cowboy. I'm just showing mercy."

"You're a fine liar. How'd you get over here anyway?"

"Rope swing at the swimming hole."

"Over to Wilder's dam?"

"Yup. I spliced in a length of rope, climbed that old willow and swung across with dry shoes!"

"You tie the rope off on the other side?"

"I'm not as dumb as I look."

"It's good to see you, Levi."

"You too, bud. How you holding up?"

Danny could feel the knot in his stomach tighten. "All right," he said, as he stared off into the hills.

"I heard about it in the school yard."

On their feet again, the friends brushed themselves off and started walking.

"Jesus, Danny, what happened up there?"

"Nothing really. It was all so fast"

"Goddamn, there's nobody could handle a team like your old man. Just don't make sense."

They paused by the south side of the barn. The mid-day sun was warm though the air temperature was dropping as the storm front scattered and the winds moved around to the north.

"Jesus," exclaimed Levi.

"What is it?"

"I guess this makes you an orphan."

"I'm too old to be an orphan."

"And too young to be anything else."

"I'm old enough to hold my own."

"So what are you gonna do now?"

"I don't know. Stay here and take care of things, I guess."

"Danny, your brother's going to sell those cows. There's two cattle trucks parked down in the village just waiting to cross that bridge."

"Water's still rising."

"Yeah, but for how long?"

"I ain't gonna let them take those cows."

"Don't talk crazy."

"That's what I know."

Levi produced a pouch and rolled a cigarette and struck a blue tip on the rough-cut siding of the barn. The boards were wet and the match weakly sparked and sputtered and he cupped it and tried to save the flame but the wind snuffed it.

"Listen, my folks always liked you. You could stay at our place, come back to school, work on the farm. Bring the horses if you want."

"How could he do this to my Dad?"

Danny fell silent a moment, scuffed at the ground with the toe of his boot. Ever since he was a boy he had dreamed of being a cowboy. He had never been much for school, he read well and devoured books about the old west and although he'd always figured he would manage the farm one day, his dreams were of frontier days; he would practice roping steers, bull-calves that would have been sold if not for the indulgence of his father. Now that the farm was slipping out of his hands and with it the entire ground of his reality, his mind took refuge in those childhood dreams.

"Maybe I'll just saddle up a horse and head west."

"Sure, you can ride off into the sunset. So what are you gonna do, go and become an Indian fighter?"

"Not likely."

"I guess that wouldn't make sense, you being part Indian."

"Not much is making sense these days."

"Damn right."

"You wanna come in for coffee or something?"

"Can't - if I don't get my ass back in time for chores, I'm dead."

"Thanks for coming over."

"I miss you, Danny. Bunch of us at school do, you know. Think over what I said about coming over our way awhile. We've got plenty of room and there's no lack of work. You don't need to go nowhere."

31

Levi thrust out his hand and as they shook their eyes met, Levi's eyes imploring, Danny's answering in gratefulness but not acceptance.

He watched as the tall fellow turned and set off at an easy run in the direction from which he had come.

He went down to the root cellar and got a head of cabbage and some potatoes and came upstairs and put together a midday meal. He ate bread and cheese and pickles with the boiled vegetables and he topped it off with a tall glass of cider.

He stepped through the well house door and looked out over to where his friend had departed. He studied the long shadow of the wooden silo imperceptibly circling the bare empty fields like the register of some giant sun dial. He looked across the fields and to the woods beyond. Maybe he should just go, just leave his troubles behind, it would be so easy.

"Out west," he said as he stared at the point where the ridge line met the sky.

He took his name off then. He stood still and with his will, he peeled his name off his body, starting at the crown of the head, pulling it off as if it were a snake skin. He folded it neat like a pocket handkerchief to keep it somewhere hidden and safe for the time when he would have need of it again.

He stood there another moment and a silence rang through him like the peals of a bell ringing through a monastery at the call to prayer. It echoed through his every cell until he became that silence.

He went once more to the brook to check the water level. It was still rising. He returned to the empty house.

He started his afternoon chores earlier than usual, finding solace in feeding and milking the cows. When he was done he fed their milk to calves, and to the cats, chickens and pigs and he drank as big a glass of it as he could stand. He was loath to dump it again.

That evening back in the farm house, he began to assemble some gear. He started with his rifle, cleaning and oiling stock and barrel. He found a supply of cartridges and rummaged out a leather scabbard from the attic. He stitched two woolen blankets together to create a bedroll and then rolled it up inside a rain poncho. A canteen, a cast iron fry pan, coffee pot, striking flint, extra pairs of woolen socks, a roll of wire for snares, fish hooks, line and sinkers, a length of good rope, a sack of potatoes, dry beans, flour and jerky and salt---he spread these goods out on the parlor floor.

He went to the kitchen and slid open a counter drawer containing a cigar box with petty cash inside. "Guess Dad won't be needing this," he thought to himself as he stuffed the moderate wad into his billfold.

In the horse barn he sorted through the tack room and found the civil war era McClellan saddle. He affixed an extra long girth on it to accommodate Rory. He hauled up three sets of saddlebags and brought out two bridles and his own western saddle. As the horses watched on in curiosity from their stalls, he cleaned and oiled the leather by lamplight; then he filled the largest set of saddle bags with oats and returned to the house with the other two slung over his shoulders.

Walking across the farmyard he was braced by the night air. There was no moon and he gazed up at the stars silently screaming a balanced timbre of intensity and brilliance. Then the cold urged him inside.

He packed the assembled goods into the saddle bags. The bedroll he would tie on behind the saddle. He worked unhurriedly at the task, placing each item in with contemplative care as a priest in the sacristy might fold his vestments.

Finally he went upstairs to retrieve one more object. From a shoe box on the floor of his bedroom closet amidst a collection of found objects and gifts, a child's memorabilia, he took out a knapped flint arrow head. In the grooves etched at the base where the point would be affixed to a shaft, there was a tiny drill hole with a silver cord strung through it, transforming the intrinsic beauty of the artifact into an adornment. He could not remember how it came to belong to him.

He placed the silver cord over his head, the arrowhead hanging at the center of his breastbone. He went downstairs and put wood into the stove box. Then he returned to his room, undressed, blew out the lamp and climbed into bed. He fell asleep with the arrowhead grasped in his fist, resting on his heart.

The late winter sun crept with cold fingers over the night black eastern ridge. He crawled out of bed, bundled up and walked down to the underwater bridge. The air was clear and the exposed hard-pack of the thaw-melted lane was frozen into weird shapes and fixed heaves. A hoar frost covered all. His breath blew white and the cold penetrated his lungs, even his bones. Standing at the brook he gauged his mark and determined that the water level was falling. "Okay," he spoke within to his nameless self. He strode with determination up to the cow barn and began the morning chores.

When all the cows had been milked, having thanked each one for the gift, and when all the calves, pigs and chickens had been fed, he went out and opened up every gate within each fence line of the farm. He opened the gate to the cow yard that gave way to the fields and hill pastures. Then he opened the double Dutch doors of the barn and unlocked the stanchions. The cows backed out of their stalls into the central alley and made their way to the open doors, just as they did every winter morning while he cleaned the barn. Only this time a couple of cows, the alert ones of the herd, found the way unbarred and kicked up their heels and raised their tails as they frolicked out onto the land. They mooed and then peeled back their upper lips to sniff at the air, elated to be loosed into the late morning sun.

Once all the cows were out, he opened the bull pen and released the herd sire. The bull trotted out of the barn and bellowed. Excitement rippled through the herd. Soon all of the cattle were out of the yard exploring their new-found freedom. He watched them from a window in the barn. As the light poured through, his eyes were drawn to the quilt-like frost patterns on the window panes etched by the artist of the night. He stood there studying those crystalline images for the space of several breaths as if contemplation of such mysteries might stave off the inevitable consequences of his actions, might relieve him of this role he felt compelled almost against his own will to fulfill.

Next he released the heifers from their run-in shed, and lastly the calves from their pens. He set about cleaning the barn in his methodical way though he did not add new straw bedding to the stalls, only scraping them clean with a flat shovel. He climbed up the ladder through the chute to the hay mow and slid open the loft door to the yard and pitched down loose hay from the stack as fodder for the cattle, the winter fields being barren.

Next he opened the door of the chicken coop and rolled a barrel out of the house on its edge, spreading its contents of scratch on the ground. He flung the gate to the pig pen wide as well, leaving the six two-hundred pound wonderlings to their own devices.

All the animals turned out, he went into the house and fixed himself a hearty breakfast of ham and eggs, oatmeal and hash browns, a jar of applesauce, butter-laden toast. He washed it all down with coffee and cream and then cleaned up the kitchen. He changed out of his work clothes and pulled on a clean pair of blue jeans and a flannel shirt over his longjohns. Over these he stepped into woolen trousers and put on a woolen shirt and then he laced up his leather boots. He pulled the broad-brimmed felt hat down snug on his head. He'd had the hat for as long as he could remember---a memento his father had brought back from out west when he had come home from the service.

With leather gloves and fleece-lined coat over all, he felt ready to brave the elements. He gathered up the bedroll, rifle and scabbard and the two sets of saddle bags, and headed out to the barn.

He got Tess and Rory out of their stalls and into cross-ties, groomed them and picked their feet. He placed a halter and straight bit bridle on the draft horse and a snaffle on the Morgan. Then he spread blankets on their backs and laid on the saddles; the western saddle for the mare with one set of saddle bags and the McClellan for the gelding, with the bedroll and balance of saddle bags tied down secure. He fixed the rifle scabbard to his own saddle so the stock would ride just behind his knee to the right. He found room where there was none for a brush, comb and hoof pick in one of the bulging saddle bags and with a long lead rope, he packed Rory off Tess's saddle and led them out to the yard.

He looked about the place and called once for the old black dog. But the black dog was gone and he knew it was gone, just as he knew his father was gone.

He mounted up and made the familiar kissing sound with his lips and pressed in his heels to start the horses moving out. They left the yard through the open gate heading south by southwest.

At midday he was on a high hill from which, looking back east, he could see the entire valley and the farm. He dismounted and waited, squatting down and holding Tess's reins folded over an arm. The horses blew and pawed, sniffed and nibbled at the pale withered clumps of grass poking through the rotting cover of snow. In a short while he saw the silvered reflection of the aluminum trailers flashing across the distance under the strengthening sun. The hauler's trucks, followed by the blue truck, crept down the winding lane and halted briefly at the bridge; then the miniature convoy proceeded across the somewhat still sunken bridge, as he could just make out a shallow wake rippling behind at the crossing.

He stepped up once again into the saddle of the tall black horse and gently patted her on the neck. He looked back on the vehicles now assembled in the farm yard and he could make out the tiny figures running around frantically after the cows, waving their arms and hopping about like ants disturbed out of their nest.

He sat the horse for a moment to watch the chaos unfolding below. And then the boy with no name turned away and smacked his lips to set the horses at a walk

*

Late in the day the four-door sedan of the senior partner was still parked out front of the realty office. "Shit," Tommy muttered under his breath. The blue pickup truck wheeled in hard off the main road into the parking lot. Out of the truck with a six-pack in his hand, he set the beer down on the pavement and stepped out of his overshoes, peeled himself out of the coveralls and set them along with the boots into the bed of the truck. He picked up the six-pack again and considered putting it back in the cab, but then thought, "To hell with it," and he tromped up the steps to the office door.

Red-faced with hands on his hips, the boss stood in the middle of the reception room, the frothing mouth shouting angry words as Tommy came through the door,

"Said you needed a half-day and instead you're a no show!"

"There were complications."

36

"I got five new listings needed to be written up yesterday!"

"The cattle got loose. We had to round up the entire herd."

"Acting like you're still a rank intern. How do you expect to make partner if you can't produce?"

"I'll make up the work tonight."

"Hell, I think you miss being an old farm boy. I guess you'd rather be out plowing your fields and milking your shitty ass cows than be setting here collecting a living wage in a nice clean office."

"I'll have those listings ready by morning."

Tommy tucked the six-pack up under his arm as if it were a football and tried to sidestep around the angry man to get to his corner office.

"Hold on. Hand over one of those beers."

The boss pulled the tab off a proffered can and took a long pull.

"What's the word on your father?"

"He passed away early morning."

"Damn, Tommy, I'm sorry. I shouldn't have flown off the handle like that. It's just I've never seen work coming in like what we got now. I had a lot of respect for him you know. He was real old school---an honest man."

"Thank you, sir."

"Don't worry about those listings; just get them posted when you can."

"I'll have them ready in the morning."

"Well, sometimes keeping to your work is the best thing for it."

"I know it."

Alone in his little office his eyes went red. His hands and his face were spattered with mud and manure, his clothes were still damp with sweat. He switched on his desk lamp and dropped down into the chair. He opened one of the beers and with shaking hands he struggled with a match book to light up a cigarette. With a wide sweep of his arm he cleared all the existing piles of paperwork to the edge of the desk and scrolled a fresh sheet into the typewriter and began to tap keys furiously. Finished, he ripped the page free and held it up close to his face to read it. Then his hands went slack and he let the sheet float to

37

the floor. He put his forehead on the lip of the desk, moaned low and pounded his fists on the desk top and finally the tears came. And for some time he wept. He picked up the listing, labeled it, and filed it away in a drawer. He turned off the lamp and sat back in his chair in the dark. He sat there a long time trying to do nothing more than breathe.

PART TWO

1

Heading Southwest Towards Pennsylvania and Points West

The boy and the two horses rode through the late winter landscape until he lost all track of time. He passed frozen fields and dormant trees with not even a chickadee to break the sound of the nothingness he felt inside. What was still alive in him was evident only in his care for the horses.

Early morning, breaking camp, he had the horses saddled and the gear packed away. He stepped the few paces to the banks of the brook to refill his canteen. There in the fine steel-gray sand left unfrozen by the rill he spied the tracks of a bear. The foot prints were fresh and the imprint true. The pads, the digits, the tips of claw, all neatly etched in an ambling script. The sight of it brought a half-smile to his face. He returned to the mounts, stepped up into the saddle, and asked Tess to walk on. Rory followed dutifully behind.

He followed the bear tracks southward along the brook's edge till it led him to the Connecticut River and the old north-south road. The horses were unused to traffic and at first they shied with every passing vehicle. He held his seat until soon even the roar and whoosh of the diesel trucks didn't faze them. At times the roadway shared concourse through the narrow valleys with the freight lines. Then he would have to dismount and hold the horses while the trains rumbled through. But after a while even these became a part of their new environment and ceased to spook them.

The river was receding from flood stage. Revealed now was the seldom seen face of its alluvial serpentine mystery, making human endeavor seem transitory and fragile in the face of its unfathomable age and power. The evidence of the massive flood surge was everywhere. Piles of broken up blue ice had become haphazard sculptures at every oxbow. Mud and debris were strewn across the road. Trees and power lines were felled and houses and barns, like misbegotten ships, rose out of fields that had become shallow lakes. Black and white cattle, huddled on an island spit, lowed like mournful castaways as he and the horses passed. The planting would be late this year. He felt a pang as he thought of his own fields lying fallow. He spurred his brother's horse on to quicken the pace. There would be no going back. As he rode on a pair of mallards flushed up out of a water-silvered field and he watched as their mirrored image winged across the surface of the land.

He traveled in the wake of glaciers. When these hills had risen from the ocean depths, they were towering jagged cathedrals. Ages of erosion had tempered their might and extreme warming and cooling trends had modified them with the giant carving tool of mile-thick ice. The great river followed the path of the ice, a rift where once two tectonic plates had converged. Having no set direction of his own, he followed the river.

Several days out he caught a glimpse of the future. From a high bluff above the river he looked down from the old road towards the vanguard of the new. An army of bulldozers, site engineers and blasting crews were wending their way up the ancient river course, leveling hills and filling in ravines. Close behind came the steam rollers and paving crews to lay the land under the dual asphalt ribbons of a new super highway, land that had been farmed by Vermonters for two hundred years and by the Abenaki people for another thousand before that. If this was the way to the New Jerusalem of which his brother prophesied, he could see no progress in it, only wanton destruction. He was glad to be leaving it behind.

Day followed upon day with hardships of inclement weather and spare rations. His body became inured to the elements. His cheeks hollowed and his eyes grew hard; he became as angular as a scarecrow in a winter cornfield. The horses grazed where they could, pawing through snow in abandoned meadows. When he needed to, he would stop in a town to purchase grain and supplies.

The course of the river steered his path through burnt-out factory towns. Towering chimney stacks were reflected in the stagnant waters of the canals. Empty machine-tool factories and silent woolen mills with broken windows stood in mute testament to a bygone age.

Acres of vacant red brick had gone to dust where an industry once powered by river turbines had been rendered obsolete by cheaper power and even cheaper labor found elsewhere.

The sight of a traveler on horseback being rare, the lone rider drew more stares the more hardened and weather-beaten his appearance became. Like a pilgrim out of time he drifted through the towns. He spoke to no one. People left him alone. He did not look right or left as he rode, no eyes for church spires, no appetite for general stores or diners. He guarded the few dollars in his billfold closely.

At night he would sit for hours under the shelter of an evergreen-bough lean-to, staring at the campfire, not awake, not asleep, not dreaming, but simply watching the dance of flames. On one such night he looked up from the flames and saw his father sitting across the fire from him. He was wearing his town clothes and the narrow-brimmed hat that he wore only to weddings or funerals. His father poked at the fire with a stick, made the logs settle and the sparks fly up.

"What's wrong, son?" he asked.

"I feel all frozen inside."

"You should go home."

"I can't, Tommy's going to sell the land."

"Maybe if you go back he won't."

"Will you come with me?"

"I can't do that."

"Why not?"

"You know why."

His father looked at him sternly but with kindness and then rose up and walked back into the night.

As he journeyed southward, redwing black birds sawed off their mating reels from the roadsides; Canadian geese flew overhead in their loose and raucous formations; coltsfoot bloomed like tiny solar flares in the ditches. As these and other signs of spring appeared, he turned off the concourse of the river and followed the old Massachusetts turnpike due west through the slate-riven peaks of the Berkshires. He rode each day following the peregrination of the sun.

41

Horses and rider fell into a routine of trail and rest. He looked after the animal's needs as best he could and their bodies soon hardened to the relentless walking. When Tess tired, he would switch the saddle bags and ride Rory awhile. While the Morgan was responsive and smooth of gait, the view from the back of the draft-cross was grand. At times he would dismount and lead both so they could glean a semblance of rest. In this way, they crossed the Hudson and headed to the southeast, riding hard through the knobs and hollows of the Catskills and down to the lowlands of eastern Pennsylvania.

He came into a county settled by Mennonites where farming with horses was still common. When Rory cast a shoe he knew he had to take both horses in for shodding. He found a blacksmith's shop, entered and pointed to the horses' feet.

"You've ridden these animals hard."

A silent nod.

"Lucky for you they've both got sound feet. No hoof---no horse."

As the farrier removed the shoes and trimmed the feet, hot-forging shoes to size, he spoke casually about the horses and the weather and mentioned which farmers might be looking for an extra hand now that planting season was upon them. The boy remained non-committal but he listened. He paid what he knew to be customary and was leaving when the farrier handed back half the sum. "Good luck to you, Cowboy!" With a nod of thanks to the farrier, he led the horses back onto the road with their new shoes clopping. As he rode, the scents of awakening earth reached his nostrils. His farmer's soul grew restless with the endless travel, yearning for work on the land.

Rider and horses entered the farming communities and he soon found work. The solemn men with their beards, black coats and wide-brimmed hats, the women in long dresses and aprons, heads covered with bonnets, were not unlike the conservative Yankee farmers he had left behind. They did not find his silence odd and respected his skills as a teamster, aware that such knowledge was rare among those from the outside.

42

He felt a natural affinity for these folk and admired the impeccable practicality in the layout of their fields, barns and houses. The first thing that struck him was the absence of utility poles and power lines, but there was something else, more subtle, in the harmonious ordering of the farms. Nothing was barren, no square inch was untended or without purpose and intent. The human and the natural were joined in a seamless garment of plain abundance, a spare plenitude born of faith-filled perseverance.

As he traveled along the hard-pack lanes, families passed him in their horse-drawn box carriages, the women staring straight ahead, the children waving shyly and the men offering the slightest nod. The plain folk clung to their ways with the tenacity of lichen to bare mountain rock. Through the centuries of their durable habitation, their valleys became an oasis of simple beauty in a world turned increasingly ugly by industrial progress and modernization.

He did not tarry in any one place---a few days here at the potato planting, a week there for the planting of corn. Sometimes his reputation as an able horseman preceded him along the route of wireless communication and doors opened to him. All the time he was moving west, inexorably drawn to the sunset.

*

The day of the burial dawned crisp and bright. Former members of his varsity football squad helped him bear the casket. The track through the field up to the hilltop cemetery had been washed out by the heavy rains, so they had to carry the box further than expected. The former athletes were breathing hard and sweating in their formal overcoats when they finally reached the crest of the hill. A rose blush of swelling buds was visible on the limbs of the maples in the sugar bush beyond the fieldstone walls. The pickets of the gated entrance were weathered as gray as the head stones. The great spreading oak that guarded the dead still held its leaves tight in the bud.

The body in the plain pine box had been entombed in the burial vault in the village cemetery, the burial having to wait for the frost to leave the ground. Now new grass was edging through the rank

43

browned-out mat of the season past. "I'll have to get up here and mow this year," Tommy made note to himself. "That is, if it hasn't been sold." They worked strapping under the box and then lowered it down into the open grave dug beside that of the dead man's wife.

The priest from the church in the village was new to his post. He knew nothing of the farmer now cold in the box other than that he'd been baptized in the true faith. He spoke just those essential words that must be uttered before the dirt can be shoveled back into the hole.

Tommy looked around him then, not so much to take in his surroundings as to find some relief from the sense of desperation and isolation he was feeling. He watched a raven fly overhead like a black crease across the empty blue sky. Next his eyes fell on the carved face of a nearby tombstone---the image of a skull with empty eyes, wings emerging from either side of its bony pate. He looked then to his wife's face and watched as her tears caught the glint of the white sun as they fell. Her eyes were cast to the ground. The morning breeze loosed a curling strand of auburn hair from underneath her black pill box hat. Her twin toddler sons stood to either side of her, holding her hands. They twitched, uncomfortable and restless in their miniature men-suits, scuffling their polished black shoes in the fresh dug dirt. The shoveling commenced and the large men made quick work of it.

Back at the farmhouse there was a pale reception attended by a handful of ancient aunts, uncles and cousins from his maternal grandmother's line---people with whom Patrick had never been close. They pecked like diffident hens at the food laid out on the side table. Their muted conversation was cropped and faded from his mind as soon as it entered his ears. They'd approved of his father no more in life than they did now in death. The unwashable stain of Papism. There were a few old men there from neighboring farms, closed-mouthed in their condolences, as well as the doctor, the judge and the local merchant from the general store. The county sheriff paid his respects, but his deputy was absent. And then looking awkward and out of place was Levi, the neighbor's boy and best friend to his little brother gone missing now these two months.

Tommy sidled his way over through the sparse gathering become a crowd in the close confines of the parlor. Levi was seated on the window box, cradling in his hands a porcelain mug of black coffee.

"How's it going?" Tommy asked.

"Okay, I guess. How're you holding up?"

"I'm all right. Heard anything?"

"Naw."

"You were the last one to see him."

"I guess."

"Sure he didn't say anything about where he was going, what he was up to, some kind of plan?"

"Like I told you, he just said something about heading west. I thought it was a joke."

"All right. Thanks for showing up today."

"Sure."

Levi looked up once and met Tommy's eyes. Then he dropped his eyes into his cup of coffee.

"You really gonna sell this place?"

"I don't know. Seems so weird to be burying the old man up there and to be talking in the same breath of selling this ground."

"It is weird."

"What else am I supposed to do?"

"Farm it."

"That isn't me."

"You sure?"

"Just right now I'm not sure of anything."

"What if he comes back?"

"I wish he would."

*

Haying season came round. He'd been working some and eating better and Tess and Rory were sleek from spring grass. He agreed to help a lone farm family with the mowing. They were a young couple struggling to pay off their newly acquired hill farm. They could provide him only with meals, a place to sleep in the barn loft and

45

pasture for his horses. But they seemed like good people and he stayed on to help harvest their few rough acres.

A barn owl flew in through a window in the loft and though the flap of its broad brush of wings was near to silent, it roused him from sleep. The golden eyes glowed in the darkness, seeming to hover in the murky half light above the gray bird's perch on the rafters, waiting for mice as he lay awake in the loose straw waiting for the sun.

He dozed off and when he woke again the owl was gone, leaving him to wonder if he had seen it in a dream. He arose and climbed down the slat ladder. As he emerged into the gray-green light of the pre-dawn world, roosters crowed, songbirds sang, an old hound lying under the porch of the farmhouse lifted its head and wagged its tail but did not stir when he walked by. He ascended the hill pasture that rose to the west behind the farm buildings. Once he reached its crest he sat and waited. The farmer's wife came out of the house, opened a gate and set off down the lane to fetch the cows. The young farmer came out moments after and started the feeding chores of the small animals. Even when a clear view was obscured, as the fellow entered outbuilding or shed, he could tell by the sounds carrying up the rise which chores the man was applying himself to---which critters were next in line clamoring for their breakfast--- the horses, the hogs, the chickens.

He felt a little strange, even somehow guilty, to be in a position of witnessing these people beginning a new day of rounds in the cycle of their farm. He moved about as a shadow while they dwelt in the full light of sun. The weight of their responsibility to their livestock, crops, pasture land and forest, to their children, to one another, sharply defined them and each passing day further carved the contour of their characters. In contrast he felt as if he were floating in a mist-enshrouded world, a hungry ghost who could only witness life but not feel the press of flesh against bone or the solid earth beneath his feet.

The first rays crested the horizon. He stood and walked back down the hill. When he reached the bottom and was about to crawl through the plank fence, the lead cow of the herd rounded the bend in the lane, the brass bell suspended on a collar around her neck ringing in time to her stately gait. He watched the cows file into the yard, mist rising behind them off the cool earth. They were soon followed by the pretty woman, barefoot and with her blonde hair covered in a blue kerchief, wearing a plain dress and apron, a willow switch swinging lightly in her hand. She stopped to greet him. He slid through the fence and stood awkwardly before her.

"Good morning, going to be a lovely day," she commented, knowing better than to wait for any customary pleasantries from him. He nodded an affirmation. Then rather suddenly she grasped his hand in hers and squeezed it firmly. "Thank you for coming here. You are such a great help to my husband. He so often must work alone. My little girls are happy to have you here as well." He held her gaze but shyly, then she released his hand and started to move on but she halted in mid-step and turned towards him again, gazed up to the brightening sky and then down to her feet stained with red clay and morning dew. She looked up and spoke again.

"My husband came here much like you---from the 'English'---to work among us. He is honest and charitable and he is an able farmer. We have come to live on this mountain because we have been shunned by the brethren of the valley. You see I am of the old order and my husband is not and the Bishop forbade me to marry him."

She hesitated a moment and touched the willow switch to the pink and white clover blossoms, making the tip of it hop from flower to flower like a pollinating bee.

He did not know what prompted her self-revelatory outburst. Perhaps in his silence he seemed more available, that through his wandering and grieving he had poured himself out as an empty vessel for others to fill with their own innermost stories.

"I don't know why I tell all this to you. I just wanted to let you know that your presence is truly appreciated here," she said and then she walked briskly on.

His insides warmed, his heart quickened from the encounter. Then he set off to the barn to help with chores.

The woman was kneading bread. With morning chores done, he sat at the kitchen table with her bearded husband and the two little girls. At first the girls had been a little frightened of him but after a few days they had grown accustomed to his quiet ways and included him in their conversation. They called him "Uncle."

The husband mopped up the last of his eggs with toast and turned to his wife, "Uncle and I will take the team up to the north field soon as the dew is lifted. With any luck we'll finish by night fall."

"That is well. The girls and I will thin the carrots and harvest radishes."

The farmer's young wife was an excellent cook and baker. The clothes on their backs were stitched by her nimble fingers. She tended the kitchen garden and put by hundreds of jars of fruits and vegetables. As the men rose to their work, she covered a mound of dough with a wet cloth, leaving the sponge to rise. She took the little girls by the hand out to the garden, its vast array of vegetables, flowers and herbs in clean weeded rows.

Mowing steady, the knives on the cutter bar were sharp, the grass was falling over smooth with the click click click of the sickle-bar passing. Two old chunk horses were pulling. The farmer drove and the boy followed behind with a scythe and a hay fork to clean up the corners and edges of the field and the rims around stone outcrops that the mower missed. The heat of the day grew intense. The horses were white with a briny sweat and needed to stop every few passes around the field to stand and blow and he would fetch a bucket of water from a nearby brook and water them where they stood.

He paused from the scything to wipe the sweat from his brow and to enjoy the sudden breeze that stirred the heavy grass heads and spun the leaves on the great oaks surrounding the field. As he rested he observed the progress of the team and just then the near-side mare collapsed and her teammate kept walking. The farmer called out his "whoa!" and the mower came to an abrupt halt in mid-pass. He dropped the scythe and ran and when he caught up to them the death-rattle was in her throat. "Died in the traces," said the bearded young farmer, "that's just the way the old girl would've wanted to go."

He looked at the farmer standing hapless by his remaining horse. He held up one finger and ran to fetch Rory from the paddock below. He led him up and they unhitched the dead mare, rolled her side to side to extract the harness, and hitched Rory in her place. Rory was twice the horse of his new mate and was rested and feeling good. The farmer handed over the lines to Danny who took a seat behind Rory on the mower. He backed the team up two paces, put the bar in gear and off they went. An hour before sunset the grass was all laid down. The farmer had summoned the knacker with his great wagon and winch and just as dark fell, the corpse of the dead horse was dragged from the field. Rory enjoyed an extra ration of oats that night.

Days later the hay from the fields had been raked, pitched on a wagon, delivered to the barn, then hoisted up into the loft. It was time for him to move on. During these last days he had thought about what the loss of their horse would mean to this young couple. Their hilltop acres were thin, their efforts to gain a livelihood from this land a struggle. Without a working team and cut off from the community in the valley, they could lose their farm. Loss was now second nature to him, grieving a way of life. When he awoke that morning and saddled up Tess, he left Rory behind in the gray-weathered barn. The joy the young couple felt on discovering this parting gift would have been complete if not for a new emptiness in their house created by the departure of the silent young "Uncle."

His progress took him beyond the measured boundaries of the Amish lands. The farms he saw now were not designed on the human scale of those who rely on live horse-power. These industrial operations were tailored to heavy equipment---not his definition of what properly constituted a farm. He felt alien and displaced and was no longer inclined to stop and look for work.

He crossed the Susquehanna River and journeyed into the Blue Mountains where the land and the farms were hard scrabble. Still he didn't stop. He was into the rhythm of a relentless ride.

Once again he demanded of himself and of his horse the resolute pace of the inveterate pilgrim. He avoided the larger through-ways, traveled on the old state highways and secondary routes. Horse and rider covered as much as twenty miles in a day. Tess was a tough and naturally competitive horse and she rose to the challenge. He and the horse had become their own solo endurance team. They rode through the heat of the sun and the whip of the rain. They made a grueling mid-summer crossing of Ohio, Indiana and Illinois.

Law officers drove past him from time to time, local police in small towns. Often they slowed down but then moved on. He was a vagrant, and an odd one at that, but he didn't linger in any one place long enough to pose a threat. The law seemed just as happy to let him pass. He received all the hard scrutiny with impassive demeanor and perhaps the fact that he didn't seem to care surrounded him with a shield of invulnerability.

Then one day he was seventeen years old. The birthday came and went unnoticed. He had no idea where he was going or why he was traveling so hard. Some daemon of flight possessed him. He charged on in absolute obedience to a mandate that was unforgiving and devoid of self-reflection. His tongue was silent. His mind was fixed. His soul was a house on fire.

2

Crossing The Mississippi Into Iowa And Onward Northwest To South Dakota

The earth had been under water, this land had once lain fallow under a sea. The black soil was ten feet deep, a rich pocket of sedimentary deposits and air borne glacial scree trod over by herds long extinct. A billion crushed bones had grown into lush fodder as tall as a man. He moved through that liminal space where forest gave way to prairie. Towns were further apart and as he left the bounds of the great eastern forest, mixed meadow and open woods gave way to what was once tall grass. Here he passed through farms as big as the township he had lived in, vast faceless farms strung along a roadway running straight as an arrow aimed into the nothingness of the prairie sky.

The waters of the Mississippi wound slow, wide and brown like a great snake lapping lazily at the cement pillars of a state highway bridge as rider and horse gazed over from a railing above. The shod feet clip-clopped sharply on the paved surface as they made the crossing. They left the highway, opting to travel the gravel tracks connecting agrarian outposts.

He walked with Tess on a lead some of the time so that she would not constantly carry all the provisions and his weight. He marked time by the shifts from foot to saddle and back again. As he walked now at Tess's shoulder, her lead draped loosely over his own shoulder, he saw his father walking alongside, brandishing a polished cherry wood walking stick which seemed to help him keep apace despite the bad leg.

"Where you going, son?"

"I don't know."

"You're heading west."

"Thought maybe I could be a cowboy."

"We're farmers, Danny, always have been, always will be."

"You can't blame a fella for dreaming."

"Dreams have their price."

"I know it."

"Your horse looks tired."

"She ain't mine, she belongs to Tommy."

"She's yours now. Best look after her, son."

"Don't worry, Dad, I will."

"You should go home."

"I ain't ready."

"When will you be?"

"I don't know. I wish you could go back with me."

"I'm dead, Danny."

"I know it."

His father stopped walking and stood still in the road. He whoaed the horse and turned to face him.

"Where'd you get the cane?"

His father held up the cherry wood as if to better consider it and then tapped its brass tipped end upon the toe of his shoe.

"Oh, just something I picked up along the way. Makes the walking seem a little less hard."

"Are you following me?"

"Maybe we're following each other; my way's been lonely, too."

"I guess that makes us both lost."

He mounted the horse and nudged her forward and when he looked back over his shoulder all he saw was an empty road. He wheeled the horse around and trotted her back several paces to study the margins of the road. An empty beer bottle, a crumpled cigarette pack and no other trace in the dry gravel. When he turned again a covey of pheasant crossed the road ahead of them. He drew the rifle from its scabbard and whispered in Tess's ear. As the single shot blew off one bird's head, the horse stood her ground. The meat, roasted on a spit, did him good that night.

Men had made of the prairie a sea of corn. As horse and rider pressed onward the land grew arid and spare. Corn gave way to wheat and wheat to rangeland and rangeland at last, to wilderness. To one accustomed to the intimate configurations of the eastern hills, the limitless and gradual undulations of the open plains were more than daunting, in fact, dizzying and almost maddening in their uncompassed excess of vista.

The endless sky surrounded him, much like the lonely and desolate sky in the wider spaces of his heart. High prairie grass, blue gamma, switch and wild rye, corn flower blue and sunflower rays and away in the distance saw-toothed mountain's jagged script scrawled across the horizon. After crossing the Missouri the creeks became intermittent. Sun-browned and frayed at the edges, relentlessly hounded by the heat, the boy and his horse took to resting by day in the shade of cottonwood, willow and oak. As alert pronghorns grazed nearby, alternately feeding and raising their graceful heads, they took their rest by those infrequent waters and walked on accompanied by the wild hosts of night.

He fished and set out snares for hare. He sometimes suffered hunger but it was never dire. He moved across the westward landscape like a shadowy spectre, lost in the errant cadence of coyote song, no longer certain of what it meant to be human.

He was out of oats for the horse and she'd cast a shoe. He ran a hand along her side as she drank. Nothing but ribs.

Tess smelled them before he saw them. Her ears pitched forward, her nostrils quivering. She let out a whinny as horse will to horse. He looked up and on the next rise he saw them, each head turned looking back at him. Fall was coming soon and the wild horses were on the move to the mountains where water would be available all winter. Horses of odd colors and markings---mouse gray, blue roan, duns with zebra stripes on their legs, bristly manes and dark lines trailing down the length of their spines. Denizens of the arid plains and desolate mountains, wraith-like, bodies lean and hard with stringy muscle, they traversed the empty canyons, their hungry passage witnessed solely by bighorn sheep, pronghorn antelope, stalking puma and the restless ghosts of ancient riders.

He turned his horse away from the road then. Always at a distance they followed the herd. After days of watching, he knew what he wanted to do.

Though the stallion was ever on the alert for challenges to his ascendancy or a predator's threat, it was the lead mare that chose the direction and duration of their ambulations. Not the most impressive specimen among the little herd, she was thin-necked and lunk-headed, but with grit and determination, she kept the younger horses in line. He knew this was the horse that Tess would have to contend with if she were to find her place in the herd.

At twilight horse and rider cantered to the crest of a hummock. The herd had grown accustomed to their presence and were grazing by a sliver of creek just below. A new moon was appearing on the western horizon. He untied his bedroll and saddlebags, and undoing the girth, he brought the saddle to the ground, resting it upright on its horn. Then he unsheathed his knife and pried off her three remaining iron shoes and gave a final leveling trim to the hoof material. In the exertion of the task he sliced into the palm of his opposing hand. "Such is the price of freedom," he mused, as he stood and sucked out the wound. He spat out the bloody wad and bent to the work again. Then he undid Tess's throat latch and removed the bridle, leaving her stripped clean. She stood by his shoulder, alert and awake, sensing the light evening breeze. Then she walked, did not run, to meet them. The medley of pounding and snorting began, some striking and biting and in the long-legged striding, a wild ecstasy of equine glee. Last he saw of her she ran as one among them, a wild horse of the plains.

He walked North by Northwest, hoping to find the road. In the lonely silence of the night his sense of self was reduced to the rhythm of his breathing, the effort and weight of each footfall. At sunrise he lowered his gaze to the ground to keep his eyes from being swept away by the fleeting mirages that washed away at the flats stretching to the horizon. He carried the saddle, the rifle and the bags and grew weary to the bone.

He heard a scuffle in the sand behind him and turned to see his father laboring to catch up. He stopped and waited. His father came up and stood leaning on his cane to catch his breath.

"You still with me?"

"Don't you know, Danny? I'll always be with you."

They set out together in step.

"Hard walking now."

"Don't give up, son."

"I won't."

"I'd offer to shoulder your load but I'm having a hard enough time just keeping up."

"I'm probably gonna have to pitch the saddle anyway."

"Too bad. But you did right by that horse, son."

"You think so?"

"I think you gave her the best chance she's got."

"I never should have brought her out here."

"I won't argue that. But you've taken responsibility for your decision and that's the most that can be asked of any man."

"You think I'm gonna make it?"

"You? I don't doubt it for a second."

"I don't even know who I am anymore."

"Well, ain't that what you set to find out?"

"I guess so. But I don't even know how to talk anymore."

"You're talking to me aren't you?"

"That's different, you don't rightly count."

"You're like I was. You'll talk when you have something to say."

His father paused a moment, pulled the narrow brim hat down to better shade his eyes.

"Christ all mighty, it's hotter than hell out here."

"Ain't it, Dad? I'm just about dying with thirst."

"Listen Danny, I'm going to have to leave you for awhile, I can't go with you on this next leg."

"Why not?"

"All this traveling is hard on an old man and besides I got business to attend to elsewhere."

"I shouldn't think you'd be so busy being dead and all."

"You'd be surprised how much work there is in being dead."

"Before you go can I ask you one question?"

"Shoot."

"How old was I when my mother died?"

"You were five."

"What was she like?"

"You said one question."

"Sorry."

"She was beautiful and she loved the land and she loved you very much. But you already knew that."

"I guess so."

"Any way, I'll see you back at the farm."

"Really?"

"You can count on it. You take care now, all right?"

"I will."

Bleached bison bones in a dry gulch, the curve of the horns pointing inward. Empty eyes staring straight ahead. Maybe I should turn around now. Go back. But what if he's sold it? He's probably sold it. Nothing to go back to. Got to go on.

He was in deep trouble now and he knew it. He dug down into his root will to survive and kept walking. The flats gave way to rough country. Sandstone buttes capped with an edging of ponderosa pines, lupine, yucca, chokecherry and sumac dotted the rolling swales of soft buffalo grass, lending a blush of color to the seasonal declination. In the dry heat the scent of the pines was all-pervading. The light of the sun was so brilliant it seemed to penetrate into sound.

He curled up in a draw beneath jack pines and unlaced his boots, half afraid the skin would peel off as he removed them. His last pair of socks had long since moldered away. With the boots off, he propped his head on the saddle and fell unconscious.

Something was licking his toes. He stirred and a little gray coyote nearly dropped dead from fright. It leapt sideways and bolted. He laced on his boots and fell asleep once more.

The badlands swallowed him. Weird spires pink and blue, pale egg shapes and myriad strata entwined and drew him in. All traces of fence lines disappeared in a landscape too forbidding for sensible stockmen and their cattle. He could measure no ordinary sense of space here and time leaked away into the eternal processes of geologic shape shifting. He had dropped his saddle miles behind. His canteen was dry and his boots were giving out. He was losing all ability to reel his thoughts into a straight line. In pain he scrambled up a rise and found himself walking on grassland. Away across the flat he spied electric lines spanning the plain and felt hope then that he might be delivered from that wasteland. He walked on the fallen ladder of a rail bed under the lines.

At nightfall he stumbled into a cow town, drawn like a moth to the lonely beacon of light on a single grain silo. He drew water from an outdoor tap and bought a loaf of bread and a brick of sharp cheese at the local gas station and drank and ate his fill. Then he wandered over to the quiet train yard.

He was ambling along the tracks looking for a place to bed down for the night when a barefoot figure hopped nimbly out of an open box car and scuttled up beside him. An older man in a tattered suit and fedora of a bygone era eyed him keenly. The old fellow tipped the hat, revealing a shiny bald pate beneath and offered a cup of coffee from a wide-mouth thermos.

"You an Indian?"

The boy shook his head, "No."

"I saw your dark eyes. Thought maybe you was."

He accepted the black steaming cup.

"Where you heading to?"

A slight shrug of shoulders.

"I know, I know," said the old man as he waved one agitated hand about his head.

"Ain't going nowhere. Just leaving places. Well, take the rails, son. That's the way to travel. Since I was a young man I worked the mines from here to Mexico. Mind you, I was no bum. A true hobo is a working man on the move. There's work to be had along the way. Everyone wants to hire a young man with a keen eye and a strong arm such as yourself. Here, let me see your hands. Ahch! you're a farmer's son, all right."

The boy sniffed tentatively at the steaming cup like a coyote sniffing at bait in a trap. He took a sip. The coffee made his blood hot.

"You climb aboard the freight on track five. Northern Pacific pulls out at 4:00am. That'll take you over to the coast. You'll find work over there."

He nodded, returned the cup and turned to go. But the hobo began to speak again, in a leisurely tone, as friend to friend, and knowing it would be a long while till the freight pulled out, he turned around and politely listened. The old fellow poured him another cup of coffee and with a sweeping gesture, invited him to sit on a discarded packing crate.

"Yessir, rode that train all the way to Mexico. Ever been south of the border, son? It's another country. Here, everything is new. Down there, roots run deep. Must've been about your age when I rode into that infernal paradise."

The hobo shook his head and rubbed a mangled hand along his grizzled jaw as the memories welled up before his eyes.

"The revolution was on then but that didn't halt the mining of silver. I worked under the mountain by day, drank in the cantina by night. Not even the coyotes could make a living in that place. There was only the work in the mine, that open bleeding vein we cut into the earth."

The hobo paused and looked at him hard before he continued.

"Raised on a farm I was, but I left the land. That was my first mistake."

The hobo studied him again until he lowered his gaze.

"Don't you worry none. You're still young, you can go back."

The boy looked up and away, his eyes sweeping over the flat lands as if gauging the distances he had crossed. Just then, an east-bound freight came chugging through, carrying in its wake a dry hot wind. They lowered their heads and covered their faces with hats and sleeves to guard against the swirl of dust. The Hobo took a sip of coffee grown cold and peered at him.

"Dynamite!---that was the only damn thing worth the while. Down in the shaft I learned the art of blasting. I've never wanted for work. It seems people everywhere have need of a man who is good at blowing things up. In all that time I only lost three fingers."

The Hobo paused and the searching depths of his eyes blazed with a magnetic pull so strong the boy could feel it draw upon underground currents in his own soul. The Hobo continued to stare and parse the thin line of his lips as if willing him to speak but his tongue remained inert.

"After all these years riding the freights, there is one thing I have learned; before there can be sight of the soul, there must first be feet upon the earth. Someday you'll think on me and you'll know that what I have told you is true. Take the train, son. Take the train and go home!"

The Hobo cocked his head to one side.

"Did you say something, son?"

He shook his head to indicate that he had not.

"That's just as well. I can't hear a blessed thing---stone deaf after all those explosions."

3

Riding The Train: South Dakota - Washington State Coast

He was sleeping in an open box car, curled up in the bedroll with the saddle bags for a pillow when the train pulled out in the early hours of the morning. When he woke the sun was rising cool and yellow over an empty land. He sat up opposite the open door and watched the long rolling movie pass by. He shifted his gaze to the confines of the dark car and among bits of refuse, crushed cans, broken packing crates, discarded clothing, he noticed a small printed folio, soiled and dog-eared around the edges and he reached for it. On the cover there was a picture of a yellow sun rising in a red sky over a blue land with a path of white light sliced through the center of the blue and above the sun the printed title: 'The Good News According to St. Luke.' On the back side was stamped the name: 'Mission House of St. Francis, Seattle, Washington'. He thumbed through the pages and browsed the script until a certain passage caught his eye: "No man when he hath lighted a candle, doth put it in a secret place, neither under a bushel basket but on a candlestick, that they that come in may see the light." He read on. "The light of the body is the eye; therefore when thine eye is single, thy whole body also is full of light. But when thine eye is evil, thy body is also full of darkness." He was sure there must be more to these matters regarding darkness and light. He put the book down and sat watching the arid lands drifting by. He looked but he did not see. He picked the book up again and this time he read it cover to cover.

By nightfall the train was leaving the short grass prairie behind, ascending in long winding curves upward into the Rocky Mountains. At midnight the steel wheels rolled over the rails that crossed the great divide.

Forest clad mountains and sparkling waters cascading from snow-fraught peaks gladdened his eyes at dawn. He saw an eagle soaring on gold-flecked wings, a ground squirrel clutched in its talons. The wind had sculpted every living thing into streamlined shapes. Thousand-year-old trees gave animate expression to invisible forces.

At noon the locomotive plunged into total darkness. For the distance of seven miles it hurtled through the entrails of the earth. Then the single eye light of that long dark tunnel opened and the house on wheels began a free fall on rails descending to the desert floor. Alone in a vacant box car rolling through an empty land of dry dust rocks and sage, a lizard's paradise of exposed ancient bone, casting his fate like dice upon the mercy of the rails.

At one train stop he saw fifty men or more climb down off the train. Leather tramps and rough men in colorless overcoats and broken shoes. They headed off singly or in small groups toward the new old town, rolling cigarettes and discarding bottles, all the while keeping a wary eye out for the Bully-Boys with their night sticks.

He lived on the train for three days and three nights. Chug and roar and whistle wail became the music of his dreams. The train was rolling down off high bluffs when he caught the first whiff of salt air wafting up from the marshlands. With all his bones aching he climbed out of the boxcar at a coastal depot and on shaky legs he stumbled down to the sea.

He could not get enough of it. Staring out over the sparkling horizon, guessing at the distances, he beheld a vast island-speckled bay. Freighters and fishing boats and ferries and tugs with their tankers plied the deeper waters of the inlet that gave way to the Pacific. Just beyond the feathered fringe of landing waves he saw sunlight in play flashing off the backs and uplifted flukes of gray whales in southern migration.

He took off his hat, dropped his meager belongings and kicked off his boots in the salt grass and trundled down a steep dune to the beach. He waded in with his arms by his sides until the pacific waves lapped round his ears and topped his head. His toes left the stony bed and he flailed to the surface gasping. He swam back to the shore feeling reborn. He was tired of running; he had run as far as he could go. He had no plan and nowhere to go, but he felt a new determination to get to somewhere.

He wrung out his clothes and laid them out on stones to dry. He sat in his nakedness cross-legged amidst the protective isolation of shallow dunes and let the sound of the waves become one with his own breathing.

61

After noon he put on his clothes stiff with salt. He ate his last crust of bread and rind of cheese and emptied the canteen. He clambered up the steep bluff and started walking the tracks, going through barren salt marsh for hours in the hot sun. The tracks finally led him past vast industrial docks that serviced the cargo ships up into the port city of Seattle.

Stinging particulate burned his eyes and noxious fumes made it difficult to breathe with air belched out of the towering stacks of paper mills and refineries so thick he could have sliced it into cubes. The water in the canals ran brown with oil and bubbling detergents thick on its surface as it limped down to the sea.

He crossed out of the industrial zone and into the heart of the city and when he came to the grille gates of a graveyard, he stumbled through to find softwood trees hovering above ornate headstones, a room permeated with a melancholic green gloom. Bright flowers and trimmed hedgerows of evergreens and roses edged the neat pathways among the tombs. Red squirrels frolicked about the tree trunks, bird song trickled down from the heights. He lay down with his head resting on the roots of a conifer as if taking his place among the dead with the living tree as his tombstone. He could scarcely tell if he was awake or dreaming, or even if he was alive or dead. He lay thus a long while, finding a strange kind of peace in that sanctuary where even nature itself seemed to prosper among the dead.

As last he rose impelled by hunger and thirst and the naked and undeniable fact that he was still alive. Out on the sidewalk he noticed wild herbs pressing their way up through cracks in the concrete, thriving in the margins; nature subdued was only biding its time to reclaim this ground.

He wandered the city streets in a trance. The bedroll and rifle scabbard strapped across his back, the saddle bag slung over a shoulder, the broad-brimmed hat pulled down tight over his ears. Averted eyes and hostile stares separated him from every stranger. He looked into a shop window full of the latest fashion and was startled to see in its reflection the gaunt specter the continental crossing had made of him.

Gone the hale farm boy. He was not only a stranger among strangers but one even to himself.

He went into an outfitters and with the last of his money bought new boots, a button-down shirt and blue jeans. As he cinched his belt round the new jeans he noted that he was down to the last notch and thought maybe he should have bought some food instead. He rummaged through the pockets of his old clothes and found a few coins and then he balled up the rags and the broken boots and tossed them in a curbside trash bin.

In another store front that sold musical instruments, a certain wooden flute almost lost amid brass horns, steel guitars and rhythm snares caught his eye. He was gripped by a strange and urgent desire to possess it. The proprietor happened to notice him and opened the door to his shop and invited him in.

"I see you are a traveling man and one as might appreciate the opportunity of an honest day's work. Are you good with a hammer?"

He answered with the affirmative nod.

"I have some shelving needs be put up. Trouble is I don't have ready cash to pay. Do you think a fella might consider bartering his labor for some portion of my stock?"

Again the minimal nod, accompanied by the slim hint of a smile.

"Well my boy, you find your way back here in the morning and we'll put you to work."

He tipped his hat and walked out the door.

Into the melee he was drawn, that dark stream carrying him to the seedier side of town. He was feeling weak now with hunger and thirst. Pressed between out of work men and working women of the night, he found himself standing in front of a two-story clapboard affair which bore the painted signboard; 'Saint Francis Good News Mission House' and beneath that, 'No one admitted between 7:00pm and 7:00am'.

He didn't know what time it was but he knew the hour was late. He wondered if this was the dwelling place of the author of the "Good News". He had left that little book back there on the box car. Now in this forsaken place all the promise in its pages seemed to elude him. If he could meet that writer he might have some questions for him. That is, if he were talking. But he wasn't talking. He hadn't willed himself to silence, silence had taken a hold of his will and for all he knew, he might never talk again; and then again, he might just talk to the next person he should meet. He didn't know what to expect of himself anymore.

He climbed the steps to the mission and tried the front door. It was locked but he could hear a murmur and clatter perhaps of plates and silverware within so he knocked once. No reply. He walked back down the steps to the landing and continued along the sidewalk. He came upon a phone booth and stepped in and dialed the operator. His own voice sounded wholly alien to him as he gave her his brother's name and state and town and told her it was a collect call. The phone on the other end of the line rang nine times and his heart was pounding and he felt queasy and weak kneed when his brother's voice came on over the line, angry, saying, "Who the hell is this?" He hung up quickly and left the booth and had gone a few steps when it occurred to him that it was probably close to midnight back in Vermont and even though he was feeling desperate with fatigue and hunger, he almost laughed at his mistake. He thought about trying again but the moment had passed.

In the median was a city park of sorts with some scant trees struggling to breathe and a few concrete benches with wooden slats. Overflowing trash cans had attracted strutting pigeons and hungry black squirrels. He crossed the street and seated himself on a bench and not trusting for his safety, he determined to stay awake through the night. In short order two figures approached the bench in a comical side-winding shuffle and joined him in his vigil. They were dressed in faded jeans and pointed boots, one wearing a baseball cap, the other a cowboy hat and sharing a bottle wrapped in a brown paper bag.

"Hey man, you wanna drink?" The short round man proffered the bottle. His white teeth glistened in his brown face. His wide nostrils were dilated, his child-like eyes swimming. The boy took a short sharp pull off the bottle. The curt brown liquid set his innards aglow with a not unpleasant sensation remembered from that occasion of drinking

64

with his brother and father, long ago in another time, in a distant country. He handed the bottle back and both men took a drink to complete the circle and form a union.

"Are you an Indian?" the short round man inquired?

He shook his head, "No".

"Well that's kinda funny cause you sure look like an Indian." He said this squinting his eyes and drawing his face close to the face of the youth.

"My name is Sugar Bear and this here is Slim. We *are* Indians. I used to be a boxer. That's where I got my name. I'd take down fellas with sweetness, just like a bear with these lightning quick hands."

With that the man faked a feint to the right, ducked his head, and jumped to his feet as he shot rapid-fire fists into the body of an imaginary opponent.

"Ha Ha! Sugar Bear was the best!"

The boy was struck at the incongruity of the stumbling drunk suddenly become an agile fighter. Sugar Bear threw a few more authentic looking jabs before he seated himself and had another drink. The bottle made the rounds again. He took another taste but with caution.

"You married?" Sugar Bear asked him.

A short negative nod.

"I got a wife and five kids back on the rez. Man, I miss them. I came here to find work. But I can't find any. Did you know I am a veteran? Yeah man, I was in the war. That was a bad time. One time they gave us machine guns and sent us into a village---ordered us to kill everybody---women, children, old people---rat-a-tat-tat! Oh man, blood and bodies piled everywhere."

The man began to sob and slumped into the bench, a figure of despair.

"That ain't nothing, Bear," the thin angular man began to speak. A white scar ran the length of his face and danced about as he moved his lips. "I was a regular killing machine in that war---you know they didn't even call it a war---called it a police action. It sure as hell seemed like a war to us. Every time I was wounded, the medics patched me up and I went back in. They decorated me with medals, Purple

65

Heart and all. You go to war, some don't come back. Others come back, but they ain't quite whole."

The lean Indian glanced at him as he said this last, his eyes shifting toward Sugar Bear.

"After the army, I ended up in the can. It was like the war. You have to kill just to survive in that place. Same thing here. I been living on these streets seven years. I've had to kill five guys to stay alive. I killed them with this knife."

The lean man proceeded to produce a formidable looking switchblade out of his pants pocket, sprung it and held it up for easy inspection with no threat intended in the action. The two men talked on and he listened. When the bottle was done, they made themselves ready to camp, each claiming a park bench for his own.

Sugar Bear asked him in a childish tone, "Hey man, can I use your bed roll for a pillow?" and he offered it and watched as the weary boxer, making ready to sleep, turned and vomited on the ground by the bench, then rolled over and curled up content to have something soft to lay his head on. The boy remained sitting upright and kept his eyes open, waiting for the dawn.

He started to doze off when he felt a nudge to his ribs. His father was seated next to him on the bench with his cane set upon his knees and a paper bag with peanuts in his hands.

"Ain't safe to sleep here."

"I wasn't sleeping."

"You were about to."

"I didn't expect to see you again."

"Well, it looked to me like you got yourself into some pretty bad straights."

"I don't much care for this city."

"No place for a farmer."

"You fit right in with your going to town suit on."

"Don't hardly matter, ain't nobody can see me but you."

His father started shelling the peanuts from the bag and feeding them out to the squirrels and then he popped one in his mouth and chewed it thoughtfully.

"I didn't know the dead could eat."

66

"There's a lot about the dead you don't know."

His father pointed with his chin at the passed out forms of the drunken Indians on the benches nearby.

"Friends of yours?"

"You might say that."

"Be careful of the company you keep."

"They mean me no harm."

"Keep your wits about you is all I'm saying."

"What do you think I should do?"

"Try calling your brother again, he'll help you out."

"I still ain't ready to talk to him."

"You must be awfully angry at him."

"I am, and I'm still mad at you for dying."

"None of that can be helped. We've got to figure out what you're going to do next."

"Got any ideas?"

"Why don't you get yourself a job, start to work your way back?"

"I can do that."

"Of course you can."

His father held out the bag of peanuts and he took a fistful. They were salt roasted and tasted like the most delicious thing he'd ever eaten.

"Dad, has he gone and sold it?"

"What do you think?"

He was about to answer when a fire truck roaring by on the thoroughfare startled him. He turned to see the commotion and when he looked back again the bench was empty, nothing save a litter of peanut shells on the ground.

The siren wails of an ambulance on the tail of the tanker startled him for a second time and he rose to his feet. His compatriots of the night before were still dozing. Gentle as he might, he lifted the head of the former middleweight with one hand, and retrieved the bedroll with the other. The man groaned but did not stir as his head was placed back on the hard wood planks of the bench. The bedroll had a streak of vomit trickled down the side. He brushed it out of the wool

67

with a dry stick as best he could, then went on his way. Though the Mission House doors were still closed, a line of the hungry devout, attired in the motley discarded finery of the affluent, had begun queuing up on the sidewalk in front of the steps,

On the corner of a busy intersection he spied a streamlined silver diner. He went in to escape the early morning chill. The smells of bacon and toast, hot coffee and eggs, set his stomach into a roaring screw. When the waitress came by he indicated his desire by nodding to the coffee pot. As she poured out the coffee into a porcelain cup, he fished into his pockets for his last bit of change. She asked about cream and sugar and he nodded in the affirmative. An older man at the grille turned and sized up the youth.

"You look like you been hitting some hard traveling. Sit yourself down, son."

He did as he was told and set his gear on the floor and straddled the round red leather-cushioned stool and removed his hat. Soon enough he dove into a heaping plate of home fries, ham, flapjacks and two sunny-side-ups while world and local news poured out of a radio on a shelf above the bonnet of the grill. When he finished he stood up and found no means to express his thanks. The cook extended a hand and the thin-lipped mouth on his hard-lined face with a cigarette dangling out of it cracked a smile.

"That should hold you for a while."

He shook the cook's hand and thanked him with his eyes.

The proprietor of the musical instrument store looked a little surprised to see him standing on the sidewalk when he arrived at his business to start the day but he opened the front door with a key on a jostling ring and soon enough put the boy to work. He was quickly absorbed measuring, cutting and piecing together the wood for new shelves according to the specifications of the merchant. Again he had pause to notice how much he had been missing the simple joy of working, absent since his sojourn among the Amish. The shelving was completed by mid-afternoon and the proprietor was well-pleased with the job and took the wooden flute from the display case. He showed him how to hold it and how to form his lips in order to produce a sound, then bade him well as he left the store with the instrument in hand.

In a city park by the cut-stone banks of a canal, he experimented giving voice through the hollow tube of wood. Faint, airy, raspy by turns, he tentatively found truer sounds to string together like colored beads on a silver thread. Fueled by the impulse of rhythm and breath, simple tunes began to sow themselves as if they had been waiting in the instrument for him to find. His stoic self-imposed muteness accelerated the learning curve and guided his finger tips to an intuitive deftness.

By evening, despite this newfound rapture, he was starving. Breakfast had stretched his stomach to normal proportions and now it began to bawl within him. He packed away his flute and headed back to the city center past a teeming farmer's market where Asian vendors displayed an array of fruits and vegetables from their truck farms. Penniless, he turned away. It was a warm night, the last of late summer. Winding down back alleys, he searched through dumpsters for something to eat but found nothing. Close by the metro he took out the wood flute from the folds of the bedroll and set his belongings down, placed his hat upside down on the sidewalk and began to play. His tunes came haltingly at first with stops and starts as he had to relocate the finger holes with their true corresponding sounds and then a strangely primitive music began to unfold from his lips. The passersby seemed to be in some way touched by it; the overarching effect of the tones sang of all his sorrows and unkindled aspirations.

Coins began to collect in the upturned hat, but he did not nod appreciation nor stop in his playing. He was a hollow reed with the wind passing through it. At midnight he stumbled exhausted out of the nearly empty square. He found an all-night pizza joint and with some of his donations he ordered and gobbled down an entire pie. Back out on the street, he ignored the sharp look of a policeman and took sanctuary in the shadow of a stone church situated between a graveyard, a supermarket and a parking lot. In a picketed alcove reserved for waste bins he found a large discarded cardboard box and dragged it over to a stairwell landing at the rear entrance of the church, curled up inside it and slept the sleep of the dead.

In the morning he checked into a cheap hotel. The clerk required that he leave his firearm at the front desk. Once established in the room he made his way down the hallway to the common washroom where he found clean towels and a claw foot tub and drew a hot water bath from the tarnished brass faucet. He stripped and eased his long suffering limbs into the healing balm. Relaxation crept into the locked crevices of sinew joint and muscle as he languidly soaped up and scrubbed away half a year's worth of travel dirt. Later in the day he went out and with the last of his previous night's earnings bought provisions and went to a barber shop. The store windows now reflected a closer semblance of who he had been when he left home.

Up three flights of rickety stairs, he returned to the hotel room, sat down on the edge of the bed and devoured a loaf of bread, a half-pound of cheese and a can of beans. Then he lay back and put his hat over his face and slept. When he first woke up he thought maybe he was in his own bed back at the farm and then for a moment he didn't know where he was. He gathered his belongings and went down to the front desk to retrieve his rifle and he set off down the road, hungry again but with his feet ready to do some walking.

*

He pulled the blue truck into the parking lot after dark. The windows of the bar were alight with neon beer and liquor signs. He went in, nodding to those seated at tables or standing around the pool table with cues in hand and took his spot at the bar and lit up. The bartender wordlessly set a shot and a beer down on the counter before him. The air-conditioner hummed. Tommy watched the ball game on the TV above the bar.

He said hello to a new cocktail waitress and she stopped and said "hello, back at you." And then he recognized her as the younger sister of a high school classmate, all grown up and nicely filled out.

"How do you like it here, Vicki?"

70

"I don't like it much but Tyler's laid off and we got two kids to feed."

He was finding it hard to take his eyes off her breasts as they talked.

"We're actually looking to hire a new secretary at the Realty. Brenda cut back to half-time last year and is thinking about retirement. And business is picking up."

The sheriff came in and sat next to Tommy. Deputy Stiles remained on his feet, resting one arm on the juke box tapping an erratic beat with his fingers. The bartender set two whiskeys down on the bar.

"Haven't heard anything; have you?"

"Christ, Tommy, don't you think you'd be the first to know if I did?"

"Sure."

"You're still tied up in knots about it, isn't that so? How long's it been now, six months?"

"Just about."

Tommy looked over to Stiles who looked back at him but remained silent. Tommy still resented that cool quiet demeanor. Even back when they'd played on the winning varsity team together, Stiles had been like that. An offensive fullback, he and Tommy had worked in close and effective intimacy on the field but Stiles would never be your friend. "Reminds me of my little brother," he realized and quickly averted his eyes.

"I should've reported him missing."

"How many times have we been over this? He was a runaway."

"What's the difference?"

"Missing means they've gone missing---we don't know what happened to them. Runaway is someone who wants to be missing. They're missing on purpose."

"It doesn't help me any either way."

"He must've been awfully sore about you selling off the cows."

"He stole my horse."

"I already told you, we could press charges for that."

"That's not what I'm looking for."

71

"You file that listing yet?"

"No, not yet."

"What are you waiting on? I heard the market's never looked so good."

"Keep thinking maybe he'll come back. Maybe he'll want to farm. It is half his after all."

"Well, that's right, maybe he will come back, some do."

"If he ain't dead already," Stiles said.

"Don't listen to him, Tommy, he can't help himself."

Tommy tamped out his cigarette, downed his shot and drained the last of the beer.

"I'll call you Vicki – about the job" he called over to the waitress on his way out.

The sheriff pointed at him as if he were about to deliver an admonition.

"Say hello to that pretty wife of yours."

"I will do that, Sheriff."

4

To The Wakima Valley, Washington State

Walking into the shining face of the rising sun he crossed a long span of bridge over a shipping lane, glad to be leaving the city behind. The road out of town passed through a college campus and he saw an ROTC recruitment office where from a plate-glass window Uncle Sam pointed his finger at a gathering of young people with signs of protest in their hands. A small dark man banged on a drum, a fellow with a red beard strummed a guitar, and a pretty blonde-haired girl in India-print skirts shook a tambourine. Others with long hair danced and sang, their bright colored clothing and strands of beads making them look like some newly discovered natives. They called him to come over.

The music stopped.

"Hey brother, you going to go fight for Uncle Sam?"

He shook his head no.

"Right on."

"You on the road, man?"

He nodded yes.

"Like Kerouac, huh?'

And he nodded again though he didn't know of whom they spoke.

Someone else said; "Hey this guy doesn't talk."

"Weird, man."

The girl with the tambourine said, "I think it's cool." And she came to stand close by him.

"Come on let's jam!" said the man with the drum.

He set down his gear and took out his flute. The girl with the tambourine twirled in her skirts around him, putting him a bit on edge. The drummer offered him a pungent smelling cigarette which he declined. He wasn't sure what the protest was about but he enjoyed adding his new found voice to their song. The music grew in intensity as did the crowd of students. Even the mainstream students in conventional clothes were drawn in.

Then someone yelled out, "Beat it, here come the pigs!"

He slipped away as the campus police dispersed the crowd. At a safe distance he cut back across the green to the road.

Leaving town, the road turned to highway. A heavy rain had started and he was getting soaked and the new boots began to raise blisters on his feet. He turned to face the oncoming traffic and stuck out his thumb and soon a trucker pulled over. The truck carried him inland and away from the coast. They drove out onto a lowland plain and as the rain cleared off he could see mountains piling up, volcanoes long quiet with ice rimmed peaks even in the height of summer. The road wound its way up into the foothills thickly forested with stands of old-growth trees. Douglas fir, Sitka, spruce, western hemlocks and red cedar.

The driver pulled into a rest stop and while the man went inside for coffee and cigarettes, he seized the opportunity to meander a few paces away into a grove of glowering Douglas fir giants. He stood before a tree so great that six men could join hands in a circle and barely enclose the trunk; its growing tips pierced low clouds two-hundred and fifty feet above. The filtered green light inspired his lungs to deep breathing. His ears, closed down against the assault of the city tumult, popped open to receive the stillness.

"Hey kid, let's roll!"

He ran back to the truck.

Farther up the road they passed through miles of acreage where the mighty forests had been laid low. All that was left in the wake of the clear-cut was a scarred and tortured landscape, a bleak and wounded ruin; burned over and twisted shapes heaved blackened corpses into the perfect sky; no creature stirred and wind prowled over the dead land like a hungry panther.

He dozed in the jostle of the cab and he woke late afternoon as the truck crossed over the last hummocks of the Cascade Range and descended into the Wakima, a wide sweeping temperate valley lush with irrigation creeks and sun ripened agricultural fields replete with fruit-laden orchards.

"Looking for work?" The trucker took off his sunglasses and lit up a smoke.

He nodded in the affirmative. The man geared down and pulled over to the side of the pavement and then pointed across the black ribbon to a gravel road that cut straight through grain fields.

"Five miles due north. Apples. They'll be needing pickers."

He gathered up the saddle bags, bedroll and rifle scabbard and opened the door and climbed down out of the truck and waved to the shrinking face in the side-view mirrors, obscured in a blue cloud of diesel as the big truck took to the road. Three miles up the gravel track the trees came into view, neat rows of sundry varieties ascending gentle slopes. The branches were heavy with the fruits. Red, yellow and green. He could see them at the picking, scuttling up the ladders that were wide at the base and narrow at the top and rapidly filling the canvas sacks that looped over their necks and tied behind their waists to leave both hands free. As they picked, tractors with hydraulic fork-lifts supporting the wooden apple boxes moved slowly down the rows until they had a full load to shuttle back to the warehouse in exchange for an empty box.

He continued along the road until he reached a group of buildings. The lettered sign on the huge weathered warehouse read: 'Putnam & Sons Quality Apples.' He approached a side door with a sign on the glass reading 'Office'.

A gray haired man smoking a cigar directed him to a younger man smoking a cigarette who outfitted him with a canvas bag and showed him the way to the worker's housing where he could find a place to stow his gear. They passed outbuildings, equipment sheds and the commodious main house where the owners lived; then they proceeded further on down the lane.

"Here's your digs," the man said still puffing on the cigarette. "Welcome to Poverty Lane." He pointed to a cluster of weathered clapboard shacks. Water for the worker's housing came from a single standpipe, and there were open fire-pits for cooking. The lone tap and a broken down privy behind the rows of shacks were the sole means of sanitation. The place was nearly empty save for a few very old people and several very young. He poked his nose into a shack, saw an unused berth in one of the double bunks and stowed his belongings. As he stepped back out squinting in the westerly sun, a little old brown woman wearing a blue shawl in the late day heat, gestured to dwellings across the way and told him, *"los gringos ya están por ahí y los Indios están un poquito más allá"*, to inform him of the established ordering along racial lines of the migrant community so he might choose to camp among his own. He nodded politely to her. He looked to the orchards and saw the pickers returning for the day. He turned and went back to his berth, kicked off his boots and fell asleep.

He was up at sunrise and quickly attached himself to a gang of pickers. He strapped on the canvas bag and entered the fray. The pay was by piecework for each bushel of apples picked. He already knew that it took a delicate twist and turn of the wrist to pick an apple clean while neatly separating twig from stem, but these workers were incredibly fast. At first he stood by and observed their technique. Within five minutes he discerned who the fastest picker was and he set his sights on him. Within an hour he was picking about half as fast as the lithe Mexican boy, head wrapped in a red bandana, who looked to be just about his age.

They took a short midday break and he dug into his saddle bags to fetch a quick bite of bread and cheese and a pilfered apple. He sat on the grass by an old Mexican who sat cross-legged on his outspread *zerape*. He watched fascinated out of the corner of his eye as the man ate an apple. After chomping through the meat of it, with index finger at the stem and thumb pinning the base, he methodically nibbled at the core until there was scant enough flesh left for the ants to make a meal. Then lunch time was over and all hands were quick back at it.

As the afternoon progressed he gained in speed and efficiency, chipping away seconds on the time required to fill one bag. He soon discovered that astute placement of the ladder was the key to a faster time. If set strategically among the branches, then the optimal number of fruits could be harvested with the least replacement of the ladder.

76

Second to this skill was a willingness to scramble out on the limbs to reach and extend on finger, knee and toe holds.

The work went on till the sun was level on the rambling horizon. As the tired throng began the slow walk back to camp, a foreman called down to him from his perch on a big green tractor. "Good work out there kid---glad to have you aboard." He answered with his practiced silent nod.

It was while walking back to camp, this passage of a sweat-streaked quietly chattering parade, that he saw her for the first time. She was walking alongside another girl and the boy with the red bandana was trailing close behind. Something about her made his heart inexplicably race. He noted everything about her; her clothing, worn but clean, the white blouse with floral embroidery around the neck and the loose skirt that flowed down from her narrow hips to her dusty bare feet. His eyes lingered on the twin black braids that descended along her slender brown neck and trailed down the curve of her spine and he watched entranced as those braids swung with the sway of her buoyant frame. As she turned to speak to her companion he glimpsed the shining whites of her eyes and the way her teeth flashed with frequent smiles and how her hands fluttered about in the air like small birds as she spoke. When he came alongside them and was about to pass, he steeled himself not to stare. But even steel has its fragility and their eyes met at a breaking point. He quickly averted his gaze, noticing the dark boy with the red bandana glowering at him.

The workers lit circles of fire in the camp as darkness fell. Although he was a boy of indeterminate origins and no words, no one treated him ill in the worker's quarters. A few even spoke or gave a short nod in greeting. Anyone who had seen him out in the orchards that day knew that he had come to work. The Mexicans made up the majority of workers in the camp. Many spoke Spanish as a second language, and in fact were Indians of another country. There were a few shacks occupied by American Indians, some other few by Whites, Asians and Negroes, and each kept to his own kind, but the Mexicans filled the remaining balance of the camp with all the ebullience of a teeming village. He blithely made his way to the campfires of these *campesinos*. He was drawn to their conviviality and in the back of his

77

mind there was the notion that the pretty young girl he'd seen earlier might appear again.

He sat cross-legged on the ground eating the last of his bread and cheese. He was a little startled when a middle-aged woman handed him a plate of steaming beans, chilies and fresh tortillas. He took off his hat and nodded in thanks. *"De nada"*, she said in return, already on her way to offer food to another hungry soul. He slowly chewed and savored the warmth of the food and flames, feeling the early evening chill on his backside. He was drawn into the singsong cadence of a language he could not comprehend which yet soothed him. Shortly musical instruments appeared in work-hardened hands. Several men with guitars began to pick and strum, a woman with a gourd rattle lightly tapped and a blind man in dark glasses eased a fiddle into action.

The music set his toe to tapping and he stood and washed his tin plate clean at the spigot and went into the shack to get his flute. When he returned to the circle of light, the girl was there on the other side of the fire, singing with the sweetest voice he'd ever heard. Their eyes met again across the flame and for the first time since he ran away, he felt something alive in his heart. And though he didn't understand the words, he raised his flute to his lips, blending with her song. Tequila made the rounds of the fiery circle. Babies wailed. Old ones smiled. The stars pierced needles of light through the black quilt of the sky.

Late afternoon of his second day at work the orchard boss came down to see first hand how the new worker was faring. The boss stood shoulder to shoulder with his eldest son, observing the boy perched on a high branch, making apples disappear into his canvas sack.

Putnam asked his son, "So what is this new guy, some kind of Indian?"

"I don't know; Half-breed maybe. He hangs around with the wet-backs. But I don't mark him for a Chicano."

"The little bastard can pick faster than a bat out of hell. If only we had twenty like him."

"Yeah, he's fast all right. He's a different sort though. Still hasn't spoken a word. The Chicanos are calling him *el 'mudo'*."

"Just so long as he keeps out of trouble."

On the morning of his third day there, they chanced to meet at the tap above the well. She was drawing water into a galvanized bucket. He stood by waiting with his canteen. She looked at him plainly.

"Buen dia, que tal?"

He gave the customary nod, then removed the broad-brimmed hat and ran his fingers through the thick brush of hair atop his head.

"Toca usted la flauta bien dulce."

Again the nod.

"Tengo que irme para preparar el desayuno para mi hermano", she began to excuse herself as her bucket was nearly full. He spoke centuries of grief and hope to her through his eyes. She stood a foot shorter than he and was slender to the point of fragility. Yet he saw such strength and dignity expressed in the resolve of her carriage. He did not wish to see her go but he felt as helpless as he felt mute. As she lifted her bucket, he stooped to the pipe with his canteen and the flint arrow head fell from his shirt and glinted morning sun off its multi-faceted surface. The light caught her eye and she examined the minuscule implement from where she stood.

"Fijense, eres un indio?"

He did not speak her language but he understood that her question shot to the heart of his loss of identity. Warriors and healers, hunters and horsemen, voices of the past welled up from within and clamored in his ears. The ancestors accosted him, urging him to speak. His breath came shallow and his heart beat fast. He shook his head and shrugged his shoulders in a confused gesture of, "I don't know."

Then she had to go. But as she was walking towards the morning cooking fire, she turned in mid-step. He was in the act of drawing off water when she said; *"Pienso que si, eres un indio."* Then she walked along to her chores.

It was on that third day that he achieved the status of fastest picker of apples at the orchard. He was on his way back to work

79

following the afternoon siesta when Sebastian with the red bandana confronted him.

"No me gusta ver usted hablando con mi hermana."

He nodded and made as if to be on his way but Sebastian side-stepped into the path of his tracks unmade.

"Mira, usted no puede llegar aquí and tomar cualquier cosa que le gusta."

Sebastian told him that he could not take whatever he wanted and then pushed him so hard that he stumbled back and landed on his seat. In an instant he was up and the locked-up fury that threatened to break long held chains of restraint sent a shimmering red heat through his veins. With open hands he charged and toppled the smaller boy like so much standing deadwood. Sebastian rolled deftly to his feet and launched in and landed two quick fisted blows to his face and then a feint and a jab and a third blow struck. A crowd gathered and among them he caught sight of her horror-stricken face. A fourth blow came in and he deflected it. He held up his hands open and empty before him. A swift blade appeared in Sebastian's hand and he began to toss and catch the hilt with deft menace, left to right and back again, the sun glinting off the blade with each toss.

He didn't look at Sebastian's eyes and he didn't look at his hands. He made no sound. He moved without forethought and with the immaculate precision of one bereft of fear. His hand grasped the wrist of the weapon-bearing hand and stalled the parry in mid-thrust. He held Sebastian's wrist with a frightening intensity and then twisted that fist up between his attacker's shoulder blades causing him to spin and face away. Then he looked to the girl so that she might see he bore no malice as he held her brother in the lock. The Mexican boy fell to his knees, emitting a gasp of pain as the knife edge clattered to the dry stony ground. When he saw Sebastian drop his eyes he let loose the wrist. The fighting was done. He was still shaking as he strode to the shack to gather up his belongings.

Sebastian dusted himself off and picked up his knife and re-concealed it. He turned towards the orchards and did not look back. The onlookers followed suit. Only his sister hesitated. Sebastian called to her to come along. *"Váyanse ahorita!"* But she shook her head and clenched her fists and stood her ground. Sebastian turned then, waving her off, and went to back to work.

She found him at the well refilling his steel canteen. She studied the surfaces, already purpling and beginning to rise where her brother's fists had landed on his face. He thought she might reach out and caress the marks but timidity stayed her hand.

"Pues, adónde vas?"

Though he could not comprehend her words, somehow he understood her meaning. He looked to the mountains whose skirts rose up in the west and whose peaks were already girded in snow.

"Algo ha herido tu corazón, verdad?" She spoke to him in an intimate way about the wound and his heart. *"Y nunca vas a regresar?"*

He shook his head so that no meaning remained clear. They stood facing one another then. He hurt and ached inside but could reveal nothing. He looked at her face, her fair and stormy eyes full of light and life, the delicate temples and defined lines of her cheek bones, her sensuous lips slightly parted. And even though he had just met her he felt like he had always known her and had always loved her and in the same instant he felt certain that such love was impossible for him, that it was something he didn't deserve, as if he had forever thrown in his lot with the outcast.

He took off the silver cord and placed it around her neck, the flint coming to rest on her breast bone. She drew her hand up to it. He put on his hat and picked up his gear and he saw that she had tears in her eyes. He reached out in a gentle gesture, not to wipe her tears away but to palpate the moisture, to touch the fullness of life so alive in each minuscule bead.

"I wait for you," she said in English. He nodded and turned and walked away.

Four miles down the road he left the dust track and strode into a wheat field. The full grain-heads parted like golden waves before him. He stood in pain. He wanted to turn back but somehow could not. He fell to his knees and was astonished by the wracking sobs and torrent of tears that poured out. He lifted his crying eyes to a sky in which he expected to find no sign of mercy. The twin peaks of the nearest mountain on the outland horizon caught his eye in a mysterious whorl. Drawn like silver dust to lodestone, he rose to his feet and pointed his steps toward that mountain.

In three days of fast and angry walking he covered more than forty miles. He was in the mountains. A river came down strong, cold and clear. He stood on the boulder strewn banks, and listening and seeing became one as he peered into the roiling swirl and spiral of the water's passage. He was empty now of all but a burning rage. He looked deeper into the river, searching for some hint or trace of her face. But he could not find it. The heat ascended from his core. His limbs trembled and the surface of his skin was sweat-soaked and dripping. He threw down his gear and the rifle in its scabbard and tore off all his clothes and stood naked on the rock. He glowered at the river while it hurried by, laughing, and all its residing force and unending strength made him feel puny and mocked. He wanted to scream but his atrophied voice made no sound. He wrenched the rifle from the scabbard and fired off three shots into the running stream, the spent cartridges pinging off the stones like drops of rain. Unperturbed the river kept on singing. He tried to scream again but either his voice was still gone or the gun blasts had left him deafened. He flipped the rifle and grasped the barrel with both his hands and raised it over his head and flung it at the river. It spun three times in the air and then hit the water with a dull thunk. A few bubbles to the surface and it was swallowed to the depths. He turned rapidly and reached over and undid the snap on the leather sheath of his belt and yanked out his knife. Blade in hand he leapt into the waters. He plunged into the icy maelstrom and he hacked at the waves. The breath was sucked out of him and he flailed about wildly in water over his head. Careening off river rocks, he was propelled swiftly downstream.

He clambered into an eddy of shallows and came up gasping with the knife still clutched in his hand. He stood in waist-deep water and watched the steam rising off his shoulders. The blade was sharp and cut finely as he incised two scarlet lines along the triceps of his upper left arm. Clean too, was the steady slash he made across his chest. His hand released the hilt and the blue steel of the blade shimmered and flashed like a sunfish as it sank to the swept-clean gravel of the river bed.

He watched his blood run from his wounds and flow with the passing waters. He stood still with the current flowing all around him until his body turned blue and he was shivering numb. He stood until the blood from the cuts congealed and then he retrieved the knife and waded to the rock-strewn shore.

Still naked, he gathered dry fallen limbs and beginning with tiny dry twigs, and progressing to pieces the thickness of his forearm, he assembled a tipi construct. He dug out his striking flint from the saddle bag and lit a fire and sat crouched before the kindled flames.

When the fire had reduced itself to a shimmering heap of red hot coals, he scooped up a handful of cooling ash from the periphery and vigorously rubbed it into the linear wounds he had carved on his arm and across his chest. He did not know why he did this; it just seemed within the natural order of things to do so.

The deed done, he dressed, hoisted the saddle bag and bedroll to his shoulder and picked up the empty scabbard. He considered leaving it but then changed his mind and took his flute from the bedroll and slid it into the scabbard where the rifle had been. As he turned from the river to the forest, he noticed a path scaling upwards into the wood, though whether braced by animal or human he could not tell. The mid-day sun percolated through boughs of spruce and fir, cottonwoods alive with spinning golden leaves and tamarack shedding out thousands of tiny bronze blades.

He never even saw her. Her force descended upon him like some devouring celestial body swallowing the sun. He saw only the cub that pulled up short in his path, whining at the sight of him. First there was the roaring in his ears. Instinctively he reached for the gunstock but the scabbard held only the flute. The bear hit him broadside with a blast of fury, like a cannon shot or hurricane wind. Her teeth clamped on the back of his neck and saber claws slashed his breast.

He descended into a free fall. His hand clutched the knife but he could wield it to no avail. Sight and sound darkened as quantities of blood flowed from pulsing wounds. The whir and buzz of consciousness was nothing but a beacon call to survival over fierce swells and dangerous shoals. The attack lasted only seconds but for him it spanned an eternity until she knocked him over a rim above the alpine river. And as he fell, from the root source of his self came a sound that swelled in intensity; borne on his will to remain in the stream of life, he unleashed a scream. The sow stopped short then and turned in search of her darling charge. Like a broken rag doll he toppled over the ridge and sliced into the cold waters. He dropped into a deep trout pool at the base of a water fall before being swept by strong currents downstream. The river mercifully deposited him unconscious but still breathing face up on a brief span of level shore. Blood flowed from grievous wounds, his body inert; yet in that interior darkness he quickened with awakened life, with an inexorable will to heal and to make all things whole.

PART THREE

1

Cascade Range, Washington State

The old man of the forest was out gathering herbs when he found him. He saw the tracks of the she-bear first and he knew her and was gladdened at the signs of her little one, that he was coming on well.

"Probably out looking for mushrooms," he mused quietly to himself. "She'll be wise to steer him clear of these spotted red caps," he chuckled, referring to the *Amanita Muscaria* that was sprouting from the humus by his moccasin-clad feet. "That cub, he be too little for vision seeking just yet."

Then he came upon the site of the struggle, and at first the marks confused him. He stooped low among the wood ferns and found the saddle bag where someone had dropped it. He carefully examined its contents to understand what had happened. He picked up the broad-brimmed hat and studied it. He could see where the bear had abruptly wheeled about and gone in search of her cub and the direction in which they had fled. When he arrived at the river bed his wizened eyes scanned the banks and his flaring nostrils inquired of the evening breeze. With an alacrity that belied his years, he scampered down to the water and made his way over the river rocks, bounding from one stony purchase to another until he arrived at the boy's side.

He passed his hands up and down the length of the supine form without making physical contact. For a moment it occurred to him that there was something familiar about the lad but he dismissed the thought in his efforts to focus on the radiant vital signs coursing through his hands. He searched for areas of activity and heat and was pleased to sense that despite the extreme coldness of the limbs, the core of the body was still warm. He scanned the length of him, detecting traces of a translucent violet aura

"I think that he is having a dream, a spirit-changing dream," he laughed quietly. The river water lapped about the boy's feet as if urging them to stir and move on. The old man opened a deer-hide pouch at his side and removed a sprig of sage which he held just under the wounded boy's nostrils, then rubbed portions of it onto his temples and the crown of his head. He gathered laced umbels of yarrow from a small clearing where an ancient tree had fallen and the herbage had grown in its wake. He moved swiftly but not hurriedly, with exacting purpose and intent. He silently thanked the plants for offering the gift of their life and then gathered copious quantities of the spindly herb and carried it back to the impromptu place of doctoring. He removed what was left of his patient's shirt. Then he masticated the bitter aseptic leaves and with his hands he formed the liquefied mass into a poultice to pack on the wounds and then plastered it over with mud from the river bank. He took note of the three slightly older marks, straight incisions with wood ash worked into them. He used his hunting knife to cut strips of cloth off his own shirttails to bind the wounds snugly. Next he fashioned a crude travois made of stout-limbed saplings, harvesting the tough wiry roots of a spruce tree to use as lashing. He secured the injured one tightly to the rough-hewn frame and tied his belongings down, then grasped the shafts and trudged uphill into the deep forest.

The pinto nickered and the wolf dog let out a single bark when after a three-mile trek with frequent pauses to rest, the old man approached his camp. A year-round creek flowed through the clearing seeded to pasture, orchards and garden, all within the shelter of the twin peaks. At the northern rim stood the homestead with its outbuildings for laying hens and cattle. As he approached the cabin he spoke to the horse corralled next to a small barn.

"See now Tequila, I've brought you a visitor. A horseman without a horse."

Stopping to catch his breath at the door, he removed his bandana and wiped the perspiration from his broad furrowed brow. He brushed back the snow white locks that fell below his shoulders, stood up straight and stretched. Despite the fall nip in the mountain air, the effort of hauling such a burden had worked him into a sweat.

"Hey little pony, I look just like you after the spring plowing, hey?" The horse put back its ears and turned its spotted round butt towards the rail fence and lifted its tail and broke wind. The old man waved the horse off and turned to the task at hand. He pushed the heavy plank door open and carried his patient in, laying him on a buffalo robe spread out on the packed earthen floor. Then he lit a kerosene lamp and carried in an armload of wood from the woodshed. The stove in the center of the room was cut from a fifty-five-gallon drum and set into the floor with a pipe-stack that ran underground and emerged vertically some paces away outside. Under a blanket of ash the coals were still red from the morning's cook fire. He stacked in kindling and larger chunks to get a good fire going to heat water and while it was heating, he redressed the wounds, adding plantain leaf, comfrey and coneflower root to the mash. He gazed down on the face shadowed golden in the cast of the lamp, intuiting that the boy was not out cold but awake in his dreaming; he could see the eyes actively rove through dreamscapes beneath closed lids.

In his dream the boy with no name was walking naked by the ocean. It was nighttime. The rare shape of a lone gull flew past and crews of sandpipers scuttled just out of reach of the incoming waves. Glancing back over his left shoulder he saw the outline of a rocky outcropping projecting into the sea. From a spot in the midst of the rocks came a faint glow, a mysterious luminescence in the dark. He had a sense that this light was something he was choosing to walk away from. He was drawn to a sound like the inhaling of a breath only intensely magnified, like a giant wave crashing against the beach. With an ominous clarity he knew there was nowhere he could run, so he surrendered himself to the massive force of the wall of water as it swallowed up even the crescent moon, the stars, and the blue-black sky.

The waters raised him up, lifting him into a green light-filled sea of sky. The dream wave carried him wide awake into his own wounded body and the swift-dimming light of day. His first sensation as he stared at the weathered leather of the healer's face was not pain but recognition. "I know him," he thought.

The healer smiled at him and said: "So you have come to see me. That was some gateway you had to pass through."

He opened his mouth as if to utter a response.

"Shush," the elder placed a finger to his lips, "Don't try to speak. The she-bear has touched you, but you shall live. That is a warrior's feat!"

"Where am I?"

"Flying Cloud camp."

"Who are you?"

"Just a crazy old hermit living in the shadow of the twin peaks. Old Joseph they call me. And what shall we call you?"

"Luke," he impulsively replied, feeling so alien to the farm boy who had run away that he did not even know whether he was giving a lie. As he spoke the name he groaned in pain, the reality of his wounds beginning to crack through the protective shield of his dream.

"Well Luke, be glad for pain. Sometimes it's the only thing let's you know you're still alive." Old Joseph helped him drink willowbark tea from a dipper.

Luke lifted his head to take a look around at this new dream. Dried herbs, leaf flowers and roots hung in neat bunches from every beam and rafter of the one room lodge. Baskets crafted of ash splints, birch bark and red willow lined the three walls and held primitive clothing, tools and household goods. There was a wide bench along the fourth wall that served as bed and workspace. A cast-iron cook stove stood in a corner nook, hard by a counter, a porcelain sink and tin wash basin. Snowshoes, a hunting bow and beaver-hide quiver of arrows, assorted traps, all hung from wooden pegs in the rough-hewn walls. A tall drum stood in hollow silence in a corner along with an ornate flute. Luke knew he had landed in the hands of someone who lived off the land and it comforted him. He lay his head back down on the robe and slept.

In the next days and weeks that followed, the old man applied his skills to mending the boy's wounds. His patient wavered in and out of feverish wakefulness fraught with hallucination and fitful dream-haunted sleep. The healer brewed concoctions to reduce fever and swelling. The worst of the wounds required stitching, so he boiled fine strands of nettle fiber in a yarrow tea to fashion antiseptic sutures to close the rent flesh and applied fresh poultices of special curatives he had brought with him when he had migrated to this place from across the prairie. By these and the more subtle means of prayers and purifications, Old Joseph helped Luke cross the bridge from crisis to recovery.

Once he'd pulled the stitches, the old man let the boy resume the use of his limbs. He brought Luke a basin of hot water to bathe himself with and outfitted him with a wool shirt to replace the one ripped by the bear.

"I don't know how to thank you, Old Joseph. If not for you, I'd be dead."

"Your wounds are severe but that bear, she let you off easy. When I was a boy I remember once they carried a man into town. He had been out hunting elk when he ran into a grizzly with cubs. Half his face torn away, rib cage crushed, limbs ripped like torn cloth and his belly laid open so you could see his guts. Yet he was such a mighty hunter he managed to crawl a great distance to the nearest cabin. And so powerful was the medicine of our healers in those days that in six months the man was recovered completely. Except for the scarring and that was a hard thing for him. He had been a handsome man, perhaps overly proud of his looks, and interested only in hunting, whiskey and women. After the attack he was a changed man. After his encounter with the bear he became a renowned healer."

"The bear helped him?"

"That's how it works. The bear always moves through the place of the wound. That is the gateway through which the bear brings healing power but sometimes people fear a person who has been given such power. Those who have been touched by the bear become part of a mysterious and sacred reality, a reality that can appear dangerous because of its freedom. All the bear wants is peace, and often as not he will run rather than fight. But once a bear is angry he has no respect for anything and that sort of energy can make others feel uneasy. In these mountains there are two unpredictable animals---the human and the bear. Of the two, the human is the more dangerous."

*

He cut out of work early for no good reason. As he rolled into his driveway the mid-afternoon sun was slanting sideways through the tall pines in the side yard of the little salt box house. She was standing in the front yard with a fan rake in her work gloves in the diminished shade of the big red maple, now past peak, the leaf lode falling or strewn about the still green lawn.

"Things were slow today," he said.

"Really, I thought business was booming."

"It was an odd day."

"We all have those."

"Where are the twins?"

"Their grandma took them for the afternoon."

"And so you're raking leaves."

"I want to. I like to. It reminds me of my father. I still love the smell of leaf piles burning."

"That's a pretty good pile you got going right there."

"Almost enough to jump in."

God, she was beautiful! Something about the fall air, something about the strangeness of being home in the middle of the day and the two little boys not being there, made him want to bed her down right then and there in the leaves. What was it that made him fuck anybody else? Was he trying to hurt himself by hurting her? She didn't seem to suspect anything but he felt certain that at some level she knew he was screwing around, however much denial might play its part in keeping that devastating knowledge at bay. His memory flashed to them as kids. Himself at her house with a couple of friends, twelve years old or thirteen maybe, wrestling, rolling and tickling in a giant leaf pile. And then holy cow! Under cover of the leaves, his hands exploring the soft silken reaches of flesh underneath her clothes and she not resisting in the least, both of them by what was happening. Until her sister caught on. "I'm gonna tell!" she shouts. They swiftly roll out of the leaves onto the next game and anyway it it's time for a farm boy to get home to chores.

She was looking at him, a shrouded inquiry from underneath the broad brim of her straw hat. He inhaled deeply as if trying to breathe in the last rays of gilded sunshine, all the sense and the smell of it, the fullness and ache of the last juices being pressed out. For the first time in a long time he felt truly sober and he saw her just as she was then---not lover, not wife or mother or some other, just this long-limbed auburn haired woman raking the leaves and she was so beautiful. God damn I am such a fool.

She started raking again and talking as she worked.

"My dad made us bag up leaves and set them around the foundation of the house for winter. Put some on the garden too. The rest he'd rake into big piles and when the ground was wet, he'd burn them. He liked to keep a big lawn, fuss over the dandelions and crab grass. Probably because he missed the farm so much."

"My old man had no use for a lawn. Hell, we had corn growing right up to the steps of the back porch."

"I guess we miss them."

"Who?"

"Our fathers, stupid."

"Yeah I guess we do. Been so busy I don't think about it."

"Still no word?"

Tommy shook his head. "Either he's dead or he just doesn't want anything to do with me any more."

"I think he's still angry."

"Never forgive me if I sell that farm."

"Any buyers?"

Tommy's shoulders dropped. "I took down the listing."

"That's a start."

"It's nothing. I just needed some time to think."

She put her hand on his arm. "About?"

"I don't know. Maybe I just need to rewrite it or something. We got another rake?"

"In the garage."

He grabbed his briefcase out of the truck cab and headed up the walk undoing his tie. He was thinking about that leaf pile again. Wondering how big they'd have to make it before they couldn't be seen by the neighbors.

*

The aspens flared golden against a serrated edge of dark fir. Days went by, each day shorter than the last. He became accustomed to being called Luke and was glad to have found his voice again, liberated from his dark solitary cell. Silence had sealed him off from a world that had meted out too much pain. Now in the generous presence of the medicine man, he didn't want to return to that unutterable void, and the old man proved a lively conversationalist, regaling him with tales and reminiscences.

As soon as he was able, Luke began to help Old Joseph with his chores. Thick red scars remained on his chest, arm and neck, a terror-wrought brand of living memory. He drew a certain dark power from the fierce aspect of the bear claw tattoo etched on his skin, though he was less certain how he felt about the scars from his self-inflicted wounds. He was glad for the work at hand that made it easy to forget--- glad to be just where he was now.

There was plenty to do to prepare for winter. Entire days passed in easy silence between them as side by side the old man and the boy labored, splitting firewood and hauling up water from the creek, tending to the livestock and mending fences, digging the root crops out of the garden. Only occasionally would Luke take to brooding on traces of his past, turning morose and listless until he turned to the one memory that could stir him to life. He would search with the eye of his heart to conjure up her face and recall the words she spoke in the orchard.

Old Joseph asked Luke no questions about his past nor inquired as to how long he intended to stay. He shared freely of the little he had and was grateful for such help as one so wounded was able to offer. The medicine man was pleased to see the boy's surface wounds were mending, and patient enough to wait for Luke to reveal the deeper wounds within.

Luke took on the care and feeding of the pinto horse and once he was well enough, he began to ride. Never had he sat on the back of such an aware and responsive mount. The mare accepted the rider as a natural extension of her own body, her sharp perceptions like heightened ones of his own. Should a ruffed-grouse explode out of the underbrush, her first instinct was to plant her hooves rather than rear up or spook.

One day as he led the pinto along a woodland path, the wolf-dog dodging in and out on the trail ahead, he spied an eagle feather lying on the dark forest ground, the white of it shining like a beacon in the lowering light of the wood. He dismounted to retrieve it and as he held it he could feel his senses open to a deeper level that allowed him see the forest as energy, to hear the woodland move out and away from him like rings in a concentric pool and to know with a certainty the connectedness between the scrape of branches, his horse's breath, the creak of saddle leather, the woodpecker's hammer, dry leaves falling, bound of red squirrel and distant raven cry. He looked again at the feather so complex and elegant, yet so spare and simple. He was suddenly aware of his feet in full contact with the ground, that soundness had returned to his limbs. He put the feather in the band of his broad-brimmed hat and returned to camp.

Luke unsaddled the horse, picked out her feet and turned her out in the paddock with a dish of oats then stored the tack away in the barn and returned to see what the old man was up to. Old Joseph had a short-handled broad axe which he was deftly wielding to shape a stave of wood. He pointed to another seasoned chunk of yew wood. "If you like, I will show you how to fashion a bow---the deer are in rut and it's time for a man to hunt."

Making the bows took two entire days. First Old Joseph demonstrated how to rough out the form with the axe and later how to refine and tiller the bow shape with a curved knife, equalizing top and bottom limbs and fashioning a grip. Next he climbed up into the stilt-cache and came down with a basket of leg tendon from elk quarry of past seasons' hunts. They split this material into lengths and soaked it in a hoof and hide glue and then carefully laid the strips to create a cohesive surface of sinew along the backside of the bow, a laborious process that would add twenty pounds of pull pressure to the hunting weapon. With the bows set indoors across rafters to dry, he gave Luke instruction in the skill of reverse-wrap twining of the finer sinew taken from the spine of a deer to fashion the string of the bow. Finally they made the arrows. Old Joseph took down an arrow from the quiver on the wall and handed it to Luke for inspection. Luke's eyes were riveted on the knapped-flint arrowhead. His heart began to pound like some ancient drum. The arrowhead was identical to the one he had given the girl in the orchard so long ago, in another country, in another lifetime.

"Did you make this arrowhead?"

"I did."

"I have seen one like it before."

"That's not likely. Each flint knapper has his own style. My arrowheads bear my signature as clear as deer tracks in new snow."

The ensuing lessons covered the art of flint knapping, fabricating arrow shafts from birch limbs and then applying the turkey feather fletching to make the arrows fly. When they strung up and tested the finished bow, it shot the arrow swift and true.

In between homestead chores Luke spent hours shooting blunt-tipped arrows into a stack of straw. The day before the hunt they fasted. Luke took his cues from the old one and spoke only out of necessity. In the evening they built a fire in an outdoor pit and covered the blaze with green wood and boughs of red cedar. Then they stepped repeatedly through the thick smoke until it permeated their clothing hair and skin.

Back in the cabin Old Joseph spoke about the hunt. He said if Luke truly wanted to see a deer, he must not look directly at it but should soften his eyes and take it in with all of its surroundings, and if Luke looked at the deer in this way long enough he would come to understand that he was one with the deer and that even before he unleashed the bow, his arrow would already have found its target.

They arose before dawn and walked into the forest. At intervals Old Joseph would make a strange high-pitched whistle to call in the deer. The morning breeze was coming down off the twin peaks and the deer would be traveling with it. They walked with their faces into that breeze, leaving their human scent trailing behind. They entered a stand of virgin timber and rested a brief spell, reclining on the gnarled bole of a giant Sitka spruce. Breaking their fast, Old Joseph parceled out small pieces of smoked meat. They heard the blowing and stamping of hooves before they saw the buck. The patriarch in his prime was trailed by three does and a yearling. Luke cautiously hiked onto one knee and raised his bow and drew an arrow in the slowest motion he could effect.

He scarcely breathed as he sighted his aim on the neck of the proud one, who unsure and fatally curious was still blowing to alert his small coterie of potential danger. As Luke gamely strained to hold back the bow, he glanced sidelong at his mentor who was shaking his head and frowning. So he took aim anew on the middle-sized specimen of the three does and let the arrow fly.

Although it took two miles of protracted chase to set her down, his aim had been true. Exhausted from loss of blood, the doe fell at last with the arrow shaft still stuck in her neck just below the point where the spine joined the skull. Luke unsheathed his knife and slit her throat. He followed Old Joseph's instructions and took a prepared offering of tobacco wrapped in a square of rawhide and held fast by a red yarn tie from his pocket and placed it on the ground where her life had departed. He spoke words of thanks to the spirit of the deer and he addressed words to the spirit-master of her tribe. Old Joseph dipped two fingers into the mortal wound and smeared blood on Luke's face, leaving twin scarlet marks on his forehead. Then he gutted the deer, leaving a feast of entrails for some roving coyote or fox and made slices between leg tendon and bone through which he strung rawhide strips to lash the legs to a bough long enough for each of them to heft an end over one shoulder. In this way they carried the deer's body back to Flying Cloud camp. Luke skinned the carcass, then watched on as Old Joseph butchered out the meat, tracing grain and line with his sharp blade. They saved out the best cuts of tenderloin to eat fresh. The rest of the meat they cut into strips and lay out to dry before they smoked it over a slow burning fire. Hooves, antler, sinew and bone were cached for later use. The remaining offal they fed to the wolf-dog.

After mid-day rest, Old Joseph showed him how to remove the deer brains from the skull and to rub the viscous brain matter into the scraped clean surface of the frame-stretched hide and work it in. The tanning was a lengthy process that took the better part of three days to complete; roughing, buffing and finally smoking the hide.

In the evening they sat with bellies full before the glowing woodstove. Old Joseph puffed on a corn cob pipe.

"Well, Luke, how did the hunt go for you?"

"I've always taken deer with a rifle. Hunting with the bow after all the steps of making it made me feel as if I shot the deer with a part of my own body."

"You have understood rightly the making of the bow. We fashion something that is an extension of our will and power; by fashioning the bow in a sacred manner, we cleanse and renew our intent. Only remember this, you did not take that doe; she offered her life so that you and I might live. This matter of killing, the taking of life so that we can continue our own life, this has never been an easy thing. If we understand that all animals are our kin, the gift becomes even more dear and we find ourselves asking, how can I live in such a manner as to be worthy of this sacrifice?"

"Why didn't you want me to bring down that buck?"

"That buck was in the fullness of his years. He will sire strong offspring because of your choice and it was good you marked out the smaller doe. Perhaps winter would have reduced her to bones, her right hind-quarter was previously injured, probably had a run-in with coyotes."

"I knew when to release the arrow. I felt power moving through me."

"It is good," said Old Joseph and he looked long at the boy with joy in his heart.

2

Flying Cloud Camp, Cascade Range, Washington State

Between them they brought home three deer that fall, two does and a spike. Old Joseph killed an aging bull elk and with all that meat and the harvest of his garden, the old man was content that the larder was well stocked for the rigors of the mountain winter.

Old Joseph charged Luke with tanning the hides and when he had completed the arduous process helped him cut and sew a shirt, smartly lined out with fringe. It became his second skin.

An inch of new snow was on the ground and the breath of the horse and the cattle white in the air when he stepped out early the next morning to fetch water from the creek. The wolf dog leaped and frolicked, her bushy tail telegraphing messages of discovery from the whitewashed canvas of the world.

"I think we are going to have some visitors." Old Joseph asked him to help set up a tipi; they struggled to drag out the stitched skin from storage underneath the stilt cache. The old man constructed the primary tripod and explained how to lay the poles in, leaving a wide margin for the east facing door. When the poles were in place he sent Luke climbing to the top with a rope to lash and bind them. "That has always been a job for the young men," he chuckled. They hoisted up the painted skin and unfurled it like a sail, then secured it together with willow lacing pins.

"Raising the tipi used to be the work of the women, and I tell you straight, we would be chilled molasses to their greased lightning if there were a contest!"

When the door was in place they dug a firepit off center towards the rear. They placed two slender poles into flaps on the outside that served as adjustable vents to the smoke hole. Next they staked the skin to the ground and hung up the interior lining for insulation against the chill. Finally, they laid in a bundle of kindling and split chunks of wood.

"Now we are ready for our guests." The old man stood back

97

and dusted off his hands with satisfaction. They went back to the cabin for their midday meal.

Old Joseph sat whittling a galloping equine form out of a piece of apple wood and Luke was softly piping tunes on his flute when they heard the sound of a vehicle bombing up the faint track of road to Flying Cloud Camp.

A rolling wreck of a two-ton truck with rattling chains on all four tires, dented fenders, doors and hood of dissonant hues encrusted in rust, roared to an abrupt halt. A driver and three passengers tumbled out of the cab whooping and hollering at the sight of the old man. The visitors embraced Old Joseph and offered him gifts of tobacco and canned goods.

Luke stood off to one side afraid that his debilitating shyness would rob him of his speech again. Old Joseph introduced him.

"This here is my young friend Luke. He's helping me out around the place for awhile."

Old Joseph then introduced each visitor by name: a somber solid man named Raphael, a tall lanky fellow with a good natured face called Jimmy White Eagle, the diminutively plump and authoritative Marguerite Moon Hawk and a small, grinning Freddie Walksfast.

Luke helped unload the gear from the truck into the tipi. In the midst of the task, he reached up to grab a burlap sack stuffed with what he thought might be dried food of some kind. But before he could heft the load he felt a hand on his shoulder. "Let me carry that, little brother," said Raphael, who wore his raven hair long and loose on his shoulders.

"That sack contains sacred medicine and I am charged to be its keeper. How are you enjoying your stay with Old Joseph?"

"I don't have the words. He's given me back my life."

"I know what you mean. He is a powerful medicine man."

"I've never met anybody like him."

"Well it's good to have you here for our gathering."

When the guests were settled in, the party went to the cabin to enjoy an evening meal together. Luke sat by quietly, enraptured as he listened to the old friends catching up on news of each other and all their relatives back on the Pine Ridge reservation.

The woman who had come along in the traveling party had the most news to share, alternately crying or belly-laughing according to the content of her narrative. He was instantly attracted by her vivacious energy, her bright merry eyes, the air of competent goodness about her. She was not "pretty" but beautiful in the way a tree or a wildflower is beautiful. She was wearing a full length calico dress with lace ruffles around the wrists and neck and her fingers, ears and throat were adorned with silver turquoise jewelry. He had already noted that this finery didn't keep her from splitting kindling for the cook fire or hauling up buckets of water from the creek.

Raphael was older than the others and from a different tribe. He spoke intermittently and then only of matters having to do with native rights and something called the "struggle." The talk went on late into the night. Luke was lying prone on the buffalo robe with his chin in his hands listening attentively until weariness bested him and he drifted off to sleep.

After chores and breakfast Old Joseph and his visitors began to prepare the sweat lodge, gathering stones and fallen branches and deadwood, choosing to collect fuel for this fire from what the forest offered up of its own accord. Old Joseph gathered the tinder to start the fire.

As the flames leapt up, the others returned with long whips of willow and the roots to bind them. Freddy Walksfast scraped and dug a second pit and Marguerite Moonhawk took the displaced earth four paces to the east and formed it into a mound. With the pit as a center mark, sixteen saplings were inserted into the ground in a circular form and then bent and lashed one to the other to fashion a dome. This was covered with skins, blankets and tarps, creating a thick shell, impervious to the light of day. Old Joseph brought out a buffalo skull and placed it on the mound of earth that Marguerite had formed with her hands. He carried a wooden bowl of water and a fistful of dried sage into the newly created lodge. The visitors sat by the fire wrapping offerings of tobacco in small squares of hide which they then tied to the outside of the lodge with red yarn.

Old Joseph took Luke aside and explained that the people were about to perform a rite of cleansing and that they wished to honor their new young friend by asking him to be keeper of the gateway. His task would be to deliver the hot stones to the pit and in addition, he was to keep watch at the door and only open it when he heard the spoken words "all my relations." When the others began to remove their clothing, he didn't know where to direct his eyes, but the people were so natural in their nakedness that he was quickly put at ease. They approached the door and walked sun-wise once around the lodge before they entered with Old Joseph coming last of all bearing a bundle containing the sacred pipe.

Luke closed the door flap behind them and listened to their muffled voices as if from a distance as they began to sing and pray within. The call came for the stones and as quickly as he could, he delivered them with a pitchfork, feeding them like burnt offerings through the dark maw of the doorway.

"Welcome Grandfather Stones!"

Luke sealed the sweat lodge door closed and listened from outside to the wild hissing and steaming of the incendiary rocks as the elder ladled water over them. Three more times in the course of that evening he was called upon to open the door. Three more times those within paused to breathe in the night air. In between times he crouched by the door and waited. The fire dwindled, the stars burned brightly, and he grew cold. He was lonely at the vigil, listening to the animated song and prayer coming from within. They sang in a language that was strange yet somehow familiar.

On the fourth invocation of the phrase, "all my relations", he opened the door and they all left the lodge and ran naked with the steam billowing in plumes off their bodies and plunged headlong into the icy creek. Trills of liquid laughter blended with the flowing of the dark waters as the revelers heaved themselves ashore like a rowdy herd of seals up from the sea. Afterwards they called him to join them in the cabin to feast and to bask in the warmth not only of the woodstove but of that singular kind generated by the singing of the stones.

The following morning they all fasted. There was to be another sweat that day and the preparations of the day before were repeated; the gathering of the stones, the making of the offerings, the collection of firewood. Midday all was ready. Old Joseph volunteered to be the gatekeeper and Luke was invited to enter the Lodge.

Once they were all settled in, White Eagle began. He addressed them as his brothers and his sister and thanked them for having the wisdom and courage to enter the house of cleansing and healing and he said that the sweathouse was like a womb, that when they exited through the door of this womb they would be given a chance to be reborn.

When he was done the others responded with a resounding, "Ho!"

"Gatekeeper!" he called out dramatically to the elder waiting outside. "We are ready for the stones!"

The door flap was flung open. What remained of the afternoon sun poured into the dark interior. The air blew in chill and cold as Old Joseph swiftly delivered the stones to the fire pit. He made four trips delivering sixteen blazing stones and then he sealed the door.

As the dry heat became more and more intense, Luke felt a claustrophobic pressure, even a buzzing in his skull as his sweat began to pour.

White Eagle then sprinkled red cedar leaf on the stones and the aromatic scent filled their nostrils. Then from out of the silence Marguerite gave her voice to the darkness. She bid them to enter through the gateway of the east, the place of the color red. She called them to journey to the source of illumination, the doorway of the sun and the home of the wolf. She told them that they could know this source within themselves.

Again the water was poured out. The rocks steamed and hissed, seething with primordial violence. Luke felt trapped and wanted to flee the confines of his own burning skin. At last White Eagle spoke the words, "all my relations." Old Joseph opened the door flap and Luke sucked in the cool stream of night air, his chest heaving with relief. The respite was short-lived as the door was closed, the darkness returned and the ladling out of water renewed the blast of wet fiery airs. Perhaps because he now knew what to expect, he could hold the panic at bay.

The boundaries of his awareness began to blur. As he surrendered to this expanded sensibility, he felt as if he were floating.

101

He was in communion with these strangers in the enclosed circle, in the shared darkness. Then Walksfast spoke:

"Oh Creator, it is your child Freddy Walksfast who speaks. As we walk through the gateway of the south, reveal to us your spirit alive in all things. In the cleansing and healing of our own bodies and minds, the renewal of the Earth begins."

For a second time the door was opened. The light outside was diminishing into the pale gray of late afternoon. Never before had Luke tasted air so sweet. This time with the singing stones and the wall of vaporized heat, he slipped into a detached and floating space.

"Oh Creator, spirit who moves in all things, it is Raphael who speaks now. Hear my prayer. We approach the gateway of the west. Give us courage to enter that doorway into darkness as warriors. You know well that it is not death we fear but our own cowardice in the face of oppression, our own unwillingness to unmask the lies, to confront the forces among men that create injustice and strife and destruction of the land. These forces represent all that is blind to the beauty and harmony of your Creation. We know this gateway to be the facing of the bear. We have here among us a young warrior who has the scars of such an encounter. Scars have the power to remind us that our past is real. Let us pray with him as he seeks to uncover the gifts contained in the wounds of one who has danced with the bear and lived to speak of it."

Jimmy White Eagle spoke next. He told them that the daughter of the Creator was coming to them from the north. He said that her name was White Buffalo Calf Woman and that from her they would gain knowledge of how to restore the sacred hoop and so bind themselves in service to one another. When he was finished he cried out: "Ho! I have spoken." And the people within the sweathouse answered in unison, "all my relations."

Old Joseph opened the door. Downhill to the creek, playful and laughing they splashed in, their silvered bodies steaming in the night air above the waters and below the winter stars. Luke started out after them at a slow trot still feeling set apart, but as their ebullient cries rang out, he broke into a sprint and plunged in. He was amazed that he could resist the cold and swim about in those icy waters. He felt cleansed within and without.

They clambered up the bank and returned to the fire to dry off. When all were dressed, Old Joseph spoke to them saying: "Now we are ready for the seeking of the deer." Old Joseph entered the tipi and all followed.

The people circled around the fire pit before taking seats on blankets spread on the earthen floor. The fire was blazing before a hearth of earth facing west and mounded in the shape of a crescent moon that served as an altar. Old Joseph handed his drum to White eagle. His pipe bundle was set before him along with a stick, a gourd, bunches of red cedar, sage and braided sweet grass.

The boy watched as the elder filled a basket of gray-green buttons taken from Raphael's sack, carefully removing the white tufts that sprouted from each of the multi-sectioned surfaces. He handed the basket to Marguerite and then gathered up the beaded wrap, untied the rawhide strings and removed the red stone pipe. He tamped the bowl and offered up the pipe with a gesture to the four directions, to the sky above and the earth below. He reached into the bank of the fire and withdrew a live coal between forefinger and thumb and placed the coal in the pipe and began a hollow-cheeked sucking upon its stem. When it was lit, he passed it to the nameless youth at his side who, surprised at its sweetness, sucked in the smoke then passed it on. When the pipe had come full circle, Old Joseph began to speak.

"I am the road man. Hear my prayer. Let us partake of this medicine meat. Chew it well. When you take this medicine, if you want to use this power, if you want to walk this peyote road, you must love everybody, treat everybody right. The Messenger has shown us that there is a black road that leads to death and a red road that leads to life. Together let us walk this good red road that leads to life."

He glanced over at the woman with a nod of his silver mane. She took up the basket and held it as a sacrament before her and she spoke words of thanksgiving and gratitude and chose out four cactus buttons and then passed the basket. Each in turn took four, spoke words of similar effect, then passed the basket on.

When the boy received the basket from the hands of the elder, he too picked out four buttons. He passed the basket and then held the cactus out before him on open palms. Words came forth then like the outpouring of rain clouds over drought-stricken lands. "My name is Daniel Sweeney. I give thanks for my life and for my name. Ho!" Suddenly he felt afraid. He looked to Old Joseph who smiled at him reassuringly and he gained heart and ate the cactus. The basket made the rounds for a second time. Again he ate the cactus. A crystalline light appeared before him, a singular diamond-like shining as captivating as the source of beauty itself. From out of the silence, from out of the void came a soft, sonorous tone, the sweetest sound he had ever heard. The sound and the light enveloped him in a singular fusion of the senses. His only wish, his one desire, was to surrender himself completely to that perfect lovely light, this utterly transcendent sound and to know the peace from whence it sprang. Then suddenly he was that light, he became that sound. He felt himself to be at one and at peace.

"Who am I?" he asked himself. He was answered by a voice that came from within and yet spoke with an authority and conviction that were not his own: "I and the land are one." And he knew he believed this, that it was perhaps the one thing he had always held sacred and true, but then doubt crept in and he questioned himself. As if reading his thoughts, Old Joseph spoke.

"The Messenger is real. He drinks from the veins of the earth. He is the body within the body. Don't judge, only witness!" he proclaimed. "There is no past. There is no future. There is even no now."

Old Joseph paused for a moment of stillness, then continued.

"Who are you? The sum of all your mistakes and all your grievances accounted with all your hopes and dreams and your every act of bravery all add up to nothing. Your life is a speck. So what? Forget it! For all that cannot even begin to add up to who you *really* are. Your little will alone can't do anything. To accomplish the acts of a warrior in this world takes great determination. Great determination doesn't mean just making an effort; it means the whole universe is behind you and with you---the birds, the trees, the sky, the moon and the six directions."

The passing of the basket and the dance of the fire gave Daniel a glimpse of a reality vaster than any he'd ever imagined. He had not ever felt more alive and aware, not even as a child in his forest refuge, that poetry of place where he was unconsciously just a part of it. Here he found himself fully conscious in the intensity of this moment.

Old Joseph spoke. "We have been given freedom of choice. We are offered this good red road. The task of the warrior is to place himself in the service of the healing powers of the Great Spirit. The Messenger has chosen each of you and is willing to be your ally. You in turn must choose to make use of his gift wisely. We must try to help those who have lost a link to the wisdom of the ancestors. The very survival of the Creation demands this of us."

Daniel felt the truths Old Joseph spoke becoming rooted in his own body and mind. As the night passed they chanted many other songs which to Daniel all sounded as one song, a song to the giver of life.

*

He was not even sure why he'd agreed to come. He'd never much enjoyed hunting. That had been something Danny and Patrick had shared. He liked eating venison well enough, but tromping around in the winter woods all alone looking to shoot some poor deer was not his idea of fun. He'd much rather watch the conference title that was to air that afternoon. But he'd let the fellas he played cards with talk him into it. They said that because Sugarbrook hadn't been hunted for a year there might be more deer wintering here than elsewhere. Well shit-all, it was cold. And now he was feeling a little disoriented. It had been a long time since he'd been up in this section of the woods and things had changed. He thought to reach for the flask in his liner pocket, then remembered he'd already taken the last sip about an hour ago. He'd been forbidden by his companions to smoke. They said the scent would tip off the deer. But dammit he was going to have one now.

He paused to catch his breath on a steep north facing slope. So far it had been a soft winter. There was an inch or two of snow on the ground, good for tracking, but the brooks and the seeps in the woods weren't yet frozen up. He'd not oiled his boots before coming out and now his feet were wet. He set his rifle against the bole of a tree. Just as he was getting out his matchbook to light a cigarette an icy rain began to fall. It made the forest come alive with a crackling riff as the pellets hit the sheet of snow. He stuffed his gloves into his coat pockets. His fingers were stiff with the cold and he dropped the match book and as he bent to reach for it he lost his footing and slid down the hill on his back tumbling into a shallow brook at the base of the ravine. He clawed his way out through the thin fringe of ice at its edge. When he regained his feet he still had the unlit cigarette clenched between his teeth. He ripped it out of his mouth and hurled it to the ground. Shit! This is why I hate goddamn stupid ass motherfucking hunting.

He trudged back up the hill to retrieve his rifle. He'd agreed to meet his companions back at the barn by dusk. It was already dusk. Now all he had to was find his way back to the barn. It would be located somewhere to the southeast. He thought of the old lore that said moss always grows on the north side of the tree. He sure enough could see that the moss was thicker on one side than the other. That gave him hope. He started walking uphill in the direction the trees told him was south and entered a lovely grove of birch trees. He crested the ridge and thought he could see a hint of luminosity in the cloud cover in what should have been the west. He started picking his way down the opposite side of the ridge. The footing was treacherous and he grabbed onto saplings for support as he went. He slipped and went down hard enough to bruise his ribs. He rolled over onto his hands and knees and went into a coughing fit. Man, I got to quit smoking.

He got his breath back and was about to regain his feet, when his attention was caught by a curious set of tracks in the snow in front of him. Looks like a goddamn cow! Momentarily forgetting the cold and his predicament, he started to follow the tracks. He ambled through the woods a ways and was about to come to the conclusion that what he was doing was ridiculous when he saw the pile of scat. Fresh enough to be still steaming. A freaking moose! He'd heard rumors that moose were making a comeback in the state but those stories were filtering down from the Northeast Kingdom. Moose hadn't been seen in these parts since some time in the middle of the last century. He knew his scat, he'd not been a boy scout for nothing. There was no mistaking it. He just had to follow.

He spotted it midway down the southerly slope. It was standing atop a mound and looking back in his direction and it was all legs and gangly and big as a horse and it was completely white. He wouldn't have seen it had it not been silhouetted against the last gun metal sheen of the westerly sky. It stomped a fore hoof and huffed out a nervous warning. Then it turned and loped off.

He stood watching after it till the pelting ice rain bit his face. He began to shiver uncontrollably. The rifle slid from his grasp and he had no awareness that he had dropped it. He shuffled and slid his way down to the spot atop the mound where he'd last seen the phantom moose. He knew this place, though it was years since he'd been here. It was the root cellar. At least that's what the old timers called it. Some damn fool academics over at the college had notions about its being some kind of Neolithic site, but he'd never bought that. To him and his buddies it had first been a neat fort, and later a cool place to come and party. They had named it the 'Troll Hole'. He went around to the southeast facing door and entered the interior so black it made the night woods seem light and as he stepped in, a calmness washed over him. I'll just set for awhile, he thought, gather my strength. But as soon as he sat with his back to the stonework, fatigue rose up and sleep beckoned. He felt a peace that was a welcome stranger. I must be getting hypothermic. I should fight sleep. But he was drifting away and his thoughts dispersed like clouds in a changing wind.

He opened his eyes to see there was a fire burning bright in the pit set at the back of the cavern. Seated cross legged with her back to the blaze was a young woman. She wore robes and jewels and her skin was an iridescent green. She held up her right hand with the palm facing out. In the center of the palm there was an eye. "Look," she said and the three eyes gazed toward the wall opposite from where he sat. His eyes followed. It was Sugarbrook farm, though whether it was a picture of the past or of some yet to be realized future he could not tell. It surely was not of the now because the farm he saw was in the fullness of high summer. Fat and sleek black beeves shared lush pastures with fawn colored dairy cows, their engorged udders causing

107

them to wattle as they foraged. Crops stood headed out in the fields ripe for harvest. As he gazed on the scene it touched a longing for health and for sweetness that lay buried like a deep seam within him. He wept.

The green woman rose and strode towards him. She knelt in front of him; her power and her beauty overwhelmed him until his whole body shook. She took his hand and closed his fist within her own hand and squeezed it tight. She raised a quartz crystal before his eyes. He pressed it to his forehead and when he shut his eyes, his mind was filled with light. Tommy, if you would be healed, you must first heal the land.

"Tommy! Tommy!"

There were beams of lights in his eyes oscillating and harsh. He sat up cold and stiff.

"He's in here!"

"Christ Jesus, we thought maybe you'd froze to death.'

"What time is it?"

"It's the middle of the night, boy, we been searching for you for hours."

Someone gave him hot coffee from a thermos cup. Someone else put a chocolate bar in his hand. They hoisted him up and got him walking.

"I remember this place."

"Yup, the Troll Hole, used to be a wicked good partying spot."

"More creepy than I remembered it."

"Come on let's get this old boy home. He's in need of a good hot shower."

"Hey Tommy, what happened to your rifle?"

"I don't know. I must've dropped it when I saw the white moose."

"Man, we'd better get him home."

3

Diffuse morning light filtered in through the smoke hole of the tipi. Someone had covered him with a blanket. He arose out of sleep as if returning from a long journey. As he stood outside and took a deep breath, he remembered that he had reclaimed his name; it felt like a favorite old coat, mended, yet somehow new.

Freddy strummed a banjo. Marguerite sang as she dipped pieces of fry bread into a pan of hot cooking oil while White Eagle brewed up a batch of strong black coffee. Old Joseph and Raphael sat together on the buffalo robe in deep conversation. Soon everyone sat down for breakfast, eating and talking all at once. Daniel sat in the afterglow of the previous night's spiritual pilgrimage.

After breakfast he went outside to split firewood when Marguerite came by.

"We leave Flying Cloud tomorrow. My grandma, she was a healer. She helped the sick by calling on the powers of flowers, leaves, roots, mushrooms, berries and bark. This medicine pouch is something she passed on to me. I want you to have it."

The pouch was of soft deer-hide, finely stitched and decorated with intricate quill and bead-work design. He thanked her and brought the precious gift indoors to put with his scant belongings stored under the bench and went back to splitting wood.

He had a fair-sized stack accumulated and had worked up a sweat in the sunshine of an unseasonably mild afternoon when Raphael came up to him in his quiet way carrying a necklace, an extraordinary piece of ten black bear claws with two incisors strung on a sinew loop. Raphael placed the necklace over Daniel's head. "One time a man shot a bear on my land and left it. To honor the bear's spirit, I fashioned this necklace with his claws and teeth. As you know I am engaged in a struggle to defend my land and my people. When I have felt too weak to carry on I have looked to the west and called upon the strength of the bear tribe to help me find courage. May it be so for you, young warrior; may this necklace remind you of the power of the bear that resides within you."

As he met Raphael's eyes, he knew that here was someone worthy of emulation, a model to guide him in his relentless becoming. Raphael returned his gaze, nodded once, then turned and walked on his way.

Daniel hefted the pole with a bucket chained on each end and headed down to the creek for water. White Eagle was there and bade Daniel to come and sit by him. They sat in silence listening to the ever same, ever changing chorale of the passing waters. White Eagle began to hum a tune, then the humming became a chant and he tapped his foot in time and gestured with an open hand, inviting him to join in. Daniel sang haltingly at first, then surprised himself as he gained confidence and chimed in. Together they sang until the song dwindled down and ran away with the water as it tumbled down the mountain.

"It pleases me that you remember the song. It is given to us by the Messenger to use in times of the dark moon. If ever evil powers threaten to overwhelm you, remember this song and your feet will be guided along a safe path."

"What do the words mean?"

Their meaning is manyfold, for this is a song of intent. It is an instrument to bring the medicine wheels within our bodies into harmony with the body of the Creator. It might translate something like this: 'Spirit of wind, I am an eagle, soaring through the rain and the snow, hey yo, hey yo!'"

"The power of the eagle."

"Yes, the wisdom of the north gate. Do not tap into the power of this song lightly; draw upon it only when there is true need. In that way you shall always honor the power of the gift."

Daniel rose and drew creek water into the buckets. Then they clambered up the path over the steep rise to the cabin where preparations were underway for their last supper together.

Daniel went about the feeding chores for horse and cattle. He collected eggs and closed up the chicken house for the night. The wolf-dog followed along behind him as was her wont, close, but not too close. He returned to the cabin with the basket of eggs and paused just steps from the door and gazed out at the early night sky. The moon on the verge of full, would soon rise in the east, and the egg yoke of the sun had just slipped behind a black evergreen script to the west. A deep azure rose into the spreading inkwell where the boldest points of light were blinking. The air held the empty stillness of approaching winter, not yet frigid but as the silver shield of the moon sliced into view, Daniel took note of the shimmering milky aura of concentric rings that augured heavy weather. For several long moments he watched the moon rise, simply breathing in the goodness of being alive.

He paused outside the cabin door listening to the music and laughter inside. He looked forward to a meal together with his new friends even as the anticipation was tinged with a melancholic mist at the thought of their imminent departure. He pushed open the heavy door and entered into the convivial warmth of that gathering.

*

She was just pulling the last of four pumpkin pies from the oven when he came in. She set it on the counter in line with the others and removed her mitts. Although she would have preferred to let it cool, she took down a dessert plate and cut and served him up a slice of the pie with a glass of cold milk. He hung up his wool overcoat and scarf and took a seat at the table.

"You're home early," she said.

"Yup."

"Slow day?"

"Real slow."

"That's unusual."

"I quit."

"Oh?"

"I couldn't take it any more. I'm sick of always having to be the bad guy."

"What do you mean by that?"

"All these farmers that keep coming in. Closed mouthed sons-a-bitches. They treat me like I'm some kind of traitor."

"Because you're not like Patrick?"

"So many of them going belly-up these days. I try as hard as I can to work them a good deal and still they despise me."

"They've got to blame someone."

"But I'm making them good money."

"None of them really wants to sell."

"I know it. Christ, I feel the same way about Sugarbrook."

"Then don't sell it."

"We need to more than ever now."

"I can find work."

"Who will be mother to our boys? "

"You could stay home."

"Very funny. Anyway, I heard there's an opening at the high school."

"You a teacher?"

"Why not? English and assistant coach."

"The coach is the part you're excited about."

"I am."

"Well, that's a good thing. I haven't seen you excited about anything in a long time."

"I'm excited about this pie."

"It's getting cold."

"I'm excited about untying those apron strings."

"That's getting warmer."

"Where are the boys?"

"Still taking a nap."

"I'll have my pie later."

*

The air had grown thick with that singular moist and metallic taste to it. Even before the noisy departing truck faded down the trail, the snow began to fall. The minuscule flakes slanting down on a northwest wind told Old Joseph that they were in for a good one. Together he and Daniel laid in plenty of wood from the shed and hauled up dozens of buckets of creek water and provisions from the root cellar. They picked up any loose tools or gear around the barnyard and stored them away.

By noon there was a foot of snow on the ground---the air was thick with it. The wind picked up and blew dry powder into drifts. The four pregnant cows and the bull stood hunkered down in the run-in shed, tails turned under and backsides pointed into the storm. The pinto horse was content in her stall relentlessly grinding up last summer's grass. They had done all they could to secure the camp in the face of the blizzard and young man and old man hurried back inside to the warm sanctuary of the cabin.

Old Joseph resumed his carving, a mustang frozen in the full extension of a gallop. His hands were always busy at something. The fingers curled around the whittling knife were like the living growth of tree root gripping stone, an animate expression of the wood he carved. Those hands spoke decades of hard work, compassionate touch and creative artistry.

Daniel sat on a square of canvas tarp and practiced flint-knapping on pieces of the black glass given to him by Old Joseph. A bean stew was slow cooking on top of the stove. At intervals they would each rise up to stir the stew pot and then gaze out the window or crack the door to gauge the progress of the storm by sighting off the fence posts of the corral to see how much snow had accumulated since the last check and then return with the cluck of a tongue, a low whistle, or disbelieving shake of the head at the magnitude of the fall.

"Old Joseph?"

"Hmmm!" the old one growled like a wolverine disturbed out of its den, so fully absorbed was he in his carving.

"How is it you came to live here alone on this mountain?"

"This place was an old mining claim. I won title to it in a card game. Back in my drinking days."

"But what made you decide to come live here?"

Old Joseph set aside his carving and rose to his feet with a stretch and a groan. He lit a kerosene lamp and stoked up the woodstove. He sat down cross-legged on the bison robe and took out his corn cob pipe and tobacco from the pocket of his vest.

"Well, Daniel, as with any story, the hardest part is to know just where it begins; it's a long story but I will start at the time when I was about your age which was a long time ago. Our people had never been farmers. Though many other nations were accomplished agriculturists, the Oglala Lakota were free-wandering nomads. Our life was all rolled up in one bundle with the life of the buffalo. However, it was painfully clear to us young people that those days were gone forever. The old ones could subsist on their memories, but the youth needed to find a new way.

"My way out was to fight in the white man's army. They declared the Armistice six months into my tour. When our braves came home from fighting the Great War for Uncle Sam, the Feds went in and broke up our tribal lands. They said they wanted to assimilate us Indians into the modern world, give us the opportunity to be owners of property. They gave each adult male a sixty-acre parcel. Having had a taste of the wide world in the service with all that a regular salary can buy, most of our young men weren't about to settle for a life of subsistence farming. That left the door wide open for the white farmers and ranchers to start buying or leasing Indian land till practically all that was left to us was the badlands. Now that they have found there is lots of the hot metal out there, they want to take even that land away.

"I should've taken a parcel but I wasn't ready for that kind of responsibility, so I sold mine off just like everybody else. I went up to stay with relatives in North Dakota. It was hard for us young guys. When there was work, it would be seasonal at best. Round-ups, hay-making, breaking horses, busting our asses for a little spare change. And you know a lot of the old ones who were still alive had been around when we were an unconquered people. The old men could tell stories of having been on the trail with famous medicine men and great warriors; Sitting Bull and Red Cloud, Big Foot and Crazy Horse. And there we were with time on our hands and no purpose to our lives.

"I don't remember whose idea it was. There was a circle of us young warriors and we were ready for something. Somebody knew where we could sell horses with no questions asked and somebody knew where we could 'find' them. So off we rode, the bunch of us, each one on some unlikely mount including an old mule fresh from the plowing. We had a few ancient guns between us. And one young brave was even carrying a bow and arrows. We painted our faces and headed up toward Elgin. One moonless night we crossed the Cannonball River at mid-night and rustled up forty, maybe fifty head off one of those big

114

ranches up there. Things were going along pretty well, we were slipping out unnoticed when a dog caught wind of us and began to raise a stink. I never knew a dog to bark that loud. Before you knew it there were cowboys busting out of barns and bunkhouses swifter than a swarm of angry bees, piling into trucks to give us chase. Some of our boys got away and took some horses with them. But not everybody was so lucky. I heard later that two warriors fell that night and a third was captured and hung."

Old Joseph paused to pack the tobacco in his pipe and light up and after a few long draws he continued his story.

"It must have been a stray bullet that nailed me because nobody stopped to finish me off. The mule I was riding got away--- her name was Lucky. Lucky for her. Two of the skins wheeled their ponies around to come back for me but by that time there were armed riders in hot pursuit. They came under such heavy fire that they were forced to turn tail and run. By some miracle the posse rode on by as I lay bruised and bleeding in a ditch.

"One of her men found me in the morning lying on the ground with a busted wing. The bullet had passed through my left shoulder and come clean out the front. Shoulder and arm have never been quite right since but I can't complain---I'm still living.

"The cowboy who found me worked for a woman known around those parts as the Widow Jane. She was one tough bird. She could outrope, outride, outshoot, outdrink and shout down the best of men. For some reason she found a tender spot in her heart for me. I'll have to admit I was a rather handsome devil in those days and that might've had something to do with it. She was my senior by a good ten years but she was one fine looking woman. Of pioneer stock, Norwegian or Swede or some such, tall and strong of bone but slender. She had sparkling blue eyes and hair the color of corn silk which she kept done up tight. I was privileged to see it brushed out and spilling down over her breasts. But I am getting ahead of my self.

"I was now a wanted man. Jane kept me hidden in the attic and she tended my wounds. Her husband had died young, murdered some said, before there were any children. She never talked about him. To that woman the past was just that. After he died she took on managing the ranch with a thousand head of cattle all by herself. Well, she had her hired hands. Those guys were all right. They could've easily blown the whistle on me---there was some kind of a reward. But they were loyal to her.

"After awhile the big stir over Indian uprisings and horse-thieving blew over. Soon as I was feeling able, I started working with the hired hands. Only truth is, the Widow Jane's candle-lit visits of healing ministrations to the attic had increased in the nature of their intimacy and duration. Looking back I would have to say that we were in love, though neither one of us would've dreamt of uttering the word. She was a rare woman. I learned a lot from her about being a man."

The old man puffed on his pipe, lost in the reverie of those treasured moments.

"I had been living on the ranch about a year and what do you know? Jane became big with child. I was grateful for all that she had done for me and I cared for her as much as I had ever cared for anybody. But I was young and full of myself and ready to eat up the world. I just couldn't see settling down even with a lady as pretty and durable as she was. So I lit out of there like a thief in the night.

"Things went downhill for me from there. I hit the road and it was all hard traveling. I couldn't stay away from the bottle in those days. I sobered up in jail, not that a guy couldn't get whatever he wanted in there. It was during my time in the hole that a dormant seed in me awakened. When I was released, I headed back to Pine Ridge. I started hanging around the old ones, asking lots of questions, observing and helping them out as much as I could. It was a good thing to be speaking the old words again. And through the practice of our ancient ways, I felt a new power coming into me.

"My old man had already gone on his journey up the star trail by that time, but my mother was still alive. She was living in the camp of my sister's husband. I was amazed at how much she had to teach me about the use of healing herbs, knowledge our old ones had kept and guarded for the next generation in spite of the suppression by the government and the churches. The old ones tended the ancient ways in secret, like coals for the cook fire, until we were ready to rekindle the flame.

"I also found a teacher, Three Moons, the antelope dancer. He was an Uncle I'd heard about but had never met. He carried the pipe that I now carry and I learned many secrets from him. After he passed on, I began to travel again. Only now I was no longer wandering without purpose. My feet were gaining purchase on the good red road.

"I thought about the Widow Jane often. I thought about going up to see her but somehow there was always something right at hand that needed doing. And yet my sense of gratitude for what she had done for me in those wild days of my youth only grew as time went by.

"Near to fifteen years had passed since I had left and when word got to me that she was in dire straits, in danger of losing the ranch, I knew I had to go see her. Even after all those years, Jane was still a handsome woman. But my heart nearly stopped dead when I beheld the angel with black braids standing in the doorway behind her mother. At fifteen she was a proud beauty. Jane had told her about me and it took her about an instant to figure out who I was. I spent all of that spring and summer on the ranch helping out. Jane bore no grudge for my having walked out on them; such capacity for forgiveness is the mark of a truly free spirit. Our daughter on the other hand was cautious about me at first, but with time her insatiable curiosity about everything overcame her reticence and we soon became fast friends. I didn't even think about trying to be a father to her; it was too late for that. But in my role as a medicine person, I taught her about her heritage and the knowledge of who we are. I taught her the language of the people and she was quick to grasp it. She was especially keen to learn the songs.

"With cattle prices down, Jane's ranch could no longer pay its way. She was deep in debt and the bank threatened foreclosure. Perhaps that's why it happened. Strong horsewoman that she was, she must have been preoccupied, not paying attention. Anyway, she was out rounding up cattle as she had done thousands of times when she was thrown from her horse and broke her neck. She died instantly. My daughter was placed in state custody but not for long. Wise Jane had left enough evidence of her paternity so that with the help of a lawyer, I was able to gain custody. I brought her to live with my sister's family at Pine Ridge.

"Although my heart was heavy with the loss of the only woman

I ever loved, and worried how my daughter would adapt to her new family, I was able to stay fast on the good red road. Everywhere I went I carried my pipe and I performed ceremonies. The first time I saw the twin mountains, I felt drawn to this place and I chose to settle here, been here more moons than I can count now. It's not so lonely. When fair weather comes, it is unusual for me not to have guests. A steady stream comes through during the moons of plenty."

"What happened to your daughter?" Daniel asked.

"The last time I saw my daughter she was living at her grandmother's house on the Pine Ridge. It pained me to note how much of the sparkle had faded from her eyes. I could see she felt out of place on the reservation. She had not been raised in the Indian way, was caught between two worlds. She ran off to make her own way in life. They say she married a white soldier and he took her back east. I hope she chose a man who would treat her right, that she was happy. Her name was Sarah Three Moons."

Old Joseph frowned, shook his head slowly and closed his eyes, looking backwards into memories still flashing across the screen of his inner vision. Daniel thought his head might explode when he heard that name, the pieces of his life falling into place.

"Sarah Three Moons was my mother. Sarah Sweeney. She died when I was five years old." He was almost shouting.

Old Joseph nodded and gazed upon his face with such tenderness that Daniel was moved to tell his own story. He told the old man everything that he could remember about his mother and then he spoke of his life on the farm and of all that had happened to him and of all the events that had brought him to the threshold of Flying Cloud Camp.

"Yes, Daniel, my grandson. I know who you are. I suppose that I recognized you the moment I saw you. A good thing has come to pass. It is the way of the Mother Earth to bring all things full circle."

"I'm sorry I lied about my name."

"This matter of changing your name is no cause for shame. There was wisdom in the choice you made then. Among the old ones it was common for a person to change names several times in the course of a lifetime. Whenever a life-changing event occurred, they believed it a sensible thing to mark such with a new name. Who knows? Perhaps your true name is yet to be revealed."

The dark of evening was settling in, the snow still falling. After loading up the woodstove, Old Joseph bundled up and pulled down two sets of snowshoes from their wall pegs. Daniel followed him out the door into a world transformed. Even trailing behind on the broken path, the fresh powder was up to his knees. The wind blew head-on and whipped frozen particles that stung his eyes.

"Stay close!" hollered Old Joseph above the wrath of the storm. Daniel knew the danger well, having heard as a child the oft-told stories of farmers who had been lost in blizzards walking the distance between house and barn. The fierce cold bit at extremities and made their blood run thick. They struggled to bed down the livestock for the night. In weather such as this, the simplest tasks became monumental feats.

Warm and safe inside, they shared a meal of black beans, chilies, venison and corn bread. Old Joseph brewed up a pot of roasted chicory root which they drank sweetened with raw honey. Thus contented, they weathered out the storm.

4

The snow continued to fall for three days running and it took them the better part of a fourth day to dig their way out. They settled into quieter routines, taking delight in exploring after each new snow to see what tracks the artist of the night had painted on that empty canvas. They followed the comings and goings of their wild neighbors. Old Joseph trapped beaver, marten and rabbit---he did not trap for profit but only to secure the few pelts he needed for winter gear. Daniel helped him work his trap lines and render the catch. In the evenings he played his flute, the music melding with the flicker of lamplight, echoing the tones of the deep well of winter.

When it was too inclement to be outdoors, they would sit together in the cabin. If Daniel should ask him a question, Old Joseph would pack his cob pipe and puff away for several moments before answering. In bits and pieces the medicine man transmitted teachings that could help him integrate all that he had experienced with the four guests. Old Joseph waited for his questions, resting in his knowledge that a vessel can only receive substance according to its present shape.

"Old Joseph, why did you and the Widow Jane never marry?"

"Well, in one sense, we were married."

"You left out that part of your story."

"It's like this---among the old ones we never stood before a pastor or judge. We came before the assembly of our own. First there was the courtship, the young brave wooed the maiden with songs played on an elk flute such as the one in the corner there by my drum. There was an exchange of gifts and feasting between the families and the young man had to acquire a quantity of horses to present to the father of the bride, but that was mostly a test of his courage and skill. Then the couple would stand before the people facing one another and clasping hands. And he said, 'I am your husband' and she replied 'I am your wife' and from that moment on they were considered married.

That is how I married Jane except that our witnesses were our horses, the pines atop the butte and the Great Spirit all about us. The giving of one's word is a crucial step on the path to becoming a true human being. Each one of us is a mirror. If a person can faithfully abide with

120

even one other person through the good and the bad of this life then such a one is drawing near to the power in which the Great Spirit enfolds our lives."

As the old man spoke his hands would be busy with small tasks, stitching moccasins, braiding rope out of pounded nettle fiber, fashioning arrows, or carving figures out of wood. Old Joseph didn't file or sand his diminutive sculptures. He left the rough-hewn marks and textures in the wood as the natural surfaces of his carved objects--- sublime imperfection. Daniel took up carving as well, eager to try his hand at liberating form out of block, knot and grain. He observed and imitated, only occasionally drawing his own blood in the attempt. And while engaged in carving, his questions would arise.

"Do you think it's important for a man to marry?"

"A warrior must be complete in himself. But the companionship of a good woman is something surpassing sweet."

"I wish I hadn't walked away from that girl in the orchard."

"You did what you needed to do. You'll meet her again if it's meant to be. Just as we were meant to find each other and just as you were meant to meet the Messenger."

Suddenly, from the near woods Daniel heard what sounded like the sharp crack of a rifle shot and jumped up with a start. The severe cold was freezing trees from the inside out, causing them to explode from the core. Old Joseph had not stirred from his comfortable seat on the floor with its crafted backrest of red willow weave. He regarded Daniel bemusedly.

"Now you know why the old ones call this the moon of the popping trees."

*

In the backroom of Smokey's bar late on a Saturday night, five former varsity ball players hunkered down on a winter's night around a card table, five card-stud in play, smoke thick and curling about their heads and fresh whiskey poured at intervals. Tommy took a handful of salted nuts and chewed them methodically as he studied his hand. Last call out at the bar. He glanced up at Stiles trying to read whether he was bluffing. How would you ever know if Stiles was bluffing? The man was born with a poker face.

Tommy folded his cards. Stiles *was* bluffing. The Deputy laid down a straight and pulled in the chips; there might have been a hint of glee playing about the corner of his thin lips or it might have been just a nervous tic.

"It's late."

"Not leaving already are you Tom?"

"He just don't want to give me any more of his money," said Stiles.

"There is that."

"Specially on a school teacher's salary."

The last spoken by Ed Brown, a science teacher. Ed had been a tackle. Now big as a house, he was known for his trick ties, stripes or checks on the front side, images of naked ladies on the back.

"What's eating you tonight? You've been about as talkative as Stiles over there."

Tommy heaved an extended sigh, poured another shot and lit a cigarette.

"It's nothing. It's been a year since my brother took off. Found myself thinking about him today."

"What made him run off like that?" asked Jason Talbot, former center, now hog butcher.

"Thought I was going to sell the land out from under him."

"Well ain't you?" asked Teddy Peaver, former running back, current diesel mechanic for the town.

"I thought I was, but I can't seem to make up my mind. The weird thing is, if he hadn't run away I most certainly would have sold it."

"You ought to let somebody farm it. It's a shame to have all that good land sitting up there fallow," said Jason.

"You're right. I've thought about talking to the Johnson's about cropping it this year. But then in the next moment I think I'm going to put it back on the market."

"Lots of farms for sale. Seems like somebody's going under just about every week," said Teddy.

"It's that regulation requiring refrigerated bulk tanks. Goddamn expensive. I warned my old man about that," said Tommy.

"Not just that. Price of milk is bottoming out. Too much competition from New York and Wisconsin," added Ed.

"I keep thinking maybe he'll come back. That's what keeps me from selling."

"He's probably in a Mexican jail, " said Stiles.

"Too funny."

"Fucksake, my little brother's shipping out to Vietnam in a week. Been six weeks in boot camp out in San Diego," said Ed.

"At least you know where he is."

"Not sure I want to."

"I hear that's a real mess over there," this from Chip Conway, former wide receiver, logger by trade.

"It's a mess all right. A lost war," replied Ed.

"No telling what kind of trouble Danny's got himself into," said Chip.

"That's the worst of it. Not knowing," Tommy stubbed out his cigarette and downed his shot.

"You still in?" asked Stiles ready to deal.

"No I'm out. Wife's gonna be wondering what happened to me."

"What *did* happen to you?" This from Stiles.

Tommy made a face. He stretched his arms overhead, gathered up his cigarettes, pulled out his wallet to even up.

"Man, when we were in high school seemed like we were on top of the world. How in the hell did things get so screwed up?"
Nobody had an answer.

Vicki poured herself a shot into his glass and downed it. She went over to the console and put on an LP. Hank Williams singing, *Are You Lonesome Tonight*. She reached for Tommy's hand and pulled him to his feet. They began a slow dance. He realized when his feet hit the floor that he was feeling the whiskey. He was feeling the way she felt close up in his arms and sashaying side to side and that was feeling pretty good. A low whistle came from someone at the table and he realized they had

123

become the evening's entertainment. He whispered in her ear.

"What do you say we take this somewhere private?"

"I'm with you, Mister."

*

As winter wore old, the afternoon sun gained a height and warmth that stirred buried memories of another season. Daniel began to take long rides on Old Joseph's pinto. It helped to take the edge off his growing restlessness. The melt-off had begun on the twin peaks---the snow was no longer impassably deep but there was still enough on the ground to leave tracks, making it possible for Daniel to find his way through the woods back to camp.

On one such morning after chores he set off with the horse, planning to return in time to fix a stretch of fence. Blow downs had done some damage over the winter and now was the time to clean up before the cattle grew restless and began to test their bounds. Old Joseph was out drilling taps into birch trees. Soon the sap would begin to run and he was fond of the boiled-down syrup.

The horse was aware of the wild herd before he was. She raised her head, flared her nostrils, and pitched her ears forward. The horses had come into the mountains off the plains of the Columbia Basin in search of water and shelter. They grazed the meadows and the open woods, pawing through the drifting snow in competition with the elk for forage. When times grew lean, they nipped at the buds of hardwoods and gnawed the bark off young aspen. This was a large grouping of mares and several yearling foals not yet weaned, a dominant stallion, and a few young bachelor stallions trailing cautiously under truce.

Horse and rider stood still at forest edge, watching the herd move upward along a sweep of meadow that filled out the saddle on the eastern spur of the peaks. One mare caught scent of them. She peered in their direction, arching her neck and lifting her tail. As she walked towards them slow and alert in an equipoise between curiosity and fear, a ripple of heightened awareness struck through the body of the herd.

124

All eyes and ears were suddenly riveted. By her side was a lively colt, white as was his dam, but spotted with reddish-brown freckles. He captured Daniel's fancy in an instant. The colt already sported a luxuriant mane and tail. Bold white rims surrounded his eye-whites, making him look perpetually startled and disconcertingly human.

The feisty bay stallion snorted, stamped and circled round, and corralled the mares and lead them further uphill. Tequila neighed and pawed the ground as they left. Daniel held her back, wheeling her around twice in the effort. "Don't worry, old gal," he told her, "we'll come back and see them again."

Return they did. He didn't tell Old Joseph where he was going nor did the old man ask him why he stuffed the saddle bags with sprouting carrots from the root cellar. With the passing days the wild herd grew accustomed to their presence. As long as he kept at a safe distance, he and the horse became a tolerable feature of their landscape. The wild horses soon learned to look for the sweet carrots left behind. He knew that he didn't have much time. The herd would soon be on the move again, heading down the slopes with the snow melt in search of new grass in the lowlands.

He was slow-handed but persistent in his method. He would dismount and tie the long-suffering Tequila to a tree branch and then walk apace with the herd. He aimed to harmonize his motion to the blend and flow of the landscape and match the pace of his movements to the rhythm and cadence of the horses, so that to the unknowing observer he might seem to be some archaic shaman engaged in a sympathetic dance of transformation.

Sometimes he would come upon the herd while they were at rest. Always one horse would be standing watch but there came a day when that sentinel did not start on seeing him. The appaloosa mare and her spotted foal were close by. Playful and sensing no sign of danger from his elders, the little one approached the accustomed figure of the man on foot. Daniel turned to face the colt---their eyes met and the colt started but his flight was only half-hearted. Daniel angled his body sideways and let his eyes trail away to the sparse snow and pale grasses at the colt's heels and retreated two steps back. The spotted colt raised his head with renewed interest and stepped forward again. In repeated fits and starts, the colt drew near. There came a thrilling moment when he ate a carrot from Daniel's hand and for the space of a breath Daniel laid his hand upon his withers and stroked him. Then the colt turned and ran back to his dam.

Days passed and he continued to befriend the colt, waiting patiently until he was sure the colt was fully weaned before he began the next phase. He carried a lead rope and a saddle blanket with him and worked to accustom the colt to the smell and feel of these things being placed on his body. Eventually, he could slip a lead rope over the colt's head and neck and then slide it off again without startling him. He would then move the rope along the vulnerable areas of the young animal's body, parts most likely to be struck by a predator, the soft underbelly beneath the ribs, the flank and the tendons above the hock.

Finally the day came when he could buckle a halter onto the lead. The little horse balked at having its delicate ears placed through the head stall and secured at the throat latch but Daniel talked gently to him and stroked his neck so that even this difficult step was accepted. From then on the work progressed swiftly. One late winter afternoon, when every creek on the twin peaks was running full and the waters raced like quickened blood, he led the colt down to Flying Cloud camp. The colt left the wild herd willingly, accepting Daniel as one of his own kind. Though by nature his dam was already beginning to let go and preparing to breed again, at the sight of her foal being led away, the white mare raced hysterically up and down over the open ground. Daniel had to steel his heart against her plaintive cries. The colt though agitated, found comfort in Daniel's presence and also Tequila's, who had the advantage of being a horse. The mare would not follow them into the shadow of the forest, and as her neighing receded behind them, the little horse settled down as they proceeded into its depths.

Old Joseph stood in front of the cabin with his hands on his hips and amusement on his face as Daniel led the spunky colt down the trail with the ever-patient pinto following behind.

"Looks like we've got a new charger to be trained. Now I understand where you've been disappearing to."

"I gave a fine horse to the wild herds. Now I'm asking them to give one back. I hope I do no wrong."

"He comes willingly enough."

"Will you help me break him?"

"No. But I'll help you gentle him. What's his name?"

"Friend."

"Who in the world doesn't need a friend?"

Two days passed and he saddled up Tequila and rode out of camp again in search of the wild herd only to find they were gone. He rode for hours, trailing them down the mountainside, but their lead was too great and he saw only the signs of their passing. He felt a strange sense of loss at their departure tinged with an element of foreboding, as if the perpetual movement of the herd was something that he too must do, an augury that the same cyclical current of growth and change would all too soon draw him out of the shelter he had found in the shadow of the twin peaks.

Work with the colt proceeded well. Under the tutelage of Old Joseph the little horse soon allowed them to pick up his feet with ease. They got him to accept a saddle and he was quick to understand the principle of being ground driven with a hackamore bit and two long lines slipped through stirrups drawn high. With good foundation work laid, all that remained was for time to grant the yearling size and strength enough to support a rider.

Buds were swelling on the cottonwoods, their spent downy catkins littered the ground, their wispy chaff carried on the breeze. Two cows dropped their calves. One was a dairy-cross, so they had fresh milk and thick butter to slather on their bread. Old Joseph got busy organizing his stash of seed stored in canning jars in the root cellar in preparation for planting season. Daniel looked on with tight-lipped apprehension. He had come to a decision and he felt a pressing need to speak of it

Working along side old Joseph, he continued to be amazed at the old man's strength and agility, strength exceeding that of any man he had ever known, even his own deceased father. But Daniel no longer threw himself wholeheartedly into the labor. His heart was awake with

127

tremendous strains of healing energy, and yearnings he could not give voice to but whose emotive pressure he could not ignore. There was the image of her face---the girl at the well---floating in and out of his inner vision with varying degrees of clarity, confused at times with antecedent images he had begun to recall.

They patched the barn roof, replacing cedar shakes that had been torn off by winter winds. The two of them were anchored by bowline knots hitched in ropes tied over the apex of the roof and secured to a support beam on the opposite side of the structure. Straight forward as a hammer striking a nail, Daniel blurted out words more concisely than the amorphous reeling of his mind.

"I'll be leaving before long."

"I have been waiting for you to make up your mind to tell me, Daniel. It is good that you are finding the strength to make choices."

"This choice brings a lot of pain. I'm going to miss you."

Old Joseph placed a work-hardened hand on his shoulder. "There is no real choice that does not bring with it a measure of pain. Any true choice involves two goods between which we must choose. I will miss you, but my blood runs in your veins and wherever you go, I will be with you."

Daniel turned his face away, hammering in the shakes.

"Where will you go?" asked Old Joseph, as he took up his own hammer.

"There is someone I need to find."

"Oh?" exclaimed Old Joseph, by way of a question, as he sank a roofing nail.

"A girl," explained Daniel.

"Ah," said the old man smiling. "There is always a woman. This would be the girl you once walked away from?"

"She's the one."

"Go to her then."

"I don't know where she is."

"To undertake any task the first thing a warrior must do is come up with a plan."

"How will I ever find her?"

"You found me."

"I wasn't looking for you."

"That's the point."

"I'm not sure that's helpful."

"It's a matter of knowing your intent."

"I'll guess I'll have to make some money."

"The green frog skins make the white man's world go round."

"If I can find her I intend to ask her to come home with me."

"And then?"

"I aim to farm."

"I understand why a young man should not stay in a place such as this. You prepare now to meet life; I prepare to greet my death. You know, Daniel, if you wish you can always go over to the reservation. They need skilled farmers and you have people there who will make a place for you."

"Thanks, but no, Grandfather. Since the day I met you much has become clear. I think I know now who I am and where I belong. I want to go back to the land where I was born and raised."

"What will be necessary for your return?"

Daniel paused before trying to answer, to grasp the handle of meaning towards which the old man's words would steer him. He laid down his hammer and took in a deep breath and exhaled a sigh.

"I must forgive my brother."

"And what must you do to forgive him?"

"Love him."

"And who else must you learn to love and forgive before you can hope to forgive your brother?"

This seemed the hardest question of all but in an instant it became clear to him; who it was he was most afraid of, who it was he had run away from in anger, who it was he most longed to understand and be at peace with.

"Myself."

"Grandson, that makes my old ears rejoice. Up to this time you have been running from your past. Now it is time to run towards your future. May you succeed in both your quests for love and for land."

Two days later he was prepared for the trail. Friend was outfitted with a surcingle to hold on the saddlebags stocked with oats, jerked meat, biscuits, striking flint, griddle, and canteen. He tied on the rifle scabbard housing his flute and the bedroll with the rain poncho wrapped around it. He wore his buckskin shirt, the bear claw necklace circled his breast, and the fleece-lined coat covered all. He had the beaded medicine pouch from Marguerite along with his set of bow and arrows slung over one shoulder and the travel-worn hat on his head. Old Joseph had sewn him a pair of moccasins with beaver pelt uppers and thick raw elk-hide soles.

Old Joseph placed a hexagonal quartz into the palm of his hand. He held it up and looked through it in the morning light. A single beam like a cupful of liquid rainbow filled his eye. Then he clasped it in his fist. The old man embraced him and as their chests were pressed firm, Daniel sensed a mysterious light swirling from the cavity of heart to heart. He gazed one last time upon the healer's face. The old man gathered him up in one last warm embrace. It was time to go.

Tequila whinnied and the colt began to stamp and paw, then nipped him on the arm. With an open hand he pushed the horse's face away in gentle rebuke, picked up the lead rope and without hesitation, turned and walked down the trail, the spirited young horse skipping along behind him. The wolf dog did not follow.

He descended the mountain by the same feint track of road the four visitors had come up on in the fall and as he crossed the snow line, shoots of grass appeared here and there and spring flowers poked through the litter of the forest floor. It was dusk when he reached river's edge by a decrepit wooden bridge. Though it was passable, he remained on the north side of the cold running rill. He watered, fed and tethered out the colt, then pitched a rudimentary camp. As he cooked his supper on a campfire, loneliness struck like a penetrating arrow, his only solace the sounds of his equine companion nibbling at new grass.

Awake with the morning sun, he tended to the needs of the colt, fixed a make-shift breakfast and packed up quickly. He studied the river high with runoff and gazed down the road that continued on the further side and chose not to cross the bridge.

Further on he found a spot where the river fanned out wide enough to ford. He took off his moccasins and his pants and led the colt wide-eyed and snorting through the icy waters, the round pebbled bed making their steps uncertain and the force of the current sucking at their legs When they hauled themselves out on the other shore, he began to retrace the steps by which he had first approached the twin peaks.

PART FOUR

1

Down From The Cascades

He didn't remove his hat when he entered the small office tucked into a corner of the warehouse of Putnam and Sons Orchards. The elder Putnam was parked in a caster-wheeled chair behind the steel desk. One of the sons sat leaning back in a metal folding chair. Hanging behind him was a calendar showing a scantily clad woman in a seductive pose. The air in the cramped space was thick with tobacco smoke.

"I'm looking for a girl that was working here last fall. Travels with her brother."

"Didn't hardly recognize you when you first walked in," said the son.

"Any idea where they might have gone?"

"Been cured of your muteness?"

"That's right. Any idea?"

"Sebastian and his little sister?"

"Sebastian and his little sister."

"Damn good workers, though Sebastian soured on us after you out-picked him and out fought him all in one day. We had to ask him to leave, if you catch my drift. Sister went with him. He watches over her like a hawk. No telling where they're off to now. If I was you, I'd go down to the Chehalis. Most of them wetbacks will be working the truck farms. Transplanting lettuce and the like. We only employ a few this time of year. Pruning and spraying and what not." He took a draw off his cigarette and narrowed his eyes. "Suppose you'll be wanting to collect your back pay? What happened to you anyway, get captured by a bunch of wild Injuns?"

"Something like that."

The elder Putnam opened a metal cash box and counted out some bills and passed them over to the son who stood and handed the money to Daniel. As he left the office door he caught a startling image of himself out of the corner of his eye. Thick locks strayed wildly over his collar and a youthful beard sprouted on his face. With his fringed buckskin shirt, bow and arrows and moccasin clad feet, he looked like a man of a century past come down from the mountain---a white man gone native or a native half taken to white civilization. He shook his head and laughed to himself in quiet wonder. He fetched the little horse tied to a fence post who eagerly awaited him. "They weren't too helpful," he said to the horse. "But at least we got a name."

It took him another three days leading the horse to walk to the nearest town which was centered in the agricultural zone of the Wakima river valley. The rich land yielded a variety of crops, hay and grain in the bottom lands surrounded by dairy and vegetable farms, orchards climbing into the foothills on either edge of the immense mellow rift, and range land beyond replete with cattle. He found a barbershop and went in to get a haircut and shave.

Outside the barbershop he took off his moccasins and stowed them in his gear and pulled on his boots. On the main street, he and the horse drew only an occasional stare and that for being strangers in a small town where the horse was still a common means of transportation. Alongside the trucks and cars parked outside of the cluster of false-front buildings that made up the commercial district stood many occupied hitching posts.

He passed a train depot backed by twin grain elevators. Next door there was an auction hall flanked by a maze of pens and gates and just beyond, an arena, its wooden palisades empty on that day. Between the auction hall and the arena stood a single-story weather-beaten building with a signboard that read; 'Garwood Rodeo Saloon' in bold letters and inscribed just below 'World famous bull shippers'.

He hitched the colt a safe distance from three saddle horses at the rail and then he eased through the swinging doors into the dark saloon. He was working on his plan.

All eyes were on him. It took a moment to orient himself in the room thick with tobacco smoke and reeking of sweat and beer. A love ballad twanged from a juke box. Tiny race cars sped around a loop on the black and white TV screen above the bar. Several men under cowboy hats and a couple of women wedged into tight jeans sat at the few tables or on stools at the bar. One woman with big hair took a drag off her cigarette and winked at him as he walked by. He could sense the man next to her scowling at his back. He followed the trail through the sawdust on the floor that led to the bar. The bartender stood with his hands spread open on that bar. Above his balding head mounted on the back wall the skull of a longhorn, perched like a giant bird, stared down on the scene through hollow eyes.

"Howdy Son."

"Afternoon," he returned with a tip of his hat.

"What can we do you for?"

"Give him a whiskey on me, Jake, seeing how he's new in town," rasped a jovial fellow, worn and lean, wearing a bright red shirt. The man turned from his seat at the bar and smiled through handle bar mustaches, flashing four gold teeth.

"I don't reckon he's of an age to be drinking. Ain't that so, son?" said the bartender.

Before he could respond, the man at the table chimed in. "Aw, go on Jake, give the whip a taste of your finest. That is unless you're thinking he's an Indian. Wouldn't be fitting to serve no Indian in here."

Daniel felt heat rising into his neck and ears. The bartender ignored the remark and looked to him.

"Can I get you anything to drink?"

"Glass of water would be fine."

"Let's just hope the Indian can hold his water," guffawed the man at the table. Those sitting with him also laughed except for the woman who had winked. She nervously brushed her styled hair back from her face and twisted in her seat as the man put his giant tattooed arm around her and patted her shoulder in a proprietary fashion.

Daniel sipped the glass of cool water. He heard it before he even remembered what it was, like water springing from a deep well, the song of White Eagle, quiet at first, building with the intensity of a steady drum beat, arising from within. Lips still, he silently sang that sacred song. He glanced sideways over his left shoulder and squinted at his aggressor. The man grew uneasy under his gaze and looked away. Daniel turned again to the bartender.

"Would you know of anybody who needs a hired hand?"

"Offhand I can't think of nobody; times been a little hard around here. Cattle prices down, gold's played out, choice lumber been cut."

"Hold on a second, Jake," interjected the man in the red shirt. "Don't go forgetting about old Zeke Burly. He's always looking for good help."

"Come on Oak, don't be sending the boy up there --- the man's tweaked in the brain."

"Say what you will, it's a money-making operation. Now listen, son," he turned to address Daniel, "follow the north bound road out of town and head up five, six miles into the Horse Heaven Hills and hook a right onto Rattler Gulch. Follow it till there ain't no more road and you'll be at 'Work Til U Drop Ranch'. That's Zeke's place. Now I won't lie to you and say that Zeke ain't an ornery opinionated old critter. But he's a straight shooter and his wife Irene is the nearest thing to a saint you're likely to meet this side of the pearly gates. So tell me, how do you feel about mules?"

"Excuse me, Sir?"

"Mules, Son! If you're going to work for Zeke, you sure as hell better love the very idea of mules because you'll not find a tractor on the place. Mules is what makes Zeke's ranch run and mules is what the sorry-assed crazy son-of-a-bitch lives for. He can't never get enough of them---mules!"

"Well, thank you sir," he tipped his hat, nodded to the bartender and turned to leave. The angry man stood up out of the shadows as he passed.

"See you later, Tonto!" he called out after him.

"Hey Charboneau, why are you picking on that kid? Wasn't your own mama an Indian?" asked Oak.

"I ain't no redskin! But he sure as hell is!" he bellowed out, as he gesticulated madly. "Goddamn Indians and Mexicans crawling all over us like red ants. Stealing jobs from decent Americans."

"I guess you're too ill-mannered to be taken for an Indian," said Oak. Then he turned to call out after the departing youth, "Mules, Boy. You gotta love them!"

Daniel unhitched the colt and led him on down the road. The tidy cottages of the town gave way to cinder block shanties with metal roofing and broken down mobile homes with gnarly mongrels chained in front. Even in this rough section of town, people kept horses on any postage-stamp sized parcel on which they could tack up a shed and stretch a wire.

As he walked on to the outskirts of town, the poverty became more visibly desperate, the decrepitude of the dwellings more complete. The few people he glimpsed were brown-skinned, children mostly, barefoot and barely clothed, with swollen bellies and hungry eyes, making child games in garbage heaps and mud puddles and young mothers, many pregnant, hauling water from a common spigot. Their homes were constructed of cast-off materials, trucking palettes and used sign-boards. The makeshift village had its own town center with a grocery, a bar, and a church. Skinny chickens and runty pigs wandered freely underfoot; old men sat at tables in the shade playing board games, moving the pieces with a mysterious languid intensity, like ancient gods who had been playing since the dawn of creation. The scents of open cook-fires filled the air. He could pick up snatches of conversation in Spanish, the language of the girl of the orchard. He began to scan the environs for a glimpse of her face. He saw girls who reminded him of her going about their chores and he strove not to stare as he haplessly sought to verify an interior image that had taken on the aspect of a visionary dream.

As he reached the outskirts of the settlement, human habitation gave way to fields and range land and he stopped and scanned the empty road that cut through it. Then he turned to the horse and asked, "So, what do you think of mules anyway, little Friend?" As if in reply, the horse lifted his tail and let some road apples fall. Daniel made his own decision and led the horse up the road at a lively pace.

Rattler Gulch was an unpaved deeply rutted track of hard curves, steep drop-offs and winding switchbacks that ambled up like a blind snake into the golden hills. He saw cows grazing in isolated herds of thirty or forty head, running with a bull. Occasionally the earth would rumble and the ground would shake just moments before a self-loading logging truck would appear booming like an avalanche around some tight corner or bend in the road and he would have all he could do to keep Friend from jumping out of his skin.

The road ascended steeply as he approached a sheer tower of limestone cliffs. The way ahead was notched through a narrow gap like the entrance to some natural embattlement erected in an age of giants. The stratified walls of the passage were rife with relics, archaic templates of shell and bone etched upon mineral prints indicative of a time when these vertical cathedrals had been the level paving stones of a diluvial sea.

The western sky was ablaze with luminous scarlet and burnished clouds when he passed through the gap and reached the end of the road. He came to a gate suspended from thick posts with a sign attached that proclaimed he had arrived at the 'Work Til U Drop Ranch'. A second hand-painted sign drawn with a skull and crossbones declared: 'No hunting---the blood you shed may be your own!'

"Guess this is the place," he said to his horse.

He took note that the fences and pastures on either side of the lane were in decent condition. The first beings he encountered were two little mules. They were joined with a lead rope through the rings of their halters and on spotting the strangers, they whirled their long ears in circles above their heads, emitted odd snorts and skipped away, their heads in an awkward sideways position as they sped in unison keeping the rope taut between them.

"Now I know we're in the right place," he remarked to his horse. They saw mules of varying size and color peeping over the buck fence or peering out of the groves of pine. A striped ass brayed so loud that Daniel wondered how so much sound could be contained in such a miniature creature. His little spotted horse was wary of them all and drew near to the shelter of his body as foal will to mare.

The approach to the ranch was lined up on both sides of the road with old farm implements and rusted out autos. What would it take to get those antiques up and running, he thought. Further on he was relieved to discover a corral containing horses. They were a spirited bunch and he guessed them to be unbroken. There were nine in all, mustangs, appaloosas, pintos and paints.

Just ahead lay tumbledown barns and sheds and a log structure of considerable dimension, its sills resting on large stone pillars. Three men were sitting on the large verandah, smoking and drinking, taking in the last light of day. The two leaning on the rail, eyes hidden in the shadow of straw sombreros, were hard and lean men in worn-out clothes, who appeared neither young nor old, only weathered. The third, a bear of a man with a grizzled beard, squint eyes and a protuberant red nose sat on a high-backed rocker. The face had surely been handsome in a by-gone era but life had bludgeoned it into pulpiness, gouged furrows into the high forehead and carved swirling creases all about the steely eyes. It was he who rose up and hailed Daniel as he approached.

"Howdy stranger! That's a fine looking colt you have in tow."

The old rancher clambered down off the porch in a jaunty bow-legged stride. The other two languidly followed.

"Yessiree!" he exclaimed, as he touched his nose to that of the horse and then ran his hands along the length of its spine and up and down its legs. "Exceptional fine specimen. Where'd you acquire him?"

"We chose one another."

"I see," the rancher stuck his thumbs in his red suspenders. He stepped back in further scrutiny of the animal and then turned to the two men who stood waiting several paces back and seemed to find some confirmation of his appraisal in their impassive faces.

"That's an Indian notion if ever I heard one," he said, and stuck out a hand to shake. Daniel winced with pain when he felt the gripping power of that hand.

"My name is Burly, Zeke Burly. I am a first class mule-skinner," he said by way of introduction, then took in a gulp of air before continuing on. "I specialize in breaking wild horses, quelling uprisings, winning wars, starting revolutions, reforming governments, taming lions, emptying bars, organizing orgies, swapping used cars, land, whiskey, manure, nails, fly swatters, or racing forms. I can play the bongo drums and if need be, I can repair windmills, though that is one job I truly hate.

"These two shiftless but amiable honchos are my sidekicks, *los hermanos* Pedro *y* Juanito. They're hanging around here biding their time till the resurrection of Pancho Villa and the start of the next Mexican revolution, at which time they shall return to their glorious but ravaged nation to become commanders of the rebel forces and lead their people in the overthrow of the fascists and in the reclamation of the illegally usurped territories of the entire southwest quadrant of these United States. Don't suppose you're interested in selling?"

"Like I said, we chose each other. He's not mine to sell."

The rancher looked at him sideways.

"Pleased to meet you, sirs. My name is Daniel Sweeney and this is Friend."

"Sweeney, that's Irish' ain't it? My wife's people were Irish. Came out to build the railroad and never left. What brings you up here?"

"Heard you might be looking for a hand."

"Who told you that?"

"Man in town wears a red shirt."

"That would be Oak. Bronc busting bad-ass and a good friend of mine. Well, there is every goddamned thing needs to be done at once around here. Horses to break, roundup coming on, planting time soon. Can you rope? Can you ride? Can you drive a team?"

"Yes sir."

"You ain't from around these parts, are you?"

"No, sir, I'm from back east."

"You mean the Dakotas?"

"I mean Vermont."

"Is that east of the Missouri?"

"Just so."

"Don't worry, I won't tell nobody! Damnation, I didn't know there was anyone still living back there. Figured they'd all moved out to California by now."

Zeke laughed long and loud out of his prodigious belly before carrying on.

"Funny, I never would have guessed you was a blue-blooded, blue-balled, long eared, drip nosed, thin lipped, tight-assed, Yankee son-of-a-bitch. Fact is, I'd swear there is something of the Indian about you. I can say this, son, because it takes one to know one."

Just then an enormous raven creased the sky directly overhead, loosed a caw of raucous rolling laughter in the fiery heights and then sped away in a line straight as an arrow shot from a bow.

"Look here, Daniel Sweeney, my good wife Irene is inside fixing up some beans and corn bread. Why don't you unload your gear; there's beds to choose from in the bunkhouse, and you can put up your horse in yonder stable. Then come on in, grab some grub and we'll see what we can do for one another."

"Thank you, sir," he said and then set about doing what he had been told.

He started work the next morning. If the brothers, Pedro and Juanito, seemed relaxed to the point of torpidity the night before, once the work day began they became virtual bundles of particulate energy unloaded on an unsuspecting world. The task at hand was the breaking of the wild horses. Zeke explained to him that the nine in the round corral had been cut out of the herd that ran on his holdings. Every spring they would break and train such a group and in the fall they sell some of them as saddle horses fit for a child to ride.

They had little time to get the horses into condition before they had to bring in the range cows, castrate bull calves and brand all the young stock. To Daniel the Mexicans' method seemed uncommonly harsh, an economy of method once dictated by a brutal feudal system in an unforgiving land. They showed him how to begin with a green horse by roping it with a lasso to the forefeet, catching it up and laying it down on its side and once down, they rolled it side to side to secure a saddle underneath. When the horse was afoot again, they wound a rope around the neck and looped it behind a rear hoof and the horse, forced to stand on three legs, would soon realize the futility of resistance. With hard cases they resorted to the 'running W', restraining both forelegs and bringing the horse to its knees if it did more than proceed at a walk.

Although he felt the pain of the horses whose proud natures fought against these harsh tactics, he did as instructed and learned much from these tough little men. Their ancestors had developed the cowboy culture in a heritage that traced its roots back to the first band

140

of Conquistadors to arrive in the New World. By such exacting means, Pedro and Juanito wore the wild horses down and forced them to accept the unimaginable---bearing a human being on their backs.

Late morning of his second day on the ranch, Daniel was being whipped about on a bucking mustang, a bay mare unbroken, and holding his own. Following the advice of his mentors, he struck her about the head with a short quirt every time she bucked and the diminutive fireball gradually wearied and began to pace about the ring until she ceased to leap and hop and fell into an easy trot. In the end she came to a walk and both she and her rider knew that something had been decided. He dismounted, with Pedro holding the horse until his feet were on the ground.

"Well done, young man," Zeke called out from the sidelines. "That nag sure was full of piss and vinegar. I believe you have a natural affinity for the horse wrangling business. That was damned impressive riding for a dude from back east. I've noted your roping skills could use fine tuning. But man, if you can't ride the wild ones, then dogs don't scratch and pigs ain't happy in a pile of shit! Ever consider the rodeo?"

"No sir."

"You ought to. Come Saturday of every month in summer there's a big yahoo down at the Garwood. Round about the half of June there is a regional shindig with professional cowboys. Not kid's stuff. A fellow can win purse money down there if he's got the *cajones* and catches a bit of luck. Fact is, I used to ride them old bulls. You know I was pretty damn good until the day I broke both wrists. Cracked my spine and ruined my knees long before that, but the breaking of the wrists---that was an evil matter."

"That's mighty encouraging, Mister Burly."

"I'm telling you straight, you've got the makings of a bronco buster. I'll be happy to teach you such tricks as I know."

"Thanks, I'll think about it."

The two mules joined by a single rope came idling by, nibbling at the grass along the fence line.

"That's my latest team. Up and Coming. I'll use them to skid logs this year."

"Why do you keep them tied together like that?"

"I tie them so they get used to doing everything together, learn to move as a unit."

The mini-mules sauntered up to the rancher. He dug around in his pockets until he came up with some sweet oats which he offered to them on the flat of his massive hands as an old man might parcel out candy to his grandchildren.

"Mules!" Zeke exclaimed, in the theatrical tones of an inspired bard, "There is no animal on God's green earth so noble as a mule. For plowing or packing, or moving cattle, they are quick-witted, sure-footed and cooler than ice. You may have heard men make claims against them that they are stubborn, but a mule is gifted with second sight. Was a mule saw the angel of the Lord and warned the prophet not to pass. She knows when a man is leading her into danger and she won't budge. Another thing you're bound to hear is that mules are kickers. I never been kicked by one of my mules and I never seen anyone get kicked that didn't deserve it. Do her a wrong turn and sooner or later she will make you pay, but treat her right and she's more loyal than the best of men. Well now, I hear Irene ringing the dinner bell. Hey Pedro, Juanito, *al ataque, vamos a cenar!* "

Along the path to the bunkhouse they passed by the paddock where Zeke wintered his permanent stock. "See that black mule? That's Moon. When I bought that mule, was more like I rescued her, she'd been treated so poorly she come close to being an outlaw. Took me all of six months just to make friends enough to where I could lead her on a halter. She's all of twenty now but can still work like a young one. I've learned more about nature and spirit from that mule than ever I did from any preacher man."

Zeke eyed him severely as if to ascertain that he'd been understood. Daniel returned the gaze and nodded once in response.

"You don't waste words do you, son?"

"Excuse me, sir?'

"Don't worry about it. I'll waste enough for the both of us."

The brothers snickered but Zeke ignored them and continued.

"You'll have to pick yourself a mount out of the wild bunch. There is one or two worth the trouble, unless of course you'd care to have a mule?"

"A horse would suit me fine, sir," he responded, too fast for Zeke's liking.

"Let's head in for grubstake," he growled.

The rough-hewn log structure doubled as bunkhouse and main house. Zeke and Irene maintained a separate apartment at the rear of the building but shared the spacious living quarters which consisted of bunk beds, dining hall and kitchen rolled into one with the hired hands.

Irene was setting out steaming pots of food on the table. She was a spare woman and at first impression she struck him as frail. But one look into her flashing blue eyes and it was obvious to Daniel there was plenty of grit contained in the bird-like frame. She had long silver hair kept up in a bun. Her movements were quick but her manner of speech was slow as a wide river.

When all were seated, Zeke spoke a simple grace, then the men tore into the meal --- platefuls of steak and onions, beans and tortillas smothered in chilies, canned carrots, peas, and pickles. Nobody spoke for long minutes as they filled their faces. All save Irene, who ate with decorum.

"Tell me, Daniel, were you raised on a ranch?"

"Not exactly Ma'am. I grew up on a farm."

"What kind of farm?"

"Dairy farm. We raised Jerseys, milked upwards of twenty when my brother was still with us."

"Oh, what happened dear, did he pass away?"

"No Ma'am, he went to college."

"That's worse!" Zeke snorted between mouthfuls.

"Ezekial, hush! Go on now, Daniel."

"We kept chickens and pigs and horses, too."

"That sounds lovely. I was raised on a farm myself. I miss the bossies. How I loved that fresh cream!"

Zeke interjected, "My stepdaddy used to milk some cows on this place when I was a sprout. That man would milk just about anything with hooves and tits! Of course, us kids had to do the milking.

143

Now a cow, that's a critter knows how to kick! Way I see it, cows don't really need us humans and they know it. They are essentially herd animals by nature. They need a critical bovine mass to maintain a functioning circuitry."

"Ezekial Burly, must you go on blabbering such nonsensical theories? I've known many folks who kept a family cow and those animals seemed perfectly happy," said Irene.

"One cow is not even a cow. It's an isolated fraction of cowness, like a missing piece of a jigsaw puzzle, the lost card in a deck, the screw that fell out of the engine. One cow is an unnatural event. Not so with mules!"

Pedro and Juanito rolled their eyes and smiling surreptitiously beneath their mustaches, lowered their heads and attended to cleaning their plates. Irene rose to fetch the coffee pot. Meanwhile Daniel was left as the captive audience while Zeke continued to hold forth.

"A mule by its given nature is a lonely creature. It knows in the depths of its soul that it is fundamentally different from other animals because it has been fashioned by the intervening hand of man. It is for this reason that a human element has taken root in its soul. You can see it in the eyes, that woeful questioning of reality. This is the cry for love at the heart of creation, a desire for completion that manifests itself through the mule."

"Is it communion of the species when the mules try to stomp the life out of the fresh-dropped calves?" Pedro could contain himself no longer.

Zeke didn't blanch, giving answer in stride. "It's up to you to keep the fence lines secure against such occurrences. Everyone knows mules won't have no truck with intruders in their territory. Any creature that has its origins in the desert is bound to pull up something mean and nasty out of its interior when necessity dictates."

Having defended the reputation of his mules, Zeke turned to another subject, "Say Pedro, how's it looking with those new nags? Have you pacified their vicious inborn natures to a workable degree?" He always addressed such questions to Pedro, who was the older of the brothers and more settled in his ways than the younger vaquero.

144

"Pues, we have two remaining who will not accept the bit. If we can't bring them around this afternoon, we'll hold them back and bring in the cows *mañana por la mañana."*

"A good plan!" concurred Zeke. He turned to Daniel, "You see young partner, we've got our grazing lands divided into sections for rotation. Makes for a lot of fence maintenance but over the years we've gotten ample returns by not over-grazing. The pastures are ready, so tomorrow morning before sunrise we'll commence to bring in the cattle from winter range. You best pick yourself out a mount this afternoon, after siesta that is."

Try as she might, Irene could not stop Daniel from doing the dishes at the sink. He started to explain to her it was a chore he'd always done but realized this might involve divulging the loss of his mother. He didn't want anybody's sympathy on that matter. She threw up her hands in mock exasperation at his obstinacy and then set to sweeping the spotless floorboards.

2

When he awoke dawn was a faint hint on the horizon. Irene put a biscuit and a steaming mug of coffee in his hands as he headed out the door. Pedro was already outside tending the flames of a fledgling bonfire. By the time the cows were in, that fire would produce coals sufficient to heat the branding iron. The horses were saddled before the sun cracked over the eastern ridge.

Daniel had chosen a sporting bay pony from the ranks of the wild herd. Juanito was riding a big paint horse and Pedro was on his Arabian. Irene mounted a fast-walking quarter horse and Zeke rode his Moon mule. Friend ran back and forth in his corral, distressed at being left behind. Two collie dogs, a mother with one blind eye and a grown son, trotted diligently ahead. Riders and horses followed, sweeping through the gates into the mist-laden pastures.

By mid-morning they were driving the first herd of black cows into a large holding pen. Pedro moved out fast ahead of the cows. Juanito and Daniel flanked them and Irene and Zeke brought up the rear. The dogs filled in the gaps. Pedro worked the gate as the first batch was brought safely in.

Juanito coached Daniel on the finer points of roping. The Mexican preferred a lariat of three separate strands made of braided raw hide over the hemp rope rubbed with black tar favored by local cowboys. Daniel only had a couple of days to train the bay pony but she was proving herself a natural. He roped his first calf and pulled up short to tug it down. As the dallied rope grew taut on the horn and he leaned back into the saddle, the pony instinctively planted herself solid as a counterweight to bring the one-hundred-and-fifty pound calf to its knees. She then stood patiently as he swiftly dismounted and secured the calf's legs in a truss. Zeke wielded the glowing iron and placed the brand on the calves left flank. If it was a bull-calf, he would hold it down as Irene deftly removed the testicles with a short sharp knife, tossed them in a bucket and doused the wound with iodine. The calves were then freed to return bawling to their mothers who stood bellowing in a distraught mass at the far end of the corral.

Daniel dismounted and tied up the bay and got himself a dipper of water from a cistern. He leaned back against the rails of the corral and looked on as the two brothers culled out and roped down more calves. Zeke called to him from the branding station. "Looks like that pony of yours is working out fine."

"Yes sir."

"What are you going to name her?"

"I'm waiting on her to tell me."

"Hmm, more Indian notions. Well, ain't those two *vaqueros* something to see? Can you imagine any dang fool not being more pleased than a bobcat in a henhouse to have such men working on their place? And yet in Garwood, way you hear folks talk you would think the Chicanos are the scourge of the nation. Dirty, lazy low-down thieves is what they call them. But I swear I never have met a more reliable hard-working people as the Mexicans. Tough as desert burros and sharp as flint knives, thick-skinned as Texas longhorns, and meaner than a scorpion if you get on their bad side."

Daniel slipped into an easy rhythm working with the brothers. At once competitive and playful, they delighted in showing off as they coached him, praising him when he performed well and correcting his errors in very colorful language. The round-up took three hot, dusty, tiring days, but they were days filled with exhilarating challenges that engendered a deep camaraderie.

The men sat on the porch smoking and sharing a bottle of tequila. Their horses were watered, grained and turned out and they had consumed a prodigious supper. With the dishes washed and put away, Irene sat inside on a rocker knitting woolen socks and listening to her favorite radio program. Daniel sat outside with the men. A part of him felt inclined to say no to the bottle; he wasn't sure he wanted any of the loosening of those inner bonds, but when it was offered he could see no gracious way to refuse.

Juanito sliced a lemon and showed him how to cover it with a pinch of salt and then take refuge in the sour and salt in the wake of the clear liquid fire in the bottle. Pedro cautioned him to take it slowly and Daniel did as the older man told him, taking a second shot but declining a third offered by Juanito.

147

The clear air of a perfect spring day had cooled to pleasant evening temperatures and the slight moisture in the atmosphere lent magnificence to the emerging stars. The descent of night had a leveling effect on their spirits, and muscles bound tight from relentless work considered the prospect of letting go. The collie dogs curled up contentedly at Zeke's feet. The men rolled cigarettes from thin crisp sleeves of rolling paper. Daniel felt green at his first inhalation but on a second try he found the flavor to be surprisingly mellow, even as the smoke still hit his lungs like a fist. It made him feel more at one with these men he'd quickly come to admire.

Juanito picked up an old beat-up guitar and began to strum, singing plaintive songs of his homeland in his gravelly sweet voice. Daniel played his flute like a breath-driven drum keeping time to the strumming of the guitar.

When their music had drifted back into the silent sources of the night, the men fell into quiet reflection. United by the circle of their lives, each yet remained isolated in the vastness of his own solitude. Hordes of tree frogs had ventured down to the rain-spawned vernal pools that lay scattered about like the shining footprints of some aimless giant who trod about the outlying woods and meadows. As he listened to the insistent amphibian mating calls, Daniel could almost hear his father saying; "When the peepers sing for three nights running, it's time to plant corn." The memory of that voice brought the shadow of a grin to his lips and the pressure of unshed tears. A cacophonous symphony of voices rose up in the east, the weird laughter and yammering of the coyote's howl. Zeke in turn broke the silence of the company of men.

"I saw signs of that wolf again this morning," he declared. In the inky darkness all eyes were upon him. "I made out a track in the mud along the banks of the creek."

In the winter past, the ranch had lost two new born calves to a predator. Pedro was certain it was the work of coyotes and Juanito suspected a pack of feral dogs. No one had seen any wolves since the government sponsored campaign of hunting and trapping ended fifty years ago but Zeke was certain that a lone male wolf prowled his rangeland. He didn't hate this spectral wolf, nor fear it as an enemy, but he considered that the economy of his enterprise justified his extermination of any creature that cut into his thin profit margin. The men had set traps and several coyotes had been caught and summarily executed and the depredations had ceased. Still Zeke remained certain that the wolf ranged in the vicinity as if the dark brooding of his soul was projected out onto the natural world and returned to stalk him.

"El lobo, he is a family man. I do not believe one wolf would come down all the way from Canada," Pedro commented.

Zeke sighed heavily. "We are in agreement on one important point, *compadre*. It is a question of belief. I've told you fellas about my Grandma, a full-blood Blackfeet from the short-grass prairie. When I was a child she instructed me that my dream-body could take the form of a raven and in that body I would be able to travel and verify facts beyond human ken. She said that I would forget as I grew older but remember again in my old age, the second childhood upon which I am now embarked. I know that some folks would just as soon lock me in the loony bin for speaking such but the raven has returned and I have seen this wolf in my dreams."

The brothers chose not to believe or disbelieve their *patron*. Daniel wondered at the tale and was fascinated by the glimpse of his past that Zeke had chosen to reveal, finding in it echoes of his own mixed ancestry.

"Were you raised out on the plains, Mister Burly?"

"Now Daniel, I told you to call me Zeke or Burly or son-of-a-bitch, but quit calling me mister!"

"Yes sir Mister Bur...ah.... Zeke."

"I was born on the great plains of Montana. My mother moved us out here when I was four years old. She had met my step-daddy, the old cowboy who carved this ranch out of wilderness, and it was true love. She didn't tell him about us five kids living back on the reservation until they'd been married for six months. I must say my step-daddy took it graciously. He worked us hard but treated us decent. I took to this life right quick and before long we both knew that one day this ranch would be mine. I learned everything I know about punching cows from that man. The fact that I was a 'breed' from the rez made me a target for every bully and would-be bully in the schoolyard. I became rattlesnake mean and I often found occasion to prove it. I thank the Creator for bringing me to Irene. That woman set me on the right road. She makes being good seem as natural as the rain. She never preached nor scolded when I back-slid into wicked ways. She won me over with the greatness of her heart."

The *vaqueros* nodded their heads in agreement. Zeke shifted in the rocker, passed a 'whopper' and loosed a low whistle as his mind turned to plans for the coming day.

"We've got fences to mend and equipment to fix. What say Pedro and I work on getting the field equipment up to snuff. It if stays dry we'll plow and seed first of the week when the moon is full and the seeds will be sure to increase. In the meantime Juanito and Daniel can ride the fence lines. What do you think cowboys, sound like a plan?"

"Si Mister Zeke, seguro!" Pedro responded with a smile.

"This is the import of what I'm trying to impart, Daniel. I want you to pack a rifle. You can choose one from the rack in the bunkhouse. If you see the wolf, drop him. Understand?"

"Yes sir, Mister ...Zeke, I understand."

"Good! I'm gonna hit the hay while I can still get up out of this chair. *Buenas noches a todos!"*

"Buenas noches"

The next day woolly weather came blowing in over the mountains from the sea with spits of rain and mist creeping over hills and into vales. Daniel and Juanito set out in opposite directions along the fence lines. Each rider and horse packed a mule behind, the mules wearing pack saddles outfitted with an array of fencing tools to deal with practically any contingency. Both riders were outfitted with a saddle boot and gun. Daniel had chosen a Remington thirty-aught-six hunting rifle from the gun rack. Zeke had sent him out with the Moon mule, who despite her irascible disposition, proved herself entirely sensible.

By late morning he'd had only to make some minor repairs. The fog still hung thick on the rolling hills and a lazy lemon yellow sun began to burn its way through, bearing brilliance to the haze. The rider and the horse and the mule approached a rambling creek that bordered a grove of cottonwood and cedar trees. One gray-boled poplar had cracked mid-way up its height during a late winter storm and the upper reaches of the tree had come down on the fence at a point where it spanned the creek---he could see the broken post and the snapped wire.

As he dismounted he noticed the ears of the horse and the mule arch forward, raising their heads and peering intently, their nostrils flared wide. He scanned the direction of their inquiry and heard a crashing through the trees. His first thoughts were of bear--- the scars flared with heat beneath his shirt.

He grabbed the rifle. The horse and mule held still as he leveled the weapon, aiming toward the source of the sound. He was fairly certain that the bay would bolt if he fired but circumstance left him little choice. When it first leaped over the bank and splashed into the creek, he thought, "Maybe it's a dog." But in his gut he knew that it was something other as he beheld the timber wolf, carefree, frolicking in the shallows. He was struck with the simple observation that the creature appeared to be playing. He had it in his sites, twenty-five paces at best but he did not squeeze the trigger. The mustang pawed at the ground and the wolf froze, its eyes riveted on his face. Their eyes locked, held. Daniel felt that he was looking into the eyes of a ten-thousand-year-old being.

He shifted his feet and in an instant the wolf was gone. Brash as its approach had been, its departure was sudden and silent. He stood still, looking and listening for long moments after all echo of it had ceased. In the quiet he lowered his rifle. The horse and mule relaxed and nibbled at the new grass. And still he stared at the locus of the vanished apparition. A huge raven flew overhead like a far flung shadow and harangued the world with an unruly cry. As its black winged form seared the yellow sky, a tail feather slowly spun to earth, catching and casting away reflections as it fell, landing just at his boot tips. He slid the rifle back into its scabbard, tied the horse to a post, hobbled the mule and unloaded the tools. After clearing the busted fence line, he selected a cedar and felled and limbed it with a broad axe; then he took up a Swede saw, sawed off two post-lengths and peeled off the fragrant bark in slippery strips with his hunting knife. He

151

chopped the butt-end of the posts to a point and dug new post holes on either side of the creek and tamped the posts in firm. He wielded fencing pliers to splice new lengths of barbed wire to the old and employed a come-along to tighten the strands; then he tacked the wire to the posts with fencing staples.

He searched the creek bed and found a suitable stone and formed a wire sling of strands set crosswise, weaving it through the strands of fence to suspend the stone over the creek to prevent livestock from passing under along the water way. As he went about these tasks, he thought of nothing else, his attention riveted on the work at hand.

He drank from the creek and loaded up the tools and followed the fence line up through the woods. He held the reins loose as the bay picked her way through the trees and the mule, though resentful of packing behind the green horse, obediently followed. It appeared that the rain would hold off. Good. Maybe they would get in planting the fields before it came.

The sun had broken through the fog and as they emerged onto open ground he was nearly blinded by the crystallized dew shimmering across the meadow. Their tracks trailed a wake through the jeweled grass. They followed the fence line along an ascending ridge grown over with clusters of juniper and sage to a view that opened out on the blue volcanoes of the Cascades, Mount Rainier cutting a diamond edge above the rest, its gleaming ice-fields ascending to a cloud shrouded peak.

He sat the horse and breathed in the scents of the earth awakening around him. To a farm boy, that awakening always felt like something holy. He thought of her then. The remembrance was imbued with a sacred quality that filled him with a deep longing to see her again.

The dark cloud moving in covered the face of the sun and brought a shadow of doubt. Whose face was it that he sought? Was this another dream? No, he had determined to stand in the truth of himself as a man both self-reliant and reliable. He would find her. He was a warrior with a plan, moving into his future, just as Old Joseph had told him.

152

He stopped for lunch at mid-day, gave oats to the horse and mule then let them graze for a short while. He unwrapped the ham and cheese sandwiches, taking care to save the wax paper and after he finished eating, he took off his hat and lay back on the knoll and watched the clouds being broken apart as the wind turned and whipped down out of the north carrying blue air in its wake. He stretched his arms above his head and drank in the sun's warmth, breathing---with all his body---he breathed.

They threaded their way down out of the hills in the lengthy purple shadows of afternoon, the new grass spread like a yellow apron upon the flats. Keeping just ahead of the shadows, somnolent under the broad brim hat, he and the horse and the mule rode back into the yard at day's end.

Zeke approached from the other direction in his rattletrap Ford with the mini-mules on board the bed and a dozen cedar poles skidding from the bumper hitch. "Hey ho, Danny boy! I figured you fellas might be necessitating more fence posts so I procured some with these here mighty mites."

Zeke unloaded the mules and employing logging tongs and a chain, he had them skid the logs to a landing in the lee of a shed. Daniel helped him unhitch and hang up the harness. As they went about the tasks of picking feet and brushing down the mules, he put forth a proposition he'd formed on the ride back in. "Zeke, I been thinking I could use a truck. I wonder if I might work on one of those rigs in the bone yard---be my pay in place of cash."

Zeke frowned and thought about it. "Funny, I never would have taken you for a gear head. You're welcome to drive my blunderbuss anytime."

"I appreciate that but I been thinking on heading out on the road. Just on my days off, to see the country."

"Planning your escape already, huh? If that's what suits you, take your pick. No doubt Pedro will help out. The man is a wizard of the mechanical arts. He comes from a land where new parts are as scarce as roses in December."

"I've an idea that green Dodge is the most promising on the lot."

"A precious historical artifact is what it is. Consider it yours!"

In the fading daylight Daniel could see the eerie blue flashes and crackling yellow sparks emanating from the shop. He shielded his eyes from the too bright light given off by the arc welder. Pedro looked like a medieval warrior, the welder's hat covering his head like a helmet, the cow hide apron girding his torso and loins and gloves that reached his elbows, the alchemical rod gripped firm. He straightened up and tilted the face guard back.

"*Buenas noches vaquerito. Como estas?*"

"Not too bad."

"What can I help you with?"

"I've worked a deal with Zeke to swap labor for that old Dodge sitting in the equipment graveyard."

"I know this truck. I will make no comment as to who gets the better end of the deal. But I will be happy to assist you in making it road worthy. When would you like to begin?"

"Whenever you're ready."

"I just finished a spot-weld on this spike-tooth harrow. Help me lift it off the sawhorse. Then we go fetch the beast!"

They were soon up to their elbows in grease. They put the truck up on lifts, drop lights were strategically placed and wrenches were strewn about the concrete floor. The parts of the dismantled engine were placed on shelving, according to the order in which they were removed. Pedro operated and Daniel assisted. Once past his initial reserve, the vaquero was amiable and talkative. As they worked he had questions about the farms of Vermont and Daniel reciprocated, inquiring as to what brought the brothers so far from home. The Mexican took pause from his labor, shimmied out from underneath the vehicle and went to the back of the shop and reached into a tin bucket and produced two bottles of pale beer. After popping the lids with a screw driver, he offered him one. "*Cerveza?*"

"Sure, *gracias*."

"*Cuando yo era chico*, we used to open them with our teeth."

He grinned, his smile revealing a mouth full of silver. *"Salud amor dinero."* He raised the bottle in a toast before taking a pull.

"Juanito and I, we come from a large family. We are *norteños* eh? We come from the mountains---la Sierra Madre Occidental. We could not find work. The great haciendas are no more. Cattle is raised but not as in the old days, so my brothers and I, we left for *la Costa de Oro* to find work and send money back home. The conditions on *las fincas grandes* were so bad; starvation wages, planes spraying poison on us as we picked, housing unfit for swine."

"Hardly farming."

"*De veras.* My brothers and I, we felt it was our duty to organize. We presented our demands to the land owners. We organized strikes. Problems arose. We had a fight on our hands."

"But you didn't start it."

"Nor is it finished. The government officials told us our duty as workers was to be uninvolved politically, but we continued in our efforts to secure a just wage and better working conditions for the *campesinos*. We held strikes and demonstrations and there were clashes. When my house was searched, I knew my life was in danger. Juanito was detained and tortured and our brother Miguel disappeared. We never saw him again. The only choice left was to pick up a gun."

"You had reason enough to."

"Si, but the time was not ripe. That is the reason we are living here with little hope of returning anytime soon, because the repression in my country grows and grows. The *norteamericanos* run the show. Everything that is produced is taken out of the country. The companies drive out the *campesinos* and take over the fertile land. The peasants are left with no access to land. All those people in the countryside with no access to land."

"So where *do* they live?"

"We have become a people in perpetual migration. We go here for the coffee harvest and there to cut cane, or we go to the belts of misery that surround the big cities, or else we come north."

"And I thought I had a hard life."

"You know they say some demons may only be driven out by fasting and prayer. I don't know. Who can say? There is a church in town. I do not go there to pray. But since I was a boy I have known that

God is with me. That is how I have strength to work and send money to my family."

"I've not seen your kind of trouble. But I'm also a long way from home and wondering how I'm ever gonna get back there."

"*Si, somos exiliados.* Here we can help each other, no? It is good you have come, Daniel. You know Zeke and Irene---they don't talk about it much---*pero su hijo era un soldado*---Thomas never came back from Korea where your country was fighting a war."

"Not my country."

"Can a man choose his country? I shouldn't think a man can change his own country any more than he could change the color of his skin."

"I ain't even sure what color skin I'm in."

"The country and the skin---they are like the layers of the onion."

"I guess I haven't much thought about it."

"There is not a day goes by that I don't think about mine."

"I guess that's how it is for me with Sugarbrook farm."

"Maybe that land is your country."

Daniel nodded in agreement and they both fell silent and took sips of the tepid beer.

"How did Zeke and Irene's son die?" Daniel asked.

"His plane was shot down. They have a daughter too, Lucy. She is married and works in the city, a nurse. She does not come to the ranch much anymore. I think for this reason they think of you as an adopted son. You bring them new life."

The next day Pedro drove the truck down off the lifts. He honked the horn, raced the engine and let out a hoot. Daniel was grinning from ear to ear.

"A little polish on the chrome and a dash of paint would go a long way!" Pedro exclaimed as he climbed out and slammed the door with a solid thwack. "Climb in and give her a whirl."

Daniel hopped in the cab. He let out the clutch too fast and stalled out, pushed the starter and tried again. This time he lurched out in second gear and scrambled to find the brakes, stopping inches short of a granary shed.

"Do you know how to drive?" Pedro asked.

"I've driven my brother's truck some."

"Okay, don't worry. I'll give you lessons."

Zeke stuck his head out the front door as they approached. "His first pickup truck!" he bellowed out to all. "He's a man now, by golly!"

The fence line Daniel was working was close by the main house, so he rode in at lunchtime and passing up the ritual siesta, worked on the Dodge, sanding the body in preparation for paint which he applied in two coats over the subsequent evenings. Then he polished the chrome to a mirror finish.

In the course of a few days Daniel and Juanito checked all the fences and did maintenance on the windmills that fed the stock tanks. Pedro and Zeke brought the tillage equipment into working order. The crew worked steadily through Saturday afternoon and all of Sunday, their usual time off, to ensure that the field work could begin Monday morning before the rains.

Sunday after the evening meal the men were gathered on the porch. Zeke reviewed the planting schedule for Daniel.

"Our field crops are corn, oats, wheat and hay. We work the fields in a rotation. Following a corn harvest we drill in the oats and under-sow clover. You can grow two crops that way---a crop to sell and a crop of fertilizer. We have Moon and Shine as one team and we'll hitch the draft mule with Juanito's paint for a second. Any questions?"

"Sounds good to me, Sir."

The cool earth was alive with rising vapors as the first rays of yellow sun struck slantwise over mountains and through the trees in energetic shafts, charging the soil in preparation for the seed. Zeke worked the paint and the mule on the ground-driven spreader. In between runs the men waited at the steaming heaps, leaning on their forks and smoking cigarettes.

Daniel worked Moon and the black mule named Shine on a walking plow. Walking behind the plow was hard work but it was hard work he had been missing. He felt elated to be driving a team once again, felt like he was connected through those leather lines not only to the mules but to the life force itself. Moon knew to follow the track of each preceding furrow so that Daniel scarcely needed to work the lines and could keep his attention focused on steering the plow. Working behind this trained team, his delight was akin to a sailor when the quotient of wind to sail is just right and the boards beneath begin to hum. The neat slices of soil turned over in the wake of the plow like waves of liquid earth.

The rhythm was set. For the following four days the men spelled each other. The teams worked with a succession of implements gliding across the field---plow, trailed by harrows to prepare the bed followed by the drill set according to seed kind. On the fifth day thunder spoke with a giant voice and lightning crashed and shook the ground. The violence of the storm subsided quickly and a steady rain settled in. The seeds swelled in their dark womb and the cowboys were driven indoors to bide the time.

Zeke laid his cards on the table. He was about to lose another hand to Juanito who sat almost hidden behind a stack of chips. Rain beat on the roof and a fire roared in the pot belly stove to drive out the damp.

"I hope we don't get too much damn rain, wash out the seed." Zeke said as he pushed his chair away from the table and leaned it back on two legs.

He turned to Daniel who was studying his cards. "Well, young cowboy with the perpetual poker face, I guess we've seen the last of our lone wolf."

Daniel was silent for a moment and he could feel Zeke's eyes upon him.

"I wouldn't know, sir," he responded without looking up from his cards.

"Seeing as you're holding onto your cards, I must confess I know for a fact that the wolf has left this country and gone back where he came from."

"If Daniel knows this wolf, he is not ready to reveal his hand," said Juanito.

Daniel laid a full house down on the table and gathered in the chips.

"*Diablos*," sighed Juanito, and went in search of the solace of his guitar. Daniel stretched across the table to rake in the kitty. The game over, he rose and went to the counter by the cook stove to peel potatoes for Irene. She was chopping onions and smiled at him through tearing eyes. Zeke went to his room and stretched out on a buffalo hide on the floor to sleep and to dream of ravens and wolves.

Day was drawing to a close as the rain ended. Daniel stepped out to work with his little spotted Appaloosa. The yearling colt had put on some size and muscle. He had been getting to know the ranch horses and mules through a fence that separated his corral from the main paddock. Daniel released the colt in with the herd. There was a lot of tearing around and kicking up of heels as Friend began to find his level within the hierarchy. He gravitated to the proud Arabian and shadowed him and began to mimic the haughtiness of the older horse, who bounced when he galloped with his tail held high like a battle flag in the breeze.

Back in the bunk house Irene was scrubbing the men's work clothes with a washboard in a large basin of hot soapy water. She kept at Daniel to fork over his worn out clothes and he finally relented when she offered him some replacements from her cedar closet. She didn't tell him that the neatly pressed work shirt and blue jeans had once belonged to her son but he guessed it. Zeke was seated at the table reading by lantern light as the radio played swing tunes over a background of static. Daniel sat down awkwardly in the pressed pants and starched shirt on the bench at the table across from him.

"What are you reading?"

"A memoir; 'Forty-eight Days in the Saddle'."

"Who's it by?"

"Major Assburn."

"Go on."

He took a close look and spied out the title.

"You're reading the book written by Luke."

"That's right, him and all his holy *compadres*; the saints, the prophets, the madmen, and the kings."

Daniel took a deep breath and stared at the dancing light in the lantern.

"I couldn't pull the trigger," he said, peering into the flame. Zeke didn't look up from the book, neither was he reading.

"Ain't the first time such has happened, is it son?"

"No, it ain't."

"Way I see it, you could be judged a coward or esteemed a warrior. I know you ain't no coward cause I witnessed you jump on the back of a wild mustang with vengeance on the brain and murder in its heart and when it threw you I saw you pick yourself up and climb back on again. You have nothing to be ashamed of, you're not the kind of man who will shoot down his own brother."

Zeke looked up with a faraway stare, shook his head and smiled.

"It's just like it says here in the good book; 'If thy eye be single, thy whole body be full of light.' I reckon we are that 'whole body' of which the Evangelist speaks. I'm glad you've come among us, Daniel Sweeney. You help an old man to see with new eyes."

3

The crops were in and life on the ranch took on a more relaxed pace. There was plenty of work from dawn till dusk but without the urgency of the round-up and the planting. Daniel decided to take Zeke up on the offer to instruct him in rodeo riding. The two brothers spoke of little else as they prepared for the day when the professional rodeo would arrive in town and people would flock from all over the region. At stake was a large purse of prize money for skilled ropers and riders, with plenty of betting action on the side for the spectators.

Zeke was impressed with Daniel's skill at breaking the mustangs. The bay pony he'd picked for a mount had settled down well---she exhibited a degree of 'cow sense' that made her an asset to the ranch. Everyone concurred that Daniel was a natural horseman and that he should enter the saddle bronco riding contest.

There remained three horses of those cut from the wild herd that had refused to accept the bit. Juanito had labeled one of them an 'outlaw'. A red roan stallion. Tall for a mustang, the stallion had a sleek coat that shone like coals smoldering beneath ash and a temper that sizzled like a burning flame. Zeke thought he would sell him to the rodeo as a bucking horse or else it was off to the cannery for dog food, so he hauled out a competition style stock saddle and with the help of the vaqueros, he put it on the twisting red roan. He then clipped a rope to the halter as he explained to Daniel the technique of the single-handed ride and the sweeping of spurs high up on the horse's shoulder to impress the judges.

Everyday after work they practiced at the game. For a solid week they trained hard. When one of the three horses showed signs of relenting, Zeke stuck Daniel on a fresh mount. By the end of the week only the roan continued to put up a fight. The other two were saddle-broke and Juanito took on the task of finishing them out. But the mustang stallion was hotter than when they began, biting and kicking and doing all he could to buck them off. Daniel got through his training with no broken bones but enough scrapes and bruises to keep Irene clucking her tongue as she disinfected, daubed on her 'potions', and bandaged, all the while communicating her loathing of the sport by her silence. While a young wife she had watched her husband destroy his body piece by piece, eating dust and offering his blood to the wrathful deities of the arena until the man could hardly stand up straight. He had lived in chronic pain since.

Daniel felt ready for his inaugural into the arena. He was eager to join the brothers at the season opener.

Under the shade of the verandah at day's end, Zeke took a slow sip of clear liquid from the ubiquitous bottle then passed it to Pedro. Daniel was in the kitchen helping Irene clean up after supper.

"I tell you, amigos, the kid has got the touch. The boy can ride anything with hair on it---rides like a full-blood Indian from the plains."

Pedro took a sip and passed the bottle to his younger brother who leaned on the railing watching the mules frolic in the paddock as the cool of the evening came down.

"Y dígame patrón, que es un indio?"

Zeke eased back in his rocker, raised his arms above his head with fingers interlocked, stretched and cracked the knuckles.

"That's a damn good question, Pedro. Way I see it, it has to do with speaking a language and I ain't referring to no spoken written language you find in a book. I'm talking about the language spoken by such a person as realizes the entire Creation is alive. Being an Indian is a matter of understanding the language of life."

"Pues, creas que Daniel es un indio?" inquired Pedro.

"The thoroughbred is known by the gallop," answered Zeke.

"Será el nuevo campeón del rodeo, verdad?" ventured Juanito.

Daniel finished helping Irene with kitchen duties and came to join his comrades. He sat gingerly in a high-backed chair and Juanito passed the bottle and he took a sip and handed the bottle to Zeke and rolled himself a smoke.

"Another week or so we'll start in cultivating corn," Zeke said. He took another pull off the bottle, screwed his face in a grimace and passed it on.

"Damnation, I'm getting too old for that stuff!"

"Too old for farming or tequila?" asked Pedro.

"I ain't never too old for farming---I'm fixing to die with my shit-kickers on! I've taken to reading the good book of late. Irene scoffs

162

at me and tells me it's too late to be getting religion after living my life like it was a footrace with demons from hell. But as I read about Jesus and his gang, it occurs to me that God's blessing is evident in fruitful lands."

"You think Jesus was preaching to the farmers? I think he was organizing among the dispossessed."

"His message is for anyone who has ears to hear. But he used the good farmer as an example of how things is supposed to work. It gets me to cogitating on what I see going on nowadays with all these people living as if nothing binds them to the land, as if living that way makes them more free, as if there were no tomorrow."

"How has it come to this, *Patrón*?" asked Pedro.

"All I know is that when I was a boy this valley was busting at the seams with farms and ranches. So many have gone under or sold out. What I want to know is what's going to happen to the country when all the farmers are gone?"

"*Pues, serán jodidos, verdad?* " said Juanito.

"It's as if nobody even remembers the dust bowl. What's coming down the pike is gonna make those times seem like an itty-bitty dust devil, that old Depression seem like a Sunday picnic in July. One of these days I'm going to lay in some dynamite---when the end times come we can blast the walls on those limestone cliffs and block the road through the gulch to keep at bay the hungry hordes that are gonna spill out of the cities in search of food and water."

"Do you really think that's going to happen?" asked Pedro.

"Unless things turn around quick I don't think there's any help for it. Nowadays the farmers are the prophets of the country because they are still in communion with the wisdom of the ancestors. We are the ancestors of our children's children's children. One day they will remember us for the choices we make now."

Daniel breathed in the night air. He was feeling mellow from the sips off the clear bottle. And though his body felt beat and exhausted from his battles with the wild horses, his heart was stirred by the older cowboys' meditations. It wasn't a safe picture of the world that Zeke painted but it jibed with all that had happened to him and all that he had seen out on the road. But just now he was feeling safe and

163

right with the world and he felt that nothing more needed to be said, so he just gazed out over the darkened reaches of the pastures and the fields beyond, content to be mesmerized by the dance of the fireflies and the magnificence of the stars. He was grateful that he was no longer imprisoned by his own silence, but in this moment he wrapped himself in it as night spread out its bejeweled cloak across the sky.

The new grass was ankle high. The cows and the mules and the horses buried their faces in it, invigorated and refreshed. Pregnant mares dropped their foals. Calves suckled with vigor on their mothers' rich sweet milk.

When Daniel came in with the ranch hands for lunch at noon on Saturday Irene was quietly humming as she went about setting the table. He noticed that her steps seemed unusually light, almost girlish, as she briskly carried out her daily ritual of feeding hungry men.

"You seem cheerful today?" Pedro commented by way of a question. She paused with a bowl of steaming potatoes held between mitts.

"Zeke brought home a milk cow," she smiled a pleased satisfaction. "Just like I had when I was a girl."

"*Que bueno*, how good he was able to overcome his horror of the single cattle unit," Pedro replied with a devilish grin; then added, "*Me gusta tanto la leche fresca!*"

Before he could eat, Daniel had to run out to the barn to take a look at the cow. As dinner wound down, he sat back, finished off a second glass of milk, and patted his stomach, stretched taut as a drum.

"Did you get enough, Daniel?"

"That's fine cooking, Ma'am."

"Pedro here is a pretty good cook himself," Zeke declared. "Only trouble is he favors those little green chilies---burn you twice---if you know what I mean!"

The routine of the ranch included time off from half of Saturday till Monday morning. As soon as lunch was finished Daniel gassed up the newly painted Dodge. He jogged back into the bunk house and unpacked his buckskin shirt, treasured for all the memories it evoked. He rustled some camp food, grabbed his bedroll and canteen

164

and drove off down the rutted gravel road. He threaded the natural gate of limestone cliffs flanked by lush pasture and rolled down the steep winding track of Rattler's gulch, turned right on the highway and drove back to Garwood. He found himself exhilarated at having a truck of his own. Possessed with a new sense of maturity and freedom he sat tall on the bench seat and switched on the radio. He hummed along to guitars and fiddles wailing, keeping beat with an open palm tapping on the steering wheel.

He switched off the radio and turned serious as he approached the immigrant shanty village on the outskirts of town; he wondered if he was being foolish to think that he would ever find the girl again. He had to admit that his days were so full at the ranch, there were times when he'd forgotten all about her and his plan to return home and reclaim the farm. But now off the ranch he was awake again to that desire and intention. He turned and drove slowly down a crowded lane bordered by margins of red clay stripped of vegetation by unfenced goats and swine. Tiny shacks and hovels were piled in tight upon each other with pirated electric lines crisscrossed above. Barefoot children stared as he passed, curious eyes in diminutive brown faces, dirt-streaked, beatific.

He cruised the impoverished neighborhood searching through that maze of misery for a glimpse of the girl, believing against all probability that their paths were destined to cross again. Several times he thought he saw her but it was always some other girl, the same loose skirts and swinging braids, but a different face.

He returned to the highway and headed north towards the Cascades. For no good reason his mood lightened---for no good reason save that he was young and behind the wheel of his first ride with time on his hands and the road in front of him. With his hat tipped back and the windows rolled down he switched on the radio again and sang along to the tunes and rolled a cigarette, so adept at it now he could do so while driving.

As he zoomed along the blacktop he stopped and looked for her at agricultural stations along the way. The highway traversed the corridor between the Rattlesnake and Horse Heaven Hills. The farms situated along the Wakima River were watered from an extensive series

165

of canals and every last one of them depended on migrant laborers to plant, cultivate, and harvest the crops. He observed the workers, whole families including small children who were expected to do their share. Every work camp held the same desolate shame. Why, he wondered, were the people who contributed most to the success of these farms treated so badly? They had no homes, their children no schools. Yet everywhere he went he heard the same laughter, saw the animated smiles, listened in on the singing and jovial banter as they went about their ceaseless toil in a spirit of camaraderie. A silent witness, he could only ponder the inscrutable. By sunset he was worn out and discouraged that his searching had been in vain. He had one more day before he was expected back at the ranch. He determined to rise before the sun and continue his quest.

The next morning he stopped at a diner and ordered a breakfast of sunnyside eggs, bacon, hash browns, toast and black coffee. A lament of lost love played over the radio. Above the booths hung common scenes of western art; trail drives; riding and roping; braves on painted ponies hunting buffalo with their short bows. He gazed abstractedly at the pictures, then had a sudden flash of awareness that he was living out his boyhood fantasies. A farm boy, who over the winter had lived and hunted and prayed with real Indians and who was now on a ranch working cattle with real cowboys. So why this hollow ache inside? He tipped his hat to the young waitress as he went out. She rewarded him with an innocent smile.

It rained all day and all day he searched through the rain. He returned to the bunkhouse after sundown. He stood for a moment in the dark room. Zeke and Irene had retired and Pedro was in his bunk snoring. Juanito had not yet returned from his weekend rambling. He lit a lantern and found a place set for him at the table. A bowl of chili, a slice of buttered corn bread and a glass of milk and by the place setting, a glass vase filled with cut wild lupine

4

Daniel and Juanito continued to ride fence lines. Their first round had focused on finding breaches but now they made a finer job of it, replacing rotten posts, shoring up gates, tacking down sagging wires and keeping a keen eye out for the well-being of the cattle.

Pedro was busy in the shop readying the haying equipment, while Zeke harnessed a single mule and worked up the ground in the kitchen garden. Irene had lots of potted plants set in window sills whose roots were itching for soil.

In the afternoons Daniel continued to practice riding the mustangs. Pedro and Juanito were getting in shape for their respective events, the younger brother for the bull-dogging, an event where the cowboys ride out after a young steer. A hazer goes first to keep the steer running a straight line then once alongside, the second cowboy leaps out of the saddle and wrestles the steer to the ground, turning it over by grasping and twisting the horns. This event requires a courageous horse along with strength and agility on the part of the rider. The brothers also worked together as a unit in the team roping event. They ride after a loosed calf; Pedro tries to lasso its neck while Juanito attempts to rope the hind feet. Daniel never tired of watching these masters with the lariat.

Mid-week Zeke showed up at the round pen with a horse trailer. "Sorry to spoil your fun, Daniel, but I need to improve our cash flow and I've determined to sell the roan stallion to the rodeo. Seems he just grows meaner and he'll fetch a better price as a bucking horse than he would at auction."

"Just when I think I'm getting the better of him, he pulls out something new."

"Ain't been a horse couldn't be rode---never been a cowboy ain't been throwed!"

So Daniel had to part with his first and best teacher at riding bronco. Although he had been growing more adept at anticipating the moves of the stallion, the horse still had plenty to teach him and he was sorry to see him go.

The following weekend the brothers scrubbed, put on clean clothes and headed to town. Daniel drove out to resume his search. Zeke and Irene wondered about his forays off the ranch but nobody asked him any questions. He returned Sunday night, empty handed and tuckered out.

The land was re-greening. The horses shed winter coats and were prospering on new grass. Mules wore coats slick as oil. Cattle grazed and men delighted in the peaceful interval that lay between planting and haying season.

Every evening Daniel practiced riding the remaining wild mares. Juanito attached a strap that girded them around the flanks and incited them to bucking. The vaquero alternately called out instruction, insults and encouragements, sharing freely of his own experience, his taciturn nature transformed into a barrage of banter, so excited was he to have a protégé who shared his passion. By Friday he felt confident that his pupil was ready to enter his first competition.

It was still dark outside on Saturday morning, but the kitchen was already alive with activity. Irene served up platefuls of steak and eggs, the traditional pre-rodeo breakfast. Zeke turned his attention to Daniel and the matters at hand. He raised a chunk of rare dripping steer on his fork and gestured at him en route to cramming it into his working jaw. "You've been looking real good out there, young partner. But remember, that arena is gonna be full of hungry fellas that can make a pretty ride. If you want to win, you have to unleash the bear!"

They loaded up the horses, then all piled into Zeke's truck, Irene up front, the hired men in the bed. Daniel sat with his back to the cab. He was feeling confident enough about the competition, but he was nagged by the feeling that maybe he should have foregone the rodeo to continue his search; as if by not doing so he was betraying the one he was seeking. Yet he reasoned if he could win a purse of prize money, it would move his plan forward. Sometimes it was hard to know the right thing to do.

Since he had come to the ranch he had been eating well and working hard and he felt as strong as he ever had in his life. But his

168

mind often felt distracted and it seemed that only when he was deeply engaged in work could he find some peace. There were moments he even wished he could just forget about the girl and forget about the farm; just bury himself in the good work and companionship he had found at the ranch. But then *those* thoughts left him feeling at odds with himself.

The men of the ranch had grown excited with his progress in bronco busting---they had coached and encouraged him to the point where he felt he was riding for them all. On the drive to town he forced himself not to dwell on his inner conflict but to prepare himself mentally for the upcoming ride. He fingered the bear claws hanging beneath his shirt.

The stands were full when they arrived. Inaugural day of another rodeo season turned picture perfect with blue skies and bright sun. He helped Juanito unload the horses while Pedro went to register them in their events and pay the stable fees. Zeke and Irene took seats in the shaded grandstand. As the competition got underway the men hung back with the other cowboys who watched from behind the chutes or sat on their saddles on the ground and worked fresh rosin into their rope lines. After the announcer welcomed everybody in, a recording of the National Anthem was played over the loudspeakers. Daniel stood when everybody else did but did not realize he was supposed to remove his hat until Pedro gave him a nudge. When the standing and singing were done, a pageant of trick riders and cowgirls carrying banners rode out in formation.

The first event was calf roping, where a cowboy rode out after a loosed calf with a 'piggin' string clenched in his teeth. As quick as he could the cowboy roped the calf and sat the horse to bring it down and while the horse backed to draw the rope taut, the cowboy would jump off to bind the calf's legs, holding them up high so that the judges could be sure it was a secure tie. All working cowboys appreciated these events because they were drawn directly from the routines of ranching life; everyone knew that the skills of these amateur rodeo riders were honed in the hard grind of earning an honest dollar punching cows.

Saddle bronc riding was next. The brothers slapped Daniel on the back and wished him luck. On his way to draw lots to determine who would ride which horse, he spied the roan stallion pacing the corral. He was disappointed to find he had drawn another horse, a chestnut mare, a quarterhorse with powerful haunches, lean and long of leg. He watched her as the wranglers roped her down and got the hornless stock saddle cinched and he could see that she was an experienced rodeo horse who offered little resistance. Throwing men from the saddle was but a job; some of the craziest bucking horses could be led like old work horses by the halter but as soon as they entered the chute with the buck strap around their flank, they were out for blood.

The first rider was Oak from the Garwood wearing his trademark red shirt. He made a respectable showing but his horse was a laggard. The second rider was thrown in two seconds and kicked in the ribs before the pick-up men got him off the ground. The third rider grasped a fistful of mane as he was falling and was disqualified for a two-handed ride. The fourth rider never made it out of the chute---he climbed on the back of a horse who hurled around so violently that the cowboy was pitched off through splintering boards and hit the ground hard, fracturing an elbow. So began the rodeo career of the roan stallion.

"Look out for Red Devil, cowboys!" the announcer called over the loudspeaker as the horse was released into the ring so he could be rustled back to the holding corral. "He'll be back next Saturday when the Professional Rodeo Circuit arrives in town. We'll see what the big boys can do with him." The horse tore at breakneck speed and made several attempts to leap the side-wall of the arena to the amusement of the crowd before men on horseback got enough rope around him to drag him back to confinement.

When the excitement died down, Daniel's horse was led into the chute. The buck strap was cinched but the horse stood still as stone. He climbed gingerly on her back, and slid his boots into the stirrups and took hold of the rosin-packed rope that ran from the nose band of her halter and wrapped it round his gloved hand. Still the horse barely moved a muscle. He could feel her between his thighs, one tensile knot of horse scarcely breathing, ears laid back flat and nostrils flared, her face poised forward in an attitude of anticipation. She was sizing him up.

Without his willing it, the white eagle song began to drum, reverberating throughout his body, calming his mind. He took a deep breath then raised his hand to signal that he was ready as he had been instructed to do by the brothers. The chute opened and the horse exploded out like a ton of touched-off dynamite.

Daniel entered into a timeless sphere as if floating and gliding in slow motion. There was a roaring in his ears like the sound of a flood-tide river or the crash of storming sea waves. The horse flung its rear quarters skyward again and again and arched its back like the curved span of an aerial bridge, curled its neck over so the head was tucked between the forefeet, jumping helter-skelter in pogo-stick fashion. He felt his frame rip and roll in kinetic fusion with this explosion of energy. He remembered to sweep his spurs repeatedly across the horse's shoulders, a command drilled into him by his coaches until it had become second nature. Otherwise he was without thought--- he was all response. Despite the stampede string, his hat went flying. He did not notice. Caught up in the heat of the ride, he resisted when the pick-up man rode alongside to pluck him off after the ten-second buzzer sounded. He returned to his senses only when he heard the cheering.

"Nice ride," the man said as he offered a hand lowering him to safety on the ground while other men caught up the bucking horse. Another wrangler offered him a mount on which to take a victory ride around the ring. A small clown in size 15 sneakers and colorfully patched overalls handed him back his hat with a princely flourish. He looked up at the stands to see Zeke and Irene up out of their seats and Zeke hooting like a bear drunk from eating too many apple drops. Irene, all decorum set aside, whistled and clapped her hands. She might detest the rodeo, but she was glad for him. Pedro and Juanito greeted him back of the corrals, pounding him on his back and knocking him to the ground with fierce joy and embraces.

171

The brothers placed third out of a field of seven in team roping. Juanito came second in bull-dogging. Not a bad day for the "Work Till U Drop' ranch and the men were ready to celebrate. Daniel collected a purse of twenty-five dollars, a week's wages for a single ride.

After the final event the brothers took him over to the saloon where they found the Burlys seated at the bar, waving to them over the heads of couples twirling and shuffling on the dance floor. Daniel couldn't help but notice a gaggle of young cowgirls by the jukebox, all talking at once and laughing and looking at him. He quickly turned away and was suddenly facing a giant of a man standing directly in his way.

"Well if it ain't Injun Joe and the blessed disciples. Don't you fellas know we don't take kindly to wetbacks and red men hereabouts? Don't matter how lucky you get in the rodeo, you'll find no welcome here. Why don't you mosey over to the cantina up there in little Mexico?"

Daniel remembered the man from his first visit to the saloon. He was aware of the brothers standing at his back, holding their ground. "I don't want no trouble," Jake said from behind the bar. "Far as I'm concerned everyone is welcome who can pay."

The man spat on the floor, just missing the toe of Daniel's boot. Suddenly a beefy hand landed like a meat hook on the giant's shoulder and when he whirled around he found himself staring into the laser pinholes of Zeke's ice blue eyes.

"Eddy Charboneau, isn't it? I worked with your old man in the logging camps."

"This is no business of yours, muleskinner."

Zeke's hand was still on Charboneau's shoulder and he smiled grimly as he spoke. "Now Eddy, these men work for me. One rule I've always tried to follow is that any man who works with me is going to be treated like a friend. My friends drink where I drink. You wouldn't be trying to tell me I can't have a drink in the Garwood, me---who was raised on yonder mountain---now would you?"

As he spoke, Zeke grasped the backside of Charboneau's neck to steer him towards the bar. He applied enough pressure to let the man know the nature of his intent but not so the action was obvious to the onlookers.

"No I wouldn't be saying such a thing, Zeke. It was a joke."

"Come on over and join the wife and me for a beer. Catch me up on news of your family."

A cowboy gave up his stool so Zeke could sit Charboneau down next to him and Jake set out a round of drinks. Someone dropped a dime in the juke box and the dancers returned to the floor. Daniel and the brothers made it to the bar and Pedro ordered up three ice-chilled mugs of draft. Jake did not question Daniel about his age.

They rolled cigarettes and they stood in silence sipping the beer and smoking. The cowboy in the red shirt approached, nodded to the brothers and spoke to him.

"That was some fine riding out there today, son."

"Thank you, Sir. You probably would have won if you'd drawn a hotter horse."

"And if a frog had wings it wouldn't bump its ass so much!" the man flashed a grin. "My name is Oak Leforge. I run a ranch outside of town---Herefords. I used to ride the 'Suicide Circuit'---professional rodeo, that is."

The man stuck out his hand and Daniel shook the iron hard grasp.

"I'm Daniel Sweeney and these are my partners, Pedro and Juanito, as fine a pair of riders and ropers as ever lived," he said, feeling a little high on the wave of his win and the beer. Oak nodded to the vaqueros with a knowing smile and they cordially acknowledged him then went to mingle with the local ranch hands, color-blind acquaintances in the fraternity of working cowboys.

"How you getting on with those mules?"

"You steered me in the right direction."

Oak nodded his confirmation.

"I understand this was your first competition?"

"Yessir, it was."

"That's a heady thing to win your first. You've got native talent, no two ways about that. Guess you know this win qualifies you to enter the professional competition next weekend?"

Daniel nodded though he hadn't thought at all about riding again.

"Think twice and think again before you go signing any contracts. Thrill of life on the road wears thin quick."

"Mister Leforge, I ain't trying to be a rodeo star. I intend to return home and farm my family's land."

"Well, all right then. I still ride a bronc now and again but just for fun. Let's an old buckaroo like me know he's still alive. That's my advice to you---only stay in this thing as long as you find joy in it. Good talking to you young man," Oak said.

"Thank you sir," he replied, aware that it was Oak who had done most of the talking. But he knew the man had spoken not only from his own experience but also from his heart.

Daniel was startled by a light but insistent tapping on his shoulder.

"Hey there cowboy, wanna dance?" a soft husky voice inquired. He turned to face a girl wearing a western outfit and in her snakeskin boots she stood as tall as he.

"I don't know how," he said.

"Permit me to show you. It's real easy and lot's of fun."

Before he could protest she had one hand around his waist and his hand in her other hand. All he could do was go along as she led him across the floor.

"Just follow my lead, one step-two step," she said breathily in his ear. "Just follow the bass line. There you go. Now you're catching on."

As she encouraged him he began to feel like he was getting the hang of it. The insistent rhythms of the music bypassed his brain and pulsed into his bones and his legs followed suit and in spite of his reserve he was on the verge of having a good time.

"I'm' awfully sorry about that bit of nastiness with my Daddy. He can be such a bully."

He felt a knot form in his stomach. He stopped dancing and stared at her dumbly.

"That son-of-a-bitch is your father?"

"I'm afraid so. But keep dancing. I'm old enough to do as I please."

As they swung and turned around the floor crowded with dancers, he stole a glance over to the bar where Zeke was sitting. Charboneau was there, glowering at him like a cornered wolverine. Irene smiled and Zeke gave a big wave.

"Shit," he murmured under his breath as the music slowed and the girl pulled him closer. Juanito and his dancing partner circled past. "*Muévate hombre!*" he called.

The second dance ended and she leaned over and whispered in his ear, "Want to step outside?"

"What for?"

"Cause I ain't wearing any underwear."

"Sure, let's get some air." His brains felt pan-fried. He could feel Charboneau's eyes boring twin holes in his back. With all the excitement of the rodeo, the beer in his belly, and her breasts and hips pressing in close to him, he felt shook up and mixed up and deep into trouble.

They went out the door with their arms around each other's waists. The evening was warm, the sky alive with gold-tinge on the feathered streaks of pink clouds. They ambled over to the corrals of the auction house to look at horses. He was giddy with the scent of her perfume and the feel of his hand on her curvaceous hip. They strolled through open sliding doors into the cavernous interior containing stock pens and feed storage. Curious and anxious, the penned livestock popped their heads up as the couple sauntered past. They came to a ladder that led up to the hay loft and she started to climb.

"Come on up!" she called in a girlish voice, "if you dare," she added seductively.

He shook his head but found himself incapable of thinking clearly with it. As he climbed the rungs and gazed upwards, he verified her statement concerning the lack of underwear. When he reached the top she grabbed his shirt, pulled him tight and kissed him. He began to kiss her back, awkwardly at first; then she stuck her tongue in his mouth and he responded in ways he hadn't known he knew. Almost of their own accord, his hands found their way under her shirt and began to explore the hidden surfaces of her body. They lost their balance and she let out a little squeal as they tumbled upon a low stack of hay bales. She rolled on top of him and started to unbutton his shirt.

"What's your name?" he asked her.

"Graciela, but everyone calls me Gracie," she answered all out of breath, as he placed his hands on her breasts.

"I'm Daniel"

"I know who you are."

Her nimble hands undid his belt buckle, button and fly. She slid her hand into his pants and grabbed hold. His hand found its way beneath her denim skirt to the warm wet between her legs. He rolled over on top as she spread her lush brown thighs. But even in his excitement the image of another flashed before him and it stopped him cold. He got up abruptly and buttoned his shirt and tucked it into his trousers.

"I'm sorry Gracie, I gotta go"

And with no further explanation, he picked up his hat and descended back down the ladder.

"Goddamn!" she said. "It's me whose supposed to say no. Daniel, you come back up here this instant."

But he was running and already out the door. He nearly bumped into the giant Charboneau.

"I'll murder you if you so much as drooled on her, you puny chigger!" and he stomped off in search of his daughter.

Next he encountered Pedro and Juanito hot on the tattooed man's trail.

."*Que chico tan travieso!*" Pedro chided him.

"Nothing happened," he said, gasping for breath and very serious.

"*Que triste,*" Juanito replied, as he punched him on the arm. "Zeke is in the truck waiting to drive us all home."

The room was spinning when he lay down in his bunk. He was overwrought, exhausted to the bone. He slept fitfully at first but gradually his limbs relaxed and his breathing slowed; his dreaming eyes roved and darted like hungry fish beneath sealed eyelids.

When he woke the next morning he was still wearing his clothes from the night before. He hadn't even taken his boots off. Irene was up starting a fire in the stove. Everyone else was asleep, Pedro raucously snoring. Daniel stretched his arms to the ceiling, his body one big ache. He mumbled a greeting to Irene and walking stiffly, stumbled his way to the outhouse where the early chill began to rouse him. He watched the sun break into the valley while he reflected on the events of the day before, right up to the moment when he remembered her face and his longing had become tinged with desperation. He hauled buckets of fresh water into the house. Zeke stomped in from the backroom, grabbed Irene and started to waltz her around the kitchen.

"Lord, Lord, he's a rodeo champion and on top of it all, he can dance!" Everyone laughed and even Daniel had to crack a smile.

*

He was driving the family home from church and this was a new thing. Sunday mornings to the Presbyterian service at the church her parents had attended. The tedious sermon, the infernal drone of the organ pipes and the well worn hymnals. They'd meet her mother there and then stay on for the social in the basement. Pastries and coffee. Kids running around. Small talk with the pastor. He couldn't stand it. He hadn't been in a church since his mother had dragged him off kicking and screaming to the Catholic Church when he was how old? Maybe nine or ten. He'd run out and walked all the way home on his own from the village and she'd not tried to make him go back after that, had only taken Danny who seemed to like going or was just too little to know whether or not he did but knew he wanted to be with his mother.

He was driving back up the road to their house, undoing his tie with one hand, and he was feeling hung up, constricted, like he wanted to rip the tie off his neck and throw it out the window. He switched on the radio---gospel hour and talk shows and top forty countdown. He switched it off again. Boys rough housing in the back seat. Trying not to be impatient, trying not to yell or lose control. She's sitting next to him riding shotgun in her church clothes. Satiny form-fitting sleeveless green dress with a button-up collar, white gloves and fishnet stockings with high heels and a yellow felted hat with a broad up-turned brim. Red lipstick on her white face, a sprinkle of freckles across the small upturned nose, and long lashes veiling those green eyes.

As they pass a broad open meadow, he spies a farmer in the distance on his tractor raking hay in preparation for the baling. Early this year. Hot dry spring. Good for making hay now, could be bad for crops later if we don't get some rain soon. He's watching the farmer's progress across the field and slows down the car and finally pulls to a stop at an outlook on the side of the road. Not thinking about it, just drawn into the contemplative pace of the oscillating rake leaving a maze-like pattern of windrows in its wake across the face of the field.

"Is something wrong with the car?" she asked.

"Huh? No I just thought the boys might want to see the farmer making hay."

"That's nice. Can you see him, boys?"

"What is it?"

"He's pulling a rake to gather up the hay so he can bale it and feed it to his cows next winter."

"Oh."

"Your Daddy used to do that kind of work when he was growing up. Only he used to do it with horses."

"Really?"

"Wow!"

"How come he doesn't do it anymore?"

"Because now he makes more money working at the school."

"Oh."

"That poor bastard is probably working sixteen hours a day and still looking at bankruptcy."

"Even so, don't you miss it sometimes?"

"Are you kidding?"

"No."

"Maybe just a little."

He turns away from the farmer and looks at her a moment but turns away quickly from the unmasked reflection of pure pain he glimpses there. He puts the car in gear and moves back out onto the road.

Later in the kitchen he gives her a peck on the back of the neck.
"Time before supper for me to take a quick ride?"
"Weren't you watching the ballgame?"
"Not a very interesting game. Sox are slamming them."
"Sure, there's time."

He's not sure why he'd bought this thing. He'd had one in college and he'd liked the freedom of the back roads, liked the way it made girls look at him too. But now? He'd barely ridden it since that day last spring when he'd bought it on a whim. He'd been making some good money at the realty and it made him feel flush to be able to go and buy something just for fun. It was just like when he'd gone and bought that Morgan filly. Hardly ever rode her. Danny had ended up taking care of her. But he had liked the idea of owning a horse.

He put on the leather jacket, the boots and the goggles and the helmet. She'd made him promise to wear the helmet. He swung a leg over, hit the kick start and revved the hell out of it. He rode around the hills for awhile, leaning into the curves, accelerating on the upgrade, enjoying the bite of nobby tires on the gravel. He found himself drawn back to the same spot where they'd paused in the morning. He parked and lit up and sat astride smoking in the shade of a hickory.

They were at the baling now, the man on the tractor joined by a substantial crew. He knew the family. The man on the tractor was as old as his father would be now. A couple of generations of uncles and brothers and sons out sweating together in the field. The farmer was kicking out the bales and another tractor hauling a hay wagon was in his tow. Some men were on foot bucking the bales onto the trailer, others on the trailer labored to keep apace with the stacking. Even at this distance and above the rhythmic 'kachunk kachunk' of the baler and the steady 'putt putt' of the tractors, he could hear the voices of the men calling out to each other in jocular banter as they progressed ant-like across the field.

"What am I doing here?" He sat and he watched for moments more.

"What the fuck am I doing here?" And still he sat and he watched.

5

Daniel and Zeke finished the first cultivation of corn. They spelled each other, taking out fresh teams on the two-row cultivator. And now the grass was coming on. Pedro toiled in the shop getting machinery in tune for the rush of haying season that was about to fall over them like a wave. Juanito continued to ride the fence lines, trailed by the collie dogs, making repairs and watching over the cattle.

Early morning mid-week while washing up at the outdoor tap after breakfast, Juanito approached him, throwing a set of keys in the air and catching them as he walked and grinning from ear to ear with the pomp and pretension of someone carrying a wonderful secret. *"Vamanos!"* he said. Daniel followed on the wave of enthusiasm but had no idea of what was going on. He was still mystified until Juanito drove into the parking lot of 'The Great Northwest Outfitters'. Juanito ushered him in. The store building was warehouse big, aisles and aisles of sundry merchandise. Juanito stood him in front of a mirror to try on hats.

"I don't need a new hat."

"Mira muchacho, este sombrero...se huele muy mal. Por favor, pon esto."

"What's wrong with this hat?"

"It stinks!"

At last he agreed to a white felt hat and by the time they were through he was neatly trussed into a white cotton-duck shirt, a tooled belt with silver buckle, blue jeans and fringed chaps, lace-up roper's boots and spurs with brass rowels---the embodiment of a professional cowboy. He stood in front of the full-length mirror, scarcely believing in his own reflection. Juanito appraised him up and down then suddenly called out, *"Esperate!"* and ran down the aisle of *banderas* and selected out a blue one and ran back breathless and knotted it around his neck.

"Not so tight!" Daniel croaked.

"Mírate, ya es perfecto!"

The check-out girl couldn't contain a low whistle as they approached the cash register, causing him to blush.

"Looks like somebody's ready for the rodeo," she said.

181

"Yes Miss, though I don't expect these fancy clothes come with a guarantee that I'm going to ride any better."

"No, they don't," she had to admit and then she made an awful face as Juanito handed over the old clothes which she dropped into a paper sack as if she were handling a dead animal. Daniel reached into the sack to retrieve his billfold from his old jeans. Juanito quickly intervened. "No, vaquero, on Saturday you will be representing the ranch. Zeke and Pedro and I---we all pitched in to foot this bill."

"You needn't make such a fuss over me."

"Daniel, for us the rodeo is a religion."

The following Saturday the grandstand was packed to standing room only and excitement ran high as the pageant began. "Ladies and Gentlemen, welcome to the annual presentation of the Northwest Professional rodeo at the Garwood arena!" blared the amplified voice from the judge's box. Ten cowgirls in blue suede chaps, white outfits and matching hats came thundering out on fine mounts, standing in the stirrups and bearing bright banners on lance-like poles. They interwove at a gallop, taking their horses through intricate crosses and figure eights then joining in two units to circle round the ring. The girl riders were followed by a parade of painted wagons drawn by big teams; six-up of dappled Percherons, four abreast of giant black and feather-footed Clydesdales, and a smart team of Belgians pulling a coach driven by the cowboy in the red shirt. Daniel's heart quickened at the sight. He was particularly impressed with the way Oak handled the Belgians, how they moved out with power and grace. They reminded him of Liam and Rory and the memory of his old team struck him with an unexpected pang.

Rodeo Stars of the circuit rode out waving their hats at the cheering crowd as their names were announced. The rodeo queen had been chosen in festivities the previous evening. She was handed a bouquet of yellow roses and sat on a white stallion to promenade the arena, laying claim to her domain. Daniel's jaw dropped when he recognized Gracie, Charboneau's daughter, tall in the saddle, flashing teeth and beaming at the crowd. He was leaning on high rails by the chutes among a gang of riders and ropers and he lowered his hat and tried to hunker down as she circled, but the Queen had already picked him out and she blew him a kiss as she rode past. He turned red as men gave him crooked smiles and jabbed elbows in his ribs. Then all stood for the raising of the flag and the national anthem and this time he knew enough to remove his hat. The announcer prayed for God's blessing and protection, petitioning that no competitors be hurt that day; then it was time to rodeo.

The competition opened with calf roping. He hardly saw the goings on. His eyes turned inward as he attempted to focus and gather his forces. Midway through the event the saddle bronc riders were called to draw lots. He took his ticket and went to study the pool of horses and he could not believe his luck. *Diablo Rojo* was in the pool and he was slated to ride him. The horse gave him the red eye when it smelled him. With a violent whirl and kick it tried to split the rail at head height where he was standing. "Good," he told him. "I'm glad you're still hotter than hell."

He looked out across the corral to observe the other horses and he sensed that someone was watching him. He lifted his eyes to the far side of the enclosure and saw a sharp brown face under a black Stetson, cool eyes peering darkly back at him. His concentration was fractured. He wanted to sprint over and ask the boy the whereabouts of his sister. Yet Daniel knew that Sebastian regarded him as an enemy and if he wanted to ask him anything, he'd first have to figure out how to avoid another fight.

The last of the calf ropers came in. There were twelve competitors on the docket for saddle bronc riding and Daniel was in the middle of the pack. He determined to try and resolve things with Sebastian after the ride. He walked off to find a quiet space behind the grandstand. He looked around to see if anybody was watching. No one but a stray yellow dog on business of its own. The muted voice of the announcer and the surge of yells and applause from the audience drifted over from the other side of the palisades.

He had taken the eagle feather off his bow and placed it in the band of his new hat. He took out the feather and set it down on the sand and began to dance in a slow shuffling gait around the feather. The bear claw necklace under his shirt clacked and jangled as he danced. He

183

began chanting the eagle song soundlessly and the chant welled up from within with the intensity of many hands beating on drums until he could contain it no longer and broke out in full voice, singing his power song to the blank wall behind him, the bare ground below, the naked sky above. Suddenly he received a hard rap between his shoulder blades. He spun around, drawn out of his trance, ready to stand and fight.

"Que haces aquí, chiquito? Ahorita estan llamandote, apurate rapido!"

It was Juanito come to fetch him for his name was being called. He picked up the feather and ran. *"Gracias amigo!"* he called back over his shoulder.

He was out of breath feeling airy and light when he reached the gates. Oak was there, serving as a wrangler and pick-up man and he pinned a paper square with a number onto the back of Daniel's shirt and offered him a hand in climbing over the rails of the chute.

"Good luck, son. You've got a live one there."

"I got just what I need, sir!"

He scrambled into the saddle on the back of the flailing Red Devil and it was all he could do to raise his hand in signal to the man waiting to open the chute. Strangely, the horse too hesitated for the space of a breath. But just that. Then horse and rider exploded into the arena. The roar of the crowd sounded distant to his ears, like the hollow crash of waves on the shore as heard from within an ocean cave. Instantly he became enwrapped in vision. As if from far away, his ears perceived the sounds of piercing cries and drum beats carrying an escalating chorus of chanted prayers. He rode with the vivid sensation that his arms were outstretched wings. His breath pounded in precise rhythm with the bucking of the horse, which reared and plunged and dove with the energy of a demon. Although he was making constant adjustments to stay in the saddle, holding on for life to the rope wrapped vice-tight in his hand, his left hand held high in counterpoise and struggling to keep up the sweep of spurs, within he felt weirdly self-contained. He was not thinking of staying on or of being thrown. He was one with the wild flux of equine energy in fluid motion, rising and falling in the reckless beauty of the ride.

The buzzer sounded and again he kept riding, the crazed horse bucking beneath him careening madly about the ring. The crowd was on its feet, unloosed by his passion. Oak rode after him, managed to get his mount alongside and grabbed him about the waist with steel strap arms. "Let go, kid. That was already one hell of a ride!" Daniel snapped out of it and hopped on behind the old cowboy. His ears unlocked from their inward state and the sound of the crowd whooping and clapping came on full volume. It took four men on horseback to subdue the roan stallion.

Pedro and Juanito received Daniel into their arms. They lowered him off Oak's horse with excited and tender emotion as if they were disciples deposing the Christ figure off the cross. Once they had brought him to earth, they pounded him on the back and embraced him with tears in their eyes.

The next five riders were either unseated or disqualified for infractions and Daniel looked to be the winner. The final rider in the competition was a wiry brown fellow under a black Stetson. Sebastian drew the chestnut mare that had been Daniel's mount in the previous competition. The horse put on an admirable show and Sebastian rode more than ably and out-lasted the ten second requirement in perfect form. But when the points were tallied, in consideration for the pure mean streak in his horse, the judges scored Daniel the winner. He was awarded the champion's prize, a silver belt buckle embossed with the image of a bronco, and he was placed in the saddle of Oak's tall thoroughbred to take a victory ride around the arena as the announcer repeated his name to the whistles and cheers of the appreciative throng.

It was a moment that most young men could only dream of and in that moment Daniel felt like he *was* in a dream. Men who had been riding the circuit for years came up to congratulate him and shake his hand. A newspaper reporter took his picture and youngsters petitioned him to autograph their event fliers. Amidst all the bustle boiling up to a pitch around him, a wordless thought came in like a pressure from the side, leaning on his heart, striving upward to his mind; "Sebastian", he spoke the name silently and scanned the tumult of the crowd and the cowboys and all the workmen behind the scenes searching for that fierce face that had so recently cast him an evil eye, but to no avail.

Zeke came down from the stands to greet the victor. Irene had stayed at the ranch this day, having had her fill of rodeo for the season. Zeke found him in a distracted state and puzzled to himself over the vagaries of youth. Daniel excused himself mumbling about someone he was hoping to find. He urgently sought the one connection he had to the girl whose image was still seared on his heart. But Sebastian was nowhere to be found. It seemed he must have quit the grounds at the announcement of the Judge's results. Daniel knew how much Sebastian hated to lose. He also knew that if he wanted to collect the prize money, he had to stay until the final event; that the money figured as a key element in his plan and that in any case, he didn't know where to begin to look for Sebastian. Little Mexico was his best bet even though he had already been there more times than he could count, but if Sebastian was still in town, that's where he'd find him. He would go there as soon as the rodeo was over.

Daniel wandered among the holding pens and stables. He spotted the contingent of draft horses brought in for the show, among them the Belgians, still in harness, who were eating hay from an open air manger. He walked over to the rails and the two turned their massive heads and plodded over on heavy iron shoes---first one then the other poked a long nose through the gap between the rails as he blew gently into their nostrils, stroked their muzzles and spoke softly to them. They were gelded, mild, in their prime and well cared for; their red dun coats glowed with a healthy spotted sheen, their flaxen manes and tails were groomed. They gazed at him with large almond eyes, dark and furtive like those of beautiful Mediterranean women peering from behind veils.

"Like my horses, Dan?" Oak was suddenly behind him.

"I'd like to make you an offer." He was shocked at his own words, even as they left his mouth.

Eyes squinted and rubbing his chin, Oak appraised the horses as if seeing them for the first time. "I love those horses."

"I would guess you do."

"However, I'm short on cash and long on horse flesh. Horses are a sickness with me. I've got a whole barn full at home. But these

186

two? I wouldn't sell them to just anyone." He gave Daniel an appraising look. "But then you ain't just anyone."

Daniel looked down at his boots.

"Couldn't let them go for under five hundred."

"Including harness?"

"Rides like a Comanche and drives a hard bargain to boot!" Oak was talking to his horses. "What d'ya think boys? You want to go home with this raw upstart?"

He turned to Daniel. "What are you going to do with them--- would they have some part in your farming scheme?"

"Just so."

"That's what these old boys ought to be doing instead of all this fancy parading. You sure you wouldn't rather buy a team of mules?"

Daniel saw the wink and gave a knowing smile.

"Forget about the harness and you've got a deal!" Oak fairly shouted as he stepped forward to shake his hand.

"I had a good feeling about you when first I laid eyes on you at the saloon. My heart will rest easy knowing my boys go with you."

"What's their names?"

"Storm and Tempest."

"Storm has that stripe like a thunder bolt and Tempest the blaze like a tear drop."

"I'll have the money for you soon as they wrap this thing up."

"No hurry."

"I'll pick them up tomorrow?"

"No problem cowboy, they're as good as yours."

As Daniel walked away he felt baffled. The last thing he'd expected to do was buy a team of horses. But there was something about those two that caught him up and made him feel as though all his actions were predestined as part of some great plan. He didn't have time to ruminate long. An official came and invited him to participate in the finale. He rode proud among the professional cowboys as he waved his white hat with the eagle feather stuck in the band. After the show he went to the offices to collect his purse of five hundred dollars. He went directly to Oak and paid him in full. Shortly Zeke and the brothers found him and astonished him by laying a nearly equal sum in

187

his hands, telling him it was his share of the winnings. "We done a little betting on the side," Zeke explained. "Out of all the long shots, you were the most unknown, the new kid on the block. The odds on you were longer than a donkey's pecker. So take your share and I won't listen to a word of your bandy-legged side-winding protestations."

Daniel pocketed the cash gratefully and proceeded to tell them of his purchase.

"They're fine looking examples of horse flesh, I'll grant you," Zeke opined. "But I could've steered you toward some little mules that'll still be plowing ground long after the coyotes have picked those giant carcasses clean and their bones have turned to dust and I can get them for half the price!"

"Basta ya con las mulas, hombre, let's get a drink!" interjected Pedro with good humored exasperation. The comrades joined the procession of visitors and locals emptying out the stands and headed for a common destination. Daniel had other purposes and intentions but he was swept up bodily into the swell of that human wave. "Fellas, I got some business I got to take care of," he told them. But Zeke and Pedro lifted him up onto their shoulders and carried him along. "First order of business is a toast to our success!" said Zeke.

The rowdy hordes hit the local watering hole. People spilled out the doors and milled about the parking lot of the saloon; someone had filled a fifty-five gallon drum with scrap wood and lit a fire. There was a band inside complete with caller and fiddler. Even with two extra helpers at the bar, Jake was swamped and running frantically to keep glasses full. It was not easy to break away from the celebration. Everyone wanted to buy him a drink, but he had to find Sebastian. Little Mexico.

Just as he stepped outside a giant shadow loomed up out of the darkness. Aw hell, he thought, not Charboneau again.

"I told you, Indian boy, you don't belong here. Go back where you came from."

Daniel ignored the taunt and giving him wide berth, he set off up the roadway. With a gesture of his craggy head, Charboneau signaled and a handful of locals followed as he trailed Daniel up the road. Oak was outside for a smoke, saw what was going on and went in to alert Zeke who was still at the bar. Zeke took a glance around for his cohorts only to discover that the brothers were gone. Left about an hour ago said Jake. Zeke reached out an arm to Oak and the two old cowboys set off to trail the gang of men.

Daniel knew that he was being followed by Charboneau's gang. He neither quickened nor slackened his pace. He thought that he should probably be afraid but he wasn't. He was back on the path of heart and he felt like there was nothing that could touch him or stand in his way. The men were well-liquored and had bottles passing between them as they stalked him. It was a fast mile from the saloon to the heart of Little Mexico. Daniel walked on and found the worn pathway that led to the door of '*El Toro Viejo*', the drinking establishment of the Chicanos. The building was second only to the church in the solidity of its construction, more like a small civic hall than a bar. A handful of men stood outside on the steps smoking and enjoying the night air. "*Buenas noches,*" he said as he climbed the steps. "*Bueno*", they duly intoned as they stepped aside to let him pass. The doors opened to a festive gathering with a five-piece mariachi band sharp as pins in their vast sombreros and silver-studded regalia perched intimately on a small stage. Women in flowing pastel skirts and brocaded blouses danced with men who wore their hats of woven palm indoors. The bar was gaily decorated with cut flowers in clay pots. Candles flickered on the tables below paper cut-outs of animals, moons and stars that festooned the rafters. All eyes fell on him as he entered. Juanito was there among the revelers and spotting him, he left his dance partner who stood with hands on her hips, her pretty face in a scowl, not happy at being left out on the floor. He edged his way through the press and clasped his hand around Daniel's arm and leaned in close so that his lips were next to his ear.

"*Que haces aquí, amigo?* "

"I'm looking for someone."

"*Aquién?*"

"Sebastian."

"*El tipo que era en el rodeo hoy en dia?* That guy you beat in the saddle bronc ride?"

"That's the one."

"*Daniel, porque lo buscas? Es un gallo de pelea* and no friend of yours."

"He's the only chance I've got."

Juanito puzzled at this but there was no time for explanation. Even as the words were leaving his mouth, Daniel's eyes scanned the patrons of the cantina and lighted on Sebastian who was glaring at him from across the hall. Against Juanito's protests, he crossed the distance over wide floorboards that separated him from his nemesis. Dancers parted out of his way and Sebastian stepped out to meet him. They stood a moment facing each other. Sebastian was ready for the rematch. Daniel kept his hands down at his sides and made an effort to see his opponent in the manner that Old Joseph had taught him. He could sense the anger and fear and as he softened his eyes, he saw an energy field flowing upward from the crown of Sebastian's head, shimmering red waves with secondary hues of violet and green.

"I come to talk."

"I know what you come for, and for that I am going to whip you."

Sebastian leaped and kicked Daniel in the stomach with the heel of his boot. The breath went out of him and he doubled over as his enemy rained down blows on his face. He shifted his center of gravity, planted his feet and managed to hold his ground. Then Daniel moved in, assuming a boxer's crouch, he feigned a right jab, then landed a sharp left with a hard right follow-up to the mid-section.

"*Que bárbaro*---but you have fast hands!" Sebastian quipped as he winced and blood began to trickle from his nose. He flashed a wicked smile and then landed a couple of quick strikes of his own. In the next moment they were on the floor in a flailing tumble.

As they fought on, the men who had been lounging outside rushed in shouting a warning that was soon followed by Charboneau with his drunken gang. The mariachis quit playing and hurriedly packed their instruments. Rapt in the deadly fascination of their combative dance, the fighters were impervious to all else. Sebastian wriggled free of a headlock and jumped cat-like to his feet and Daniel rolled and regained his own legs, barely escaping a boot tip to the ribs. He caught Sebastian by his shirt front and lifted him up against the

190

wall. Juanito stood close by to make sure that no one intervened in a fair fight. Sebastian looked searchingly into Daniel's eyes, facing defeat once again, he was torn between rage and fear and the hope that if he could just regain a pin-point of balance, he might yet find an opening.

Daniel returned his gaze, trying his best to quell the manic surge that had possessed him. It was not his nature to be the aggressor. For him there could be no victory in vanquishing the other, only the ruination of his hopes and dreams. He looked at Sebastian with the respect and affection he felt for him. He lowered his fist and released him. The lithe contender still had some fighting tricks up his sleeve but he sensed the change within Daniel and he was unsure of what to do next. This was a challenge of a new kind. His enemy began to intrigue him, but then he looked beyond Daniel and what he saw caused him to scream.

Charboneau came roaring through the ring of spectators and smashed a chair down on Daniel's head. Daniel raised up his hands but too late and the splintering wood dropped him like a weighted sack to the floor. He lay in a heap and blood flowed from a wound to his head. Without thought, Sebastian leapt up and struck the tattooed man in the jaw, stunning him with the element of surprise. Juanito joined forces with Sebastian and broke a wine bottle over the thick skull. Zeke and Oak arrived and got into the brawl with Charboneau's drunken gang aided by several Mexicans who took no little delight in the unexpected Gringo invasion. Pedro appeared out of nowhere and waded into the fray. Daniel came to but wasn't ready to stand. He crawled under a corner table while all about him men roared and women screamed and ran for cover. The brawlers busted up furniture and smashed windows as they battled. Much as he loathed to, the proprietor summoned the law. A squad car arrived manned by a sheriff and a handful of on-the-spot deputies with nightsticks in hand. With several shots fired in the air and wood to the heads of the intractable, they subdued the rumble and the sheriff radioed in for the station wagon that served as both county ambulance and paddy wagon. Anyone who was too hurt or too drunk to flee was slapped into handcuffs and hauled away.

The proprietor identified Daniel as the instigator. He struggled to make it on his own power into the back of the wagon. Sebastian was picked up too. The brothers slipped out seamlessly into the warren of the shanty town. The sheriff delivered Zeke and Oak a reprimand but didn't detain them out of deference to their status as elder residents of Garwood.

Daniel watched from the back of the wagon as they tried to arrest Charboneau, who was so berserk that it took four deputies to bring him down after which they determined it prudent to drive him to the hospital for X-rays and stitches before they hauled him off to jail.

*

Christ, it had been ages since he'd been in this store. With state sales tax rising and the new highway access, he, like just about everybody, shopped on the tax free side of the river these days. Lots of big box stores had been built there to meet the demand. A bell on the back side of the door made a little tinkling sound as he came through. He'd always hated that damn bell. Probably put there by old Mister Wilder to warn him when little shoplifting hooligans like himself and his buddies came in. They'd only ever tried to steal some penny candy for the thrill of it and Mister Wilder's wrath contributed to the thrill. Tommy could see the shop keeper seated on a tall stool behind the counter with his spectacles perched on the end of his long nose going over some accounts. The old bastard never aged, never changed. He looked just the same as Tommy remembered him.

He ducked his head to avoid eye contact and headed for the hardware section. Or where it used to be, except the old bugger had rearranged things in the store and he had to go looking among the cluttered aisles stocked to the ceiling with what all.

As he was wandering he saw Vicki with a hand basket of groceries. He prayed she didn't see him.

"Tommy?"

Oh shit! Not here, Vicki. Now he knew he had Wilder's attention. He started walking toward the back of the store and she followed him apace. She looked good out of uniform---short shorts and a halter top, her hair loose on her summer-browned shoulders. But he was trying not to notice.

"Why haven't you called?"

"What and get Tyler on the line again? I'm running out of fast talk."

"And you don't come to Smokey's anymore. It's been weeks. I know when I'm being avoided."

"Vicki, we gotta cut this off."

"I knew you were going to say that. I just wish you would've been man enough to come out with it before now."

"Well, I just did."

"Like you think I'm gonna beg now?"

"No."

"Or cry?"

"No."

But it was too late --- she was already crying.

"I wish this had never happened."

"Asshole."

She stomped off and he wished he hadn't said it like that. It wasn't how he meant it; yet he was glad it was finally over. Fuck all.

When he got up to the counter and Mister Wilder looked up, he realized that the man before him was not Mister Wilder but Mister Wilder's son. How could a young man look so old? They had been in high school together.

"Tommy."

"Jay-Jay."

"How's things?"

"Not too bad."

"Will that do it for you today?"

"I'll just throw one of those cedar posts out front onto the rig."

"Okay. Coaching ball I understand?"

"That's right."

"Team shaping up?"

"Too early to say. We lost a lot of talent when the seniors graduated."

"Maybe you'll play your second bench more than the last coach."

"That's right."

"Heard anything from your little brother?"

"Not a thing."

"I guess the old man dying threw him for a loop."

"They were pretty close."

"Danny was always a little strange."

"What do you mean?"

"So quiet like."

"He's all right. Just a little moody is all."

"He loved that farm."

"Yes he did."

"Must've teed him off something awful when you made noise about selling it."

"Yes it did."

"Anybody interested?"

"Interested in what?"

"I mean do you have any buyers for the land?"

"There's one retired couple from downstate."

"Value of that land is only going to increase with time."

"I know it."

"You still going to sell?"

"That's what all this is for. I'm going to paint a 'For Sale' sign."

"Why don't you just get one from the realty office?"

"They don't talk to me over there anymore and I don't talk to them."

"I see. Should I put this on your account?"

"Do we still have one?"

"Sure do."

"Please do then. "

He got a couple of planks out of the garage and dragged the lawn mower up into the bed of the truck and headed up to the farm. It was a hot and muggy day and it was difficult mowing the overgrown moist rank grass---the mower kept choking on the cuttings and stalling out. Each time he'd have to flip it over and clean clumps off the blades and then work the rip cord for several pulls before it would start again.

194

The easy twenty-minute job ended up taking more than an hour. Soaked in sweat and barely containing his cusses he did manage to reclaim the front yard of the farmhouse into the semblance of a lawn.

He found the tools he needed for erecting the sign in the workshop of the barn.

"Why am I putting up this stupid sign? Christ, we're out here on a dead end road. Who's even going to see it?"

He set the post, tamped it in with a spud bar, and then gave it a few whacks with a ten pound sledge. He still enjoyed the feel of it, the energy coming up through the earth and passing through him as he sunk the post right into the ground. Nice that the body still remembered how to do that. Though he guessed he'd pay for it in the morning.

He had a pre-primed section of plywood which he nailed to the post. He then carefully inked his message onto the board with the bright red paint. He had to use his shirt tail to wipe off a few drips, but the final lettering came across neat enough. He stood back to admire his work. "Well, that's done."

He was about to leave, when on a whim he decided to walk up to the graveyard. Half way up the hill he got winded and stopped. He couldn't catch his breath. His chest gripped tight and he doubled over with his hands on his knees, sucking for air. He thought for a moment that maybe he was having a heart attack and the panic fed the constriction in his lungs. Then he fell to his knees and began to sob and with the sobbing he got some air and began to feel better. When he stood up again he desperately wanted a cigarette but he'd left them in the truck.

"Christ, I gotta stop smoking."

He looked up the hill to where the headstones stood beneath the tall maples and the giant oak.

"This was a bad idea. He wouldn't want to see me right now anyway."

He turned around and headed back down the hill with the intention of some heavy drinking forming in his mind.

PART FIVE

1

Garwood Jailhouse, Town of Garwood, Washington

He awoke under the glare of a naked bulb, stretched out on a bunk bed with metal springs and a straw tic mattress. On bunk beds lined along the cell walls other men snored their way through various states of the unconscious. Sebastian was sitting cross-legged on the lower tier of a bunk opposite, studying him. His face looked as bad as Daniel's head felt and though the night was not unduly warm, he wore no shirt.

Daniel swung his legs to the floor and sat up, bumping his head on the frame above. He reached up to his aching skull and found that it was wrapped in strips of cloth and realized that the strips were the vestiges of Sebastian's shirt.

"Thanks," he said.

"*De nada*. They should have brought you to the doctor instead of that pig with the designs from hell tattooed on his arms."

"He wound up in the hospital?"

"He got what he deserved. *Caramba*, look what he did to you! That pissed me off, you know? I was about to whip your ass."

"You probably would've."

"You think so? I am not so sure. First you best me at the picking of apples. Then you defeat me in the rodeo. I've never seen anybody ride like that. It was a thing of great beauty."

"You had a pretty good ride yourself."

"Not good enough."

"It wasn't your day."

"I did not feel so bad about it when I heard that you are half-breed. It would have been worse to be defeated by *un mero gringo*."

He blushed at the unexpected praise.

"My name's Daniel."

"I know your name. Guess we can't call you '*el mudo*' anymore

196

now that you are talking. I am called Sebastian."

"Fellas at the orchard told me your name."

"*Pinche cabrones.*"

"Sometimes I think things would be easier if I'd stayed quiet."

"But you didn't."

"Nope."

"Where did you learn to fight like that?"

"I'm not much of a fighter."

"*Que chiste*! *Aye yai yai*...not much of a fighter. Why is my nose feeling broken and my eye swollen shut, heh? Since I left my country I haven't had a choice. I've had to fight to survive."

"I didn't come to fight."

"Why did you come?"

"You don't want to know."

"Why was this tattooed man so eager to shed your blood?"

"He thought I was after his daughter."

"Were you?"

"She's not the one I'm looking for."

"It's best we don't speak of it or I may have to fight you again."

"Sooner or later we will."

"But not yet. Tell me, where did you learn to ride like that?"

"My father put me on a horse when I was very small. I held the lines, he steered the plow."

"*De veras*, you were raised on a farm? *Que bueno*, so was I. What kind?"

"Dairy farm."

"We had just the one cow and a donkey by which to travel and of course the *milpa* where we grow the corn. But not only corn, we grew everything there. Mama would sell the crops from a stall *en el mercado* and Papa would hitch the donkey to a cart to haul the coffee beans."

"Just like my Dad. He'd hitch up the team to haul the milk cans down to the creamery."

"All that was before the troubles, before the bad times that befell us."

"Seems there no getting away from it."

197

"There is not."

"You working the rodeo circuit now?"

"*Si,* but some day I will have a farm of my own."

"That makes two of us."

"It is the only life. Not for nothing do my people call ourselves *the people of the corn.*"

"We grew corn on our land, sweet corn in the kitchen garden and shell corn for the cows, and we tapped the maples."

"What means to tap the maples?"

"To collect the sap from the trees and boil it down for sugar."

"You made sugar from trees? We get our sugar from the cane. Every year Papa had to travel to *la costa* and chop sugar cane. It was hard on him but I never heard him complain."

"Where is your father now?"

"Men came for him in the night with masks over their heads. We never found his body. We found the body of my mother on the side of the road."

They both fell silent a moment and it struck him like a blow to realize how pale his own losses seemed in light of what this boy and his sister had been through.

"Why were they after your folks?"

"My parents were teaching their neighbors to read and write and Papa organized a cooperative of furniture makers."

"I don't see his crime."

"His crime was being an Indian who tried to help his people. And how came you to leave your land?"

"My father passed on last year and I guess I sort of ran away. But my plan is to return and farm our land."

"How I wish I could return, but in this moment, it is too dangerous. It's strange, you and I are not so different, but now I suppose you are going to ask me the question that is burning in your soul?"

"Sebastian please, where can I find her?"

The shirtless man, lean and muscular as a wild cat, stared with unblinking eyes as if appraising his prey before the pounce; then he looked away and studied the barred door a moment and when he turned back his gaze had softened.

"Go to the Priest, Padre Benito, at La Iglesia de San Jose. Tell him, *'Estoy en busca de mi alma.'* He is a good man. He will help you."

Sebastian spoke with the sly hint of a smile and then he looked Daniel in the eyes and his face turned serious and he spoke with gravity.

"You must promise me you will take good care of her."

"I promise," said Daniel and he reached out and they shook hands. Sebastian sat back and stretched himself out on the bunk, pulled up the threadbare blanket and turned his face to the wall.

Daniel lay back down too, but his sleep was fitful and his head was pounding. The bulb in the ceiling burned through what remained of the night.

At dawn the Sheriff emptied out the cell, leaving only Sebastian behind bars. The lawman released Daniel on the condition that he help to repair the cantina. Daniel shifted uneasily in his boots as he stood before the front desk to receive a parting admonition.

"I can't fault a fella for taking a crack at these wetbacks but you can't go around busting up private property."

"Can't you let that boy go, the one I was arrested with?"

"In the first place, I ain't arrested you, yet. And second, what concern of yours is he?"

"He is my friend."

"He's an illegal is what he is, no green card, no papers, no nothing. I'm gonna send that little fire-ant back to Mexico where he belongs. Immigration is on their way to fetch him now."

"They'll kill him if you send him back."

The sheriff smiled. "That's not too likely, son. Fact is, they'll loose him on the south side of the Rio Grande and he'll be back up here in a matter of weeks. We've got to make an example of some even if it just sets them back a little. We can't have them making a laughing stock of the law. Now you go on, get out of my hair. And remember this, if you want to make it in rodeo, best keep your nose clean."

Daniel turned on his heels and exited through the plate glass doors. He was limping and his vision was still blurry from the blows to his head as he squinted his eyes against the morning light. His hat and the feather were gone - lost in the scuffle.

The streets of the town were empty as he walked over to the arena to check on his new horses and there found Pedro and Juanito with Zeke's truck and trailer loading them up. He was surprised at how glad he was to see the brothers, how strong a bond he felt with them.

"You guys are too much," he said by way of greeting.

"Don't thank us, Amigo. We figured since you were in jail, we would come down and steal your horses. Now you've caught us in the act," Juanito laughed.

"How's Zeke?"

"Hung over bad. Irene's ready to chop off his nose she is so mad." Pedro said. "*No te preocupes,*" Juanito jumped in. "We told her it was all your fault."

"I made a mess of things."

"A man in love should not be judged as any other," said Pedro.

Daniel wondered what he knew and how he knew it.

"I have to bust a man out of jail."

Juanito closed the swinging tailgate behind the horses and latched it.

"He will be all right, Daniel. *El es un indio de Chiapas.*"

"Is that in Mexico?"

"It is, but it is like another country."

"It sounds like an awfully hard place."

"That's what makes him so tough."

He rode in the bed of the pick-up, glad for solitude and cool wind to clear his head. He had his mandate to work at the cantina but he was determined to settle in his new horses first and besides that, he couldn't get Sebastian's plight off his mind. They unloaded the horses; they leaped and bucked and galloped about then rolled on their backs, all four legs flailing at the sky, and with that done, they ventured to meet the resident horses and mules across the fence line.

The brothers went on their way. Daniel stood in the sun-baked yard scanning the ranch in a moment of rare quietude, taking it all in with its rambling, ramshackle functionality. It was the closest he'd felt to a home since he'd left his own. He went to the outdoor tap for a drink, took off the blood-soaked bandage and let the ice cold water gush over his still throbbing skull. He changed his clothes, grabbed his old hat and headed into the kitchen. While he filled up on leftovers, he stood at the window to watch Irene in her garden venting her anger on potato bugs and weeds. He could hear Zeke snoring in the back room.

A sunbeam slanting through the window illuminated a framed photograph hanging near the door. He had looked at it a hundred times but had never really seen it until now---a young pilot in his flight suit, helmet tucked under his arm as he descended the steps of a jet fighter flashed a handsome grin---the son who was never going to come home. Daniel stepped out quietly, climbed into his truck and drove back to town.

He idled slowly round the sheriff's quarters and the jail house. It was a single story cinder-block building surrounded by a chain link fence with a formidable defile of razor wire along the top edge. He had a wild thought, fleeting, of driving his truck into the cinder blocks to break Sebastian out. He parked across the street and sat, watching.

Before long an unmarked van drove in and stopped at the front entrance. Two men in green uniforms emerged and entered the building. They exited a few moments later with Sebastian in handcuffs walking between them. They had dug up a white over-sized T-shirt for him, lending him the look of a child in his father's clothes. For all that, he walked jauntily, head held high. They brought him around to the rear and stuffed him into the already brim-full van that swallowed him up as the doors slammed shut.

Daniel sat in mute witness feeling hollow inside. He scarcely knew this boy, yet he felt as though another person was being snatched away from him; as though his every relationship had to end in loss.

He headed out of town and turned down the dirt lane to the little white stucco church. He entered and was standing at the foot of the altar when a gentle voice hailed him from the dark recesses of the sanctuary.

"*Como puedo ayudarle?*" the voice wished to know.

He struggled to recall the words given him by Sebastian.

"*Estoy en busca de mi alma,*" he managed at last. A figure emerged from the darkened sacristy, the Priest he had seen on his first

201

visit to the church.

"De veras? Pues venga conmigo, vamos a charlar un poco. "

Daniel stepped onto the small podium not realizing he was entering the holy of holies reserved only for the ordained and his chosen acolytes and followed the Priest beyond the altar and through a narrow doorway that led to the sacristy. The Priest motioned him into yet another room which lay off to one side. Daniel marveled at the labyrinthine spaces within spaces inside the little church.

It was a spare room with a lone window, a single cot, a writing desk and a book shelf. As he stood in the doorframe, hat in hand, two items on the wall caught his eye. The diminutive crucifix above the head of the bed was hand-carved in wood, the beardless face of the effigy plainly meant to represent an indigenous person. His eyes lingered longer on a second image above the writing desk, a black and white photograph of a nude woman standing in profile beside a cascading waterfall, pine trees and mountains in the hazy distance, a lovely slender figure with dark hair descending to the small of her back.

"Pasa, por favor. "

The Priest offered him the desk chair and sat down on the cot.

"Me llamo Padre Benito. Como se llama usted? "

"Daniel Sweeney."

"Ah Sweeney, *eres el nuevo campeon del rodeo, verdad?*"

"I wouldn't of guessed you a fan of the rodeo."

"It is my business to know everything that goes on in this town."

"Just like the sheriff."

"Así es. De donde viene usted? "

"I'm from Vermont. And I'd prefer if you'd speak American."

"*Oh...lo siento...*that is, forgive me. When you addressed me in the chapel, I assumed you were a *paisano.* I've seen you once before, no?"

"I poked my nose in here once."

"What draws you to the church? Are you truly in search of your soul?"

"I guess I haven't given it much thought."

202

"Then why did you tell me so?"

"What I spoke back there in the church? That's what Sebastian told me I should say. I'm looking for his sister."

"You are referring to our little Sebastian who was picked up this morning by the Federales?"

"I feel real bad about that. The whole thing was my fault. I went to the cantina to find him but just to talk. Somehow all hell broke loose."

"*Cálmate* Daniel, these kinds of incidents are all too common around here. So tell me, why are you looking for Alma?"

"Alma?"

"Why Sebastian's little sister, *por supuesto*."

"Alma," he repeated in a whisper. "All this time I've been looking for her I never even knew her name. Now I'll have to tell her of all the trouble I got her brother into."

"You are not the source of his trouble."

"Who is?"

"That's a long history."

"I'm in trouble myself."

"You are in love?"

"All I know is I have to see her again."

" Ah, you *are* in love. That cannot be bad. But before you do anything, you must first ask yourself some hard questions. You have some Indian blood, am I wrong?"

"My mother."

"And yet you live in the white man's world as we all must. Alma is not of that world. Not of this land. She is of another country. Where will you take her? How shall she fit in that place?"

"I'm going back east, to the family farm."

"If Alma decides to go with you, she will have many challenges to face. She speaks another language, even the Spanish is not her own. And of course there is the color of her skin, and *muy importante*, she is in this country illegally. These are daunting issues for ones so young to face."

"How do you know her?" Daniel asked.

"Alma and Sebastian came here early last winter, out of work and nowhere else to turn and we gave them temporary shelter. I could see there was a special light about her. Sebastian on the other hand was wrestling with some terrible darkness. This matter of the rodeo---I'm sure he took losing to you hard."

"Yup, the aching in my ribs tells me so."

The Priest reached with both hands to remove his glasses and took a linen cloth from the breast pocket of his black shirt to wipe them clean. He put them back on, smoothed back his thinning hair and sighed deeply.

"I saw you looking at my Lucia, no doubt wondering what a priest was doing with such a picture hanging on his wall. Once long ago I knew an ardor of the heart such as I see burning within you. I did not set out to be a priest you see."

"What happened to her?"

"She left me. We had met at the national university. She was studying to be an actress and although I started out as an art photographer, I was drawn into documenting popular social movements. Through my picture taking I became an advocate for the struggles of the poor. That is my job now, of course. I try to be a voice for those who have none."

"I never knew that's what a priest was supposed to do."

"Unfortunately most priests do not know this either. But for my Lucia, art came first and the revolutionary tendencies of my work threatened that. One morning I awoke to find her gone."

The priest then went on to talk about his life after he entered a missionary order and was sent to a mission in the remote southern highlands which he said was like stepping back centuries in time. The people still held their lands in common and governed themselves according to ancient natural laws.

"I was welcomed into the village with all the deference befitting my holy orders. But I came to gain their hearts when they understood that I had come not only to administer sacraments but to incarnate myself into their daily struggles. I labored alongside the men in the fields. Together we constructed a church and after that a clinic.

"In my third year I accompanied the men to the coast to work on *las fincas grandes*. When we returned to the village there was trouble afoot. In a neighboring town a Mestizo landowner had tried to usurp grazing and timber lands from the Indians. When they resisted, soldiers came in the night and dragged the men from their homes wearing nothing but their underwear and held them for a week. All my inquiries to authorities fell on deaf ears. The men were suspended by their thumbs, stunned with cattle prods and burned with cigarettes.

"After they were released, from out of nowhere a band of revolutionary fighters appeared on the scene, masked men wearing homemade uniforms and poorly armed. But in the hearts of the people this army of outlaws walked in the footsteps of the warriors of old. When the *Fincero's* men tried again to run his cattle on Indian land, they were driven back and word of it spread from village to village like wildfire. An uprising had begun. I resolved to walk at the side of my people. At first the fighting was not open. One only noticed that at certain times there were fewer men in the village. Distant crackles of gunfire occasionally trickled down off the forested hills like the staccato call of some strange bird. Incidents were reported; a bridge taken here, an armory robbed over there. Prisoners captured by the government forces rarely saw the light of day again.

"In response the wealthy landowners formed para-military units and joined forces with the national army. Choppers began to crisscross the skies giving the children nightmares. News filtered back to us of those who had fallen and the tally of widows in the village grew almost daily. The median age of *los guerreros* tilted from men to boys. Then an unexpected event occurred. Our rag-tag army walked in and took the state capital in broad daylight. Suddenly international attention was riveted on our remote province."

"So the good guys won for a change."

"It happens sometimes. It was at this precise moment that the superiors of my order issued me a summons to return to our mother house for a review of my mission among *los indios*. How could I leave my people in this hour of victory? Yet I was not ready to disobey Mother church.

"I took the train to Mexico City and underwent the review of my mission and though I was admonished to stay out of politics, I was granted leave to return to Chiapas."

From there the priest recounted what he found on his return--- the unspeakable horrors that had befallen the people of his and many other villages. Men and boys had been rounded up to dig an open grave and executed on the spot; infants were ripped from their mother's arms and their skulls dashed against the trunks of trees; women and young girls were raped out in the open. Those who survived the attacks were herded into churches or other communal buildings which were then set afire. Homes were burned. All the livestock were slaughtered. Fields were laid waste.

"As I picked my way over the scorched land and the charred corpses, I had a vision of Christ crucified not once but hundreds of times in the bodies of each of these poor little ones. The only way to describe what happened next is to admit that I lost my senses. I wandered into the upland forests, cursing God as I wandered through the mountains like some reckless beast, feeding on roots, berries, carrion, losing all sense of time. Then when I had lost almost all hope, I chanced upon a band of guerillas, several of whom turned out to be compatriots from my village who had joined the populist army. They were heading to a rendezvous with other contingents for an offensive to re-take the Capitol. No warrior myself, I traveled with them as their chaplain and tended to their wounds received in nighttime skirmishes."

"How long did the fighting last?"

"Daniel, this fight has been going on for five-hundred years. The second attempt on the Capitol was a failure. *La lucha* dragged on for another year with much death by bullets and by starvation. I saw fatigue and desperation eating away at the warriors' hearts. However at the bargaining table the government was forced to grant concessions to indigenous rights before the rebels would agree to lay down their arms."

"You won."

"No, in such a conflict there can be no true winners. But neither did we lose. As the rebel bands dispersed and the warriors of the

206

mountains began to return to such villages as remained, *de repente,* I was a shepherd without a flock but I clearly sensed that for me something had been completed; a new phase of my calling was about to begin.

"By clandestine means I made my way back to the mother house. I was sent here to this apostolate among our migrant workers. I came driven by necessity just as so many of my people have come to *el Norte* and though I personally have no illusions of finding a better life here, this is my village now and I am not discontent."

They fell silent for a moment.

"Are you all right, Daniel?"

"It's just too hard is all. How can there be so much evil in the world?"

"It's an age old question, Daniel. I have no answers, only my faith. I tell you this story because through it you can know the story of Alma and Sebastian. What I have seen they have seen and more."

"I didn't know."

"I hope this has not overburdened you."

"No. It helps me to know where I stand."

"Then I have succeeded."

"One more thing."

"Yes."

"I think that you are a warrior."

"Gracias."

The two men sat in the tiny cell with their eyes falling into the brief space between them as though peering into the depths of a pool, listening to the wan voices of ghosts murmured up into the waters of the living. The Priest clapped his hands once loudly as if attempting to dispel all that he had conjured.

"After Sebastian began to ride the rodeo circuit, Alma had no place to stay. I brought her to the sisters at the Saint Francis Indian mission. It is not far from here on the Wakima reservation. Last I heard they had not yet made a nun of her. The sisters give shelter to the children that I bring up there. They offer them schooling and there is a farm managed by the Indians. I will write you out the directions."

He reached for note pad and pen and as he wrote he asked Daniel. "And where do you live now?"

"The Burly ranch."

"Ah, then you work with Pedro *y* Juanito, *son buena gente, muy simpáticos.* "

"You know them?"

"Como no? They do the work of God's angels in this forsaken place. They bring food to families, medicine for sick children, supplies to our infirmary. They have repaired our community building. Whatever the need, those two are there."

"Pedro said he didn't care much for church."

"Si,si, he won't set foot in church. He refers to our *capilla* here as the church of the enslaver. Though I am a priest and Pedro denounces Mother Church, still I believe we are cut of the same cloth."

"You mean Pedro is like a priest?"

"Pedro is a burned man--- burned by the power of love. That fire has made of him a man of deep conviction who is committed to action."

The sound of the steeple bell reverberated through plank and stone into the room where they sat. The Priest emitted a drawn-out sigh, and pressed his palms onto his knees and stood to his feet.

"I'm afraid it is time for me to prepare for Mass. I will change my homily. Today I must speak of the seeds of redemption contained within romantic love."

He reached out his hand to Daniel who received the neatly folded piece of paper into his palm. The Priest placed his other hand on top of the clasped hand and shook it with vigor and warmth.

"It has done me good to speak with you, Daniel Sweeney, and it is my hope that it has done you some little good as well. May God's blessing be upon you in both your quests---for love and for land."

Daniel walked across the way to the cantina and spent the remainder of the day helping the proprietor clean up and repair the damage to his establishment. Other men from the shanty town fixed furniture and replaced window glass. By the end of the day he had made some new friends. The woman of the house invited everyone in for the evening meal with the family.

As he drove back up the mountain to the ranch, he reflected on all that the Priest had told him. The man of faith had shaken his own faith in the world. Maybe that was the secret of the Priest; his faith was not dependent on this world. Daniel felt very unsure of the ground he stood on. But his heart lightened now that he had reason to believe he would find Alma and he was determined to do so even though he could not square his memory of the young girl with the bright eyes and beautiful smile to the stories of loss and devastation he had heard from Sebastian and the Priest. How would she react to the news that her brother had been deported? How would she feel about him when she learned of his role in Sebastian's arrest? He forced himself to remember the words she had spoken to him at the well: "I wait for you." He thought again about what the Priest had said concerning matters of faith, and although much remained obscure to him, he knew that he had faith in her words.

2

As ardently as Daniel wanted to make the trip to the Indian mission, he remained faithful to his obligations at the ranch. The haying was upon them and everything counted on the timing. The grasses and legumes were at peak ripeness. All eyes kept a watch on the sky. The rains for which the ranchers had so long prayed now became the enemy. Once the grass was laid down it required two days in the field to cure and if heavy rain should fall, the crop would be a loss.

His new horses, Storm and Tempest, came in as key players. With their size they could mow down the flats faster than any other draft animals about the place. When it came time for baling, Zeke added two draft mules to the team. The 'four-up hitch' tromped along steady as a tractor, the big machine chewing up the windrows and kicking the square bales out behind. Pedro had devised a baler with the engine mounted on board the carriage so all the team had to do was tow the implement behind a cart.

As the youngest members of the crew, Daniel and Juanito were sent up to be stackers in the mow. Pedro unloaded bales off the wagons and onto the elevator as fast as he could, trying his best to bury them in hay. Dripping sweat like open faucets, the two would compete against him to keep on top of the stacking.

At the end of a hard week of long days the first cutting was in. Late afternoon found the gang driving down the road in Zeke's pickup ready to hurl themselves into the creek. Irene had packed a picnic basket with lemonade and cold beer. Zeke eased the truck into a swale and parked by the swimming hole, a place where the creek ran unhurried and wide. Irene swam in a sun dress which she put on in the shelter of a copse of trees. The men jumped in naked. Although it was the height of summer, the waters ran icy cold with the runoff from the Cascades. Untold layers of grit and dust, sweat and grime peeled off them and the penetrating chill was a healing balm to over-heated muscle and bone.

Long strands of sun rays were stringing through the cottonwood weft of branch twig and leaf by the time they finished their lunch. The men sat on a cloth spread on the ground smoking and sipping beer. Juanito idly strummed his guitar in time with the passing waters and Irene had her knitting. Pedro was absorbed in flycasting and Zeke read an agricultural bulletin. Daniel was going over in his mind the directions he had received from the Priest. He hoped those directions might lead him homeward, yet everything the Priest had told him had left him feeling older and less certain about anything in the world; the one certainty he had was that there could be no turning back.

Across the creek up on a rise, Daniel spied a group of black cows moving across the bleached hills like a herd of living shadows. The afternoon breeze had brought them out of their mid-day ruminations to graze and he could hear the sideways shearing as they pulled the grass into their mouths. A red squirrel approached the blanket's edge and he tossed it a piece of biscuit, watching it stuff the morsel into the pouch of its cheek like a cowboy putting in a plug of tobacco before scampering away. Daniel sipped the cold beer and listened to Juanito's guitar chords humming above the river song and he felt an ache in his breast so pure that it was akin to pleasure. He knew it was a wanting and a missing of her; yet in that same moment he wished he could just sit by this river in the shade with his friends for a little bit more of forever. He lay back on the blanket and watched the sky-dance of aspen leaves in the breeze.

The next day he was rolling down the lane in the green Dodge, the sun just coming up over the mountains, the air chill, the cloudless sky fiercely blue. He turned off Rattler's gulch and drove north into Garwood. It was time to go find her but there was one more loose end needed tying, something that had been gnawing like a trapped mouse in the cage of his heart.

He got directions to her place at the gas station in town, as he well knew that none of his workmates at the ranch would have obliged him. Before leaving he had rummaged through his things and found the crystal Old Joseph had given him at the moment of his departure from the camp beneath the Twin Peaks.

Charboneau's ranch was just a short stretch north of town. The truck rolled over a cattle guard and up a narrow winding side road that leveled as he climbed. The operation was more orderly than he'd imagined, with mended fences and pastured red and white cattle of fine aspect. Sun-beaten men on horseback heading out to the day's work nodded at the incoming stranger as he passed. There were several trucks parked by the equipment shed but he didn't know if one of them belonged to the tattooed man.

She was curled up in a white wicker chair out on the front porch of a tidy ranch house still in her night dress and wrapped in a blue shawl taking her morning coffee. She watched him approach with steely eyes as he warily stepped down out of the cab.

"Good Morning, stranger," she said.

"It is."

"Nice rig."

"Runs all right."

"You gonna take me for a ride?"

"Not today."

She took a sip of coffee, fighting hard not to let him see that her hand was shaking as she raised the cup to her lips. She had no makeup on and her hair was loose about her shoulders and he thought he'd never seen her look so pretty. He looked at his boot tips and then all around at the barns and outbuildings, stock and fields, anywhere but at her eyes so hardened to him.

"Nice spread."

"He knows how to do some things right."

"Your old man around?"

"Why, you looking for him?"

"No, just wondering."

"They're still holding him down at the county jail."

"What for?"

"Assaulted an officer."

"Sorry about that."

"Don't be. It's peaceful around here for a change."

He looked her in the eyes, thought he saw a hint of softening but wasn't sure what to do with that so he stuck his hands in his pockets.

"How are you doing?"

"What's it to you?"

"Well, I brought you this."

He pulled the crystal out of his pocket and putting one boot on the porch step, handed it up to her. It caught the sun, refracting a splintered rainbow into her palm just as she took it. She held it up before her face, looked at it with one eye shut and grimaced.

"Worth anything?"

"Not to sell."

She cocked her arm back and threw the crystal at him. He didn't try to catch it---just let it bounce off his chest with a thud. Then he stooped to pick it up and handed it back to her, wordlessly. She took it then. He almost smiled and turned to leave.

"You coming back?"

He stopped and stood still with his back to her, tracing his boot tip in the sand.

"You know I'm not."

"Why not?"

"I'm not the one you need."

"That's not what I asked."

He turned to face her again and lowered his hat brim as the sun crested fully over the roof of the house.

"I'm going home."

"What are you going back there for? Seems to me things been going pretty good for you right here."

"It's the right thing to do."

She nodded, looked at the crystal, folded her fist around it.

"You need not of come here."

"I know that."

"Could've been trouble."

"I ain't afraid of that."

"No, and there's your trouble."

"How do you mean?"

"Well, ain't you just the troubled kind?"

"I guess you're right. That's me, nothing but."

They looked at one another for what seemed like a long moment, a

213

softness now in both their eyes.

"Well, go if you're going then."

"You take care, Gracie."

"Get along, Daniel Sweeney."

He turned on his boot heels and strode back to the green truck. She called out to him midway and he stopped to listen but he did not turn.

"Hey, maybe you ought to quit trying to do the right thing and just get on with living your life."

He raised a hand but still did not turn and made no reply as he walked on again. She held the crystal tight against her breast bone as she watched him pull out and thread back on down the narrow lane. She felt like she was going to cry. But she didn't.

Even though he'd memorized its content by now, and it had been handled so many times in and out of his pocket till it was about to tear at the folded seams, he had the paper with the Priest's handwriting set on the bench seat. He was carrying a week's worth of provisions, a borrowed army surplus canteen from Zeke, and a new bedroll and a cast-iron fry pan Irene had given him --- and his flute.

The sign was simple, hand-lettered, the rectangular board hanging by strands of chain from the iron pipe cross-piece of a gateway. The main house was surrounded by a high concrete wall faced with field stone, creating a miniature sanctuary within. He parked the Dodge on the roadside and got out and peered through the bars of the wrought iron gate. The structure was a three-story clapboard with chimneys rising out of either end of the four-square roof. The grounds around the main house were manicured with flower beds and sculpted shrubbery; a white marble Virgin presided over a fountain set amid a tame briar of roses. To her left stood Saint Francis, his raised hands serving as a perch for a congregation of songbirds. A small stone chapel adjoined the house and a series of sheds, outbuildings and barns trailed out behind to the border of pasture and cropland. The skirts of the mountains rose up abruptly beyond the fields to peaks still capped with snow.

Two beagle dogs came bolting around the other side of the house, spotted him and started baying like sawed-off hounds. He ducked out of sight and hopped in the truck and drove further up the road.

The concrete wall soon gave way to cattle fence. Once he gauged himself to be a safe distance beyond the beagle patrol, he pulled over again. He took his flute with him and clambered over the barbed wire and set off across the fields. He noted that the pastures were bearing a healthy stand of clover and he could see dairy cows grazing in the distance. They were a breed unfamiliar to him and as they raised their heads to look at him, he could see their stout inward curving horns and it pleased him to contemplate the chocolate brown bulk of them, their white muzzles looking as though they'd been dipped in cream.

He crossed another fence into an extensive planting of potatoes where an Indian drove a single mule down the rows. The mule dragged a hiller, throwing the black dirt to cover all but the tops of the plants. The Indian stopped the mule at his approach.

"We don't allow no hunting on this land," he said. Daniel glanced back quizzically, then he saw the man's eyes fix on the scabbard. He took the flute out and blew a single note.

"I'm looking for Alma," he said.

The Indian tilted his straw hat back and wiped the sweat from his forehead with a kerchief then motioned in the direction of another field back towards the main house where a planting of sweet corn was coming into tassel.

She was knocking out weeds within the rows, the blade of her hoe slicing through the uppermost crust of soil to avoid the shallow roots of the corn. There were three other girls working rows of their own further back along the line. Busy at her task, she had yet to notice his presence thirty paces away at the end of her row. His hands were shaking and his breath came short. Would she even remember him? A part of him wanted to turn and walk away. Instead he crouched behind the stalks and took out his flute and began to play. She ceased her labor, cocked her head and stood to listen. He could see beads of sweat glistening on her brow in the afternoon light. The breeze was toward

215

him, making his song faint so that she alone could hear it; her co-workers, unaware, kept on hoeing.

He watched her as she stood and listened. He stood to his full height and she saw him and he knew by the amazement in her eyes that she recognized him. He walked toward her, stopping a pace or two before her. She was even more beautiful than he remembered. His eyes fixed on the flint arrowhead glinting in the sun, a talisman of greeting.

"Has venido por fin," she said. "I always believed you would."

"You speak English," forgetting for the moment that her parting words had been in English.

"You speak," she retorted. "It is good to hear your voice," and she laughed.

He stared at the tips of his boots and then in anguish he looked into the deep wellsprings of her eyes.

"They've taken Sebastian and it was my fault. I'm so sorry. I was only trying to find you."

"I know what happened, Padre Benito sent word. He is doing everything he can to find my brother."

He nodded in relief, breathing in the earthy air scented with corn pollen earth. He gazed beyond her, his eyes reading the near distances of the tended fields.

"Appears to be a fine farm," he said.

"They treat me well here."

Without knowing where the words or the courage to speak them came from, he beseeched her: "Come with me."

She looked into his earnest eyes and recognized what she had first seen and loved in him. She tensed and bit lightly on her lower lip.

"Wait," she said and laid her hoe on the ground. She sprinted toward the first of her companions still working on the corn rows. He could not hear what passed between them, but as he watched and waited the two girls began gesturing as if the discussion had become heated and she turned and pointed his way and the other looked at him and then nodded. Alma embraced her and ran across the black earth through the corn.

"I am ready," she said breathlessly.

"This way," he said. He felt a deep joy to have her walk beside him. He didn't notice that she shed tears, salt water drops of hope and sorrow.

He held down the fence wires to help her across and she steadied herself by placing one hand on his shoulder while hiking up her skirt with the other. He was electrified by her touch. She sniffed at his shirt and that worried him.

"What is it?"

"You smell like horses."

"Guess I could stand a bath."

"I like the smell."

He opened the door of the passenger side for her before he walked around to the driver's side. She did not ask where they were going and she did not look back when they pulled out onto the road.

They drove for awhile in silence, he watching the road, she gazing upon the passing scenery of forest and wild meadow. He felt wrapped up inside himself, unsure of what to say. He was wholly devoid of that glibness that often passes for charm. His father had been a man who spoke when he had something to say and even then he often held his tongue. His older brother was a master of that superficial oratory that eases social tension. He would have to find his own voice, pass through this liminal space where he could leave his boyhood behind.

He turned the truck heading southeast on the highway where the valley opened onto a wide sweep of rangeland, rolling hills infrequently cut by scant creeks and irrigation ditches. They passed run-out-of luck homesteads, old barns, gray, crumbling, some gone half-way back to earth. The empty cabins and outbuildings and fallen split rail fences bore silent witness to the broken dreams of pilgrims who had ventured to a new land hoping for a better life.

As he pondered the ghost ranches he thought about all he had seen and done since coming to this land and gratitude welled in his breast. For him the journey west had meant new life and with Alma sitting here beside him, everything now seemed possible.

As they approached the limits of Garwood he slowed for the passage through town. He sensed her eyes magnetically drawn to the barrio with the little white chapel at its center.

"Want me to stop?"

"No, gracias, I was just thinking of Padre Benito."

"I never met anyone like him."

"*Es un verdadero* man of God."

She looked at him, her eyes large in her delicate face and he saw that those eyes contained a depth of sorrow most often veiled by the tender mirth of her heart.

"*Es un hombre quemado,*" she continued, "he has been burned by the fire of love until nothing extra remains."

Daniel recalled that the Priest had spoken in those same terms when he described Pedro.

"I would be burned by such a flame."

"That fire is within you, Daniel."

His ears thrilled at hearing her speak his name.

"I saw it from the start---*el fuego interno*---that light is in you."

He wasn't so sure and wished he could have as much faith in himself as she did.

"How do you know?"

"When you came to us at the orchard, I watched you."

"You were watching me? I thought I was the one doing all the watching."

"That's what men always think. I watched the way your feet greet the earth when you walk. I listened to you breathe as you worked the lever of the well pump. I watched your hands receive the water from its spout. When you stepped out the door at first light, I was there in the shadows to see a thousand questions cross your face as you looked up at the sky. In such small acts I saw the burning in your soul."

"Alma," he spoke her name, "until I saw you I didn't even know I had a soul."

"Our souls recognized one another. When we stood by the well that last time, I felt as though

you knew my every thought."

218

"I only knew you were the most beautiful creature I'd ever laid eyes on."

She dropped her gaze and he looked away down the black ribbon of highway unfurling before them. He had thought to head back up to the ranch, but as they approached the turnoff to Rattler's Gulch he had a sudden change of heart and doubled back the way they had come. Still she did not question him regarding their destination.

They drove north for an hour or more and they passed the turn off to Putnam and Sons Orchards and they drove until he could see in the near distance the twin peaked mountain where Old Joseph made his camp. He drove until he recognized the truck stop where he had once stopped for gas and had breakfast. He paid the attendant for a full tank, and then parked the truck.

"You hungry?"

She shook her head no.

"Come on," he said, "let's get something to eat."

He walked around to give her a hand as she got out of the cab and his eyes drank in the length of her as she stepped down with her floral print cotton skirt cascading in lengths to the graceful attenuation of her ankles, her slender torso in a sleeveless peasant's blouse gathered at the waist, her graceful arms lean with the muscles of a field laborer. The glint of afternoon sun on silver caught his eye and he noticed that her ears were pierced, each lobe bearing a turquoise mounted in an oval of the precious metal. She smiled shyly at him as she allowed him to take her arm in escort to the door.

The woman at the register looked up with a frown.

"She can't come in here," she stated with flat finality.

"Why not?" he asked in defiance. The woman nodded at the 'No shirt-No shoes-No service' sign.

"Got no shoes on her feet."

"Daniel, let's go," Alma spoke in a small voice from behind.

"Can she come in to buy shoes?"

The woman nodded yes but her expression did not change.

Alma found a pair of boys' work boots that fit. He thought the boots looked impossibly cute on her and told her so.

"*Prefiero huaraches*, but they have none."

219

He paid for the boots and they went into the diner. A young couple with small children occupied one booth and a group of men in coveralls and visored caps held another. He sensed conversations trailing off and eyes following them as they slid onto the vinyl benches of a vacant booth. He recognized the pleasant young waitress who brought menus and poured coffee and found himself grateful for her simple civility. Alma could read some English from schooling she had with the nuns at the Mission. She chose sausage and scrambled eggs with toast.

"Chorizo con huevos revueltos y tostada" she explained to him "that is how we call it."

He ordered a double stack of pancakes with a side order of hash browns.

"And these," he asked as the waitress set the platter down, "how do you call them?"

Alma looked at the tall stack of steaming flap jacks in serious concentration.

"Pancakeys," she said and all three laughed as he realized how it could make his heart sing just to see her smile.

Daylight was on the wane. He had no plan but as they pulled out in the Dodge he felt an impulse to head north again and he watched for and found the dirt road that led to the high place where he had camped on one of his search missions. At the end of the road they parked and packed in the food, water, bedroll and the sheepskin coat he had brought from the ranch. She walked quietly beside him, even now not inquiring as to their destination.

At the top of the rise in the open meadow they turned to drink in a view of hazed blue mountain folds lifting into a golden sea of sunset sky. He spread out the bedroll and laid out the provisions on a folded paper sack. They sat side-by-side on the woolen blanket and gazed up at the water color pictures painted on the horizon. They ate sparingly, an easy silence between them. Warm air came streaming up the swale as the first stars emerged out of deepening blue. Twilight worked magic all around them, the last light of day glowing with an aura of living spirit.

The stomping and the blowing caught them by surprise and their quiet repose was transformed into alert stillness as the vanguard of the herd verified their presence. Moving into the breeze, the black-tailed deer were on their nightly foray from upland forest to field. The lead deer, a high-stepping stag, proceeded down the mountain and soon the deer were all about them. Daniel and Alma felt a sense of privilege, as if visited by magical beings. He turned his head slowly to meet the girl's gaze. The glowing intensity in her eyes startled him. How could eyes be at once so dark and mysterious and yet shine with such a clear and healthy light?

"Alma," he spoke her name in a near whisper. "May I kiss you?"

"Yes," she said and her hand clasped his as their lips met. They were beginning to intertwine the first loops in a knot that would bind their lives into one bundle. They lay back to watch the stars and as the dew began to fall, he covered them both with the sheepskin coat and he took her in his arms. They lay in silence for a long time, not sleeping, just holding onto one another; not yet engaged in the impassioned embrace of lovers, they held each other as two lost children might huddle close in a cave or hollow tree, drawing such solace and comfort from the nearness of the other that a warmth and peace protected them from the dangers of the night.

A pale light was behind the forested mountain to the east when he woke. To the west the full-bodied moon wrought golden by gathering daylight descended like a naked bather to the sea. The girl curled up next to him breathed steadily in repose. He lay still for several moments, savoring the wonder of awakening in her presence, drinking in the music of songbirds giving voice to the new day. He carefully rolled away to one side and stood up. She stirred but did not waken.

He stretched to his full height and felt the cool air open his lungs. He watched the moon slide below the silvered edge of the saw-toothed peaks and he watched her as she slept. Surely the spirits of this magic meadow had been watching over them during the night. It was alive with wildflowers, Indian paintbrush in orange and scarlet strokes, the lights of strawberry blossoms come late to these heights, the yellow and violet of brown-eyed Susan and lupine. The perfumed air assuaged his inner tension and he stood in easy vigil over her as the morning stars faded. She woke with a smile as light as a hummingbird upon her lips and sat up and yawned and rubbed at the corners of her eyes. Despite their intimacy of the night before, he found himself suddenly shy.

"I must be dreaming," she said. "For so long I have dreamed of sleeping in your arms."

He gathered up the gear and they set off downhill to the creek among the cottonwoods. They stopped to pick blackberries from a thicket until their hands were stained purple and their bellies full. At the water's edge he took off his boots and rolled up the legs of his trousers, took off his shirt and waded into the roiling shallows. She looked at him from the sliver of gravel, at once admiring his lean and muscled form and appraising the history of the encounter with the bear that had been carved into his flesh, along with the trace of ashen tattoos from his self-inflicted wounds. His skin was bronzed from hours of farm labor under the summer sun and the scars now blended into his body as if they had always been a part of it. He had grown unconscious of their existence until this moment when he felt her eyes on him.

Eres tan guapo, Daniel, as a warrior of ancient times. So proud you bear your wounds."

"It happened after I left you. I was attacked by a mother bear with cub."

De veras, has peleado con una osa?"

"I was hurt pretty bad. Probably would've died if not for my grandfather."

"He is an Indian?"

"He is. He found me and healed me and he told me stories about where I came from. Out of all that I guess gained some hope about where I might go."

"Where might you go Daniel?"

"Home. Back to my land, if you'll come with me."

"I will come."

She pulled off her boots, hiked up her skirts and jumped in the creek and he watched as she splashed water on her face and arms. He took a step closer and reached out his hands as she turned to face him and they stood in the middle of the stream clasping hands.

"My grandfather told me how the people used to marry. He said the couple stood before the tribe holding one another's hands and they looked into each other's eyes and the man said to the woman, you shall be my wife, and the woman said..."

She held up a finger to his lips to silence him and finished the line: "And the woman said to the man, you shall be for me a husband. You and I, Daniel, we have the creek, the sky, and the trees as our witness. Everything I had in life was taken from me; my family, my land, my country. But you give yourself to me. I will go with you."

For all the depths of her sorrow, her face was radiant and he did not attempt to shield his heart from the truth and purity of her expression but opened himself to the promise of renewal he saw there; he wrapped his arms around her. The top of her head just reached the underside of his chin and he was surprised in one who seemed so delicate at the strength of her arms as she hugged him tightly. As they pressed their bodies close he felt a surge of desire. He released her and stepped back. She whirled around and splashed him, then leapt up on the shore and danced among the boles of the cottonwoods like a woodland nymph.

They spent three days together on the mountain. They explored the wild meadowlands and the deep forest. Still in innocence, they shared shy caresses and kisses and spent the days like children in the garden at rest and at play and for the moment free. Only when their provisions ran low did they face return.

On the morning of their last day, they hiked to the height of the meadow and Daniel could hardly get enough of the snow capped summits striking a jagged line across the horizon, volcanoes of the Pacific rim still alive and growing in the clash of tectonic plates, searing and primal to one used to the tame and rounded knobs of the northern Appalachians.

And then it was time to go. The truck turned over at the push of the starter and he was thankful for its reliability. As they pulled out he spoke a silent goodbye to the meadows and the forests of this place of unexpected gifts.

"I want to head back to the Burly's ranch where I've been working. Tie up loose ends."

He looked over at her expectantly.

"Si vámonos," was her quick reply.

The men were working in the field when the Dodge rolled up the drive. Zeke was driving a mule team on a riding cultivator through the corn and, absorbed in checking the mules' progress along the row paths, he did not notice the truck. Daniel pulled in by the shop and Pedro emerged from his cavern of grease and iron.

"Hola compañero, que tal?" he called, and then his eyes adjusted to the sunlight and fell upon the girl.

"Dios mio, que haces aquí hijita?" he inquired with familiar affection.

"Estoy con Daniel ahora."

"Que bueno," he sanctioned her saying. He dropped his welding gloves and removed his work apron and as she stepped out of the truck he embraced her and then he shook Daniel's hand.

"Que bueno," he said again with a silver-toothed smile. "I see you inside, heh?"

He put on his gear and turned to be swallowed by the glowering forge once more.

Daniel guided Alma towards the bunkhouse where he could see Irene beneath a straw hat hoeing lettuce in the kitchen garden.

"Pleased to meet you darling," Irene declared. "Come inside. I'll fix you something to eat."

Just then all turned to a hilarious whoop from someone coming up the drive. It was Juanito in saddle on the little Appaloosa, Friend. They came at a brisk trot. The freckled horse had prospered on spring pasture, no longer all sticks for legs, his neck and rump had filled out, giving a glimpse of the solid horse he would become.

"I put him under saddle while you were gone. I hope you don't mind."

"If it's you starting him, I know it's done right."

"I used the hackamore so as not to harden his mouth. He is gentle of heart. He will be a horse to make a man proud."

224

Juanito spoke with enthusiasm about the horse. Then he turned to the girl.

"*Eres la hermana de Sebastian, verdad?* " he asked.

"Si," she confirmed

That evening all gathered around a table overflowing with the bounty of the land. In the center a vase spilled over with fresh-cut flowers surrounded by heaping bowls of hard-boiled eggs, tossed salad and cooked vegetables, fresh cheese, hot biscuits and a platter of steak. Even with a guest among them the men ate in silence, forking in mouthfuls as if they had just been liberated from famine.

"*Bienvenida,*" Zeke finally spoke gently to the girl, a rare softness covering his eyes like a veil. "Glad to have you with us."

"*Gracias,* Senõr Zeke. It makes me happy to be here."

"Consider yourself among family now; *nuestra casa* is your *casa,* eh? "

Zeke took a sip of cold beer from a bottle and swished it round his mouth like he'd never tasted beer before and then he spoke again.

"You two lovebirds fixing to get hitched'?"

He winked at Daniel who smiled bashfully at the girl.

"Why Zeke, they're still so young!" exclaimed Irene.

"How old are you, honey?" Zeke asked Alma directly.

"*Pues, enero era la fecha de mi quinceanera.* "

"Fifteen years old. You see, she's only a child," said Irene.

"In our culture she is already a woman," said Pedro.

"We married ourselves," said Daniel

Everyone at the table raised their eyebrows but only Zeke was not at a loss for words.

"Surely it will require every ounce of fortitude you can muster for you two innocents to survive all the ignorance and prejudice of this country. It'll be about as easy as swimming through stone. But if ever two young people were up to the challenge, it's you. Blessings upon you."

Daniel reached under the table and squeezed the girl's hand and he told them all then that he aimed to return to the farm in Vermont where his father's bones were buried.

Everyone at the table was quiet for a moment. Then the unflappable Zeke started up again. "Now that's an Indian talking if ever I heard one," he said as he opened up a second cold sweating bottle.

Daniel's plan was taking shape but he wanted to have enough money in his billfold before taking to the road, so for the moment he threw himself back into the work of the place. Alma found plenty to do helping out with ranch chores, the garden, and the household. Irene was delighted to have her company. High summer was upon them and the days fell into a sun-drenched sameness. The livestock took refuge under the tall pines, putting their faces into each other's tails in an effort to repel the biting flies. The solstice light lingered into the borderland of night. Solar energy flared in the limbs of the working men and the food that the women served was abundant with its vibration. Oblivious to fleeting dreams, turning shoulders to labor like oxen to yoke, they were in the rhythm of the season, each day ready for the early dawn as each day turned the wheel of their world toward peak ripeness. Still, Daniel felt a restless urgency tugging at his heart.

3

Daniel downed a cup of coffee with the rising sun and before the dew was off the fields, he drove to town. He came bombing back up the drive at midday as the men were straggling in from the fields. The truck was hauling a stock trailer and there was a passenger in the cab. The girl was descending the steps of the bunkhouse porch and when the passenger climbed out of the truck she let out a muffled cry. The basket of fresh-washed linens she was carrying fell to the ground as she flung her hand to cover her mouth and ran toward the truck. The passenger, wearing a big black hat that obscured his features, stepped out quickly. He looked up at the start of her cry from underneath the brim of his hat and she stopped short in her tracks, crestfallen. He was not the one she had been hoping for. She turned to retrieve the laundry.

Pedro and Juanito came and stood alongside Daniel, his face turned towards the fields to hide his pained expression.

"*Quién es?*" inquired Juanito.

"Fella looking for work," he replied.

"*Pobrecita,* she was thinking it was her brother," said Pedro.

"Him gone missing is just about killing her."

"*No te desesperas.* He'll make it."

Zeke caught up with them, grit and sweat running brown rivers along the vast geography of his body.

"Fine looking trailer. Guess this means you'll be leaving us soon?"

"Afraid so," he said, looking now at the pastures where the mules stood in a group dozing in the shade of a ponderosa giant.

"We'll sure enough miss you around here but it seems you've set your heart on heading back home."

"I don't even know if I have one to return to. My brother might have gone and sold it. All I know is I got to go back."

"What will you do if your land has been sold?"

"I'll get it back somehow. Buy it back. Fight for it. Whatever it takes."

"Just remember, you and the little lady have a home right here if and when you need one."

227

"I appreciate it."

"Don't be too proud to ask if you could use some help, son. We're your family."

Daniel met the gaze of the old rancher, looking gratefully into the flinty sparks that shot out of the weather-scarred mass of flesh that served for a face.

"Where'd you find him?" Zeke asked, gesturing with his thumb.

"His name is Carlos. He was walking up the road with nothing but an old guitar strapped on his back. Said the spread he was working at got raided by Federal agents."

"Well, with you fixing on leaving he comes at a good time."

"Next time *los federales* come around he can hide inside that hat," Pedro laughed.

The men proceeded to greet the newcomer. Then all went inside to eat the meal Irene had prepared with the help of her new girlfriend.

The air was cooling and the light fading as Daniel leaned on the rails of a fence looking over the horses with the girl by his side. The bay mare he'd been riding was showing signs of heat. Though gelded, Pedro's Arabian was demonstrating keen interest. He followed her like a shadow and drove off any interloper who drew near, striking with fore hooves, neck arched, tail held high. The mare was equally feisty. Every time the gelding approached she would stamp her feet, squeal and whirl her hind quarters around threatening to kick. They carried on, well matched adversaries in the courtship dance.

"The gelding was cut late in life, no?" inquired Alma.

"Yup, still much of the stallion in him."

Alma continued to observe the defiant love games of the mare and to study her savage lines.

"*La yegua se comporta como una bruja.* She has the flea-bitten horse under her spell."

"What does the name mean?"

"*La bruja* is the witch."

"*Bruja*", he repeated the appellation. "That horse has been waiting on a name."

He slipped his hand into hers and squeezed it. She left to return to the bunkhouse, but he stayed behind to study the horses as night enfolded him in its darkness. He felt then that if he were struck dead by lightning he would die content, that so far all had happened as it should and his passing would not be an unhappy end. Yet a deep anxiety nagged at him for what lay ahead, about the choices he was making.

Later that evening everyone gathered on the front porch. A lantern hung from a rafter casting a benevolent glow and in the circle of that light Juanito and the new man Carlos picked and strummed their guitars, Daniel played the flute and Alma sang. No gathering seemed more like what a family ought to be than this, Daniel thought.

Dawn came, a pale sliver, a lost thought in the vast mind of sky etching a ragged silhouette of spruce tips on the mountain. Daniel was first up. He stoked the cook stove and filled the kettle then went outside to liberate Irene's chickens from the coop. They popped out of the cut-out door like sailors too long at sea and swarmed about him as he doled out corn like a god letting manna fall.

Next he went to the well, pumping it until it croaked and sighed and filled pails with the cool water for the hogs; then he returned to the kitchen for slops. The hog hunger bordered on naked passion as they squealed in anticipation, clambering over one another to be first at the trough.

When he went back to the kitchen Alma and Irene were both up and the aroma of fresh coffee filled the air. Yellow tortillas were sizzling in a smattering of oil, beans soaked overnight were boiling, bacon was frying. Irene nodded thanks to him as he fetched a milk pail from a shelf above the sink. The other men were just stirring in their bunks as he headed out the door.

The brown cow was waiting at the door of the barn and as soon as he slid the door open along its suspended track she walked straight to her stanchion and placed her head through the irons. He fastened the top latch of the stanchion and fetched hay and grain for her and she stretched her long neck to reach the feed. He began the rhythmical splashing, the sound of the milk jet softening as the depth in the pail rose. He hummed a tune as he milked. The rising sun came streaming in slim shafts between cracks in the siding; motes danced like tiny solar systems.

After breakfast they had cattle to move. The new man, Carlos, saddled an idle horse to join in the task. He sat the horse well. The men discovered a breach in the fence line where the cattle had spilled over onto timber company land. A few of the cows panicked and broke ranks and they had to ride up some steep ground among the trees to flush them out and bring them down safely. Daniel was impressed at how well the new fellow was able to keep his seat as they herded the animals over the rough terrain. Once the cows were secured, Carlos and Juanito finished out the morning at fence repair while Daniel and Pedro shifted the cattle to an adjacent paddock.

Later that morning Daniel brought the Dodge into the shop. Pedro had written out a checklist for him and he went over each item in detail. With the aid of his mentor he was getting a handle on the intricacies of the combustion engine. The truck had a long haul ahead of it and he aimed to apply preventive medicine.

The days rolled swiftly by shortened by the sun's elliptical decline. With Carlos serving as an extra hand they finished the cultivation of field crops in short order. Zeke drove to town mid-week and returned with a load of cedar shakes. All the men climbed a ladder to the roof of the bunkhouse and began ripping the old rotted ones off with hammer-claws and crowbars. Irene and Alma picked up the discards and heaped them onto a flat bed wagon to be hauled to a burn pile. The task brought everyone together and the work went easy. Daniel felt bittersweet pangs; he was already missing his friends as he realized this would be the last time the ranch crew would work together as a team.

The day of departure arrived. He and the girl packed the Dodge with such gear as they possessed and provisions provided by Irene. He secured the stock trailer onto the ball hitch and loaded up Storm and Tempest and Friend. Everyone then gathered by the truck for their good-byes except for Zeke. They made conversation, stilted by his unexpected absence. Shortly he came tromping round from the back of the barn leading the bay mustang, *la Bruja,* outfitted with a hand-tooled saddle and carrying a thirty-aught-six Remington in his free hand, the same rifle that Daniel had chosen when he rode out to encounter the phantom wolf.

"Any sensible man requires a sound horse and a good rifle," Zeke said as he placed the reins and the rifle in Daniel's hands.

"I might've given you a mule but I didn't have any to spare, least ways none I could bear to part with," he added with a wink.

"Zeke, this is too much!" Daniel protested.

"I ain't giving you nothing you don't deserve," the old rancher said and looked back at him sideways with a hint of menace. Daniel studied the rifle a moment and then handed it to Alma, who held it awkwardly as a thing alien to her. He stepped forward and embraced Zeke, stretching his arms around the extensive girth as if he were paying homage to some ancient and holy tree. Zeke took a step back and looked kindly on him.

"You've done well for yourself here and you've made us all proud. You're a natural horseman. Always remember, as far as horses and mules are concerned, you and I are no better than predatory monkeys. It is our task to improve upon this basic assumption."

"Some are more monkey than others," said Pedro as he nudged his brother in the ribs with an elbow.

Zeke ignored their joking and carried on, "We're going to miss you around here, Daniel, but it's good what you're choosing, returning to your daddy's land. Don't forget everything I've told you. My ideas will still be around a hundred and fifty years from now. They are forged out of three-quarter-inch iron."

Irene could not contain herself a moment longer. "Hush now, Ezekial, the young people are ready to move on."

"I won't forget any of this," Daniel made a sweeping gesture with his hand to take in all that surrounded him. "Not a word that was spoken, not a piece of what each one of you has given me."

He let the lead rope fall to the ground, trusting the mare to stand. Then he went around the circle and embraced each of them in turn. When he stood before Pedro his eyes were met with a face of burning inquiry.

231

"You will take care of her?"

"I will love her as I love my own soul," Daniel responded. The weathered *vaquero* held his gaze and then nodded curtly.

"*Bueno,* it has been an honor to know you" he said and the two men placed their arms around one another's shoulders in a formal embrace. Next it was Alma's turn to say goodbye and as he had done, she embraced them all. Lastly she stood with Irene holding her in her arms. Alma wrapped her arms fervently around the older woman and bent her face to the earth and fought back her tears. And then they were parted.

"*Buena suerte.* "

"Come back to visit"

"Don't forget to write."

"*Vaya con Dios.* "

The words trailed on behind them, the Dodge rolled out and down the lane, the tires crackling over the dry gravel. Daniel leaned on the horn and watched them all waving in the rearview mirror till the truck glided around the first bend and they were out of sight. The collie dogs chased them downhill, barking at their wheels for a quarter-mile until they reached the gate. Then the dogs did an about-face and trotted back up to the ranch.

They threaded the needles' eye of the limestone cliffs, the truck hurtling through that natural gate, then came bursting out of blue shadow onto the yellow-lit hard pack road on the open side. The shadow of a raven passed over low as they made the turn off Rattler's Gulch.

He reached across the bench and grasped her hand. She squeezed his hand back and her tears turned into uncontrollable sobs.

"What is it?" he asked in alarm at the depth of her distress.

"I will never see my brother again."

He was taken aback at the force of her outburst. He felt as if he himself had delivered her a wound. A grievous weight of responsibility landed on his shoulders. "Alma, it doesn't have to be that way. We'll see him again. Who knows maybe some day he can come work with us on the farm."

"No, Daniel," gaining control of herself, she spoke with finality. "I know it in my bones. I will never see my brother again."

Helpless in the face of her grief, he drove relentlessly on.

At length she spoke again and her voice was composed.

"We always knew we would have to part. When I went to the mission he did not visit often. I think he was making ready for this day. He and I are all that was left of the world from which we were torn. Now that tie is broken."

"I had a falling out with my brother, but you love yours so."

"Do you not still love your brother?"

"I suppose I do. It depends."

"Does true love have conditions?"

"If he sold our land I won't forgive him."

"Yes you will."

"You think so? Why should I?""

"Because he is your brother."

"It's not the same between me and him as it is between you and Sebastian.

"You might be surprised."

"I need you, Alma. I only hope we are doing the right thing."

"What do you mean?'"

"Us leaving the ranch, me taking you away from here."

"*No te preocupes mi amor*, this is what I have chosen. It is what every woman must choose if she desires to give herself to a man. I do not grieve for myself. I grieve for Sebastian."

"He's one tough character."

"That is the face he shows to the world. Sometimes in this strange land he loses himself in the need to prove his worth. All that he does is really an attempt to defend our culture and our people. My brother follows the way of Techuaman, the last great warrior who led the people in revolt against the Spanish invaders. Do you know of the quetzal bird, Daniel?"

He shook his head to say that he did not.

"The quetzal bird is a creature of rare beauty. It lights up the forest with its tail feathers like a sickle of turquoise longer than my arms" and with that she extended the elegant arms of a dancer.

233

"It happened while Techuaman lay dying on the battlefield. He believed the conquistador of the red beard and white horse to be one single creature, so he plunged his lance into the breast of the horse. The soldier hacked him down with his sword and as he lay dying a quetzal landed on his breast. The quetzal was his *Nagual*, his ally in the spirit world. The breast of the bird was stained crimson in his blood. Every quetzal bears the marks of that wound to this day. *Así es con mi hermano*, he was born into this world bearing such wounds."

They drove past the turn off to the township of Garwood and took the cutoff east to begin the long haul that would take them across the dry land coulees of the Columbia Basin following the Snake River to the Rocky Mountains. They coasted through the lower gates of the verdant valley of the Wakima, the valley which nestled the orchard where they first met and the memories of all they had thus far shared. The magical and mysterious ache of their first encounter returned to them as they left that geography behind.

"I remember the first time I saw you," she spoke to him. As she spoke he could not have told whether she spoke now in English or Spanish or in some proto-symbolic utterance common to their ancestors. Her words became like the clear waters of a mountain stream and he no longer had a sense of hearing them but of drinking them, absorbing them like a thirsty plant in drought soil.

"You were different from others who came. No one could pin you down. I knew at once that you were not occupied with the things that captivate most boys. I could see sparks in your eyes, sparks that kindled fires in my soul."

"You were the one with all the tinder. It was the dream of seeing you again that kept me going, kept me alive even."

"Most men live their lives in refusal of dreams. But you *live* your dreams. Sebastian sensed that, too. I think that is why he feared you. You were all that he was attempting to deny in himself because it did not fit with Gringo culture."

Daniel could only shake his head upon hearing her words.

"Alma, I don't recognize myself in your words but they warm my heart."

"Eso no me importa, Daniel. You may not think such thoughts but I am certain that you know them in your soul. You are one of the chosen whose task is to restore the ancient ways."

"How do you know these things?" he asked her as he stretched and strained to grasp at the meaning of her words.

"I listened to the elders of my village. Many of them cannot read or write and have never traveled farther than to the market in the next town but their vision reached into the heart of Heaven."

"You really think I'm like your brother? Seems like we were at odds right from the start."

"Everything he had was taken from him, *su tierra y su cultura y hasta su propria identidad.* Do you know how that feels?"

"I do."

They both fell silent and for the first time he felt that she understood his silence and that she could exist in that silence with him, that it no longer set them apart.

He gazed into his rearview mirror and spied a glimpse of the receding volcanoes of the Cascades, the mountain fastness where the old man of the forest made his home. He felt the strong presence of his grandfather inexplicably near him. He felt an urge to turn around to go see him one more time. But he resisted it. He sensed the urge itself to be a resistance to the seeking of his own destiny. He held fast to the steering wheel and kept rolling on as the black road rose straight as a speeding arrow to meet the next rise of mountains.

The travelers began to place masses of continent between themselves and all the people, places and events that had brought them together. From here on for Alma all would be resolutely new and untried. For Daniel the road was like a river---he was a salmon following the primal urge to swim upstream to its place of origin. The runaway was coming home.

They soon established a rhythm to their travel. They held to the state highways and they parked at truck stops by night and unloaded the horses and grained and watered them and staked them out on grass at the fringes of the tarmac. The girl prepared meals over a cook fire while he refueled and serviced the truck and filled a reserve tank of water for the stock. Their lives were reduced to a litany of sparse routine dictated by the demands of keeping the livestock, the vehicles and their own selves fit to withstand the rigors of the road. They slept out in their clothes side by side, under covers, beneath the stars and they slept yet chastely as sister and brother, a sleep short, swift and deep. They rose early to be back on the road with the rising sun.

They crossed out of Idaho into Montana by way of Lolo Pass and then through the mining and logging and cattle towns of the eastern slopes of the Rockies and across the Great Divide

Five days out they had made the crossing of the great plains of Montana and passed through the Little Big Horn country of eastern Wyoming. As the morning wore on they drove into a strange country. To the east serrated mountains arose out of rolling plains and range land. Thick forested and well watered, the peaks looked like dark islands rising out of a pale sea of grass. Everything in that open country seemed to point and be drawn toward those hills as if they possessed some vast magnetic power. As the road wound through that island in the plains, Daniel caught echoes and tattered fragments of ancient songs whispering around the secret corners of his mind. He remembered then of hearing Old Joseph and his friends speak of this place---the sacred Black Hills of the Lakota.

They camped that night by a hot spring and eased their travel weary bones into the bubbling sulphur waters. After they had taken their supper Alma rose from the fire and with a paper sack in hand she began to gather herbs on the nearby hillside. Daniel went to the bed of the truck and rummaged through his belongings to find the deer hide medicine pouch given to him by Marguerite Moonhawk. He helped her fill the pouch with sage and then they returned to camp under the most brilliant canopy of stars he could ever remember seeing.

The following day the towering black spires receded behind them and they came into the weird and tortured formations of the badlands. He drove as if in a dream as the road followed twisted scapes and descended into bone dry gulches that seemed to challenge life itself by their lunar starkness. The varying colors of exposed strata wove and wound over egg shapes and arches; willow and juniper sprouted from the millennial-paced pools of erosion. In the rampant tumult of heaved and worn hills, his sense of size and dimension were skewed, his perspective sundered. He felt he would be lost save for the white lines painted on the black road, cutting its diamantine causeway through the ever shifting chaos of the nightmarish landscape.

At last the ribbon of road wound up and out to a barren rangeland and he was relieved and calmed by its flat normality. Nothing but raw umber hills under a cerulean sky for a hundred miles or more. They passed a sign announcing their entrance into 'Indian Country', the birthplace of famous chiefs and territory of the sovereign Oglala nation. As dusk was settling they rolled into Pine Ridge. While still on the outskirts they passed ramshackle cabins and run-down mobile homes. He noted the absence of electric lines and the outdoor privy and cistern in every yard. He saw bony horses and even hungrier looking cattle crowding around out-buildings for water and shade. The first building that came into view as they approached town was a bar, then a grocery store, a post office, a school and a church. He saw groups of men assembled outside the store as if convened for a meeting, young and old together, passing what he knew to be open bottles in paper sacks. As they were leaving town a band of barefoot children, half naked in soiled clothes, crossed the road in front of them clutching makeshift toys.

He felt there must be more to these bearings than the stark misery that first struck the eye---the heaps of burnt-out cars, the pot-holed road, the dilapidated government housing, the empty shells of down-trodden people shuffling along the streets---everywhere signs of a heart-rotting idleness and decay.

"This is the place she came from," he mused to himself. "This is the place he brought her after her mother died and she was no older than I am now."

His eyes searched the bleached swales of the outlying hills dotted with stands of lodgepole pines keeping watch over the rangeland like bands of posted sentries ossified in their long vigil over that vast waste. Surely there must be something hidden there still abiding in that measureless and mysterious land outlying the town, a healing medicine the old one had imbibed, some ancient quality still alive and carried within as a medicine of the heart. But this was not his place. He knew it as he knew his own name. To acknowledge that fact was not a betrayal of his blood. Maybe it had not been hers either. Maybe she had never found her place in this world. He was returning to the place where he now knew he belonged and he believed that somehow that was the greatest good he had to offer.

They were out on the plains now with nothing to see, nothing to hear but the sound of their own wheels on the tarmac, nothing to break the monotony of grassland unrolling beneath an endless sky. The waters of the Missouri were in their late summer idle when they crossed and began to leave the rangeland of the Dakotas behind and head into farm country. Tall grass prairie turned over to wheat and corn, alfalfa and soy. They passed vast expanses of cultivated acreage, punctuated by islands of farmhouse and barn and silo tucked into small copses of trees, and the long straight lines of windbreaks marking the divide between fields. Daniel took note of which crops were sown and he enjoyed catching glimpses of farmers at work, creeping across the breadth of the land like ants in their tractors of red, blue and green.

Soon after they crossed the Minnesota state line Daniel began looking for a place to camp for the night. He crossed the highway and ventured a short distance up a side road and pulled in near a thicket of willows that stood by a creek bordering a fenced pasture. They watered the horses and then tethered them off a stretch of fence line so that each had a spit of grass to graze for the night. Next Daniel lifted the hood to check and replace the fluids in the truck and later he came in to camp under a load of dry wood collected from broken and discarded fence posts, scrub brush and fallen branch. As night fell they sat around a small blaze sopping up platefuls of chili with hot biscuits and then early to sleep to ready themselves for another long day of travel.

When he awoke at first light he looked across the smoldering campfire out onto an empty stretch of pasture broken only by a straggling wind break and a line of locust fence posts marching off into the distance like a defile of war torn infantrymen marching homeward. They fed and watered the horses and loaded them on the trailer. The wide bowl of farmland was filled to the brim with liquid golden light pouring in over its easternmost edge. Bold purple shadows lengthened out and swiftly fled. Alma was in the cab waiting as he checked the campfire to make sure the embers were squelched.

They drove into an orange hazed sun which drew into a sharp edged disc as it rose. They traveled a short distance in silence before she spoke.

"Pull over, Daniel. You look tired."

"I don't want to stop. We're making good time."

"Pull over and switch seats. Do you not know that I can drive?"

"Where did you learn?"

"De vez en cuando en los lugares where we worked. Sebastian taught me. I hauled produce and cattle. I drove the two-ton behind a corn chopper before we went to pick the apples."

"Say no more!"

He pulled over and they switched places. He made an earnest effort not to watch too closely or appear nervous as she slipped in the clutch and put the engine into gear. She gripped the wheel till her knuckles turned white and she could just barely see over the dash.

"Hold on a minute," he said.

"*Mande?*" she shifted into neutral and pulled on the hand brake as he went around back and grabbed two saddle blankets from the trailer.

"Here, sit on these."

"*Ándale pues*, much better."

With the elevated seat she could see the road ahead. She worked the clutch and shifted smoothly and they both relaxed as the truck accelerated. He leaned back and drank in the passing vistas. In another moment he was fast asleep.

Late afternoon of the following day they were in the Blue Mountain country of Pennsylvania, driving east along the same rode he had ridden his brother's horse west over a year and a half ago. He was behind the wheel again and Alma was asleep beside him with her head resting on his shoulder. He recognized features of the landscape that reminded him of the hill farms of his home town. His sense of purpose was constant, but he could not deny his anxiety rising at all the uncertainties they would soon come face to face with. He glanced over at Alma sleeping and on the bench seat by the passenger door next to her he saw his father sitting with the rosewood cane between his knees and his narrow brimmed hat upon his lap. The felt hat was brushed down and his suit looked clean and pressed and even his shoes were black and shiny.

"Your town clothes don't look much worse for the wear."

"The other side has its benefits."

"I can hardly wait."

"Nice truck, you've done well for yourself, son."

"Thanks, she's running fine."

"Why didn't you stay? Seems like things were going well for you out there."

"I have a plan."

"Plans can be changed. It's not too late, you could turn around right now and go back to that ranch."

"Dammit, what's with you? You're the one has been telling me all along I should go home."

"Don't curse, son."

"Excuse me, but I just don't get it."

"I suppose you could call me the Devil's advocate."

"You really think I should turn around?"

"I think you should stop asking me and start listening to your own heart. Seems like a nice gal you've got here with you."

"She is."

"Reminds me a lot of your mother."

"That must've been so hard on you when she passed away."

"The hardest part is wondering about all the things I might've done different if I'd only known how soon she would be taken. Do you love her, son?"

"I do, Dad."

"Hold on to that, it's the only thing that lasts forever."

"All right."

"So, you're finally coming home?"

"I am."

240

"What will you do if Tommy has sold the farm?"

"I don't know, take it back at gunpoint."

"You know better."

"Then I'll find work and earn enough to buy it back."

"Your brother is going through some changes. I think he is still trying to find his own heart."

"Trying to find out if he has one."

"Still mad, huh?"

"I guess."

"Anything else you want to know?"

"Like what?"

"News of Gloria and the twins, maybe?"

"Sure, I miss her…them."

"She misses you. Okay, you can let me out at the next crossroads. I'm heading south from here."

"Where are you going?"

"I'm going to see the coal mines where your grandfather Aidan got his first job after coming to America."

"What for?"

"If you want to know where you're going, you've got to know where you come from."

"I know what you mean."

"Daniel, you're a fine son and I'm glad that you're returning to the land."

"Thanks, Dad."

"You take care, son. Most likely I'll see you back at the farm."

"Will you?"

"With any luck we'll all be together again soon."

His father put on his hat and took up his cane and stepped out.

Alma woke up as he put the truck in gear and pulled back out on the road.

"Who were you talking to?"

"Huh? No one, just talking to myself."

PART SIX

1

Stoneford Village, Vermont

It took them twelve days to complete the crossing. His heart nearly burst when he saw the tectonic seam of the Connecticut River, the architect of the upper valley where he was born and raised. The road wound along the river's edge, sporadically crisscrossing through the titanic pillars upholding the overpasses of the new super highway. They circled the round-shouldered flanks of Mount Ascutney where in the narrow bottom lands bordered by the bluffs of the knobby hills, farmers were combining small grains or bringing in the rowan. He glimpsed the tall steeple of the church jutting above the white pines before the truck rounded the bend onto the main street of the village.

"Is that *la Iglesia Católica?*"

"No, the Catholic one's a stone church down that side street by the mill. I'll take you there sometime if you like."

"I'd like that."

He was struck by how small the place had become, as if the entire community had shrunk down a notch in his absence. He swung the truck and trailer to curbside and parked in front of the general store. In his riding boots, blue jeans, the rodeo belt buckle and the broad-brimmed hat, he looked like a cowboy come to town off the range. He saw townspeople he had known all his life who only glanced curiously his way and gave no sign of recognition. He moved stiffly after days in the truck. They climbed the granite steps to the plate-glass doors of the store and the copper cow bell attached to the inside frame rang as he pushed the door open.

"Afternoon, Mister Wilder," he addressed the frail but smartly-dressed merchant standing behind the counter. Old Mister Wilder peered at him, squinting over the spectacles perched low on the bridge of his prominent nose.

"Danny Sweeney, is that you, son?"

242

"Yessir, last time I checked."

"By Jesus, it is, how've you been?"

"Still living."

"Goodness, what a surprise to see you! Me and the missus, we were so sorry to hear about the...uh...troubles that befell your family. Your father has been sorely missed in the village."

Daniel responded by looking down to his own boot tips.

"Where've you been, son?"

"Out west."

"Won't your brother be happy to see you."

"Hope so."

An awkward silence fell between them and he could sense Alma fidgeting beside him.

"This is my wife, Alma."

Wilder nodded nervously to the girl, somewhat beside himself but making a gallant effort to remain composed.

"Young lady," he managed to stammer by way of greeting.

"Guess we'll be needing some supplies."

It struck the proprietor then, except for the bronze cast of his skin, how much the boy had come to look and sound like the deceased father. The girl turned to examine the lady's hats perched like exotic birds atop a rack. Dresses elegant as colorful waterfalls hung on wooden hangers beneath the hats. Daniel saw her looking.

"One day, when our farm prospers, I'll buy you fancy hats and dresses."

"Oh, I don't need such things. It diverts me to look at them."

"One day, Alma."

Wilder turned his mind to the practical matters at hand and took up a pad and pencil.

"What will you be needing today then, Danny?"

"Hmmm...let's see...about a half-gallon of cooking oil, a pound each of salt, sugar, butter and coffee, twenty pounds each of flour, rice and dry beans...anything else, Alma"

"Cornmeal."

As the merchant set about measuring and sacking the goods, Daniel's eyes drifted over to the shelves with the large jars of penny candy. The first wave of nostalgia hit then. He could see Tommy and himself standing there as boys, looking with wonder at the variety of sweets in the glass jars. Each boy stood with a nickel in his fist, and a brown paper bag, the grimace of a difficult choice on his face. One penny counted for five of each kind, five cents amounted to a fortune in treats for a child. The old man is there at the counter with his purchases, lanky in his faded overalls, the cap pushed back on his head, flannel work shirt rolled up at the sleeves. He and Mister Wilder chat about the weather and the crops, weddings and births, about anything and everything except for the recent burial of his young Indian wife while he waits patiently for the boys to make their decisions.

"Will that be all, Danny?"

He looked up startled out of his reverie.

"Yes sir...ah, hang on a minute."

He reached into his pocket and dug out a quarter. He placed the coin on the counter and escorted Alma over to the shelves of candy and together they filled a paper sack with treats.

"All set," he said, back at the counter.

"Shall I put that on your account?"

"We still have one?"

"Sure do."

"I'll pay cash."

With Wilder's help they managed to carry all the goods to the pickup in one trip.

The merchant cracked a wry smile. "Full load of horses," he commented, nodding to the trailer.

"Yes it is."

"You plan on doing some farming?"

"That's my aim."

"Well, it's good to see you back here. Lots of young people leave nowadays. Not so many return."

"Thank you, sir. It's good to be back."

They got into the truck and proceeded down the main street and passed the barber shop with the red and white pole out front, and the bank, the post office and the all-volunteer fire station. They drove around the central green and on the far end they passed the realty firm where he supposed his brother had taken the position he had been so eager to get licensed for.

His hands on the wheel went clammy when he spied the sheriff's patrol car. The black and white was parked facing them on the opposite curb of the wide street. The chief officer was sitting in the driver's seat reading the morning paper and his deputy was just edging his way through the door of a diner with two coffees to go. The girl wrapped her arms tight around herself and sunk low in her seat, staring wild-eyed like a frightened animal. Daniel tried to maintain a casual aspect as they rolled on by, noting that the lawman was examining their out-of-state plates. He drove the last stretch out of the village center with one eye vigilant on the rearview mirror.

"Don't appear to be following," he breathed a sigh.

As they neared the outskirts of the village, the road began to climb away from the Connecticut and into the uplands. He glanced at his mirror and saw that the patrol car was riding right behind them.

"Damn."

"*Qué te pasa?*"

"Sheriff's tailing us."

The road took them past a development of residential homes that had sprung up like a malignant strain of giant mushroom in what used to be a cow pasture. His brother had purchased a new home in that location shortly before Daniel had run away. He made the turn onto the paved drive and he shifted the truck to low gear as the patrol car drove on by.

"Don't worry, they must not have been following us."

"*Espero que no.*"

He couldn't remember exactly which of the dozen or so salt box homes was Tommy's. To him they all looked alike. Then he spotted the blue pick-up and the gray Rambler parked in the drive of a single story ranch house with a brick patio and two-car garage. The tidy house had a picture window and a TV aerial on the asphalt roof. He could see the twin's toys scattered around the half-acre lawn, two of everything; miniature construction vehicles in a sand box, tricycles, balls and bats. The bay door to the garage was open and the toys of an older boy were in evidence too---a lawnmower, a chainsaw, and a motorbike. He guessed they must be inside having dinner and he closed his mind to the scene and kept his eyes on the road. What did his brother's family have to do with him? His sole mission was to reclaim what he had left. He shifted up and pulled back out onto the main road.

As the road wound on up into the hills, he noted changes at neighboring farms; rebuilt sheds and mended fences or conversely, fields uncut and roofs in disrepair, the condition of the livestock, new or old equipment in the yard, all the details caught his eye. Some of the farms were recently abandoned as evidenced by 'For Sale' signs and the bright colored tape of surveyor's markers fluttering in the wind like the leftover decorations of a festive gathering.

They were getting close and the excitement and nervousness began to scuttle around like a mouse in his innards. Again a quick glance to the mirrors and this time stirred into the pot with the fear, he felt a flash of rage.

"Sons-a-bitches!"

Alma gasped as the red lights flashed and the siren was sounded. Daniel pulled abruptly to the side of the road gone to gravel and the dust crested over them like an angry shroud. He didn't wait for them but hopped out of the truck like the seat was on fire.

"Don't move. Don't say a thing," he told her. He saw the terror in her eyes and it only fueled the ire in his gullet.

"*Cuídate, mi amor.*"

He nodded once and turned to face his pursuers.

"Afternoon, son. What's your business in town today?"

"It's me Sheriff, Daniel Sweeney. I'm just going home."

"By Jesus, it is you. Hey Stiles, it's Danny Sweeney come back home," the sheriff spoke back over his shoulder to his deputy who was busy inspecting the trailer.

"Can I go now sheriff?"

"Hold onto your britches, Danny, we have some business to conduct here."

"What kind of business?"

"Can I see the registration for this rig?"

He reached across Alma's lap to the glove box and retrieved an envelope. They both pretended that she was invisible. He handed the

246

envelope to the sheriff, who slipped out the contents and gave it a quick read.

"What about the trailer?"

"It's just an old trailer I bought from a guy."

"Yes, but you are required by law to have it inspected and registered with the state."

"Nobody told me."

"Ignorance of the law is no excuse."

"It ain't an excuse."

"No registration on a rig with four horses." The sheriff took off his hat and scratched his head and then put the hat back on. "What I want to know is how in the hell did you make it all the way across the country without being stopped?"

"Free country isn't it?"

"For law abiding citizens it is."

Stiles came up beside the sheriff and directed himself to Daniel.

"You got papers on them horses?"

"On the geldings and the mare."

"What about the other?"

"No."

"Why not?"

"I just kind of found him."

"As I remember you have a bit of history with horse theft," the sheriff jumped in.

"It ain't like that. I set her free. This one is her replacement."

Stiles circled round the front of the cab to the passenger side window.

"Hello, Miss. Do you have some identification I can see?"

"I don't have it with me."

"Well, where do you have it?"

"I lost it."

"Where did you lose it?"

"I don't know. I lost it."

"Where are you from?"

"From my village."

"Yes, but where is your village?"

"Far from here."

"She's from Washington," Daniel interjected.

"How old are you, honey?" Stiles pressed on.

"She's old enough."

"Old enough for what?"

"Old enough for whatever it is your asking."

"Let her answer the questions," the sheriff said.

"Just leave her alone," Daniel said staring down Stiles.

"Easy, son."

"Can we go now?"

"Look Danny, like it or not, we've got our job to do. You work with me and we'll straighten this thing out, all right?"

"I guess."

"No, you'll do more than guess. Look, out of respect for your father and for your brother's sake, I'm going to let you go home for now. But I don't want either of you kids to leave that property, understand?"

"I don't intend to."

"What's the young lady's name?" Stiles asked.

"Alma."

"That's it? What's her last name?"

Daniel just glared at him.

"Let it go for now, Stiles," the sheriff said.

Daniel got back into the truck.

"Don't go anywhere," the sheriff said. "You can expect a visit from us soon."

Daniel did not respond. He fixed his eyes straight ahead and turned the key in the ignition, pressed the starter and spun away as quickly as the weight of the fully loaded truck and trailer would allow.

"The bastards!" he slammed his palm upon the steering wheel then shifted the gears up with his foot on the gas.

"*Calmáte,* Daniel. Getting angry won't help."

"I'm sorry."

"I'm scared. What will they do to us?"

"Maybe nothing. Maybe I'll just have to pay some fine. I didn't know there were so many laws just to own a truck and trailer."

"*Sobre todo es un país de leyes.* I hope it is that simple. "

He sucked in a deep breath and blew it out again.

"All I know is, I won't let them touch you."

He was quiet for a moment. Then he turned to her.

"So what is your last name?"

They both broke out in nervous laughter.

"*Soy* Alma Maria de Jesus Coatlicue."

He tried to pronounce it but failed.

"*Eso no importa, ahora me llamo* Alma Sweeney."

*

When they wheeled the patrol car into the school parking lot and pulled up by the athletic field they could already see the assistant coach standing beside an open metal basket brimming with footballs. One after another with the ease and grace of a ballet dancer he fired off perfect spiraling arcs to the line up of receivers at the ready to his side. The law officers got out of the car and strolled across the playing field. Just as he cocked back his arm ready to throw, the deputy yelled sharply, "Watch it, Sweeney!" Startled he misfired and the pass fell short by several yards.

"Losing your touch, Coach?"

Tommy spun around and almost said something but held his tongue. Stiles again. He'd been a lean mean player but not big enough for college ball. He'd never get over the fact that Tommy got a scholarship and he didn't.

"Got your roster filled yet?"

"Just about. Some of the farm boys don't make it in for summer sessions, making hay and whatnot."

"How's it looking?"

"We've got the makings of a team."

The sheriff nodded approval; the deputy said nothing, keeping his eyes hidden in the shadow of his broad-brimmed hat. Then the sheriff's face turned serious and he searched out Tommy's eyes.

"Heard the news?"

"What's going on?" Tommy asked.

"Danny's back."

"No way."

Tommy held a fist up to his mouth, dropped his chin to his chest and closed his eyes. He filled his lungs to the brim and breathed out full before he looked up again.

"We saw him come in ourselves about ten this morning. Didn't know who it was at first. Out of state plates and hauling a livestock trailer without plates. Followed him up to your place. He drove round the cul-de-sac then headed up to Sugarbrook. That's when we stopped him."

"Christ Jesus."

"He's got that trailer full of horses."

"He always did love horses."

"Not all of them have papers."

"You think he stole them?"

"At this point nothing would surprise me."

"He's full of surprises, isn't he?"

"This isn't funny, Tom."

"I know it."

"There's more to it."

"Go on."

"He wasn't alone."

"What do you mean?"

"He's got a pretty young gal with him appears to be Mexican or some gosh darned foreign country I don't know all."

"Young and pretty and brown as a berry." Stiles piped in.

"We spoke with old Josh Wilder. Apparently they stopped in there first and bought sundry comestibles. Seem to be planning on staying put for awhile."

"What's the problem?"

"Aren't you aiming to sell that place?"

"That still hasn't been decided."

"Well, the problem is your damn fool brother drove across the country with an unregistered rig, and as if that weren't enough, the young gal he has with him appears to be undocumented."

"So he's in trouble."

"Enough.

"And most likely under age," the deputy added.

"Before you do anything, will you let me get up there and have a talk with him."

"I think it's best if we go out there with you. Mediate the matter."

"I appreciate it."

*

They descended into the saddle of the valley and as they approached the bridge, the brook was like a ghostly trickle of itself, nothing like it was when he had last seen it eons ago. He felt the rough rhythmic roll of the tires across the wooden planks of the bridge and then they were there.

"My land," he thought to himself and then, "Our land." He gazed over at Alma. "This is it---Sugarbrook Farm."

The white clapboard house with its green shutters, the tall wooden silo, the big red gambrel barn, all glowed brilliantly in the long strands of late summer sun. He was struck by the sameness of it all, as if time had stood still. Even the apron of lawn before the front porch had been recently mown. His eye picked up a darker shadow beneath the tall pines close by the horse barn and he half-expected to see the old black dog but it was only an overturned wheel barrow. Then he saw it, sticking out blatantly as a fly on a white-washed wall, a blemish on an otherwise flawless face. Inked in neat letters the sign tacked to a post stated flatly: 'Farm for Sale.'

"Well, at least he ain't sold it yet," he remarked in a tone dark and low. He pulled the truck forward around the circular drive and parked in front of the barn.

They unloaded the horses into the barnyard paddock. The animals were beside themselves at being loosed after so many days of confinement. They cantered about, kicked up their heels and there was all manner of snorting and prodigious farting. Storm and Tempest took their turn rolling in the grass. Friend and the spirited Bruja continued to gallop to and fro making a game of horse tag, nipping at each other's hocks. Daniel fed out the last of the hay from the trailer and hefted bucketfuls of well water to the overturned stock tank which he had righted. It calmed him to see the long faces of the horses transformed into hollow sucking tubes like straws, their nostrils quivering as they drew in air between long swallows.

He escorted Alma to the front door of the porch and found it was unlocked. As she began shuttling their belongings inside, he went back out to see about the sign. He struggled to loose it from the earth, but it wouldn't move. Whoever had put it in the ground was likely used to setting fence posts meant to stand for twenty years.

He stood for a moment breathing hard with his hands on his hips, then went out back to a lumber rack by the rear of the shop and pulled off a half-dozen or so scraps of old barn board and set them up tipi-style around the post. Then he brought over an armload of cordwood off the porch that he and his father had stacked there two winters ago and set the pieces in among the boards. He doused the boards with kerosene and stepped back to toss a lighted match upon the pyre and stood there until he was satisfied the sign would burn.

He set his rifle on the glossy formica surface of the kitchen table and went to the parlor to grab a handful of cartridges from the drawer of a bureau beneath the gun rack. Alma watched him but said nothing. Her experience had taught her not to come between a man and his weapon. He cocked the rifle, slid the bolt and checked its smooth action. Zeke had cleaned and oiled it before passing it on. He loaded a cartridge in the chamber, set the safety and laid it back on the table.

The interior of the house was just as he remembered it---not a single item had been moved out of place. The wind-up clock above the mantle of the fireplace with its frontispiece bearing an image of a tall ship at sea had run down and stopped, he assumed, seven hours after his departure and had not been rewound. The bold-faced clock in the kitchen had stopped some time after that with the shutoff of electricity. Yet the house was immaculate, cleaner than when he left it, tidy as only a woman would have it; he guessed it was his sister-in-law, Gloria, who was keeping it so.

He showed Alma around the house. They entered the master bedroom last. He cautiously opened the door to the room where his father had passed away, opened it reverently, as if it were a sealed crypt. His brother Tommy and he had both been born in this room on this very brass bedstead now covered with a checkered quilt.

Alma stood behind him, uneasy, sensing the unresolved history contained within those walls. He smiled at her partly to reassure himself and then walked across the floorboards to a cedar chest set underneath the lace-curtained window. The key was in the lock of the chest and he turned it with a tiny click and lifted the lid. While his father had occupied the room, the boy had scarcely ever set foot in it, let alone dare open the trunk. He couldn't remember ever having much curiosity about its contents, but now it had a mysterious draw on him.

The first object he saw was an old photograph in a gilt-frame lying on stylish dresses of another time and antique suits neatly folded and packed in moth balls. There were shoe boxes containing ladies and men's dress shoes and one box contained jewelry, cufflinks and ties. But he barely registered these other items as his eyes were drawn back to the picture.

Alma came up behind him and he stepped back and put his arm around her waist as they contemplated the image together. A couple stood beneath an arbor entwined with a climbing riot of morning glories and he recalled that such an arbor had once stood at the entrance to the kitchen garden on the south side of the farm house. The craggy yet handsome man was dressed in black suit and tie, a carnation in the lapel, the suit a size too big and a generation out of date, making him appear even lankier than he actually was. The reserved smile on his lips belied the melancholy in his eyes. The face could have been Daniel's face, only leaner and more careworn, perhaps leavened with the sorrow of one who had survived a war. The woman stood beside him, their arms linked stiffly like figurines carved of wood. Her perfect dark skin stood in stark contrast to the white of her bridal gown; hair, black as night under the veil, was braided and circled by a wreath of wild flowers; light almond-shaped eyes looked out as if they could see a thousand miles beyond the camera to some unseen realm; the full mouth was unsmiling; the high cheek bones accentuated the dignity and upright bearing of her frame. She held a bouquet of cut flowers in her free hand and on the laced bodice of the gown lay a knapped flint arrowhead suspended from a silver chain, the very one that Alma now held pensively between her right forefinger and thumb.

"She is beautiful," Alma commented. *"Desde luego tu sangre india viene de ella.*

He slowly lowered the lid back down as if the trunk were a coffin and, still holding her around the waist he turned her to face a mirror that hung above a tall bureau on the other side of the room. The reflected image that stared back at them bore an uncanny resemblance to that old wedding photograph, right down to the pride on her face and the melancholic cast of his eyes. He turned to her and they embraced.

"I never really knew her," he said. "For a long time after she died, I couldn't even recall her face."

"I am with you now and I will not leave you to live in this house all alone."

"We can make a good life together. This no longer needs to be a house of mourning. Now that you are here."

He leaned over and kissed her on the forehead and he closed the door behind them and they went down the stairs.

They went out through the kitchen into the enclosed well house and he drew up a bucketful of water from below. He offered her a taste from the ladle then took an uncommonly long draught himself.

"Ah, that is sweet water." He set the bucket down and hung up the ladle and they walked on to the empty barn.

As they passed through he explained to her how the milking system was set up and showed her the milk house where the machines still hung in place. He grew excited as he spoke, his voice taking on an uncharacteristically animated tone. In his mind's eye the barn was already full again with cows.

They walked out the east door into the late afternoon light of the yard. The fire around the sign had burned down. He fetched a bucket of water from the barn and poured it out around the perimeter of the burn to prevent its spread though the flame had blackened out the grass and then retreated, leaving a self-contained barrier of ashen ground. He took the girl by the hand and they set off around the house through a gate down into the bottomlands knee-deep in timothy and orchard grass.

Their tracks cut a line across the field. He paused and kicked away at the rank growth with the toe of his boot until he could grab a fistful of soil. He sniffed at the dirt and even tasted it with the tip of his tongue. Alma stood patiently by, mildly amused by him.

"My father used to say that the only stone in this field was the one he kept in his pocket to knock off the clods that built up on his plow share. He told me this valley was carved out by glaciers. Imagine---ice a mile thick---right here where we stand. Dad said he figured that brook over there must have crisscrossed this bottomland at least a dozen times since that ice melted, dumping silt as it went. We are really blessed; most farms around here yield a bounty crop of fieldstone."

"I've never seen earth so black."

"It is good land. Mellow and with heart."

He placed the sod chunks back over the scar he'd made then tamped them down with his heel and they walked on.

At field's edge he helped her to negotiate a woven wire fence and they crossed the brook on the trunk of a fallen hemlock and climbed the slopes of a south facing hill pasture. The bowl of the valley was resplendent with the last light of day. After the crossing of dry western lands, the verdant landscape was an oasis, a mirage of green and yet he could spot the faint mineral undertones of copper and ochre in the leaves and knew that soon they would be turning and ready to fall. They filled their lungs with the cooling air of a shadowed swale and continued their climb. By no intent or design, he suddenly realized that they were approaching the graveyard. The draw of it was inexorable. He walked with her now into that place of the dead, dreading all the while the sight of what he knew he must find there.

The ancient track of road swerved around a picket fence. Most of the whitewash had flecked off the pickets, leaving the gray weathered wood bare to the harsh north wind. He inhaled sharply and entered. Despite the warm wind, Alma felt a chill but she resolutely followed. Within the fenced-in quadrant of graves the trunk of a spreading oak heaved up from the hill of bones and flung enormous muscular branches outward in all directions. Beneath the tree lay the long-standing gravesites of people he had never known. Enshrouded in local lore these were the members of the first families to breathe human life into these acres. The memorials of hand-etched granite slab were inscribed with simple plaintive epitaphs concerning the rectitude of their earthly conduct and the certitude of their final destination in the celestial abode. These carved words were accompanied by cryptic images of winged skulls of the soul and angels with sightless eyes.

Daniel walked along the narrow path through the overgrown grass to the familiar headstones of his grandparents and from there it was short steps to the tombstone of his mother.

At last he forced his eyes to look upon the mound that lay next beside it, the gravesite of his father. The chiseled epitaph read as clear as the morning headline: 'Honest man---Faithful husband---Able Farmer'.

The site was tended with flowers planted around the stone and fresh-cut blooms laid in front of it, indicating that someone still living had visited only lately. Daniel dropped to his knees and lay prostrate on the grave. He could feel the sacred and penetrating mystery of that earth aching in his own breast. The warmth of her hand on his back felt like the touch of a small bird and he rose to that touch and she embraced him.

"Let us return to the place of the living," she said, "death comes soon enough to us all."

Alma discovered there was still some gas in the tank and she got the stove lit and heated water in a large pot to draw herself a bath. Daniel went down to the deepest pool of the brook above the bridge where it ran through the pines and he stripped down and jumped in. Then he went back to the barn and saw to the horses.

He lingered in the horse barn after feeding out hay and grain and his eyes wandered over the leather harness hung on pegs in the tack room just as he had left it. It would require repair and a good cleaning and oiling before it would be supple enough to use again he mused to himself and once set in motion, his mind began clicking with thoughts of the one-hundred and one things to do to get the farm up and running again. He ambled out to the equipment shed, the broad-brimmed hat set back on the crown of his head, his hands in his pockets, hands that soon would be more than busy. Not just yet. He would allow a little space for reverie and inspection. Dust had settled on the machinery but nothing had been used or moved over the course of his absence.

He knew that every implement was field-ready; his father had always been diligent in overseeing that winter work. As he remembered his father as he was in life, the image of the fresh grave was dispelled from his thoughts. How vigorous his crippled form was whenever he turned his hand to the plow and walked behind a team. With those last two, Liam and Rory, his father had formed a near mystical union so that the three acted as one, man and team moving out across the land with the choreography of a flock of swallows winging in concert.

In the cow barn, Daniel took a stair by the door to the milk house that led up to the mow. In a quick glance he estimated that there was still plenty of usable hay in the stack. Then he opened the latched door of the seed room at the top of the stair. Mice had been into some of the bins but he reckoned them well-stocked with winter wheat, red clover and cereal rye.

"And so we will plant this year," he spoke aloud, not clear if that 'we' referred to himself and his father or to him and Alma or maybe to the three of them together. He ran his hands through the myriad clover seed of an opened bin and could feel the near-abandoned potential of its content running over his palms and through his fingers like a thickened liquid. He closed the bin and went downstairs.

He was inspecting the condition of the stanchions in the barn when he heard her call him from the kitchen window. He was met by the welcoming fragrance of fresh bread as he walked into the kitchen.

The table was set with candles and a mason jar served as a vase for a bunch of wildflowers. She had found her way around the kitchen, instilling a sensible order to everything she laid her hands on and had prepared a simple meal of flat bread, rice and beans spiced with salt and dried chilies and a salad harvested of such wild greens as she recognized growing in the backyard. They ate in silence. He was itching to tell her about all his plans for the farm that were fermenting in his brain, but the intimacy of the candle-lit kitchen momentarily subdued his fervor. He got no further than looking into the serious and soulful beauty of her eyes.

When they first met there had been a child-like lightness about her, but now this veiled mysterious nightshade of her personality began to draw him in. He knew that he needed her light the way seedlings require sun, but he had not expected to discover himself hungering to enter into moon fields of spiritual darkness with her as well. In one moment he could feel as if he had known her forever and been with her from the beginning of time and in the very next moment the newness and suddenness of their being together would overwhelm him in waves of uncertainty and shyness. Now he found himself poised at a paradoxical crux between those two extremes. He reached across the table and grasped her hand. They sat in the circle of the candles and breathed in the wonder and contentment in that shared moment of pure presence.

The electricity had been shut off since the house had been uninhabited. His father had often preferred not to use it and there was still a lantern with oil and wick in every room. Daniel lit a lantern above the sink, fetched a pail of water from the well house and washed the dishes. Night had fallen and with it came the rising of the moon waxing fat above the east hill. The moonlight cast silvered squares through the window panes on to the walls and floors of the dark house. They moved from the kitchen through that crazy quilt of fractured moon surrounded in a soft yellow cocoon of lantern light and side by side they climbed the creaking stairs.

He hesitated at the landing, pausing in front of the door that led to his old bedroom with its single bed, and then continued down the hallway to the master bedroom. Again he paused a moment. He felt her press close behind him as he slowly opened the door.

He set the lantern on a night stand by the brass headboard and walked across the wide floorboards and raised the window sash above the cedar chest. A night wind brought lively air into the room. The girl stepped up close behind him and he turned to face her. Her full lips slightly parted held his gaze while she removed her cotton blouse and stepped out of her ankle-length skirt and underclothing. She stood in her nakedness before him except for the obsidian arrowhead blacker than night upon her breast. Illumined in the contrast of golden lamp and silver moon, she appeared to him to be at once utterly vulnerable and completely inviolable. She undid her twin braids letting her hair spill like a silken river over her shoulders, pouring over her upturned copper nipples and down to the curve of her slender waist. He drank in the sight as if first tasting a healing elixir or precious wine. She reached for him and began to unbutton his shirt, then to unclasp the rodeo-prize buckle on the tooled belt that girded his jeans and he stepped out of his boots and clothes.

A short eternity passed before either one ventured to touch, to search out with fingertips, the flesh of the other. Their lips met and their bodies pressed in. They made their way over to the bed and the first half of the night was spent in gentle exploration. His hands moved gently over her like a carver feeling out the lines in the grain of wood. Timid herself, she was emboldened by the tenderness of his caresses, and unfolded herself from within. In full trust she gave herself over to his strength, yielding as water to stone, yet guiding and shaping the flow in the very act of receptivity.

Deep into the night they discovered the key. During the consummation of their lovemaking, the girl gave forth a short cry of pain and Daniel tensed, frightened that he had somehow hurt her. Then he felt her body renew its hunger for him, fluid and supple, she rose upward to draw him in.

Long past midnight with the pregnant moon descending in the west, the lovers entwined in one another's arms followed that silver light down into the depths of sleep. A peaceful oblivion cloaked their minds, their hearts beat in rhythm, their breaths came as one.

2

A quiet joy was upon them as they surfaced from sleep. For long moments they basked in the sensation of waking in each other's arms. Then the promise of the new day called to them. Daniel hopped out of bed and climbed into his lived-in clothes and bounded down the steps with the same clomp and clatter of his boyhood. He went to the outhouse and washed at the outdoor hand pump then stood and looked to the east to see the morning star rise out of fog thick like the breath of an ancient dragon rising up from the river. He saw to the horses. Alma caught up with him in the barn and on a whim he asked her, "Do you ride?"

"Como no?" she responded with enthusiasm. They put a bridle on the bay mare and on big Storm and set off riding bareback along the fence lines of the farm. Little Friend and Tempest created a stir of protest, running about and whinnying at having been left behind.

The sun was rising clear and temperate over the east hill and a steady breeze brought pleasant air out of the north. The girl seated herself well on the perky mare. Storm was heavy of foot but willing and they rode out with spontaneous exuberance. Even so, Daniel's eyes were keen to register those places where fallen limbs or rotted timbers had taken out sections of fence line as he surveyed the pastures, lush in their fallow, noting where wild rose, thistle, or pioneer saplings were striking open ground. He eyed the unfinished roof of the sugar house remembering with sadness his father's calculations as to how many board feet it would take to finish it. They continued to ride the perimeter of open land and as he swung down off his horse to work the cattle gates, he wondered who had come and taken the time to close them all and supposed it must have been his brother.

They galloped up the hill pasture as the green illumination of the sun on grass blades descended into the hollows of the valley. They crested the highest hill, only wheeling their horses around when they reached the woods edge. The whole of the farm was laid out before them, blanketed in the immensity of high summer's rapture. They sat their horses in silence as the blowing and the breathing stilled and they drank in the view. She seemed so happy and he desperately wanted to be happy with her but as he squinted his eyes and surveyed the horizon he sensed some unnamed and hidden threat lurking just below the sight line, and what he felt in his heart was not contentment; he was watchful and on guard. He almost spoke and then thought better of it.

As they rode slowly down the hill the girl remarked, "*Que linda*---I never guessed it would be so beautiful. Is all this really your land?"

"One-hundred and twenty acres; thirty-five in pasture, twenty tillable, and the balance in woods."

"My family owned *dos hectáres* and our neighbors thought us rich."

"This is our land now, Alma, yours and mine."

"I feared I would be a stranger here, that I could never belong to a place so distant from my homeland. But this morning I believe this is my home."

"If you believe it, it must be true."

"Because of you, Daniel, I believe."

They dismounted and walked the horses over the last stretch letting the breeze cool the sweat on their mounts slick with brine. Together they prepared a breakfast of beans, rice and tortillas and hot black coffee poured out into white porcelain mugs.

He reacted to the distant vibration of the motor hum even before he realized its full import. He jumped up abruptly from the table and grabbed the firearm and headed out the front door through the parlor.

"Daniel!" she cried out to him. He halted in mid-track and turned.

"Why the gun?" she finally dared to ask the question with pleading in her eyes.

"I can't stand to lose this place a second time."

"To pick up a gun---is not everything then lost?"

"I ain't leaving here again. I'm through with running."

"But why the gun?"

"Stay inside."

He turned again and ran out the door and down the walk and to the bridge, the rifle clutched with a firm grip. By the time he reached the near side of the span, the blue truck and the county patrol car were parked on the other side. He stopped short of crossing and made ready to stand his ground. His brother climbed out of the blue truck. He had on dress pants and shirt, but was not wearing a jacket or tie. Daniel could see nothing different about him. He appeared unchanged.

The sheriff and his deputy emerged from the patrol car, looking uncomfortable in the August heat in their tan uniforms with shining badges and holstered guns. The three of them approached the bridge. Tommy repeatedly ran a hand through his hair. The deputy laid his right hand on the grip of his pistol and the sheriff assumed a wide-legged stance, his arms folded across his chest.

"Danny," Tommy spoke his brother's name by way of greeting.

He nodded once but made no other sign of overture.

"I hardly recognized you for the beard."

Daniel reached up and felt his face as if surprised to discover that a beard had sprouted there.

"Just what do you think you're doing carrying that rifle, son?" the sheriff asked in authoritative tones.

"I've got the right to bear arms in defense of my land," he responded in a voice soft and low.

"Not in defiance of a duly appointed officer of the law you don't."

"Where's the Indian girl?" the deputy chimed in.

"What's it to you?"

"We have reason to suspect she is lacking the legal documents necessary to reside in this country."

"She belongs to this land now as much as I do."

"Way you're heading, son, the only place you're going to belong is in a prison cell," the sheriff declared.

"Tommy, have you gone and sold the farm?" he asked his brother directly, ignoring the menace of the sheriff.

"No Danny, but I've got a serious buyer ready to sign."

"That is not what is at issue here, Danny Sweeney," the sheriff interjected, pointing his finger at him to emphasize his meaning.

"He's got no right to sell it. I'm of age now and this land belongs to me every bit as much as it does to him."

262

"You weren't of age when your father died; that's all that matters in the eyes of the law."

"Then as far as I'm concerned, the eyes of the law are blind."

"The disposition of this land is by no means decided, Danny, so just try to settle down," Tommy cajoled, raising up both hands in a pacifying gesture.

"Listen, you two, we've got multiple issues here to deal with. There's the matter of no plate or title on the trailer. There's the matter of a young girl with no apparent documentation. And then there's this quarrel over whether or not you're selling this damn land. I should probably lock Billy the Kid up right here and now but I'm going to give you one week to sort things out between you, and after that I'm going to have to intervene." the sheriff stated with finality.

The brothers locked eyes, searching warily for signs. Then Daniel turned on his heels and walked at an easy pace back up the drive to the house, the relaxed pace of his stride belied by his clenched jaw and fists.

"You hear me, Danny? One week." The sheriff shouted to his back and then the men turned and climbed into their vehicles and left.

The girl came out onto the front porch to meet him. He stood at the bottom of the short steps, looked up at her and then turned and looked back down the empty road where the dust was settling. When the sound of the engines receded, he turned to her again, her eyes still squinting at the bend in the road.

"*Quién es?*"

"That was my brother, come here with the law."

"What did they want?"

"You, me, the land, everything."

"Will they come back?"

"Oh, they'll be back all right."

"Then we must leave."

"No Alma, we can't leave. This is our land."

"Not if your brother sells it."

"Well, he hasn't sold it yet and I ain't leaving even if he does."

Their eyes locked for an instant, and then simultaneously softened in the depth of mutual affection there between them.

"Then I stay, too," she said in a calm voice tinged with sorrow. He walked up the stairs and hugged her, with the one hand and the rifle held in the other.

"*Tienes mucho coraje,* Daniel, *pero a veces me parece que estas un poco loco. Tal vez es por eso que te amo.*"

He took two steps back down the stairs and tried to hand the stock of the rifle to her and asked her to hold it for him.

She shook her head in the definitive negative.

"Suit yourself," he said and leaned the gun upright against the banister of the porch and headed off to the barn. She stood looking after him with her arms folded across her middle, small and self-contained, like a woodland creature hunkering down in the face of a gathering storm.

He came back from the barn pushing a wheelbarrow with a rake and a flat shovel and used the tools to gather the ash and cinder of the spent burn that remained of the sign. He wheeled the debris out to the adjacent field and spread it there, rendering the destruction of the sign absolute. He was aware that she hadn't moved from the porch; that she stood there and watched him as he worked. He put the tools away and returned to the porch and put one hand to the rifle and placed the other lightly on her shoulder. And then he walked past her into the house and put the rifle back on the kitchen table and she followed him in.

"Daniel, *por qué*---why the gun?" she asked him again in plaintive tones. He made for the door to the well house and without turning around, echoing Zeke Burly, he said, "Every sensible man requires a sound horse and a good rifle."

He went out to the horse barn and took down Liam and Rory's old sets of leather work harness and laid them out on the floor. The girl came out of the house and found him there. He felt bad about the way he'd spoken to her back in the house but his pride and the pressure he felt under from his brother and the law held back words of amend; instead he pulled out two milking stools from underneath the bench in the tack room, gathered up saddle soap, neat's-foot oil, curved needle and awl, and the two of them set about repairing and restoring the leather.

With the harness hung on pegs, supple and restored, they took their lunch in the shade of a grand old butternut tree in the backyard. After they did the dishes, they headed to the horse barn again and brought in Storm and Tempest and he showed her how to harness up the horses. She had to stand on the milking stool to get the rigging up and over their steep withers. After a few minor adjustments fitting snaps and buckles, he clipped on driving lines and drove the team out of the barn bay and over to the equipment shed. After their long hiatus on the road, the big horses were fired up, so he drove them up and down the drive to the bridge a number of times to take off their edge. Then he tied their leads to a hitch post off the side of the shed.

"Wait here and watch the horses," he said and ran back to the house like he was running to a fire. He came back again as quickly with the scabbard that had once housed his grandfather's rifle and then his own wooden flute. He'd left the flute in the house and placed the gift rifle in the empty scabbard and strapped the assembly across his back. With the aid of the girl he dragged out the sickle-bar mower. His movements were rapid and efficient like a soldier preparing for battle. He re-greased the points and checked the oil level in the enclosed gear box. He didn't have to check the ledger plates on the cutter bar, confident that his father had left them in excellent condition, sharp for the swathing.

The mowing of the hay was not an easy go. It was late season and the crop was rank and time and again the cutter-bar bogged down in the clover blooms and heavy seed heads and then he would have to stop the horses, command them to back up a pace, then climb off the metal seat and use his hands to free up the bar. Even so, Storm and Tempest were drawn into the work. They cut for the better part of two days. With that much grass down, he began to watch the sky like a hawk and to sniff at the air for signs.

The strong sun of late summer worked to cure the grass. He enjoyed the work on the dump-rake best of all. It was an easy pull for the big horses and they seemed to glide as they sculpted the downed grass into neat lines across the sloping fields. As he worked the horses he had the rifle strung across his back keeping a vigilant ear toward the crossing at the bridge.

What he didn't know, what he could not see, was that each day after football practice, Tommy would park his truck over at the Benson place and hike to the farm over the wooded hills from the backside of the property. He'd stop at the forest edge on the west hill field and from that overlook he would observe his brother's progress, torn within himself, yet somehow enthralled to watch Daniel with his team of horses working the land.

Once Daniel had the hay all raked in windrows, Alma joined in the work. Despite some trepidation she learned fast, and was soon driving the big team hitched to a flat bed wagon and then she walked them down the raked-in lines while Daniel pitched heaping forkfuls of hay onto the wagon. Back at the cow barn they hitched the team by rope to a grapple with a trip lever suspended from a block-and-tackle assembly to a beam above the outdoor entrance of the hay mow, and thus working together over the course of many trips they brought the loose hay into the barn.

Daniel barely took time to catch his breath before he started plowing five-acres of bottomland that had sat fallow with corn stover. He was in a rhythm with the team by now and the plow turned the soil over much like the prow of a canoe creates a wake as it moves through still water. After plowing they disced and harrowed the fields and with that considerable work done he was ready to sow down winter rye. He hitched the horses to the drill and adjusted it to the proper setting, the rolling box slicing open the earth, dropping seed and then enfolding it to the proper depth; only in the wounding of the earth does new growth come forth.

He worked steadily at these tasks and was pleased and proud at the responsiveness of the team. He felt a modest ecstasy welling up from within at the visible tally of accomplished deeds piling up in their wake.

Alma pitched in where she could and otherwise looked to the establishment of their fledgling household. He caught glimpses of her as he was going about his own work, spied her as she washed their clothes in the brook and spread them out on the clipped grass of the lawn to dry or as she dragged the rugs out of the house and raised a cloud of dust beating them over the fence rail with a broom. She

266

seemed content in these tasks, even happy as she busied herself at putting the house in order. He felt some guilt at leaving her on her own as much as he did, but neither did he pull himself away from his self-imposed rounds; there was so much that needed doing all at once and that was just the way it was with this farming life he'd chosen.

On the evening of the seventh day of their labors, one week out since the encounter with the law at the bridge, Daniel walked the fields at dusk, playing plaintive melodies on his flute to the newly buried seeds. Thunder rumbled in the western sky and heavy air charged the valley in anticipation. Later, standing out on the porch, he leaned against the column and spoke to his world: "Picture perfect," he said, "hay in the barn, seed in the ground and rain coming on like a blessing."

"Yes," she came out the screen door and spoke in hushed tones from behind, "let us receive it as a blessing."

He turned to face her.

"What more can we do?"

"Nothing, it's perfect as it is."

"We do have that, come what may."

"It is so peaceful here."

"Too peaceful."

"What do you mean?"

"I mean it's weird that Tommy hasn't shown up since all that with the sheriff at the bridge."

"Maybe it's a good sign."

"Maybe so. Whatever it is, it's buying us some time to get this place on its legs again."

"Maybe that's what he intends."

"Too many maybe's."

"Sorry."

"Don't be, I hope you're right."

"And if I'm wrong?"

"There'll be a fight."

"That's what I fear."

"Don't be afraid. Just look at this storm; the powers of the directions are with us, you see?"

Lightning flashed and the ground shuddered and heavy raindrops were whipped down on the wind and even under the shelter of the eaves, the porch became a storm-tossed boat wetting their faces with sea spray. He reached his hands out to her and she took them.

"Let's go in and get some sleep."

He was up before the dawn. A liquid golden sun was rising through the white pines and purple and green clouds scudded like reefs below the surface of the low ocean of sky. He sat out on the porch and drank his coffee, gobbled down a few cold and chewy tostadas left over from the night before, then went upstairs and kissed the sleepy girl goodbye.

"Look to the horses, okay? You'll be safer staying put than going out with me on the road. If anyone comes, run up to the graveyard and wait under the great oak so I'll know where to find you."

"*Adónde vas*, Daniel?"

"I'm going to buy some milk cows."

"*No me digas?*" her worries disappeared and her face was alight and she clapped her hands.

"Can you buy me some chickens, too?" she chimed.

"I will."

"*Un momento* Daniel, didn't the law man forbid you to leave?"

"He won't know about it."

Her worries were upon her again.

He picked up the rifle on his way out and put it behind the bench seat, fired up the Dodge and let it idle a few moments, then drove down the drive with the stock trailer in tow.

He stuck to the back roads and headed north and crossed the iron bridge to the New Hampshire side and drove up the river road to the auction house. He arrived early before the proceedings began, so he had time to look over the stock. There were some sound cows up for sale. He looked first to their feet and then studied the conformation of the udders. He peered into eyes and poked into mouths to feel for wear of the teeth and to get a look at the color of the tongue and he smelled their breath and placed his ear on the rumen side and listened. He was on the lookout for Jerseys, a breed his father and grandfather before him favored. He bid on four cows, two bred heifers and two cows just freshened and he bought them for what he considered a fair price.

He enjoyed being one among that company and even though he had found what he came for, he sat with interest through the remainder of the bidding. He kept his hands quiet and face still as his father had shown him, lest a random gesture be taken as a bid. The auctioneer stood before the assembly and shot off his rapid-fire speech. What any bystander might mistake as a scratch of the head, a rub of the nose, a nervous tick of the eye, were individual signs by farmers and stockmen to indicate that the animal on show had caught their attention. They stood or sat alternately in their barn boots and coveralls and caps, smoking or chewing tobacco, familiar and largely silent witnesses to an ever increasing parade of cattle and equipment coming before the block, a procession that would ultimately spell their own demise, for it was the cattle of small farms gone under that comprised the majority of livestock for sale.

Daniel remembered to purchase an additional ten barred-rock hens and a rooster. He packed them into crates and with the help of hired men on hand then he backed the trailer up to the loading dock, cut out the four cows and got them safely on board and headed home. He by-passed the iron bridge and headed to the farm supply store in Old Lebanon to buy cracked corn for the chickens and milled grain for the cows and whole oats for the horses. He felt a new strength surging in his limbs as he loaded the hundred-pound sacks onto the bed of the truck.

On the way home he switched on the radio and found a country station and even as he drummed his fingers on the wheel in time to the guitar, fiddle and bass, it struck him how foreign the cowboy culture seemed to him now that he was back in his native place. He continued south and crossed the long span of the covered wooden bridge over the Connecticut to Windsor. The antiquated advisory posted above its entrance, 'Walk your horses or pay a two-dollar fine,' admonished the travelers of a bygone era. As he emerged out the other side he caught the weather report but switched the radio off when the world news came on. He turned north on the old state road but quickly turned off it again and drove the backroads to reach Stoneford and the farm.

He felt sucker punched as he rounded the bend and saw the gray Nash rambler parked in the drive. As he geared down for the descent to the bridge he could see Gloria and the twins out on the porch chatting with Alma.

He was glad to see Gloria, he knew that well enough. Yet the sight of her opened up a gulf in the pit of his innards. If he had once loved her, if he loved her even now, he did not want to know about it.

To the twins he could not remain diffident even for a moment. They had grown into little boys, remarkably changed from the toddlers he remembered. Tow headed and robust Aidan and pale, dark-haired Patrick ran down the path from the house clamoring and anxious to see their half-forgotten Uncle, perhaps no less eager to see the trailer packed with boxed birds and brown cows.

Gloria removed her sun glasses and came down off the porch after them. She had let her wavy auburn locks grow long again. She was wearing a green summer print dress with red high-top sneakers, making a fashion statement all her own, an outfit that was all Gloria, all woman and all girl. She carried her tall frame with an unstudied elegance, yet somehow managed to maintain the bounce of the vivacious cheerleader she had once been.

When Daniel stepped down out of the cab, the rascally boys came rushing to meet him. He shook hands with each of them as if they were little men. Then he picked each boy up in turn so they could look through the slats into the trailer and see the cows. When they clamored in demand for a second viewing he told them, "Hold onto your britches little cowboys, we'll be unloading these here cattle right shortly," and they delighted at his feigned western twang.

Gloria came up to greet him with Alma trailing close behind. She stood before him tremulous but contained, peered at him from beneath the brim of a straw hat and smiled that pretty twisting close-mouthed smile as she looked sideways at him.

"My my, Danny Sweeney, time and I don't know what else have made of you a man." She looked him up and down till he could feel himself blush. "Yes indeed, you've done some serious growing up." She put her arms around him and hugged him close and everything that

270

could ever be said was said in that embrace. He wrapped his arms full around her and pressed his body tight to every generous contour.

"And just where have you been?"

"Out west."

"That so? Well I'm so glad you've come home and that you've brought this lovely girl back with you." She turned to include Alma. "I always wanted a little sister."

She slid a long graceful arm around the girl's waist and pulled her close. Alma's face shone and he was pleased to see her shy smile, shades of the animated songbird he had first beheld.

"Sorry I did not follow your directions, Daniel. When I heard the motor I started to run as you told me but when I looked back and saw a woman with children, I believed I was safe."

"It's okay."

He backed the trailer up to the double-Dutch doors of the cow barn and with Gloria and Alma's help, he unloaded the crates stuffed with speckled birds. They carried them to the hen house and set them loose in the caged-in run. When the rooster set upon a hen as quick as he was out of the crate, Gloria shook her head and said, "Now ain't that just like a man." They all laughed, though Daniel blushed more than laughed.

He hurried inside to the kitchen to set his rifle on the table. Looking at that rifle now with those little boys around, he saw it as the dangerous thing it was. He double checked to see that the safety was on and then poured himself a tall glass of water and stepped back outside to see to the cows.

He went to unload the grain. Alma set out water and scratch and placed fresh straw in the nest boxes in the coop. Back at the barn, Daniel slid open the track doors at the opposite end of the drive-through alley. The large panels gave way to the cow's winter yard but in his absence even that barren corner was lush with greenery. He reckoned it could provide the miniature herd with a couple of days grazing. That would buy him the time he needed to repair the fences around the grazing paddocks.

With the twins contained at a safe distance, he swung open the gates at the back of the trailer. The two heifers took one glance and a whiff of their new surroundings and skipped down the ramp, tore down the alley with their tails aloft and kicked up their heels as soon as they hit open ground, beside themselves to see sky above and grass below. The two mature cows came sedately, even regally, and picked their way down and strode out into the sunlight as casually as if they had made the trip a thousand times before. The young cows explored the extent of their new bounded freedom, heads raised and ears pitched forward. The lactating cows put their heads to the ground as soon as they were in the grass, the shearing of forage audible to the onlookers standing in the shade of the barn.

Daniel was first to spy a lone figure wending his way across the coarse stubble of the recently mown fields. He peered until the recognition was secure, then he gave a little whoop. "I'll be back," he said to Alma, "here comes an old friend."

He set off loping across the cow yard and cleared the double strands of barbed wire at the far end with the ease of a sprinter clearing hurdles. The two young men met in the middle of an uncut section of the field held in reserve for grazing, waist high grass scattered throughout with a rich inlay of wild flowers. They wrestled as if they were the same school boys and had seen each other only yesterday. The visitor was the taller and heavier of the two but was surprised at the strength his friend had gained during his time away. Daniel quickly gained the upper hand by pressing the other in a knee-lock to chest and he dumped him harder than intended and at once felt sorry and ashamed when his friend let out a grunt on impact. Something raw simmered beneath the surface of his actions but the tall fellow on the ground shook off the sting and gave him a welcoming smile. Daniel thrust out his hand to help his friend to his feet and then stooped down and picked up his ball cap, dusted it off and handed it to him.

"Levi, damn it's good to see you." The two embraced and slapped one another on the back.

"Danny, I just couldn't believe it when I heard you were back. The whole village is buzzing about it. Hell, you look good. Wish I could grow a beard like that. Of course, even if I could my old man would beat me till I shaved it."

272

Levi tugged at the wispy hairs sprouting on his own chin. "So, tell me cowboy, did you shoot up all the bad guys out there?"

"Oh, maybe just one or two," Daniel smiled evasively. "It ain't all like what you see in the movies. You still working for your old man?"

"Yup, but I got myself a paying job at the general store, that's where I heard you'd come back. Old Mister Wilder said you brought home a squaw."

Daniel's face darkened and Levi was quick to apologize.

"Just kidding, Danny."

"She's an Indian, but not of this country," Daniel replied. "The sweetest girl a fella could hope to know," he added, and there was a seldom heard note of passion ringing in his voice.

"Don't you beat all. Sounds like you're in love. Is it true you two are married?"

"It is."

"Shoot, you're the last one I would've figured to get hitched. I mean you weren't exactly what we'd call a lady's man."

"You got yourself a girl?"

"Me? Nah, my number came up last month, though I was planning to enlist anyway. Only way I can figure to keep from being stuck forever in this cow town."

"There's worse things could happen."

"Like what?"

"Too many to name."

"Well, that's all right for you but you got out and saw something of the world. It's my turn now. I'm off to war."

"What war would that be, Levi?"

"By Jesus, you haven't been gone that long! Don't you know there's a war on?"

"Isn't there always?"

"Well, this time it's a war against the commies over in Vietnam."

"It doesn't matter to me."

"Me neither, but Uncle Sam sure as shit needs me there now. Could be he'll be calling you up soon, too."

"I ain't going off to fight somebody else's war."

"From what I hear you already got yourself a little war going on right up here on the hill."

"I'm here to stay."

"I can respect that. Why just last night we had my Uncle Elijah over to the house celebrating his birthday, ninety-five years old and still milking cows. Talk at the table turned to you and my uncle said he understood why you were taking a stand. Said that any true son of these Green Mountains could do no less. But my old man said he didn't envy you your one-man revolution and he forbade me to come up here. Said he wanted to send me off to the Marines in one piece."

"Can't blame him."

"Is it true you drove the sheriff and deputy off your land at gunpoint?"

"They left of their own accord."

"Watch out for that Deputy Stiles. He's a first-class prick. He busts our asses for doing all the same things he was busy at himself before they gave him that stupid badge. Back roads ain't hardly safe for drag racing anymore, he knows all our hot spots." In the trade of such banter it was almost possible to believe that time and its changes had not carved any distance between them. A light breeze carried a prescient silence which lingered a moment in their midst.

"Listen, I've got cows to milk. Want to help?"

"I'd like to stay but I've got to get back to chores of my own before the old man finds out I've been over here. I'll be back though. I want to get a look at that truck of yours and meet the new wife."

"All right."

"Hey Danny, it sure is good to see you."

"Come back and visit before you go off to your war."

Levi made a fist and pounded it to his breast with a thump then topped the gesture with an ersatz salute. "I promise," he solemnly proclaimed. Daniel stood and watched as his friend loped across the fields, watched as he leapt the brook and disappeared into the woods, then he turned and walked back to the barn.

As he waded through the tall grass, he parted his way through a mixed smattering of wild flowers making a luminous tapestry of the rank green carpet. Finches skipped about from blossom to blossom like thrown stones and a ruby-throated humming bird hovered above his head like an animate jewel loosed from the bounds of gravity. He flushed up a kestrel no larger than a red-breasted robin out of the tall grass still clutching a vole in its miniature talons.

He looked up to the cupola of the barn and noted the copper horse weather vane trotting to the Northeast. The leaves of the trees in the barnyard were turning their silvered undersides upward to mirror the slate-gray of the thickening sky. The barometer was dropping and humidity was on the rise and the sweat was dripping off his brow by the time he came back to the barn. The twins had climbed up into the mow and were jumping about in a stack of loose hay.

"Just stay out of that green hay, boys. I don't want you knocking the leaves off that good forage." His own words reminded him immediately of his father.

"This hay is for those stupid cows?" Aidan called down in a peeved tone.

"It is and a cow ain't stupid. She knows everything she needs to know, which is a lot more than I can say for a lot of people." Or so his father had always told him.

Gloria and Alma were sitting and chatting on milking stools set down in the alley way.

"Those stools were made for milking cows," he said in mock seriousness. "What do you say we bring in those cows?"

"Look who's the head farmer now," Gloria exclaimed as she rose off the stool and brushed bits of straw from her dress.

He liked hearing her say that but turned quickly before she could read that on his face.

They had no difficulty in luring the two fresh cows inside. Honed to a fine line of hunger by the demand on their bodies to produce milk, a little grain in a pail went a long way towards convincing them to stick their heads through the stanchion irons that would keep them still for the milking. Once they had eaten the grain, he put hay in front of them but after having tasted the fresh grass, they turned their noses up at it. With the heifers it was another story. Even though they were not yet in milk, he wanted to get them into the routine

275

of coming into the barn. He got a halter on one and tried dragging her while Alma and Gloria pushed from behind. The twins cheered them on from a safe distance, thinking it a choice bit of entertainment to see the adults so vexed. The cow planted her forefeet, making herself as immovable as a ton of concrete. Alma suggested that they try pushing the heifer from the front as if they wanted to back her out of the barn and it worked; when they tried to force her back out of the barn, she bolted past them and found her place in a stanchion next to one of the older cows.

The second heifer was in a panic at being left alone outside but refused to come in. And again Alma came up with a solution---that they all leave the barn and once they were outside, the little cow trotted in and took her place beside the first heifer as if it were a practiced routine. "Why I'll be..." Daniel muttered aloud to himself as he crept in cautiously to lock the irons. He rewarded the heifers with a scoop of grain and more for the mature cows so they would not wrench their necks in an attempt to steal from the young ones. He went into the milk house to fetch two stainless steel buckets and some clean wet rags and then took a place at the side of one cow. Talking gently, he stroked her flanks and when she accepted that he began washing her udder with a rag. Although the cow was facing straight, he could tell that her bulbous eyes were watching his every move, her ears pinned back to detect every sound.

Alma and Gloria sat on either side of the other cow and he could hear the hypnotic splash of milk squirting into the bottom of the empty pail. The seasoned cow aimed swats to the side of his head with the brush of her tail but she did not kick as he began working the teats. Once into the milking she made a couple of threatening motions with her back hooves but he spoke to her in calming tones. For reasons of her own, the old bovine settled in and began to chew cud. They milked the cows in the quiet of the barn, the twins gone to roughhousing outside. Gloria told him how good it was that he had brought cows back to the farm.

"Why's that?" he asked.

"Cause I'd say it's pretty certain your big brother has changed his mind and isn't going to sell. He hasn't come right out and said it, but he has been making a lot of calls. You see he had this contract drawn up with some people from down state…..."

"Flatlanders."

"Anyway, he kept putting them off and creating delays for no good reason. I know for a fact that he has been talking with Judge Benson about changing the title to this place."

"What for?"

"He wants to look out for your rights too."

"I don't need the judge to tell me my rights."

"But you do need Tommy's help now."

"You think so?"

"I suspect he has been having second thoughts about all of this."

Although she knew he could not see her, she impulsively gestured with one hand to encompass the entirety of the farm. Daniel was listening but all the while steeling his heart so he would not hope for too much.

"He's sorry for what happened."

"Tommy ain't the kind to have regrets."

"Give him a chance, Danny. He really changed a lot after you left, you know?"

"How so?"

"For one thing, he quit the real estate firm. He said that work was a waste of his education. He went back to night school to get his teaching certificate and he's begun teaching English at the Union High School and he's the new assistant coach for the football team."

"Always did love his football."

"More than once he's expressed his doubts about selling the farm. I believe he felt responsible for you running away like you did."

"I'm glad you told me, Gloria," he said and there was a conciliatory note in his voice, but as soon as the words left his mouth he felt a frightening vulnerability and shifted his inner stance back to the implacable. When he continued there was a grainy harshness in his tone.

"I only hope that part about not selling is true. Because one thing he ought to know---he can only sell this place over my dead body."

"Danny, I wish you wouldn't talk that way. It certainly is no way to be talking in front of your new wife."

"Don't worry about her. Alma ain't afraid of the truth. Pretty near everyone she's ever loved has died fighting for what they believed in."

The girl remained silent.

"I'm sorry. I've said too much," Gloria replied in a chastened voice. The milking of the cows continued in the ensuing silence. The twins came jostling back in and approached Daniel and looked on in curiosity.

"Can I have a try?" asked Aidan.

"Me too. Me too," chimed in little Pat.

Daniel showed them how to take hold of the teat and to squeeze it from the top down. As each little boy tried and then succeeded to coax a jet of milk into or over the side of the pail, he would let out a squeal of delight. The cow accepted this with resignation for awhile, and then began to fidget. Daniel massaged the last bit of milk out of her quarters and slid the bucket to safety and sat back on the stool, stretched his arms over head and addressed Gloria across the gulf that was yawning.

"I'm grateful you came, Gloria. It means a lot to me. You've been good to me ever since I was a little kid."

She smiled to hide the fact that her eyes were tearing up.

"I remember the last time I saw you, you said the land means nothing to Tommy. I've been thinking about it on and off since you left. I think he does value the land, it's just that he's never identified with it as deeply as you. Do you know what I mean?"

"I'm not sure."

"I couldn't understand at first why you ran away, but then it occurred to me you were trying to carry the land inside of you just as it was rather than see it sold into the hands of others. As I see it, the only way you could figure to protect the land was to run away with the memory of it intact."

"Well, you understand me better than I do."

"We are what we protect."

"How do you mean?"

"We become what we stand up for."

"I get it."

"Believe me, it's something a mother understands."

"I believe you."

Alma was quiet during this exchange and Daniel wondered what she made of it.

They carried the brimming pails to the milk house and Daniel rinsed off a ladle and gave each boy a drink.

"How's that?

"Mmm...good," they smiled through white mustaches. He put a jar aside to take back to the house before he poured the remainder of the pails through a paper filter into a tall can and hefted the can to the spring-fed cooler. "Wonder what happened to all the barn cats," he said as he glanced around. "They must've got pretty skinny with all the cows gone."

He stood watching from the milk house doorway as Gloria and Alma took the twins by the hand and headed back to the farmhouse to see about cooking supper. On the way Gloria opened the trunk of the Nash. It yawned like a gargantuan maw as she began extracting cardboard boxes full of house wares and clothing that she thought the young couple could use to set up a home. Then she brought in brown paper bags stuffed full of groceries as if she were determined to put some meat on the bones of her lean brother-in-law and his waif-like wife.

Daniel released the cows one by one from the stanchions. The heifers pulled back in panic trying in vain to pull their heads free as he approached. "Easy girls," he tried to cajole them. As he loosened the slide-catch on top of the stanchions they flung themselves back hard, tripping up in the gutter behind. Next he released the mature cows. Slow and careful, even gracefully, they eased themselves out of the stanchions, turning their heads sideways to fit their horns through the irons. Stepping backwards out of the stalls and over the gutter, they calmly paced out of the barn, switching their tails at flies and licking their muzzles in anticipation of sweet grass. "Good ole' bossies," he spoke after them. "Next time I'll let you out first so you can show the young ones how it's done."

After tidying up after the cows he made himself busy in the horse barn. He sensed it best to keep out from under foot of the women in the kitchen and let them get acquainted on their own terms, and besides, he was glad to have a little time alone. He took a halter off a peg and went out and caught Friend and brought him in and hitched him between cross-ties and he got out a hoof-knife, nippers and a file to give his feet a trim. "Foot, give me the foot. Steady Friend. You stand. Don't lean on me, I can't hold you up. No nips now." He kept up a gentle but lively banter with the young horse as he persuaded him to trust enough to let each foot be held. Whenever he bent over to work on the front feet with his back to the horse's head, Friend would reach around and steal the kerchief out of the hip pocket of his jeans and then he would drop it from the hold of his raspy lips, paw it into the dust of the stable floor and laugh his silent horse laugh. "That's mine give it back here," Daniel would tell him in a good-natured reprimand as he rescued the sullied cloth for never the last time, a willing participant in a game that he could only lose.

Mouth-watering scents wafted from the farmhouse kitchen as he was finishing up the trim work. He gave the colt a treat of oats and molasses as a reward for his patience and set him loose in the paddock. He put away his tools and swept the floor and closed up the barn. The smell of fried chicken made him realize how hungry he was as he crossed the farmyard to the front porch.

The twins were playing with tot trucks on the parlor floor. They asked Daniel if he wanted to play, as if he were another boy just bigger in size. He escaped by mumbling something about helping out in the kitchen. Both women were up to their elbows in work, each wearing aprons that Gloria had brought over, and it appeared to him that they were using every pot and pan in the place. He noted the rifle was not on the green Formica table top. Alma saw him looking and in a neutral voice she told him, "It is on the rack with the other gun." He nodded, glad that he hadn't had to ask.

He decided to busy himself by setting the oval dining table at the far end of the parlor. He couldn't remember when the stately oak piece had last been pressed into service. He searched through the linen closet for a table cloth, found one precisely folded, yellowed in places, with a border of delicate needlework and guessed it was something his grandmother had made. He placed candles into tarnished silver holders and set them on the table and then he put out china and crystal from a cabinet whose doors has not been opened within living memory and soon realized the whole lot needed a dusting. Next, he found the felt-lined chest containing silverware and made a concentrated effort to remember the proper order of placement.

He went out and around to the back yard where the lawn had been left untended to pick a bouquet of wildflowers growing in the shade of the hoar old butternut tree. He was critically engaged in arranging the flowers in a mason jar when he heard a vehicle approaching from the far side of the draw. He impulsively went to the gun rack and started to reach for the rifle when he became instantly aware that the little boys had stopped their play and were watching his every move. His brother came up the drive and parked the Chevy next to the Rambler. All his instincts were on the offensive as he went out to meet him.

"Danny."

"Tommy."

"Something sure smells good in there," the elder brother remarked, shifting uneasily on his feet as he sniffed at the air. Daniel avoided his brother's eyes, staring instead as his silver watch band and gold wedding ring. In his other hand he was hefting a six pack.

"I see you burned down my sign."

"It was a bad sign."

Daniel gazed beyond his brother's face to the fish-scaled sky noting the mounting evidence of a change in the weather. The horses felt the change too. The whole little herd began frolicking in their paddock, charging round and rearing up in display. Tommy glanced over to the paddock and studied the animals for a moment.

"What's with all the horses?"

"That's what a warrior does."

281

"What's that?"

"Brings home horses."

"Are you a warrior now?"

"I am."

"Well, there doesn't have to be a war."

"There's always a war."

"Speaking of war, you need to take a look at this."

Tommy reached into his trouser pocket and pulled out an envelope and handed it to him. Daniel quickly scanned it, saw that it was from the Selective Service Board and that Tommy had already broken the seal.

"What's this?"

"Draft board. You'll have to let them know where you can be found."

"To hell with that."

"I can't blame you for feeling that way. It's a rotten war."

"What war isn't?"

"Yeah well, you haven't been drafted yet, but you have to report."

"For all they know I could still be out west somewhere."

"Sooner or later they'll find you. You're going to have to deal with it."

Daniel slipped the envelope into his back pocket and changed the subject.

"I guess the women must have supper about ready."

He turned to go in just as the twins came bursting out the screen door.

"Daddy, Daddy! What did you bring us?"

Daniel watched as his brother naturally unfolded into his role as a father, producing as if by magic hard candies from behind the boy's ears.

"What do you say?" Tommy asked.

"Thank you, Daddy," they replied in perfect chorus.

"Now save them till after supper or your mother will have a fit," he admonished, although the wrappers were already flying and the sweets en route to their mouths.

The brothers and the boys came inside just as Alma came from the kitchen bearing a platter of fried chicken garnished with savory herbs. Gloria was on her heels with a heaping bowl of mashed potatoes. There's more to haul from the kitchen, she told Daniel in transit and dutifully he went to find it.

They all stood before their places at the table, Daniel at one head, Tommy at the other. Gloria asked Tommy to speak a grace and all held hands and bowed their heads as he began. "Oh Lord, blessed are we for these gifts which we are about to receive from the bounty of your hands, Amen."

"And thanks to the land and the farmers who work it," Daniel threw in during the ensuing moment of silence before they seated themselves. Tommy lit the candles, then went out to the kitchen and opened a beer.

"Can I offer anyone else a cold one?" he called out.

"I'll have a glass of wine please, honey," Gloria replied.

"Danny?"

"Sure."

Tommy came in from the kitchen bearing the two beers and the glass of wine.

"Alma, can I bring you anything?" This was the first he had spoken to her.

"*No gracias*, water will be fine," she smiled demurely and Tommy took a nervous pull off his beer. Gloria rose and went to the kitchen and came back with a tall bottle of orange soda pop. The little boys squealed with delight and the girl, looking pleased, held out her own glass after they had been served.

Tommy dished up heaping plates and passed them around. With the chicken and mashed potatoes there was corn on the cob smothered in butter, green beans, hot biscuits, gravy, green salad with slices of fresh onion, cucumber, tomato, and cranberry relish on the side. Aidan spilled his glass of pop and Gloria ran to the kitchen for towels. They ate mostly in silence save for the incessant chatter of the twins which fell from them like rain. Gloria made a valiant effort at small talk, mostly about the weather they'd been having and the health of family members and the presence of the twins helped to ease the

283

underlying tension. Alma ate sparingly. Daniel had seconds of everything. Tommy was first to praise the cooks and Daniel helped to clear the table to make room for blueberry pie and coffee.

For just a moment Tommy and Gloria were alone with the twins in the parlor while Daniel and Alma tended to things in the kitchen. Tommy sat drinking his beer while Gloria scraped leftovers onto a plate.

"I still can't believe it, Danny married. Christ, he never even so much as went out on a date. And she's a looker, too."

"You were always so self confident. I found that attractive. But Danny is so sensitive and vulnerable. Some women find that irresistible in a man."

"You call it sensitive and vulnerable. I call it screwed up."

"Picking on him won't help."

"I know it."

"What is it between you two?"

"I don't know. I was the one who did everything right. Danny was the fuck up. But I always felt Dad favored him."

"Because he loved the farm."

"And it's not like I don't. I just don't want to give my whole life over to it. And that's what it takes."

"It takes what it gives."

"What's that supposed to mean?"

"I don't know. It's just something I said."

After pie, Danny went into the kitchen, rolled up his sleeves and dove into the mountain of dishes.

"You are a lucky woman, Alma," Gloria commented in a voice loud enough for Tommy to hear, "to have a man who scrubs the pots and pans."

Clean-up done, they returned to the parlor. Gloria had another glass of wine and Alma sipped at a glass of mint iced tea while Daniel and Tommy each worked on a second bottle of beer. Aidan sat on his Daddy's lap and little Pat sat with Daniel.

"Daddy tell us a story,"

"Aidan, my pockets are empty of stories right now." Tommy pulled his pants pockets inside-out and made a sad clown face to demonstrate the veracity of his testament. "Maybe your Uncle Danny has one or two in his pockets." He looked to his younger brother in a leading way.

At first Daniel resented having the focus shift to him but the beer was beginning to loose his reticent tongue. He closed his eyes for a moment and suddenly the face of the old freight-hopping Hobo he'd met early on in his travels flashed into his mind. He recalled what the whimsical mystic of the rails had told him regarding the importance of home. How little he'd understood the man then but how clear the words seemed to him now.

He opened his eyes and began to rummage in his pockets. "No stories in here," he said. The twins registered obvious disappointment. "Wait a minute, it feels like there might be one little story hidden up in my sleeve. Undoing the button at the cuff, he reached up his right shirt sleeve with his left hand. "Oh yeah, here's one I can tell," he said, drawing the invisible story out gently into a cupped hand as if it were a baby snake. The little boys looked on in fascination, trying to see the story in his hand.

He told them of how he had ridden Tommy's horse to the Dakotas and released her to the wild herd and of riding the train and of his meeting Alma in the orchard. He told them of the attack by the bear and of being found by his grandfather and then he spoke of his time at the ranch and his foray into the rodeo. Finally, he told them of finding Alma again and of his coming home.

Though they did not understand the half of it, the boys were pleased with the story. "Tell us another one Uncle Danny, please," begged little Pat, kicking his feet and clapping his hands.

"I'm afraid my sleeve is all emptied out." He flapped the material of the sleeve to show as proof. "Maybe next time you come I'll tell you the story of your great grandfather. I'll bet you didn't know that he is a medicine man and a brave warrior who once stole many horses and cattle from his enemies."

Tommy and Gloria glanced at him with raised eyebrows and questions on their faces but he said no more. "What a story," said Gloria. "You never cease to amaze me."

Tommy shook his head in an expression of disbelief. "It's incredible that you found our grandfather."

"He found me."

"He must've taken it hard when you told him about mom committing suicide."

"What do you mean?"

"You didn't know?"

"Know what? Dad always said she got sick."

"She did, and when she got too sick to take care of us and him, she took her own life. I always figured it was an 'Indian way' kind of thing. She went up into the woods with a rifle, Grandpa Aidan's rifle, the one you took with you."

Everyone fell silent and Daniel dropped his eyes to his plate. He felt like his center of gravity was dropping through the floor. Alma reached under the table to grab his hand and he gave her hand a squeeze back as he wrestled with his confusion and pain.

"How could he have kept that rifle after what she done?"

"You know Dad, never one to let a good tool go to waste."

"Let's change the subject, Tommy," said Gloria. "This is not the best story for the boy's to hear."

"They're old enough to understand that people die in this world."

"Tommy, please."

"She's right, Tommy," said Daniel.

"Can't we hear more stories?" pleaded Aidan.

"Yours was a fine story, Danny," Gloria said. "The others will have to wait for next time. Too many stories and little boys will be unable to sleep." She stood and began to gather her things.

"Tommy dear, I'll take the boys home now and give you and Danny some time to talk."

The two Sweeney brothers looked at and then away from one another. Gloria gave Tommy a peremptory peck on the cheek then she approached Daniel where he sat and leaned forward and gave him a quick but full kiss on the mouth leaving him with a look of surprise and the taste of wine on his lips and he found himself blushing and not for the first time that day.

"Take good care of yourself," she told him and she squeezed his hand tight. Alma helped her to assemble her things and together they managed to coax the reluctant twins into the car. When Alma returned to the house she discreetly busied herself in the kitchen unpacking and putting away the utensils, linens and clothes from the boxes that Gloria had brought over.

The brothers took their beers and went out to sit on the slat furniture on the porch. The night air was warm, shimmering with the sporadic flux of heat lightning and erratic breezes blowing up from the southwest. They sat in silence for awhile, each sipping the cold brew. Tommy lit up a cigarette and smoked it as he drank, his face appearing in the orange glow each time he sucked the smoke in. Crickets fiddled in the night. He finished the cigarette, tamped out the butt on the porch rail and flicked it out onto the lawn.

"I've done some talking with Judge Benson over the course of the week," the elder brother broke the silence. "He's going to talk to some people in Montpelier to fix the situation with your unregistered rig. I've also asked him to look at our legal affairs; you see, I've been doing some hard thinking, really, ever since you left, but even more now that you are back."

Tommy took another pull off his bottle and swished it about in his mouth as if he were at some tasting of brews and then he started up again.

"I admit I've been in conflict over all of this; you, me, the land. Hell, everyone has their own private wars waging on the inside. Even Dad had to struggle, what with the blood of the Irishman on the one hand and the Yankee on the other. It certainly wasn't the Yankee coming out on top when he decided to bring an Indian bride home after the war."

He paused and rubbed the cold bottle across his sweating brow. He didn't seem to notice that his brother had yet to speak now that the train of thought was building up steam inside him. He looked at Daniel speculatively, as if they were in a card game and he wished to read whether or not his brother was bluffing.

"You really think you could farm this place?"

"It's what I know."

287

"Why'd you have to go and run away like you did? And not one word in all this time."

"I meant to write."

"Christ, Dad wasn't even dead yet! Who do you think had to stay behind and bury him?"

"He was dead, Tommy. I was there in the middle of the night. I saw the spirit go out of him."

"Jesus, Danny, sometimes I think you're half-mad."

"Half-breed is all."

"I wanted to sell the land before you went away. It was only after you were gone that I wasn't so sure."

"What changed?"

"Well, for one thing I was too damn paralyzed to make any decisions after all that had happened, Dad dying, you taking off. Then I began to see that the changes coming to the valley aren't all for the good. I thought the new economy that the highway would bring would solve everything. But I found myself negotiating to sell farms out from under people I've known since I was a kid. I didn't have the stomach for swinging those deals. Once I thought that change would only better our lives. Heck, the old man wouldn't even get a telephone out here."

"He said that if somebody had something important to tell him they would come and say it to his face."

"That was our Dad. I know what this farm meant to him and maybe what it means to you. I've only been trying to do what I thought would be best for all of us in the long run, but I'm not so sure I know what that is anymore."

Daniel looked down at his boot tips as if he couldn't bear to hear words of promise from his brother or even to look at his face as he spoke them.

"You blame me for the old man dying, don't you?" said Tommy.

"That's not it. If anything I've been punishing myself over that."

"What is it then?"

"Maybe it's just you being who you are and me being the way I am and both of us wishing the other could be different."

288

"The trouble is Danny, aside from the business with the land, you've got yourself in serious hot water with the law. I'm sure we can work out the trailer and all that, but what were you thinking coming down to the bridge carrying that rifle?"

"I wasn't thinking, I was just doing."

"Well listen, I don't know how it is out west, but now that you're back here, you'd better let go of that frontier mentality."

"The last frontier is right here beneath our feet."

"That may be true but you can't go around making up your own set of laws. You know, the sheriff probably wouldn't have given a hoot about your bringing Alma back here until you got him all riled up."

"Who brought him out here to arrest me?"

"Nobody came to arrest you. We just wanted to talk, that's all. I didn't even want them to come. The sheriff thought he could be useful as a mediator between the two of us."

Tommy stood and set one hand on his hip, gazed around and then cast his eyes to the porch floor. He rubbed his other hand up and down the back side of his neck. He fumbled in his shirt pocket for another cigarette but the pack was empty. He crumpled the pack and stuffed it into his pants pocket and sighed deeply before he began again.

"Look, first you steal my horse, you loose the cattle and then you run away and we don't hear from you for more than a year. You come back here like some outlaw with your child bride, toting a rifle. What did you expect me to do, welcome you back with open arms?

"I ain't done nothing wrong."

"You ain't done nothing right. This is not some game of Cowboys and Indians we're playing here. Those are real guns, with real bullets and terrible consequences. It's your own damn fault the law got involved with this in the first place. Now all folks in the village are talking about is how you drove the law off the land at gunpoint. I guess that makes you a hero in some people's eyes but the way things stand now, the sheriff is feeling a lot of pressure to do something about it."

"Like what?"

"He'll be out here tomorrow and will probably want to bring Alma in for questioning with the agent from the border patrol. The

289

Judge told me they might detain her for a few days, just till he can work things out with Immigration. He said he would be happy to help her file for a green card. That shouldn't be a problem seeing as how the two of you are already married."

"That ain't exactly legal yet. We don't have any such papers."

"Well, that could be a big fucking problem. How come you told old Mister Wilder over at the store that she was your wife?"

"Because she is. We were married Indian-style."

"Jesus Mary and Joseph, I don't even want to hear about that."

"Why can't they just leave her be?"

"Because she is from another country."

"What do you mean she might be detained?"

"They might keep her at the county seat for a couple of days, just until we get her situation straightened out."

"You mean jail! I can't let that happen, Tommy. If they send her back she'll be killed."

The older brother shook his head slowly, ran a hand through his cropped blonde hair and finished off his beer and took a seat again.

"Little brother, you've got to try to relax and work with these people on their terms. I'm not a lawyer but I know a little something about the law. I'm sure we can get through this...you, me, and the girl."

"I've got to protect her and I will in the way I know how."

Tommy stood up and slammed his palm down on the rail. "Dammit! There's no talking to you is there?" He flung his empty beer bottle into the hedge across the drive and by chance it hit a stone and shattered and he turned again to face his brother who sat impassive and unimpressed. Tommy took a deep breath and struggled to get a hold on himself and his voice was measured when he spoke again.

"Don't get me wrong, Danny, she seems like a really nice girl and everything. But there are laws in this country and she's got to abide by them same as anybody else."

"The more I learn about the law the less I want to know."

"Just don't do anything foolish. And for Godsakes, keep that rifle where it belongs---gathering dust until hunting season."

Tommy reached his arms up and stretched and groaned.

"Listen, you've got to be a little patient with me and with the law. We're trying to work with you but you can't go around threatening people. Do you understand?"

Daniel met his eyes and Tommy could not tell which held the greater measure in his brother's gaze---the innocent plea for help or the mad defiance that was congealing in his soul.

"I'll be back with the sheriff and we'll get everything settled, Okay?"

"I'll think about it."

"Good night, Danny."

"Night," Daniel said, standing up to shake his brother's proffered hand.

He stood out on the porch till the taillights of the truck disappeared around the bend in the road and left the valley to its quiet dark. He poured out his half-empty bottle over the rail onto an evergreen shrub. He pondered Tommy's words, struggling to decide just how much he was willing to trust the lifeline his brother seemed to offer. A part of him wished to grasp it but he was up against a stubborn streak in himself, a core of ancestral iron that was perhaps his greatest strength or maybe his worst flaw, or both. Maybe Tommy's intentions were good but wasn't he dancing with the devil? Hadn't that always been his problem? In the end an inborn mistrust of the law persuaded Daniel to withhold his hand. He would follow his original intention. As his father Patrick and grandfather Aidan before him, he would stand firm on this ground. From this place where his roots ran deep he would not be moved.

3

The pre-dawn light was blood infused. As he lay awake in bed he could smell the imminent rain, hear the staccato laughter of a barn owl coming down off the wooded hill. He leaned over and kissed the girl lightly on the brow. She smiled dreamily. He left her to sleep. After washing at the outdoor pump, he came in and put on water for coffee. He got the deer rifle off the rack in the parlor where it sat above the 'twenty-two' of his childhood, the one he used to take in an effort to keep up with his father who was often up and out before chores with the black dog hunting rabbits.

He sat out on the front porch savoring the sweetened coffee topped with fresh cream, the rifle laid across his knees, as he watched the sun rise in a billowing globe of hot orange haloed in lavender clouds.

He went back in to rinse his cup and heard her coming down the creaking stairs just as he was heading to the barn. The imprint of her body was still a palpable sensation on his skin. He felt an ineffable satisfaction being back in the barn of a summer morn milking cows again, even it if was just this germinal herd of four with two in milk. As he worked he began to think about how he would market the milk now that the farm was back in production, how he could use his truck to haul the cans down to the depot or perhaps he'd make the trip the way his father had always done, hitching the team to the buckboard. Sure, it would take a little longer but wouldn't it be grand to make the ride that way once more. And this time it would be with Alma at his side as he drove the horses.

Soon she joined him and began milking the second cow. They worked side by side in a quiet reverie that was punctuated only by the sounds of the cows chewing their grain and the blue-hooded swallows active in the eaves. When the milking was done, she went to look after her chickens and then in to prepare breakfast

He stole a few moments to himself, walking meditatively over the ground of the horse pasture. His eyes grew soft as they swept over the broad expanse of bottomland, the newly seeded ground, the hay fields and the permanent pasture; he lifted them up to the hill fields crowned with thick woods on the ridges and beyond all of it the forested hummocks tumbling up into the gathering of gun metal clouds harkening rain.

The impetus of return that had smoldered within like a slow burning fuse erupted now into a conflagration of desire. He stood with hungry eyes, the bridegroom before the beloved. He closed his eyes and felt something akin to vibration emanating from the ground, a subtle sense of the land's awareness of his presence; the entirety of the place opening itself up to welcome him home. Feeling the energy flow up into his feet from the ground, he let his arms hang loosely from his shoulders, the palms open without tension; he could feel his body enfolded in an integument of diffuse light, moist wind, brook song and the random movement of the large animals grazing on the grass, and it seemed that even his breathing was part of the vaster breathing in and out of a whole living system, as if something far greater than he was alive and afoot in this land, something that might uphold him, actively guide him to nurture the good and the true within the land itself which would in turn nurture the good and true within the human soul.

Then he heard a soft voice calling to him from beyond the barn. The voice called his name again and he savored the personal and particular sweetness of it.

He came in to the kitchen to a farmer's breakfast laid out on the table, fresh flowers in a jar at its center.

"We have eggs this morning---*huevos revueltos,*" she said proudly as she lifted the lid off a steaming pan of yellow eggs and then she set down the lid and drew him in close and held him tight before they sat at the table. But he wasn't as hungry as he had thought. Back now in the house he suddenly felt nervous and distracted and could not give himself over to the bounty of the table she had spread. Where was the Holy Spirit now? Gone avenging.

"I had a good time *con su família* yesterday."

"Uh huh."

"I like your brother's wife very much. Gloria es *muy simpática.*"

"I always felt she was someone special."

"*Y los gemelos*---the twins---so adorable."

"Little fireballs. I don't know how she keeps up with them."

"*Y su hermano,* he is trying to make peace, no?"

"I think so, Alma. I just don't know if I can trust him."

He looked at his plate and ran a hand over the bridge of his nose and rubbed his forehead and his temples then raised his eyes to meet hers.

"I can't get over what he said about my mother."

"Daniel, even if your mother did this thing it does not mean she loved you any less."

"I just never knew."

He gazed out the window, his eyes searching expectantly up the draw. She reached across the table and touched his hand.

"Your brother is not a bad man. He just seems a little confused in his loyalties. Give him time. He is of your blood."

"The law has gone and fixed us a deadline."

"I think maybe making peace with your brother is more important than saving the land."

"Nothing is more important than the land."

"But laws must be obeyed."

"The law of this land is given by the land itself."

"I don't know Daniel. In a land with no law there will be war."

"I didn't start this."

He paused a moment and glanced out the window again. Sweat began to bead on his brow. He thought he heard something in the distance. He listened intently for a moment and then turned his attention back to the room but instead of meeting her inquiring gaze he studied the pattern of the table top and when he spoke again his tone had softened.

"New cows are doing well. Five gallons between the two of them just this morning."

"*Increible!* After breakfast I will make some fresh cheese."

"We'll have to make a run down to the village. I was thinking we could hitch the team up to the buckboard to haul the cans to the creamery."

Even as he spoke he thought he heard the sound of vehicles making the approach up the far side of the draw. He stood and listened. He could scarcely hear for the hammering of his own heart. The girl grasped his hand and felt the iron tension. Their eyes met searchingly, each sensing the other's fear. Then his ears confirmed that someone was winding up the road. He let go of her hand and he looked at the rifle and he looked back at her. There was nothing more she could say. He drew near and he stooped to kiss her but she turned her face to present her cheek only and as he pecked his lips there he noted the tears welling behind her tightly rimmed lids. He backed away and grabbed the rifle.

He moved now as in a dream, as one stripped of volition, indifferent to the horror of following the arcane choices of a small and jealous god. "Don't worry," he said to her as he undid the safety, "just stay inside." She nodded and turned away as he left through the parlor, the screen door slamming behind him.

The wind was picking up, tattered furlings of cloud scuttled before it like a dispersed and panicked flock of sheep. The first few smatterings of rain pelted down. The black and white patrol car pulled up shortly with its gold star emblazoned on the doors and the blue truck came up close behind and the dust of the still dry road kicked up a small cloud behind it but the momentum of the dust was immediately dampened by the fat drops splattering on the ground. The three men looked up while still in their vehicles to see Daniel descending toward them with the rifle in hand.

The sheriff and the deputy got out first and walked swiftly to the foot of the bridge. The deputy carried a long rifle with a scope and the sheriff drew a heavy pistol from the holster at his side. A sudden gust of wind blew the stiff hat off the deputy's head and it rolled on the edge of the brim till it was perilously close to the edge of the brook. He did not chase nor stoop to fetch it but kept his eyes trained on his subject.

Tommy clambered out fast on their heels just as Daniel was about half the distance down the drive. For some inexplicable reason, the law officers did not cross the bridge, as if the flood waters were still taking it or some imaginary battle line had been drawn. Daniel halted as they did, still about thirty paces back up the drive.

Tommy waved excitedly to his brother from behind the lawmen. "Danny!" he cried out, frantically waving some papers that he held in his hand. Before Daniel had a chance to respond the sheriff barked out an order in no uncertain terms, "Dan, drop that gun." Daniel held fast the rifle. He set his chin to the warm wet wind in his face. The hat was blown off his head but held to his throat by the stampede string.

"Danny Sweeney, I'm only going to say this once; you've got to hand that rifle over to me right now," the sheriff told him and the dangerous edge in his tone exceeded exasperation.

"I can't!" Daniel cried with a note of hysteria. "It was a gift," he added but in a voice so low that the storming winds carried it away and no one heard.

Deputy Stiles raised his rifle and fired off a quick shot that deliberately struck the road some twenty odd feet in front of him, spraying up gravel to the toes of his boots. Out of sheer obdurate reaction, Daniel planted one foot back in a wide stance to brace against the kickback, then returned fire. He aimed way high over their heads to a distance back up the draw from the brook into the branches of a tall white pine.

Out of the crown a flock of crows exploded in all directions, cawing bloody murder and scattering their fleet black shapes into the fey wind. Mesmerized by the shot, the silence and the loud whirling sky dance of the crows, Daniel looked up in wonderment and in that instant his inner eye was opened and in that moment layers peeled away and he perceived an intricate web of energy extending in every direction at once; he could see how each person present was connected to the others within that web, so that his brother, the lawmen, himself, Alma, and the crows spinning and scattering away in the turbulent sky were all caught up together in this net of energy, all of them trapped within each precise act of this drama and he understood that all the players were standing in exactly the place they were meant to be, and he was virtually standing on a mountain and could see it all from a great height and with this expansive vision came a heart opening wave

296

of compassion, a comprehension borne of the one ground of being that sustained them all and in that moment he knew in his very bones that all he wanted was to belong, to be at peace. As he slowly knelt to place the rifle on the ground beside him, he understood that all he had ever wanted was peace.

**

Acknowledgements

Thanks to Sally Brady for her insightful and generous coaching as this book began to take form and to Anne Leslie, without whose untiring efforts, this book would not have come to print.

ABOUT THE AUTHOR

Stephen Leslie lives with his wife Kerry Gawalt and daughter
Maeve in Hartland, Vermont, where as members of the eco-
village at Cobb Hill, they own and operate Cedar Mountain
Farm, a small horse-powered organic dairy and vegetable farm.